THE SILVER STAR

BOOKS BY GILBERT MORRIS

THE HOUSE OF WINSLOW SERIES

1. *The Honorable Imposter*
2. *The Captive Bride*
3. *The Indentured Heart*
4. *The Gentle Rebel*
5. *The Saintly Buccaneer*
6. *The Holy Warrior*
7. *The Reluctant Bridegroom*
8. *The Last Confederate*
9. *The Dixie Widow*
10. *The Wounded Yankee*
11. *The Union Belle*
12. *The Final Adversary*
13. *The Crossed Sabres*
14. *The Valiant Gunman*
15. *The Gallant Outlaw*
16. *The Jeweled Spur*
17. *The Yukon Queen*
18. *The Rough Rider*
19. *The Iron Lady*
20. *The Silver Star*

THE LIBERTY BELL

1. *Sound the Trumpet*
2. *Song in a Strange Land*
3. *Tread Upon the Lion*
4. *Arrow of the Almighty*

CHENEY DUVALL, M.D.
(with Lynn Morris)

1. *The Stars for a Light*
2. *Shadow of the Mountains*
3. *A City Not Forsaken*
4. *Toward the Sunrising*
5. *Secret Place of Thunder*

THE SPIRIT OF APPALACHIA
(with Aaron McCarver)

1. *Over the Misty Mountains*

TIME NAVIGATORS
(For Young Teens)

1. *Dangerous Voyage*
2. *Vanishing Clues*
3. *Race Against Time*

9701

THE SILVER STAR

GILBERT MORRIS

BETHANY HOUSE PUBLISHERS
MINNEAPOLIS, MINNESOTA 55438

Published by Bethany House Publishers
A Ministry of Bethany Fellowship, Inc.
11300 Hampshire Avenue South
Minneapolis, Minnesota 55438

Printed in the United States of America.

Library of Congress Cataloging-in-Publication Data

Morris, Gilbert.
    The silver star / by Gilbert Morris.
        p. cm. —(The House of Winslow ; bk. 20)
    ISBN 1–55661–688–0
    I. Title. II. Series: Morris, Gilbert. House of Winslow ; bk. 20.
    PS3563.O8742S55   1996
    813'.54—dc21   97–4647
                                                                     CIP

To Bruce and Kathy Tippit

God has blessed Johnnie and me with many fine friends.

You two have been a blessing to us both!

Thanks for the memory—

GILBERT MORRIS spent ten years as a pastor before becoming Professor of English at Ouachita Baptist University in Arkansas and earning a Ph.D. at the University of Arkansas. During the summers of 1984 and 1985, he did postgraduate work at the University of London. A prolific writer, he has had over 25 scholarly articles and 200 poems published in various periodicals, and over the past years has had more than 70 novels published. His family includes three grown children, and he and his wife live in Texas.

CONTENTS

PART THREE
A Fork in the Road

PART FOUR
Victors

THE HOUSE OF WINSLOW

★ ★ ★ ★

THE HOUSE OF WINSLOW

★ ★ ★ ★

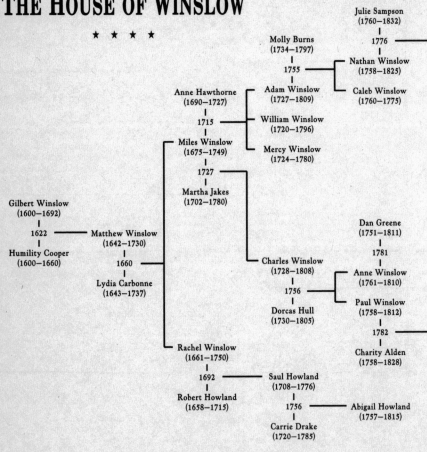

Julie Sampson
(1760–1832)
|
1776 ——————
|
Nathan Winslow
(1758–1825)

Molly Burns
(1734–1797)
|
1755
|
Adam Winslow
(1727–1809)

Caleb Winslow
(1760–1775)

Anne Hawthorne
(1690–1727)
|
1715 ——————
|
Miles Winslow
(1675–1749)

William Winslow
(1720–1796)

Mercy Winslow
(1724–1780)

|
1727 ——————
|
Martha Jakes
(1702–1780)

Gilbert Winslow
(1600–1692)
|
1622 ————— Matthew Winslow
(1642–1730)
|
Humility Cooper   1660 —————
(1600–1660)
Lydia Carbonne
(1643–1737)

Dan Greene
(1751–1811)
|
1781
|
Anne Winslow
(1761–1810)

Charles Winslow
(1728–1808)
|
1756
|
Dorcas Hull
(1730–1805)

Paul Winslow
(1758–1812)
|
1782 ——————
|
Charity Alden
(1758–1828)

Rachel Winslow
(1661–1750)
|
1692 ————— Saul Howland
(1708–1776)
|
Robert Howland   1756 ————— Abigail Howland
(1658–1715)   (1757–1815)
|
Carrie Drake
(1720–1785)

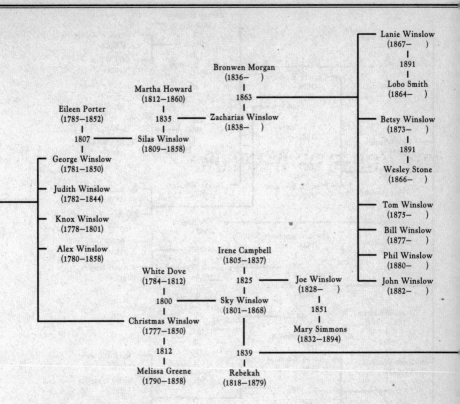

Lanie Winslow
(1867—   )

1891

Lobo Smith
(1864—   )

Betsy Winslow
(1873—   )

1891

Wesley Stone
(1866—   )

Tom Winslow
(1875—   )

Bill Winslow
(1877—   )

Phil Winslow
(1880—   )

John Winslow
(1882—   )

Bronwen Morgan
(1836—   )

1863

Martha Howard
(1812—1860)

1835

Zacharias Winslow
(1838—   )

Silas Winslow
(1809—1858)

Eileen Porter
(1785—1852)

1807

George Winslow
(1781—1850)

Judith Winslow
(1782—1844)

Knox Winslow
(1778—1801)

Alex Winslow
(1780—1858)

Irene Campbell
(1805—1837)

1825

Joe Winslow
(1828—   )

White Dove
(1784—1812)

1800

Sky Winslow
(1801—1868)

1851

Mary Simmons
(1832—1894)

Christmas Winslow
(1777—1850)

1812

1839

Melissa Greene
(1790—1858)

Rebekah
(1818—1879)

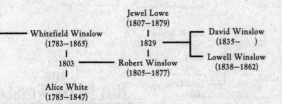

Jewel Lowe
(1807—1879)

1829

David Winslow
(1835—   )

Whitefield Winslow
(1783—1865)

1803

Robert Winslow
(1805—1877)

Lowell Winslow
(1838—1862)

Alice White
(1785—1847)

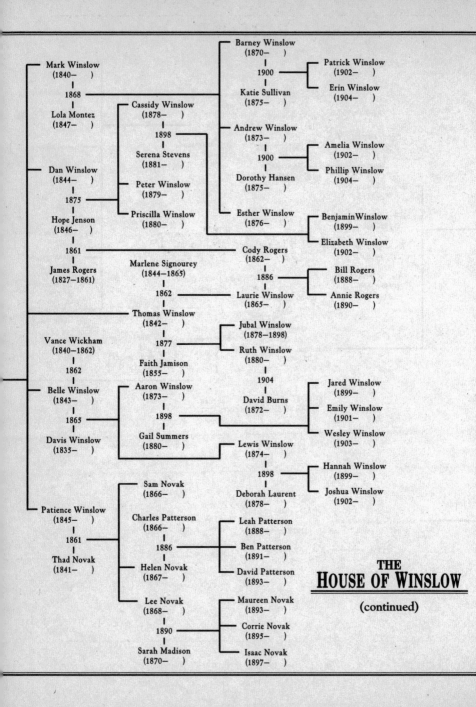

Mark Winslow
(1840–)
|
1868
|
Lola Montez
(1847–)

Dan Winslow
(1844–)
|
1875
|
Hope Jenson
(1846–)

James Rogers
(1827–1861)

Vance Wickham
(1840–1862)
|
1862
|
Belle Winslow
(1843–)
|
1865
|
Davis Winslow
(1835–)

Patience Winslow
(1845–)
|
1861
|
Thad Novak
(1841–)

Cassidy Winslow
(1878–)
|
1898
|
Serena Stevens
(1881–)

Peter Winslow
(1879–)

Priscilla Winslow
(1880–)

Marlene Signourey
(1844–1865)
|
1862

Thomas Winslow
(1842–)
|
1877
|
Faith Jamison
(1855–)

Aaron Winslow
(1873–)
|
1898
|
Gail Summers
(1880–)

Sam Novak
(1866–)

Charles Patterson
(1866–)
|
1886
|
Helen Novak
(1867–)

Lee Novak
(1868–)
|
1890
|
Sarah Madison
(1870–)

Barney Winslow
(1870–)
|
1900
|
Katie Sullivan
(1875–)

Andrew Winslow
(1873–)
|
1900
|
Dorothy Hansen
(1875–)

Esther Winslow
(1876–)

Cody Rogers
(1862–)
|
1886
|
Laurie Winslow
(1865–)

Jubal Winslow
(1878–1898)

Ruth Winslow
(1880–)
|
1904
|
David Burns
(1872–)

Lewis Winslow
(1874–)
|
1898
|
Deborah Laurent
(1878–)

Leah Patterson
(1888–)

Ben Patterson
(1891–)

David Patterson
(1893–)

Maureen Novak
(1893–)

Corrie Novak
(1895–)

Isaac Novak
(1897–)

Patrick Winslow
(1902–)

Erin Winslow
(1904–)

Amelia Winslow
(1902–)

Phillip Winslow
(1904–)

Benjamin Winslow
(1899–)

Elizabeth Winslow
(1902–)

Bill Rogers
(1888–)

Annie Rogers
(1890–)

Jared Winslow
(1899–)

Emily Winslow
(1901–)

Wesley Winslow
(1903–)

Hannah Winslow
(1899–)

Joshua Winslow
(1902–)

**THE
HOUSE OF WINSLOW**

(continued)

PART ONE

GOING WEST

★ ★ ★ ★

CHAPTER ONE

"I DON'T NEED A MAN!"

★ ★ ★ ★

The Great White Way in New York City had enjoyed an extraordinary year. The country was enjoying a financial boom, and New Yorkers were anxious to spend their cash. The year 1904 had played itself out to the month of June, and three major plays dominated Broadway. The most successful of all was James M. Barrie's *Peter Pan*, starring Maude Adams. Her youthful beauty alone would have made her successful, but she was a fine dramatic actress as well and a welcome addition to the Great White Way. The play had opened in the Knickerbocker Theater almost at the same time that George M. Cohan's *Little Johnnie Jones* opened at the Liberty. In between these two theaters was the Belasko Theater—not as large as the other two but known for the fine quality of its productions. The marquee outside proclaimed in large script, *ALL THE FAIR YOUNG LADIES, starring Priscilla Winslow.*

A derelict passing by the theater moved toward the door, but his way was blocked by a truculent attendant who put his hand on the man's thin chest, saying, "Move along, buddy! No handouts here! Don't linger now!" As the derelict stumbled off, the doorman watched him and muttered, "Too bad. Too bad." Wheeling briskly around, he stepped inside the theater, stopping at the doors that separated the lobby from the auditorium, then shook his head. "They're still applauding. That must be at least six or seven curtain calls for Miss Priscilla." He opened the door cautiously and peeked in, letting the roar of the standing ovation spill into the quiet lobby. Shouts of "Bravo!" and "Well done!" echoed throughout the theater.

Up on the stage Priscilla Winslow gracefully curtsied to the audience, cradling in one arm an enormous bouquet of crimson long-stemmed roses. Her beautiful figure was enhanced by the lavender off-the-shoulder silk dress with pearls draped over each shoulder, the low neckline adorned with a pink silk rose-and-bow trim, the narrow waistline cinched tightly with a belt. Long, flowing sleeves fell to just below the elbow, and the narrow-paneled skirt was lavishly decorated at the hem with ribbon, lace, and pearls draped between small bows. The effect was stunning and made her appear much taller than she really was. Her honey-colored hair was elegantly arranged and interwoven with metallic braids. Her large blue-green eyes sparkled in the stage lights, and there was a delicate beauty in the curve of her lips as well as in the lustrous quality of her complexion. She curtsied one last time and motioned for quiet. When the thunderous applause died down, she said in a clear voice that carried to the very last rows of the theater, even to the doorman who stood listening, "I thank you from the bottom of my heart for your kindness. None of you will ever know how much it means to me to have you come for my performances. I would be less than honest if I said that I did not enjoy the money and the small amount of fame that has found me, but I will tell you that my greatest pleasure comes not from these but from the response that you have so graciously given me. . . ."

She continued to speak, and the audience remained silent, captivated by the simple honesty and vibrancy that emanated from her. It was for this reason that many of them had come again and again to see her perform in what the critics viewed as "a very average sort of play." As she went on, the hush continued, and finally she said, "As you may know, this is my farewell performance." She smiled at the murmur of protest that rippled through the audience. "I can do no more than say it has been the greatest joy of my life to bring you some degree of pleasure, and I would hope that you would remember me. Thank you . . . and goodbye."

With a winsome smile and a sadness in her eyes, Priscilla waved to her audience and left the stage, the curtain closing on this chapter of her life. She was immediately surrounded by her fellow actors and actresses, all pressing close to wish her well. She smiled and murmured a reply to each as she steadily made her way toward her dressing room, lingering a moment to speak with Claude Parker, her leading man, before disappearing behind her dressing room door.

Claude watched her intently until the silken skirts slipped completely out of sight. "I hate to see this play end," he said to Alice Payton, an actress who had played a minor role in the production. "You don't find a star like Priscilla very often. Most of them have heads as big as elephants and are impossible to work with."

Alice had to agree. "Priscilla is sweet," she said, turning her large, expressive brown eyes on the tall man. "You tried your best to work up a romance, didn't you, Claude?"

"She turned me down flat," the actor admitted frankly, shrugging his broad shoulders. "I liked her the better for it. She's had a rough time with that braggart Eddie Rich. I thought I could just bring her a little comfort."

Alice grinned broadly and took his arm. "You can comfort *me*!" she nodded. "Come along. Let's go out on the town and celebrate being out of a job."

Inside her dressing room Priscilla placed the roses carefully on the dressing table, then straightened up and for one moment stared at herself in the mirror outlined by bright lights. Now that she was offstage her face relaxed, but there was still a tension that expressed itself in the erect quality of her stance and the stiffness of her shoulders.

"Well, that's over!" she spoke quietly to her reflection. Her voice seemed to fill the room, and for a while she stood motionless; then she began to undress slowly and thoughtfully. Laying aside the stage costume, she opened her small chifferobe and slipped a satin robe off its hanger. After wrapping the silky garment about her, she sat down before the mirror to remove her stage makeup. She had barely begun when a knock sounded at the door. "Come in!" she said, not turning around.

The door swung open, and Phil Donner, the playwright of *All the Fair Young Ladies*, stepped inside. At thirty-five, he was a rather short man with black hair stiffly parted in the middle. His mustache was clipped short and was almost as black as his eyes. Dressed in a stunning evening suit, he came over and put his hands on the actress's shoulders with a gesture of affection. "That was a magnificent farewell performance, Priscilla."

"Thank you, Phil." Priscilla looked at him in the mirror and offered him her smile. She reached up and put her hand over one of his and squeezed it. "It's been wonderful working with you, Phil."

"The same here." Donner removed his hands, pulled up a chair to Priscilla's right, and spoke enthusiastically of the performance. He was a successful playwright in a commercial sense. Although having written nothing truly great, his plays were popular and had done well at the box office. It had been at his insistence that Priscilla be chosen to star in the play, and now Donner turned his head to one side and rubbed his mustache with a habitual gesture. "I've come to talk you out of leaving New York," he said. An enthusiasm came to his face, animating his narrow features. "I'm almost through with the new play. I've written it with you in mind, Priscilla. It's better than anything I've ever done. You have to stay and help me with it."

Priscilla listened to him carefully, but now that she had removed the last of her makeup, she wiped her hands on a towel slowly, then turned to face him. "I can't do it, Phil," she said quietly. "We've been over all this before."

"But . . . but, Priscilla! It doesn't make any sense!" Donner got up and began to pace the floor nervously. "You've worked hard to get where you are, and it's just the beginning for you. Why, you can be even better than Maude Adams!"

"I doubt that."

"Well, just as good anyhow." Coming back to her, he reached out and took her hands and pulled her to her feet. "I know you've had a difficult time," he said quietly. "You've pulled through it magnificently, but you can't run away and hide now. You've got to go on with your career. Never mind about the past."

Dropping her eyes, Priscilla Winslow had a sudden recall— one of those unexpected moments that summons to attention a part of life one would rather keep locked away. Eddie Rich now invaded her thoughts—Eddie, whom she had met outside a theater and had been so charming she had not been able to resist him. She thought of how he had managed to get her a small role in a play, and how a measure of success had come quickly. Those were not bad memories. Then she thought of how Eddie, who was only a small-time actor and would never be anything more, had proposed marriage to her. When she had accepted, he became her manager. Then the bad memories flooded her mind. She saw the very room where she had stood when a woman came to tell her that Eddie Rich was already married, and that he was deceiving Priscilla as he had deceived her. Pain pierced her heart like a dagger as the memories did their work. Priscilla turned away quickly from Donner and sat down, clasping her hands together to conceal the trembling. Her lips were stiff, and she said slowly, "I can't do it, Phil. I've got to get away from New York for a while."

Donner opened his mouth to argue, and then seeing the stiffness of her back and hearing the tremor in her voice, he knew that it was hopeless to try to get her to change her mind. He put his hands on her shoulders again, gently, and said quietly, "You'll find somebody else."

Turning quickly, Priscilla shook her head. "I don't need a man, Phil."

"Every woman needs a man."

"No. That's not true."

Phil Donner knew when he was defeated, but he tried one more time. "Every woman needs a man," he repeated, "and every man needs a woman. The trick is in finding the right one." He grimaced slightly and said, "I've made the wrong choice twice. It hurt pretty bad both times, but you can't live in a hole and be alone forever. You've got to have someone to share your life with."

"I'm going to Wyoming to see my family," Priscilla said. "Maybe someday, Phil, we can work together. But now I've got to get away from New York."

"Are you still thinking of going to Los Angeles to do that motion picture thing?"

"I'm thinking of it. It might be interesting."

Donner shook his head. "That motion picture stuff is just a fad, kid. Stay with the stage. That's the real thing."

She put out her hands, and when he took them and kissed them, she smiled warmly, true affection showing in her eyes. "You've been wonderful, Phil. I'll never forget you."

"I'm not giving up," Donner insisted. "You'll be back to the Great White Way, and one day you'll be in the biggest theater on Broadway starring in a Phil Donner play. You just wait!"

★ ★ ★ ★

"I don't know who thought up things like formal weddings—but I know whoever it was, she wasn't a man!"

Dr. David Burns stood stiffly in the middle of the small waiting room at Calvary Temple. He was not a tall man, no more than five nine, though his trim carriage made him seem taller. He was not handsome, either, but his bright blue eyes and his thin, almost delicate face, with the Highlanders' look, gave him a pleasant air. He ran his hand nervously through his sandy, reddish hair and stared gloomily at Jan Kruger, who was lounging against the wall, watching him with a slight smile on his face.

"You're enjoying all this, aren't you, Jan?"

Kruger smiled and nodded. When he spoke, it was with a slight German accent. "Why, as a doctor I hate to see suffering, but this isn't like having a leg cut off, David. You'll get over it." He was a tall man, lean and strong, with tawny hair, hazel eyes, and a squarish face. He had a real affection for David Burns and now came over and slapped the smaller man on the shoulder. "You'll be all right. I talked to the minister. He said even if the church roof falls in, he'll plow right along. Whatever happens, no matter how bad, you'll be married when you leave here."

"Confound it, Jan! I wish you'd be a little bit more understanding! You don't know what it's like! Have you got the ring?" he asked tensely.

Kruger's face suddenly went blank. He slapped his pocket and muttered, "The ring—!"

"You didn't forget the ring, did you?" There was almost a note of hysteria in Burns' voice. He was ordinarily the calmest of men, but he had lost this assurance the moment he had stepped inside the small room with Kruger, waiting for his summons to meet his bride at the altar. "You can't have forgotten it! I told you—" He stopped suddenly, seeing the bright humor flickering in the other man's eyes, and watched as Jan reached in and pulled a ring out of his vest pocket. "Oh, you!" he said. "Don't torment a man at a time like this!"

"I'm sorry, David," Jan said contritely.

"Your turn's coming, and I hope you're just as miserable as I am!"

"Not for a year," Jan said. "I'll have time to work my nerve up by then." He hesitated, then said, "You're all right, aren't you? I mean, you're not going to faint or anything on the way to the altar." The door opened even as he spoke, and both men turned quickly to face the minister who stood there.

Reverend Charles Turner was a tall, thin man with gray eyes

and an abundant thatch of brown hair. "We're ready now," he said quietly, then turned and walked out to the front of the church.

Kruger gave Burns a shove and whispered, "Come along, David."

David Burns walked mechanically through the door, trying to blot everything from his mind except the need to stay upright and to make the proper responses to the minister's words. His eyes swept the large auditorium, and he almost panicked when he saw that every seat was filled and people were even standing at the back of the church. His legs felt rubbery, and his stomach seemed to turn over, but somehow he managed to get to the front, where the minister turned and smiled at him confidently. He felt Kruger standing beside him, pressing against his arm, and he swallowed hard.

At that moment the organ music swelled, and at the opposite end of the auditorium, a young woman stepped out of the foyer and moved down the center aisle with a stately cadence. Burns studied the face of Priscilla Winslow, Ruth's maid of honor. Even with the turmoil in his own soul, he thought, *She's not happy.* Outwardly, there was little to tell the young physician this, but he and his soon-to-be-bride, Ruth, had become close to her cousin Priscilla, and he knew the tragic events that had scarred the young woman. She took her place at the front to one side, and then the second bridesmaid moved down the aisle, wearing a companion dress to Priscilla's—a sapphire blue gown made of tucked linen and sheer white lace with a velvet ribbon belt. All eyes were now upon her, especially those of Jan Kruger. David knew that his friend's interest was not in the beautiful dress but in the woman who wore it—Esther Winslow, who would be *his* bride when he qualified as a physician in America.

Esther was a tall, shapely woman with a Latin look inherited from her mother. The daughter of Mark Winslow, an executive of the Union Pacific Railroad, she had made quite a name for herself recently as a successful news photographer. Her courage to cover the most difficult stories had garnered her the name of "The Iron Lady." David Burns glanced at Jan beside him, noting that the tall South African was wholly attentive to the young woman as she came and stood on the other side of the minister. *They're a fine match, Jan and Esther. They'll be happy together.* But then Burns had no more time to think, for Tom Winslow appeared at the far end of the aisle with Ruth, his daughter, on his arm. As the organ fanfare announced the bride's entrance, somehow Burns became completely and utterly calm at the first sight of the pair. He noted the beauty of the wedding dress, thinking of how much time Ruth and her mother, Faith Winslow, had spent on it. The dress was of the finest white silk available. It had a high-boned neckline and a loose bodice covered with sheer lace and pearls, accentuating it all the way to the waist. The full sleeves gathered at the wrist, trimmed with a row of delicate embroidery and pearls. Both the neckline and the train of the long skirt had been embroidered and were accented by tiny pearls.

As father and daughter drew closer and came to stand directly in front of the three men and two women who now waited, Burns had a sudden gush of well-being. He had been a lonely man until he found Ruth, having had one unhappy attachment to another woman. But now as he met Ruth's eyes watching him from behind the sheer white veil, he suddenly thought, *If the world stops tomorrow, I'll be happy.*

Ruth stood holding her father's arm until the minister asked, "Who gives this woman?" Her father murmured, "Her mother and I," then handed Ruth over to David, who stepped beside her and took her hand. She squeezed it and turned to look at him with a placid smile, though excitement brightened her cornflower blue eyes.

The ceremony started, and Burns tried desperately to fix every detail of it in his memory, but all he could remember was promising to love, honor, and cherish Ruth, and the sound of her quiet, assured voice promising the same to him.

After the minister said, "I now pronounce you man and wife. You may kiss the bride," he lifted her veil, and she leaned against him. Her lips were soft and yielding under his with a hint of promise, and he vaguely heard the applause as it burst out over the auditorium. Then the two made their way out, followed by the bridal party, going at once to the reception room.

As soon as they stepped inside, Kruger came forward with a smile on his strongly handsome face. "I will be the first to kiss the bride!" he announced. He then turned to Esther, and before she could move, he pulled her forward and kissed her squarely on the lips.

For once Esther was flustered and pushed him away. "You mustn't do that!" she protested.

"In my country, it is always customary for the best man to kiss the bridesmaid first."

"I don't believe a word of that!" Esther replied, but her eyes filled with laughter. She watched as Kruger turned and gave Priscilla a resounding kiss, then took his arm. "That's enough of that," she said pertly. "I don't believe a word you say!"

★　★　★　★

The reception had been as brief as David Burns could make it, but as he and his bride emerged from the church, they were showered by rice from the laughing members of the wedding party who had remained. "Come on! Let's get out of here, Ruth!" he cried, and they ran toward the big yellow Oldsmobile.

Tom Winslow was holding the door open for Ruth, and as the bride got in, he whispered, "God bless you, daughter. You've got a good man, and he's got a good woman." He leaned down and said, "Try not to wreck this thing. It cost Mark a fortune, David."

Burns could only nod nervously, and although he had practiced with the big touring car Mark had insisted they use for their honeymoon, David had to fumble while the car was surrounded by the party. When the large engine suddenly broke into a roar, he shouted, "Good-bye!" then jammed his foot on the gas pedal. The large automobile lurched forward with tires screaming and almost hit two of the well-wishers, who leaped back frantically. Overcompensating, Burns yanked the wheel to the left—resulting in a grinding crunch of metal as the fenders scraped another automobile—then careened back into the center of the street.

"Don't kill us before we have our honeymoon, David!" Ruth protested.

David Burns took a deep breath and put his foot on the brake. When the car slowed down to a reasonable speed, he turned to her and smiled. "Don't speak to your husband like that! Show a little bit more confidence."

Ruth Winslow moved over closer in the seat. She reached up, ran her hand across the back of his neck, and squeezed it affectionately. "All right, husband," she whispered. "I've just promised to love, honor, and obey, and I'm anxious to get started with it."

David turned to her, removing his eyes from the busy street. "You'll never be sorry. We're going to have a fine life together," he assured her, then turned back and said, "Now, let's get this honeymoon underway!"

Back on the pavement in front of the church, Mark and Lola laughed with the others at the wild exit of the couple. Seeing Priscilla standing slightly apart from the crowd, Mark took Lola's arm, and the two made their way over to where the young woman stood. "When are you going back to Wyoming?"

"Day after tomorrow, Uncle Mark. I was going with Uncle Tom and Aunt Faith tomorrow, but I couldn't get a ticket for their train."

"I wish we were going with you. I'd like to see Dan and his family."

"Why don't you come with us, you and Aunt Lola?"

"Can't get away," Mark shrugged. They spoke for a while, and then Mark moved away to speak to Jan Kruger. He had a real affection for this future son-in-law of his and was financing his final training at a New York hospital. Kruger had been qualified in South Africa as a doctor but would have to requalify for a year and a half, or perhaps two, in an American hospital.

"How are you, Priscilla?" Lola asked. She was, at the age of fifty-seven, an intensely attractive woman. Her black hair showed only a few strands of gray, and her blue eyes made a startling contrast. She and Mark had met in a jail in a town in the south of Texas near the border, and their courtship had been difficult but extremely romantic.

"Oh, I'm fine, Aunt Lola," Priscilla said.

Lola reached out and pulled Priscilla's face around, studying the girl's countenance carefully. "I'm fine," she mocked Priscilla. "That's what we say when we're dying and don't want to tell anybody how we feel. It's one of those meaningless statements that we make every day. How are you really?"

Priscilla felt a brief rush of anger, but she knew in her heart that her aunt and uncle had a very genuine affection for her. Her lips trembled for a moment. "We do say silly things like that, don't we?" She hesitated, then said, "I've made a terrible mistake, Lola. I can't stop thinking about what a fool I was."

"We can't go over our past mistakes, raking them up. That does no good."

"I suppose that's true," Priscilla whispered, and her voice was barely audible over the hubbub of talk. "But I just can't forget. I don't see how God can forgive and forget the things we do."

"I don't think God keeps very good records about things like that," Lola remarked. She was truly concerned about Priscilla. She and Mark had talked about it often, both of them being rather astute students of the human character. Though Priscilla smiled a lot and had achieved success in her chosen profession on the stage, each of them had noticed that there still was a fragility about her. "God forgives," Lola said, "and that's the end of it. He won't come back after we've asked for forgiveness a week later and say, 'Now, about that sin.' That's what you and I might do, but not God. The Scriptures say He throws our sins into the deepest sea." She saw Priscilla taking all this in, then asked, "Are you bitter at Eddie Rich for the way he deceived you?"

Priscilla was silent for a moment. She did not like to talk about Eddie Rich, but now confronted by Lola's dark eyes, she said honestly, "It's not just Eddie—it's me. I keep thinking if I was a fool once, I could be one again. After what he did, I don't want to get too close to anyone."

"That's not a very good way to think. You've got to be close to people. Even when you run the chance of getting hurt." When the younger woman did not answer, Lola asked, "What about Jason?" She spoke of Jason Ballard, the young man who had followed Priscilla all the way to New York from Wyoming. He had been her father's foreman and had a hopeless love for Priscilla Winslow.

"I don't need a man!" Priscilla said almost sharply. Then she smiled tremulously and suddenly leaned forward and kissed Lola on the cheek. "You've been so wonderful to me, but right now I just need to be alone."

Later, as Mark and Lola were on their way home, Lola recounted her conversation with Priscilla to Mark. "I'm afraid she's headed for trouble. She's closed the door on everything—especially on men."

"She's young. She'll get over it," Mark said hopefully.

"I don't know. She's a very stubborn girl, but she'd better get over it. She has a bitterness for Eddie Rich. She seems to think that every man is as untrustworthy and worthless as he is. Part of her heart tells her that's not so, but still, she's built a big wall around herself. She's determined not to be hurt again."

The two rode on for some time before Lola spoke again. She took Mark's arm in hers and squeezed it. "Sometimes it's not much fun growing up, but Priscilla's got to learn that she can't live alone."

Mark turned, and his gaze was affectionate. "Yes, she does," he said slowly, "and the quicker she learns it the better."

CHAPTER TWO

HOMECOMING

★　★　★　★

As the locomotive pulled into the station at Mason City with a grinding of brakes and an explosive huffing of escaped steam, Priscilla stared out the window and felt a sharp stab of apprehension. So much had happened since she had left her home—and much of it not good—that she had a sudden impulse to simply remain on the train and make her way to Los Angeles. It was, she knew, a ridiculous notion, for all the letters that had come from her parents were warm and encouraging. *They'll never mention Eddie and the fool I made out of myself.*

As the car made a final jerk, throwing her forward, she steadied herself, then rose and left the car. Several men, who had been highly aware of her during the long trip, allowed their eyes to follow, and one of them murmured in an audible voice, "Now there's a real pippin!"

Ignoring the remark, Priscilla stepped out of the car, and the conductor lifted his hand and assisted her to the ground. He was a tall, grizzled man with hazel eyes and a sweeping, Custer-style cavalry mustache. He brushed it now with his free hand and smiled. "Been nice having you on the train, Miss Winslow."

"Why, thank you, Sam." Priscilla turned and returned a smile for his compliment. She was wearing a charcoal gray cotton day dress with striped fabric trimmed in a brilliant yellow. She wore a matching hat and carried an umbrella, making a fetching picture as she turned from the conductor and searched for her father.

Instead, she saw her brother Peter striding rapidly across the cinder surface of the station and at once felt at home. "Hello, Pete," she smiled and took his kiss. Then he squeezed her until she cried out, "Pete, be careful! You'll break every rib I own!"

Peter Winslow grinned down at her from his six-foot, two-inch frame. He was wearing a pair of scuffed riding boots that raised him another few inches, and a flat-crowned Stetson was shoved back over his auburn hair. He had hazel eyes, wide-spaced and deeply set in his wedge-shaped face. The corners of his wide mouth turned up in a smile as he said, "You look good, sis. I'll get your luggage, and then we'll be on our way."

Priscilla waited, looking over the station as Peter disappeared into the train. The train station was a single rectangular building with a low-pitched roof painted an ugly dark red color. The station master, Tim McGivern, gave her a wave and a "Welcome home, Miss Priscilla!" as he unloaded freight from a car.

Priscilla returned his greeting, then Peter was back carrying her two bags easily, though they were large and heavy. "This way," he said, nodding his head. As they made their way to the side of the station, Peter grinned. "How do you like the vehicle?"

Priscilla laughed aloud. "It looks like you made it from a dozen wrecked cars, Pete."

"Just about right!" Peter laughed, then heaved her luggage in the rear seat and helped her into the front. When she was settled, he cranked the engine to start it. Once it caught, he raced around the side and jumped into the front seat. The engine burst into a roar, and Peter released the brake. Priscilla grabbed the side door to hold herself steady as the car shot into the roadway and headed south, leaving a rolling cloud of pale white dust spiraling into the air behind them. Grabbing her hat, she blinked as the air bit at her.

"Oh, there's some goggles on the seat beside you, sis," Peter shouted over the noisy engine. He reached down, handed her the goggles, then put on a pair of his own. "Hang on now! I'll show you some speed!"

Priscilla did hang on for her life, for her brother delighted in running the car at full speed. As they sped along, the noisy car succeeded in frightening several teams of horses so badly they reared. More than one farmer shook their fists at him and called out loudly what they intended to do to him if they ever caught him.

"Slow down, Pete!" Priscilla gasped. "We're not in that big of a hurry!"

Peter obediently slowed the speed of the car, and soon they were chugging along at a more moderate rate. "Glad to be home, sis?" he asked, finally turning to glance at her.

With only a slight hesitation, Priscilla nodded. "Yes, I am." She glanced around, taking in the familiar landscape. Suddenly she realized how much she had missed the rolling expanse where a person could see for a hundred miles. Far off to her left were the Indian Head Mountains, and to her right the land fell away, marked only by small spirals of smoke that rose from ranch houses. They passed several large herds of cattle, and finally she said, "I didn't realize how cooped up I was in New York."

"You're right about that," Peter said. "I miss all of this, but I have to go where the action is." He shifted in the seat, twisted the wheel abruptly to avoid a pothole, then when he had the car running evenly again, he said, "I've been to St. Louis."

"Oh, did you go to the fair?" She referred to the St. Louis Louisiana Purchase Exposition that had been the highlight of 1904. She had read that twenty million Americans had already gone to visit the place, viewing exhibits on air travels, the telephone, and more than one hundred of the latest models of the automobile.

"It was like nothing you ever saw, sis," Peter replied. "And everybody was singing the song about the fair. Have you heard it?"

"The one about St. Louis?" Priscilla smiled. "Yes, I've heard it." She lifted her voice and began to sing the theme song of the fair that had swept over the country. Peter joined in with her, and their voices rose above the rattling of the car as it made its way along the rough road:

Meet me in St. Louis, Louis,
Meet me at the fair.
Don't tell me the lights are shining,
Any place but there.
We will dance the hootchy-kootchy,
I will be your tootsie-wootsie,
If you meet in St. Louis, Louis,
Meet me at the fair.

"Well, I didn't know I was such a good singer. Now you'll have to give me a part in your next musical play."

"That'll be the day," Priscilla said, smiling at her brother.

He began to speak of the fair, and most of the way home he described in detail many of the new cars that had been on exhibit there. "And they had a giant ferris wheel imported from Chicago's fair, and a death-defying roller coaster. I got on that contraption, but I was ready to get off before the thing stopped. It's a wonder it hasn't killed somebody by now."

As they were approaching the house, Priscilla asked, "Are you going to stay here on the ranch?"

"You know better than that, Priscilla. Next week I'm returning to Detroit. I took a little vacation, but I'm going back to work for Mr. Ford again. I'm going to learn everything I can about building race cars."

"Is that what you want to do, Pete?"

Turning to her, he suddenly put one hand on the back of her neck and squeezed it, a gesture of affection he had done since they were small children. "You're already rich and famous, Priscilla," he said quietly, "and I'm going to be, too." Grim determination stretched his lips into a straight line for a moment, and two parallel marks furrowed between his eyes, a sign that he was deadly serious. "I'm going to build the fastest car in the world, and then I'm going to race it and beat every man that drives a car!"

All this was no news, of course, to Priscilla. Reaching up, she covered his hand with hers and squeezed it. "I hope you do, Pete. You've got more energy than any man I ever saw—and you're smart. One of these days I'll be saying, 'That's my brother, Peter Winslow, the famous race car driver.' "

Peter squeezed her neck again, laughed, then put his hand back on the wheel. Soon long, low buildings came into view, with the corrals all in the back, and the bright glint of flowers that her mother always had blooming in the front yard. As they pulled into the driveway, Peter asked suddenly, "What about Jason?" Priscilla turned her head away, and when she said nothing, Peter insisted, "He's in love with you. I think he always will be." He braked to a stop and shut the engine off. "Don't you care for him at all?"

Slowly Priscilla turned back toward him. Her eyes were half-lidded, and there was a stillness in her expression that revealed nothing at all of what she felt. She had learned to wall out everything painful that came into her life, and now she said quietly, "I am not thinking about Jason or any other man, Pete. I just want to get on with my life. Please don't say any more."

"All right, sis." Peter climbed out of the car and walked around and helped her to the ground. He watched as she moved forward to meet their parents as they came swiftly out of the house, smiles on their faces. He saw her return a smile as they embraced her, and yet at the same time he knew this was not the same Priscilla who had left Wyoming for New York City. *She's been pretty badly scarred inside*, he thought as he gathered her bags and carried them into the house. *She's going to have to get over that*.

Dan Winslow studied his daughter as Hope led Priscilla inside. When Peter came in with her bags, Dan saw that his son's eyes were on the young woman as well. Dan ran his hand through his brown hair and followed as they went into the kitchen. Hope bustled about, setting out coffee and slices of fresh pumpkin pie.

After serving them all, Hope sat down and began to sip at a cup of strong black coffee. She was happy to see Priscilla after so long—she had spent many sleepless nights praying for this beautiful daughter of hers. She listened as Priscilla spoke with animation of the play that she had been in, and then Hope said, "Cass and his family will be here, maybe tomorrow." She spoke of their older son with considerable pride in her voice.

"Oh, that'll be wonderful! I'm so anxious to see them. Are they coming on a visit?"

"I don't know," Dan Winslow murmured. "Something mysterious about it. We got a letter from Cass that just said he was coming. Nothing else."

"He can be pretty closemouthed about things when he wants to," Peter observed, shoving an enormous wedge of pie into his mouth. After he had washed it down with half a cup of coffee, he said, "How long are you going to stay, Priscilla?"

"Not as long as I'd like." Priscilla reached over and took her mother's hand. "I ought to stay and help you with some of the work. And I want to visit Cody, Laurie, and their family."

Cody Rogers was Hope's son from a previous marriage. He had married Laurie Winslow, and they had settled near Dan and Hope on their own ranch. Laurie's parents, Tom and Faith, had also settled nearby after Tom's recent retirement from the army.

Hope Jenson Winslow, at the age of fifty-eight, still had traces of her youthful beauty. She had fair hair and blue-green eyes, and her skin, though tanned by the hot Wyoming sun, was still clear and finely textured. "I wish you never had to go again, but I suppose you do."

They talked for a while, then Priscilla said, "That train ride was long and tiresome. I think I'll have a bath and then take a little nap."

"Been a few changes since you been here, Priscilla." Dan Winslow locked his hands together and nodded. "We've got an indoor bathroom now with a copper tub and all. I'll get some water heated for you."

When her father had filled the tub, she went into the new bathroom and closed the door. Taking off her travel-stained clothes, Priscilla lowered herself into the hot water with a gasp. For a long time she lay there, soaking and letting the fatigue drain out of her. It was quiet in the house. She could hear Peter outside calling out to one of the hands. Sleepily she wondered about how he would do with his venture into race car driving. It was dangerous, she well knew, and she feared for him, but her brother was a headstrong young man who did not know the meaning of fear and would do as he chose. Then she thought about Cass, her older brother, and about his wife, Serena. She did not know Serena too well, but her impressions of her were that she was a strong-willed young woman with a great deal of emotional force.

"I've got to get out of here or I'll melt," she muttered and rose out of the copper tub and toweled herself down with fluffy white towels that her mother had laid out. She put on a knitted cotton chemise and a robe, then went to her bedroom and lay down at once on the bed. Just before she dropped off to sleep, she looked around the room, noting all the familiar things. Dotted swiss curtains that her mother had made framed the window, and the wallpaper with tiny roses that she had put up herself still covered the walls. Over against one wall was a large bookcase full of the books she had grown up with—schoolbooks, novels, poetry. There were books about the theater by the dozens. Even as a young girl she had always been fascinated by acting and the stage. Along the wall hung various items from her childhood, including a small trophy she had won for reciting a poem at a school contest when she was only seven years old. It was the statue of a woman holding a torch over her head. Made of some inferior metal, it was now tarnished and turning green. As she lay there, eyeing it sleepily through half-closed eyes, Priscilla remembered how proud she was the day she had gone up to receive it. Her parents had been proud, too. Her father had hugged her until her breath left her body, and her mother's eyes had filled with tears. "I don't think they'd have been so proud," she murmured aloud, "if they had known I was going on the stage." Thoughts of Eddie Rich invaded her mind, and she shut them off, closing her eyes. *It seems like a hundred years since I left here* was the last conscious thought before she dropped off to sleep.

★ ★ ★ ★

Priscilla awoke to a loud banging on the door and Peter's voice calling out, "Sis! Get up and get your clothes on! Cass and his family are here, and supper's on the table!"

With a start, Priscilla sat bolt upright, uncertain as to where she was for a moment. Then she leaped off the bed, threw open one of her suitcases, and began pulling out clothing. They were all wrinkled and would have to be pressed, so with a grimace of disgust she walked over to the closet. A smile came to her lips as she pulled out a pair of faded blue jeans. She slipped them on and then pulled on a checkered blue-and-white shirt that had once belonged to Cass. She had always liked to wear her brother's hand-me-down clothes. Now as she pulled on a pair of socks and well-scuffed short riding boots, she felt at home for the first time. Glancing at herself in the mirror, she studied the image, thinking, *I'm different than when I wore these clothes—when I was growing up.* But she shoved that thought from her mind, went down the stairs, and greeted her brother Cass.

He had tawny hair and blue-green eyes like his mother, and his skin was tanned a deep golden brown from years in the open. He put his arms around her, squeezed her, kissed her on the cheek, then said, "You look great, sis. I've sure missed you."

"I've missed you, too, Cass." She hugged him and then turned to go to Serena, who was waiting, a smile on her face. She was a tall young woman of twenty-six, with blue-black eyes and dark hair. She was wearing a two-piece jacket of a light orange with darker orange horizontal stripes around the skirt. Her shoes were white, and she wore white hose, which was unusual.

"Welcome home, Priscilla," Serena said.

"Thank you, Serena. You look beautiful."

"She *is* beautiful," Cass said. "You didn't think I'd marry an ugly woman, did you?"

At that moment a young boy suddenly appeared in front of Priscilla. His dark eyes had a brash look, and his hair was the same tawny color as Cass's. "What's your name?" he demanded.

"I'm Priscilla. What's your name?"

"Why, I'm Benjamin. Don't you know that?"

"Ben, calm down!" Cass admonished him. He put his hand on the boy's shoulder and shook his head, a look of mock despair on his face. "Watch out for this one, Priscilla. He'll run over you if you let him."

"You were just a baby the last time I saw you, Benjamin," Priscilla said. "I held you in my lap and changed your diaper a time or two."

"Ah, I don't remember that!" There was an electric energy about this young boy, and he began at once moving about the room examining the various pictures and the guns that were in the rack on the corner.

"I better watch that boy," Dan grinned. "He's liable to shoot one of us."

"This is Elizabeth." Serena reached down and picked up the two-year-old who was standing behind her sucking on her thumb. She glanced bashfully at Priscilla with her blue eyes and then buried her face in her mother's shoulder.

"She's very shy," Serena said. "I wish she had some of Ben's gall."

Priscilla was enchanted with her niece, who was, indeed, as shy as any child she had ever seen. She made it her business to win her affection, and by the time supper was ready, Priscilla was holding Elizabeth on her lap and reading to her from a storybook she had gotten from her room.

Hope came to the door and called them all to supper, and they went into the large dining room where Priscilla had taken almost every meal of her life until she had left home. She glanced around at the enormous rack of antlers mounted on one wall and the Mexican blanket on another, then took her old seat at the table, surrendering Elizabeth to her mother.

As everyone took their seats, Benjamin continued to pump Peter with questions about automobiles. Finally, Dan Winslow said, "Doesn't that boy ever give his tongue a rest?"

"Not very often." Cass shook his head ruefully. "Be quiet, son. We're going to have the blessing."

"I'll ask it," Benjamin said loudly. "I say good blessings, Grandpa."

Dan laughed aloud and winked across the table at his wife. "All right, Hope. It looks like we've got a resident blessing asker. Go right ahead, Ben. Turn that tongue of yours loose."

"Dan, what a thing to say!" Hope scolded. "You go right ahead, Benjamin."

They all bowed their heads, and Benjamin said in a clear, determined voice, "Thank you, God, for all this stuff to eat. In Jesus' name. Amen."

The brevity of the prayer took Dan Winslow off guard. "Well," he said, reaching for a plate, "that's what I like. Get right down to business. I don't think God is too impressed with our long, flowery prayers anyway."

The table was loaded with food. In the center was a large plate of hot, savory beefsteaks, some of them two inches thick, surrounded by steamy bowls of boiled potatoes in their jackets, butter beans, corn, and carrots, all tender and succulent. The aroma of Hope's fresh-baked bread permeated the room. At the head of each plate sat full glasses of rich, cold milk. The clanking of knives and forks against the china was covered up by the sound of good humor and childish laughter. Priscilla listened as everyone exchanged family news. She let the pleasant atmosphere soak in and realized, with a pang, how much she had missed her family. *I've got to leave here as soon as possible, but I'm going to miss all this.*

"Well, it looks like good ol' Teddy will be our president for another four years," Cass said as he sliced a bite-size chunk of meat with a sharp knife. He considered it for a moment and said, "I haven't minded having a cowboy president these last three years."

Dan nodded, a smile on his broad lips. "He is a cowboy, isn't he? A real one from everything I hear. Teddy Roosevelt's my kind of man."

"So you think he'll win?" Serena asked, looking at her father-in-law.

"Yes, I sure do," Dan nodded. "His campaign is running strong. I don't think there's any doubt that he'll be reelected. He's made some mistakes, and he'll make some more, but they'll be honest ones. He has the majority of people on his side."

For some time the talk went on about politics, and then Serena said, "Tell me about the wedding. I wish I could have been there."

"Oh, it was beautiful," Priscilla said. She went on to describe David and Ruth's ceremony, including a detailed description of the bride's dress, and then she saw that Benjamin was frowning. "I don't guess that you are interested in fashions much, are you, Ben?"

Benjamin suddenly grinned at her. He was an attractive boy with his father's charm already evident and traces of his mother's smooth beauty in his large eyes. "Will you take me for a ride, Aunt Priscilla?"

"I sure will. Tomorrow morning. First thing."

"Tell us about this movie business," Cass said, leaning forward with interest.

"I saw *The Great Train Robbery* at the nickelodeon," Serena said. "It was so real." Her eyes grew wide and she laughed. "When that actor pointed the gun right at the camera and shot it, I nearly jumped out of my seat!"

"She sure did—right into my lap!" Cass laughed heartily. "Of course, I nearly jumped out of my seat, too. It was pretty real."

After Priscilla had spent some time explaining the process of making movies, she said carefully, "Jason's already out in Los Angeles. He went there to work with a producer."

Dan shot her a quick look. "I miss Jason around here. He was the best foreman I ever had. I don't suppose he'll ever come back now, though. Once you get a touch of big-city excitement, I guess the ranch seems pretty dull."

"Not for me," Cass said. "I've had enough of big cities. Seattle's not as big as Chicago, but people are packed in everywhere you look."

"How's the lumber business, Cass?" Priscilla inquired. Her brother had gone to the Gold Rush in the Yukon and shortly afterward had married Serena. He had not made a huge strike, so the two had returned to Seattle, where he had gone into the logging business. He had done fairly well, Priscilla knew, but now she saw a sparkle in his eyes.

"I've sold out. I'm not a lumberman anymore."

All the adults looked at him with surprise. Dan Winslow leaned back and examined his son carefully. "I thought you were being pretty mysterious in your letter. So that's what this is all about."

His mother asked hopefully, "Do you want to come back and

be a rancher? Plenty of land around here, and the beef prices are good."

Cass picked up a coffee cup, drained it, then shook his head. "No, I'm going a different route." He reached over and picked up Serena's hand. "We've talked and prayed and thought about what to do, and finally it came to us. Tell them about it, Serena."

Serena was also excited. Her eyes beamed, and she leaned forward as she said, "We're going into the orange business."

"Orange? You mean oranges that you eat?" Dan inquired.

"That's right," Serena nodded, looking over at her husband. "We've bought an orange grove just outside of Los Angeles."

"How wonderful!" Priscilla exclaimed, a delighted smile on her face. "We'll be in the same town. That makes it a lot better. It won't be like going to a place where you don't know anybody."

"That's right. I was saving it as a surprise, sis. Maybe we can get a big house and all live together." He looked over suddenly at Peter and said, "Pete, you come, too. Why, the three of us Winslows could take that city!"

Peter shook his head instantly. "No, I'm glad for you, Cass and Serena, but I'm going back to Detroit. I'm going to race cars."

"You'll get killed in one of those crazy things! Now, the orange business is quiet and restful. Not a lot of hard work like this ranch." Cass went on for some time attempting to persuade Peter, but it was useless, for his brother was determined to return east.

Peter began to speak about his ambitions to build the world's fastest car, and in his excitement he rapped on the table, saying, "I can do it, too! I've learned a lot from Henry Ford and his engineers. One of these days you'll see my name on the front page. Peter Winslow, the fastest race car driver in the world."

"Next thing you'll be wanting to go up in one of those airplanes," Cass said, shaking his head. "I read in the paper that they managed to stay up in one of those things for fifty-nine seconds. Well, that's not enough to do anybody any good."

"It *will* be, though," Peter said. "You keep your eye on those Wright brothers, and keep your eye on me, too. Peter Winslow, the fastest driver in the world."

"Can I ride with you in your car, Uncle Pete?" Ben broke out.

Peter reached over and ruffled the boy's hair. Grinning broadly he said, "You sure can. Who knows, you might be a race car driver yourself one day."

The meal ended, and the men retired to the parlor, leaving the women to clear the table and wash the dishes. As they worked, Serena suddenly reached over and put her hand on Priscilla's arm. "I'm glad we're all going to be in Los Angeles together. I never had a sister. Now I do."

Priscilla was warmed by the young woman's honesty and forthrightness. "Yes," she said, "it will be good. We'll have a fine time when we get to Los Angeles."

CHAPTER THREE

A New Sort of Minister

★ ★ ★ ★

Jason Ballard had no trouble seeing over the crowd that had gathered to meet the incoming train at the Los Angeles train station. At six feet three, and wearing high-heeled boots, he easily looked over the crowd as the passengers disembarked. He was the target of many eyes, for he wore a typical western garb consisting of jeans, a colorful red-and-white checked shirt, a buckskin vest, and a fawn-colored Stetson. His red hair showed beneath the brim of the hat, and his steady gray eyes targeted each passenger getting off the train. When a young woman stepped off, he straightened slightly and shoved his way through the crowd, ignoring the looks of protests. When he came to stand before her, he removed his hat, and the afternoon sun brought the red glints out even more prominently. A scar beside his mouth deepened as he smiled and said quietly, "Hello, Priscilla. I'm glad you're here."

"Hello, Jason." Priscilla looked up at the tall man and thought fleetingly of how he had been attracted to her ever since he had come to the ranch. She had treated him shamefully and now was sorry for that. "Thanks for coming to meet me," she said, smiling up at him.

As always, any kind word from this young woman drew a flash of gratitude from Jason Ballard. He shuffled his feet, saying, "I'll get your luggage." He hopped on the train, then exited almost at once, his long legs spanning the space easily. "I've got a carriage out here."

They made their way through the station grounds, and when they got out front, Priscilla was amused to see a team of matched bays harnessed to a black surrey with shiny brass fittings that flickered in the sun. "I thought you'd be driving a car by this time."

"Not as long as there's a horse and carriage around," Jason grinned wryly. He helped her into the surrey, then mounted quickly to the opposite side. Taking up the lines, he spoke to the horses. The team moved out smartly, their hooves clattering on the hard-surfaced road. The traffic was mostly horses, buggies, and wagons, but a few automobiles also moved down the broad street.

"I hate those blasted automobiles!" Jason said. "All they're good for is to scare horses!"

"You might as well get used to them. They're here to stay," Priscilla said. She looked around as they drove down a wide boulevard into the main part of the city.

"So this is Los Angeles," she said. "It's not as big as New York."

"No, and I hope it stays that way. I never did like crowds."

"No, you never did." Priscilla turned to him and studied his profile. He had a large nose with a slight break in the middle of it, and his neck was thick and strong and tanned. She let her eyes fall to his hands, which were large and obviously powerful. There were scars on his hands from years of working with ropes and cattle, and they looked tough and competent.

"How were your folks?" he asked and turned to watch her. She was wearing a simple blue dress and had a small hat on that was pinned down firmly with hat pins.

"They were fine, but I do have some news. Cass is moving to Los Angeles. He's bought an orange grove somewhere around here. I have the address. I want to go out and see him as soon as I can."

"Anytime you want to go, I'll take you, Priscilla," he offered.

As they drove through town, Priscilla was charmed by the Southwest-style architecture—the many adobe buildings and red-tiled roofs, landscaped with flowering tropical plants, varieties of cactus, and splashing fountains. Many of the broad streets were lined with palm trees, and they teemed with people going about their business or simply enjoying the delightful California sunshine—among them quite a few Mexicans and Orientals, Priscilla noticed. From certain vantage points she caught her first glimpses of the sparkling Pacific Ocean and was awed by the beauty of the rugged San Gabriel Mountains in the distance, which served as a magnificent backdrop to the scene before her. As they made their way into the heart of the city, she could hardly believe her good fortune in coming to this exotic place.

"Tell me all about the studio," she said, excited to know more about the movie-making business. "What have you been doing?"

"Mostly getting a crew together and a remuda of horses."

Priscilla listened intently as he proceeded to tell her of his activities, speaking in an easy voice, his eyes alert as he threaded the surrey through the traffic that was getting heavier. He sat loosely in the seat, almost idly, but Priscilla knew that he could change in a moment, for she had seen him leap into action with startling speed.

"Do you like it here, Jason?"

"Not as much as the ranch, but it's better than New York. A man can stretch around here." He lifted his eyes and gestured to his right. "I spend a lot of time down at the ocean watching the boats. Never was around water before. I've even gone out on a couple. Scares me a little bit. I can't swim, and if that boat sinks I'd be a gone goose." Then he motioned to his left. "Plenty of spaces out there, though. All the way to the mountains. It's a nice valley, Priscilla. Lots of ranches, but a lot of people are startin' to put in orange groves like your brother. I think he's pretty smart getting in on the ground floor like that."

"I hope it works out well for him."

"What about Pete?"

"Oh, you know Pete. He's on his way back to Detroit. He plans to build a race car and win every race in the world."

"I bet he'll do it, too." Ballard motioned with his right hand. "There's the hotel. I figure you might want to rest up from your trip. It's too late to go to the studio today." He pulled up in front of a hotel that appeared to be new. It was made out of gleaming white stucco with large pillars in the front. A doorman wearing a military-looking uniform came at once to take their luggage. Ballard turned to her and removed his hat again. He hesitated for a moment, then said, "Would you like for me to take you out later and show you the town?"

"I'm pretty tired, Jason. Maybe another time."

"Sure." He nodded, and his face did not change. "I'll see you tomorrow morning. I'll pick you up about eight."

"Come for breakfast," Priscilla said, looking up at him and smiling. "We'll try some of this orange juice that's going to make Cass rich."

"That would be fine." He watched her move gracefully up the hotel steps, and when she disappeared through the front door, he clamped his hat over his head and climbed back up into the surrey. He slapped the rumps of the horses with the lines, saying, "Get up!" and settled down as they broke into a fast trot. He drove through town until he came to the outskirts where a low bungalow sat to one side of a large corral filled with horses grazing and switching their tails at the flies. Ballard leaped out of the carriage, then handed the lines to a short, fat man dressed in overalls and wearing a white Stetson. "Unhitch the team, Charlie," he said. "Grain 'em down and turn 'em out in the pasture."

"Okay, boss."

Ballard entered the building, which was in effect a bunkhouse. The largest room ran for almost twenty-five feet and was filled with tables, chairs, and lamps. Everything was illuminated by the brilliant afternoon sunlight that filtered through the large windows across the front of the room. At least two poker games were going on, and a few men were asleep with their feet propped up against other chairs. The room was filled with cigar smoke and the pungent smell of horses from the clothing of the men.

"All right, you yahoos!" Ballard called out, and at once everybody turned to look at him. They were a fairly rough crew, and Jason had been obliged to educate two of the rougher members with his fists. He slowly reached into his pocket and pulled out a box of gingersnaps. Removing one, he put it into his mouth and chewed on it for a moment. "All right, Miss Winslow's here. She's a fine lady, and I'm giving you the law of the land. You say one word out of line to her, and I'll pound you into the ground!"

A tall, lanky cowboy sitting at one of the poker tables shoved back his high-crowned white hat with one finger and grinned. "Ah now, Jason. You don't have to make us a speech like that." He looked around the room and winked secretly at the crowd and then said innocently, "We're all gentlemen here. I thought you knowed that."

Jason grinned at the cowboy. "I made this speech especially for you, Mike. You're the ladies' man, but it won't go with Miss Winslow."

"She pretty special, is she?" Mike Smith inquired. He leveled his brown eyes on the foreman, and his fingers toyed with a whiskey glass in front of him. "I had a friend that seen her on the stage in New York. He said she was as pretty as a speckled pup."

"You can look—but don't touch, and watch your mouth!"

Another cowpoke spoke up, an older man with gray hair and a pair of steady blue eyes. "Don't worry, Jase. We'll behave."

Jason ran his hands through his hair, studied them, and then grinned as he went over to take a seat across from Mike Smith. "I'll just relieve you of some of that big money you been earnin'," he said.

Jason Ballard had a way with the men. He could be hard and tough, but he was one of them, and they all knew they could come to him if they needed help. Smith studied him carefully, started to say something about Priscilla Winslow, then decided against it. He picked up the cards and began to shuffle, and the game went on as the humming sound of the men's voices filled the room.

★　★　★　★

Priscilla rose before dawn. She never slept well in a strange room. Feeling the need for a walk, she slipped into a violet-colored cotton dress with a tiny white-flowered pattern trimmed in dark purple. Leaving the hotel, she walked around as the sun came up, throwing its first crimson rays of light over the city. She returned feeling invigorated and found Jason waiting for her in front of the hotel. "I went for a little walk," she said.

"Wish I'd known that. I'd have gone with you. Ready for breakfast?"

"That sounds good. Let's try some of that orange juice I've heard so much about."

The two stepped inside, and Jason led her to the restaurant. The elegant dining room was well lit by the early morning sun streaming through the large windows, brightening the dark red walls and the red-and-black patterned carpet. The tables were covered with white linen cloths, a folded red linen napkin at each place setting, and in the center of each table sat a Hampshire pottery lamp with leaded glass shade. Jason and Priscilla chose a corner table behind a potted palm, which afforded them some privacy, and sat down in the sumptuous red leather oak chairs. They ordered ham and eggs and large glasses of orange juice. When the juice came, Priscilla picked up her tall glass and looked at it carefully, then tried it. "Why, that's wonderful, Jase!"

"The best in the world, I guess. Although, folks down in Florida might argue with that," he grinned. His face glowed from a shave, and he looked roughly handsome in his royal blue shirt and string tie. As they ate they talked at length about the motion pictures that were going to be made, and he gave her a quick rundown of the crew. Neither of them spoke of New York nor of their early days together on the ranch. Finally he said, "Well, if you're ready we'll go see the studio."

"I'm ready, Jase."

The two left the hotel and climbed into the same surrey they had ridden in from the train station. During the short trip to the studio, Priscilla plied him with questions about the men and the horses. As he spoke she had to constantly remind herself to be on her guard. It was uncomfortable knowing that he was in love with her. After what had happened with Eddie Rich, she was determined to have no close relationships that might lead to anything serious. The old saying that her mother had often used jumped into her mind: *A burnt child dreads the fire.* She had heard her mother say that a thousand times, but never had it seemed more real than it did to her at this particular time of her life. It was a strange feeling, for she had everything she had always thought she wanted—plenty of money, some recognition, acceptance in the theater, which had been her dream—and yet something was still missing, but she could not identify it nor put her finger on it.

The sun had come up now and was beating down upon them, yet it was not uncomfortable. "I know I'm going to like it here better than New York," she said. "I couldn't stand another one of those cold winters."

"No cold winters here, so they tell me," Jason said. "Just sunshine all year round. Heaven on earth, the natives say."

"I doubt that. They may have good weather, but no place is heaven on earth."

He looked at her, surprised. Usually she was a cheerful girl, but now he saw a disturbed look in her eyes. He hesitated and, not wanting to upset her, merely said, "How have you been, Priscilla?"

She knew exactly what he meant. What he actually wanted to ask was, had she gotten over Eddie Rich? Since she could not answer honestly that she had, she put him off, saying, "I'm feeling very well. I had a good time at home. I got to relax and be with the folks a lot. I'd almost forgotten how to ride, but I picked it up again in a hurry. Benjamin, my nephew, is going to be a great rider. I gave him some lessons. We went out riding every day."

"Is he like Cass?"

"Very much like him. Only he's a little bit too fresh."

"Ah, he's just a kid. He'll change."

"I suppose so." They drew up in front of a large structure that appeared to be a barn. Priscilla stared at it with amazement. "Is this it?"

"This is it. There's more of it around over there. Mr. Porter bought up quite a bit of land here. He keeps building what he calls 'sets.' See anything funny about this building?"

She looked at it carefully. "Why, it doesn't have a roof!" she exclaimed.

"That's right. Come on in and take a look." Jason jumped out of the surrey, tied the horses up, and came back to extend his hand. When she put hers in his, he held it for a moment with an odd look on his face. Then without another word, he led her to the door of the set and opened it.

When she stepped inside, she saw that the structure was subdivided by walls, but overhead there was no ceiling. "Why, this is crazy!" she said. "What's to keep it from raining on everybody?"

"Nothing," Jason drawled. "When it does rain we go someplace that's got a roof."

"Why doesn't the place have a roof on it?"

"Them cameras need lots of light, and this way they can shoot an indoor scene right at noon. Look, they got everything in here. All kinds of sets, living rooms, bedrooms, kitchens. Everything's kind of waterproof, though. It does rain once in a while, but not a lot." He turned quickly and said, "Look, there's Mr. Porter."

Priscilla turned to see Edwin Porter approaching. He was a short, hefty man with an abundant crop of brown hair. He was not fat but rather stocky, with the kind of muscle that comes to wrestlers and heavyweight boxers. He had a pair of sharp gray eyes that were fixed on her now, and he was smiling as he came to her. Before she could move, he reached over, took her by the arms, pulled her forward, and kissed her soundly on the cheek.

"Hey, Priscilla!" he said. "It's good to see you. How was your trip?"

She was somewhat accustomed to the kisses that many of her theatrical friends bestowed, but she had never liked them. Still,

Edwin Porter was a fine man, and she had learned to trust him absolutely. "Very good, Edwin," she said. "Jason was right there to meet me. He's been showing me around a bit."

"Everything all right with those cowpunchers of yours, Jason?"

"All ready to roll, Mr. Porter."

"I guess we can start this afternoon. Stan will tell you what we need."

"Who's Stan?" Priscilla asked.

"Stanislas Lem. He's a big director from Europe—Germany mostly. He'll be directing the picture. Come on. I want you to meet him right away."

"I'll hang around until he tells me what to do," Jason said.

"I'll send him right over as soon as I introduce him to Priscilla, our star." He took Priscilla's arm and propelled her through the sets, speaking briefly to those he passed. Turning to Priscilla, he said, "Let me give you a word about Stan. He's a genius with a camera, but he's got a temper like a blowtorch. Just don't pay any attention to him."

"I'll try," Priscilla agreed. As they approached a different set, she was surprised when they met a tall, lean man with hollow cheeks and a shock of black hair. He was about forty, she guessed, and there was an electric energy about the man.

"Stan, this is our new star I've been telling you all about. Miss Priscilla Winslow. Priscilla, Stanislas Lem."

"I'm glad to know you, Mr. Lem." Priscilla put out her hand, and he took it and squeezed it so hard that she winced.

"I'm glad to see you, Miss Winslow." He bowed from the hips in the European fashion, and his smile made his Slavic features less grim. "You can't be as fine an actress as Edwin here has been telling me, I don't think."

"I'm sure he's been much too kind, but I promise I'll do my best for you."

"Fine . . . fine!"

"Stan, why don't you go and get Jason lined up on the details for that scene we're going to do out on the prairie. The one where the wagon trains are jumped by the Indians."

"Where is he?"

"I left him back by the door. I think he's waiting for you."

"I will go at once." He turned to Priscilla. "Have you seen the script yet?"

"No, not yet."

"I'll get you one." He waved to a young man who was standing at some distance holding a megaphone and a sheaf of papers. "Billy, give Miss Winslow a script. Go over it with her." He turned then and left abruptly.

The young man came forward and grinned. "I'm Billy Winters," he said. "Here's the script. If you have any questions, I'll be glad to answer them for you, Miss Winslow."

"Thank you, Mr. Winters."

"Just Billy is fine." The young man wheeled around and briskly walked away.

"What did you think of Stan?" Mr. Porter asked.

"He's got a lot of energy, hasn't he?"

"He sure does. And he's a perfectionist. He doesn't want anything to go wrong. Well, come along. I'll introduce you to the wardrobe woman, and you can pick out a costume. You'll be in that scene out on the prairie. Can you ride a horse? But of course you can. You grew up in Wyoming."

"Yes. I grew up on a ranch. As a matter of fact, Jason taught me a lot about riding. He was my father's foreman."

"That's right. I forgot."

The day was fascinating but terribly demanding for Priscilla. Porter was constantly at her side, explaining how he intended to make the Western story into a new art form. Expecting to have some sort of run-in with Stan Lem, Priscilla was surprised when he did not display the temper Porter had warned her about. Though he was very demanding down to the last detail, the director was extremely kind every time he spoke to her.

The prairie scene had been shot with a group of Indians—not real ones, but merely some of the cowboys dressed in Indian garb and made up with war paint. There had been a great deal of shouting and jeering and laughter among this group, which did not matter since their voices would never be heard in the theater. Jason handled the riding scenes well, and when it was time for Priscilla to ride in, he stood holding her horse while she mounted.

"Don't fall off and make a liar out of me. I've been telling everybody that you're the best rider in the state of Wyoming—except for me."

Priscilla laughed. "I'll do my best, Jason, but like you always said, 'Never was a horse couldn't be rode. Never was a rider couldn't be throwed.' "

He grinned up at her suddenly, and his broad smile made him look like a mischievous boy. "That's right, but you hang in there. We'll show these movie-making people a thing or two."

Everyone was impressed with the ease with which Priscilla handled a horse. When the day finally ended, she changed out of her costume and went back to her hotel. She was too tired to do more than eat a quick supper and fall into bed. She lay there thinking of the day, and her last thought was of Jason and his open smile and the light in his eyes. "I can't hurt that man," she said. "He's too good for that."

★ ★ ★ ★

The first picture went quickly. It was only two reels long, and Lem was a hard driver. When he wrapped up the picture, he came to stand precisely before Priscilla in his Prussian manner. He took her hand suddenly and kissed it. "You are not only a fine actress, you are a sweet girl. If all actresses were like you, my dear, the theater would be much more pleasant."

"Why, thank you, Stan," Priscilla said. She had trusted this director from the first day, for she sensed he knew his business backward and forward and respected him for it. He knew how to get the most out of his actors and actresses, and as he left she told Porter, "I hope you always keep him as my director. He's so easy to work with."

"Not everyone says that," Porter grunted. "Just the good ones. He's terribly impatient with anything less."

During the filming of the picture, she had received two letters from Cass. He insisted that she come for a visit as soon as she could, and she was eager to do so. Jason had offered to take her, but she had said, "You're too busy, Jase. I'll take a cab." She had seen the disappointment in his eyes, but he had not argued.

Rising early the next morning, Priscilla dressed carefully in a bright yellow-dotted Swiss cotton day dress trimmed in black and went downstairs and asked for a cab. A little while later, a loud automobile with a short, fat driver pulled up.

"Yes, miss? Where can I take you?"

Handing him the address, Priscilla said, "Do you know where this is?"

Glancing at it, the man nodded. "Yes, ma'am. I know exactly. I'll get you there in no time."

It took a little longer than the man had promised, for Cass's orange grove was located some ten miles west of Los Angeles. They passed through several other large orange groves, and finally the cab pulled up in front of a white frame house surrounded by trees. She got out and paid the driver. "Are you sure this is it?"

"Yes, ma'am. I guess those folks are looking for you."

Turning quickly, Priscilla saw Cass and Serena come outside, followed by Benjamin and Elizabeth. It was Benjamin who ran forward, crying out, "Aunt Priscilla!"

Priscilla reached down and caught him up, hugged him, and gave him a kiss. "I'm finally here," she said. She put him down and then turned to greet Serena and Cass. They led her into the house and insisted that she eat breakfast with them. Cass wanted to know all about the motion picture she had just made and how Jason was doing. Sipping on a glass of fresh-squeezed orange juice, she told them all the details of her new job. "And Jase is fine," she said. "He's awfully busy, but he said he'd be out to see you soon."

"Will you go riding with me again, Aunt Priscilla?" Benjamin demanded. He came around and tugged at her sleeve and looked up at her with confidence. "You will, won't you?"

"Of course I will, Ben. We'll have to find some horses, though."

"I keep three horses," Cass said. "I've got a car, too, but that only runs half the time. I sure wish Pete were here to fix it up."

Priscilla saw that Elizabeth was still bashful, but she had made it a point to bring small gifts for everyone. When she produced a doll with lifelike hair, it broke through all the girl's barriers. Elizabeth's eyes opened wide, and she grabbed it. "Her name is Prilly," she said, looking up at her aunt with a big grin. "Like you."

"Why, I am honored, Elizabeth. Now you and I can play dolls and house, and we'll have a fine time."

After the long days working at the set, Priscilla enjoyed the visit with her brother and his family that day. She and Serena hit it off marvelously well, and the children adored her. The next picture would not start for a week, so she found herself coming back every day to visit. After the lonely time she had spent in New York, it felt good to be around Cass's family. One day Cass grinned sarcastically and said, "It's no wonder these kids adore you. You do everything they tell you. You're just their big toy."

"They're such sweet children, Cass. They're so beautiful and well behaved. You must be proud of them."

"Well, Ben has his moments," Cass said with a resigned grin. But despite such comments, it was obvious by the tone of his voice and the look in his eyes that Cass was indeed very proud of his children. He said to Priscilla, "Sis, I'm glad you've come. I've missed family. I wish we all lived in one town where we could see each other every day."

"Most families aren't like that. They used to be at one time, I suppose. But now kids grow up and leave and go off to make their own careers. That'll happen to yours one day, I suppose."

"I hate to think about it," Cass said, looking down at Benjamin, who was playing in the dirt, and at Elizabeth, who was playing with her doll, giving her tea from a cup. "You're going to church with us tomorrow, aren't you?"

"Why . . . I suppose so."

"You'll like it. It's a fine church. A little bit bigger than we're used to, but we feel at home there already, even though we've only been going there a few weeks. The people are very friendly."

"I'll be glad to go. Is it close?"

"No, it's right in the middle of Los Angeles, but we don't mind the drive. Why don't we pick you up at the hotel in the morning and we'll take you?"

"That will be fine. I've missed church." She hesitated, then said, "After I made such a mess of my life, I thought it was all over for me, Cass." The two were sitting alone in the kitchen, and she thought about the times she had confided in him when they were growing up. Unlike most boys with younger sisters, Cass had always listened carefully and with understanding. He did so now as she told him for the first time what a horrible experience she had had with Eddie Rich.

" . . . and so I thought I was married. Then this woman showed up one day at the apartment and told me Eddie already had a wife. Cass, it was horrible. That made me an adulteress. I couldn't stand it—"

"It wasn't your fault," Cass said.

"In a way it was. I should have had more insight, but I was so naive, and I wanted to go into theater so much. Well . . . he had a way about him."

"I'll bet he did," Cass growled. "I'm surprised Pete didn't punch him out."

"He wanted to, but I wouldn't let him. Eddie was only interested in himself. He's what he is, and I made a big mistake."

"Sure, that's what it was, sis. A mistake. We all make them."

"Anyway, after that I hit bottom emotionally, and spiritually I was dead. But Esther helped me a lot. She taught me how to pray and how to seek after God. She led me to the Lord, and I was saved, Cass. I never was before. I went to church all my life, but it was just something I did. It didn't mean anything to me."

"But it does now, doesn't it? I can see that." Cass was studying his sister's face, and he saw a change that had not been there before. "I can't quite describe it. You seem sad, and yet there's a difference in you."

"I guess I'm still struggling. I'm a Christian now, but I don't know how to put the past away. I try, but it keeps coming back."

Cass moved across the room and put his arm around her. "We'll see it through, sis," he said. "And you'll like the church. I know you will." As Priscilla smiled up at him he thought to himself, *I can see you've changed, little sister, but you're not out of the woods yet. I've got to help you all I can.*

★　★　★　★

Faith Temple was much larger than Priscilla had imagined. "Why, this is as big as a New York City church!" she exclaimed as the car drove by the magnificent building. The front was faced with pink marble, and the spire seemed to pierce the clouds. "It's enormous," she exclaimed, craning her neck to see the top of the spire.

"There are a few very wealthy people who put up most of the money," he said. "They had a fine pastor, from what I understand. People say he was a terrific preacher, but he just left a month ago."

"Who's the preacher now?" Priscilla asked as she got out of the car.

Serena waited until they were all out before answering Priscilla's question. "The associate pastor is Reverend Nolan Cole. I think you'll like him."

"Is he an older man?"

"No." Serena shook her head. "I think he's about thirty."

"That's young for such a large church, isn't it?"

"Well, he's not the pastor yet. The church is looking around," Cass said. "I expect they'll ask him to stay on after they've looked awhile. I don't know where they'd find anybody that can preach any better."

The sound of hearty singing drifted out from the large doors that stood open. As they stepped inside the foyer, Priscilla stopped and looked around, amazed at the sight. "Why, this looks like the lobby of one of the large theaters in New York!"

"I hear tell that the former pastor believed in doing things right. He always said, 'God's house ought to be at least as beautiful as a theater.' " He looked around at the gleaming marble, the floors, and the ornate statuary that lined the walls. High overhead large windows let in yellow beams of sunlight that fell like golden bars on the surface below. "Must have cost a mint, I guess. Wait until you see the sanctuary!"

When they stepped inside the spacious auditorium, Priscilla almost gasped again. It was a very large building, made to seem even more so by the lofty height of the ceiling. "Why, it's like the pictures I've seen of cathedrals in Europe."

"It is something, isn't it?" Serena said. "Come along. I always like to sit down close to the front."

They made their way down the aisle to within ten rows of the front and took their seats. The building was filling up rapidly, and by the time the service started, it was almost full. Up on the rostrum a large choir clothed in white robes lifted their voices, and Priscilla found herself joining the singing.

"They always sing the old songs. I like that," Cass whispered. "They've got a soloist here who could get a job with the Metropolitan Opera, I believe."

Cass's words proved true, for right then a young woman stepped out from the choir to the front and began singing "Amazing Grace." Her voice was more beautiful than any Priscilla had ever heard on stage, and she had listened to some good ones. It was not just her voice that seemed to move the audience. The young woman's face glowed with love as she poured her heart into the song.

The song service went on for some time, and it was better than any Priscilla had ever been to.

"That's Brother Nolan Cole coming to the platform now," Cass whispered.

Curious as to what the minister would be like, Priscilla kept her eyes fixed on the man who came to stand behind the large oak pulpit. She was surprised by his masculine good looks. He was strongly built, and his broad shoulders fit well into the charcoal gray suit that must have come from a fine tailor's shop. He had blond hair with a slight wave in it and a very strong-looking square face. His most outstanding feature was his eyes. They were blue—an electric blue that seemed to sparkle as he began to speak. His voice was a deep, pleasant baritone that filled the room without any effort. He welcomed the visitors, his broad lips smiling as he looked out over the congregation. He made a few jokes about himself, gave some announcements about the church's activities for the coming week, then without preamble began the sermon.

After listening for a few minutes, Priscilla realized that Nolan Cole was a better preacher than any she had ever heard in the small churches of Wyoming. She had not gone to church much in New York, but she knew instinctively that this man had the gift that most men lacked. There was an ease in his manner, and yet as he read the Scriptures, his voice crackled with energy. And he did not stand behind the pulpit as most preachers do. Several times during the sermon, he would pace back and forth. One time, when he was making a point, it looked as if he might plunge right down into the audience. He was completely filled with his message, and a few times Priscilla had the notion that he was looking directly into her eyes, speaking only to her. She knew that this was the gift of an actor. The thought flashed through her mind, *If he weren't a preacher, he'd be a marvelous actor. Better than almost any I've seen.*

His message was simple, filled with homey illustrations, and yet he quoted from the Church Fathers, including St. Augustine, and even used modern history to illustrate his sermon. When he was finished he invited those who wanted prayer to come forward, and soon the altar was filled with men and women on their knees, praying and seeking God.

Priscilla was touched by the sermon. It had been a simple but stirring message about the love of God for those who had failed Him. The story of the Prodigal Son had formed the heart of the sermon. Reverend Cole had spoken fervently of how much the father in the story yearned for the return of the son who had gone off and offended him. At one point, Reverend Cole left the pulpit and walked across the front of the auditorium, dramatizing how the father must have risen up and squinted his eyes when he saw his son coming yet a long way off. He had acted it out—the old man going forward to embrace the wayward boy, the tears in his eyes—and his voice had sounded like thunder as he cried out, "Bring out the fatted calf! Put the best robe on him! Put a ring on his finger, for this is my son who was dead, and now he is alive again."

Never had Priscilla been quite as moved by a message. She had a desire to go forward, for she knew her need for more of God, but she was held back by timidity. As the pastor pronounced the benediction, she promised herself, *I'll go forward the next time.*

Finally the service was over, and as they filed toward the door, Serena leaned closer and whispered, "He's almost too good-looking to be a preacher."

"I don't suppose that hurts, Serena."

"I suppose not. Look at the crowd waiting to shake hands with him."

"So I see," Priscilla said as she noticed all the attention certain parishioners, especially the women, were giving him.

Cass insisted that they join the line to greet him. When they were finally standing in front of the preacher, Cass said, "I'd like you to meet my sister, Priscilla Winslow. She's come to Los Angeles to make motion pictures."

"Is that so? I'm very happy to know you, indeed, Miss Winslow."

Priscilla felt her hand enclosed by the strong, warm hand of the tall minister. He did not squeeze hard, but there was firm pressure to his grasp. She looked up into his eyes and saw that he was smiling at her.

"I'd like to come sometime and see how those things are made. I've never seen a motion picture."

"Why, I'd be glad to have you come as my guest."

"That's a date, and you'll be back for the service tonight, won't you?"

"Indeed I will if my brother agrees."

"Yes, we'll all be here, Brother Cole."

"Fine. I'll look forward to seeing you—and to my visit to see you at work, Miss Winslow. Thank you for coming."

As they filed out the doors of the church, Priscilla was slightly dazed by the personality of the man. "He's not like any preacher I've ever seen," she said.

"I agree," Serena said. "He's a new sort of minister for me, too." She grinned faintly and said, "Watch yourself, Priscilla. In the short time we've been here, I've seen the effect he has on women. He's better looking than some of your matinee idols."

"He can't help it if he's good-looking," Cass protested. "I can't help it, either. Us good-looking fellows just have to do the best we can." He grunted as Serena drove an elbow into his ribs.

As they climbed into their car and drove away, Priscilla thought, *He is a different sort of preacher. I wonder what he'll think of actors and movie making.*

CHAPTER FOUR

BUMMERS

★ ★ ★ ★

When Peter Winslow returned to work at the Ford Motor Company in Detroit, he was filled with enthusiasm and looked forward to learning everything there was to know about racing cars. In his mind he had tied himself to Henry Ford, the genius of the automotive world, and felt confident that he would rise in the company rapidly and become its star driver.

He received a rude shock on his first day back at work, the first week of September, when he ran head on into his new boss, Cecil Pennington. Pennington was new to the Ford Company, having been hired by Ford away from the Winton Automobile Company. He was a hard-driving man with little patience for anyone who disagreed with him. He looked more like a professional wrestler than a mechanic, standing over six three and weighing nearly three hundred pounds. He had a broad red face, small eyes deeply sunk under beetling brows, and a shock of almost white blond hair. His voice could rattle the windows, and his profanity was blasphemous beyond belief. It was perhaps this latter quality that turned Peter against him. He had never liked profanity, thinking it marked a man as incompetent with the English language. When Pennington stooped over Peter's shoulder that first day, then shoved him aside cursing strongly, Peter had to resist the impulse to slam a wrench down over the man's head.

"You're going to strip these bolts off!" Pennington yelled and cursed loudly. He shouldered Peter aside and gave him a lesson that Peter did not need. And when Peter argued that he knew what he was doing, Pennington's face grew brick red. With another blasphemous burst of profanity, he shouted, "Shut your mouth, Winslow! I'm the foreman here, and you'll do exactly what I say! If I tell you to sweep the floor, you'll sweep the floor! If I tell you to clean the toilets, you'll do that, too! You got that clear?"

"I didn't hire on to be a janitor. Mr. Ford hired me to work on cars," Peter said.

"Mr. Ford put me in charge of this shop, and you'll fall in line or else you can pack up your tools and get out!" For a moment it seemed to Peter that Pennington was going to grab him, but the big man contented himself with another blistering stream of profanity, followed by a final warning. "Shape up or you'll be out on your ear, Winslow!" Then he turned and stomped away.

"Better watch that guy." Peter turned to see Gerald Ramsey, a short, tubby man with long, dexterous fingers that could tune an engine to its finest pitch. Ramsey shook his head. "Been some changes since you been gone, Pete. I don't know why Mr. Ford hired that guy. They say he's a genius, but he's a mean buzzard! He punched Shorty White out last Thursday—busted his nose. Don't give him any lip. Ford backs him up, but I don't know why."

Peter took all this in, then nodded shortly. "Thanks for the warning. I'll watch myself," he murmured, then turned back to the engine he was working on. As he worked he considered his options. There were plenty of other automobile companies looking for good mechanics; since the turn of the century the manufacturers had proliferated. But in his mind Henry Ford was the up-and-coming man in this growing industry. As he tightened the nuts on a bolt, Peter thought about Ford's history.

Ford had built a quadricycle in 1896, using a buggy-type chassis, bicycle wheels, and gas-pipe hubs. It went twenty miles an hour but had no reverse. Three years later he built another quadricycle while working as superintendent of the Detroit Automobile Company. In 1901 he built a third car with fancy fenders and a steering wheel. He also built his first racing car powered by a twenty-six horsepower, two-cycle engine. It had been a fast car, averaging forty-three miles an hour, beating a Winton in a race at Grossepoint, Michigan.

When the Detroit Automobile Company folded that same year, Ford organized the Henry Ford Company but did not stay long. In 1902 he organized the Ford Motor Company with twenty-eight thousand dollars capital and joined the mad race to provide cars to Americans who were demanding them in record numbers.

The first cars were rich men's toys, and every wealthy man had one or two as a plaything. Paved roads were nonexistent, and cars ran no faster than a horse's gallop. The novelty soon spread, however, and by 1900, America had eight thousand cars. The public was fascinated by these frail, costly, bulky contraptions that shook, trembled, clattered, spat oil, fire, and smoke, and smelled terrible. For a time it was not certain that the automobile would replace the horse, and even the name for these strange vehicles was uncertain. In a magazine contest the new name for the wheeled vehicle was "Motorcycle." Runners-up included "Petrocar," "Autobat," and "Motorfly."

After the first popular American car debuted in 1901, the gasoline engine Oldsmobile business picked up and it became a male sport. Perhaps the car embodied the age-old male cravings for power and exploration. It was almost entirely a man's world. From the very start, society took a negative attitude toward women driving; some steering wheels carried the warning "Men and boys only." There were reasons for this exclusivism: roads were often muddy ruts and cars were tremendously hard to handle.

As Peter continued working, he thought about the history of the machines that had so engaged his dedication. When he reached for a wrench, he suddenly became aware of Cecil Pennington peering over his shoulder. He did not work any faster, nor did he turn to look at the man, but kept his attention on the engine in front of him. He knew Pennington was trying to intimidate him and did not give evidence that he was aware of the foreman's presence. Finally Pennington snorted and stalked down the assembly line. Peter could hear his raucous voice cursing Gerald Ramsey and then others farther down the line.

I'm going to have trouble with that fellow, he thought. This worried him because he had great admiration for Henry Ford. He had met Ford in New York almost by accident and begged him so hard for a job that Ford said, "If you can find your way to Detroit, I'll give you a chance." That had been all Peter Winslow needed. He'd packed his suitcase and was waiting when Ford returned from New York. He went to work in Ford's factory and had been happy there. Although he had little contact with Ford himself, the factory had always been a pleasant place to work. Now, however, the shadow of Pennington hung over everyone like a dark and brooding thundercloud ready to burst at the slightest provocation. There was none of the loud joking and rough horseplay that Peter remembered from before. The camaraderie among the workers was gone now, and every man feared for his job.

All day long that first day back on the job, Peter became more and more conscious of the gloom in the section of the plant where Pennington was foreman. As Peter left that afternoon, walking beside Gerald Ramsey, he muttered, "Not a very happy place anymore. I don't understand why Mr. Ford hired that clown."

"He's some kind of topnotch engineer," Ramsey shrugged. "They claim he practically invented the Winton over there. Ford paid a lot of money to get him here, but I don't think he knows how Pennington treats the hired help. That big lug is always great around Mr. Ford, smiling and speaking quietly. Never a curse word do you hear when Ford's around."

"He's not worth it, I don't think," Peter said as they walked along.

"No, but Ford will find out someday. Pennington's already fired three of the best men in the shop because they wouldn't kowtow to him." He looked nervously around, as if Pennington could overhear, and shrugged his thin shoulders. "I'm leaving myself, Pete."

Surprise washed over Winslow's face. "Why, you can't do that, Gerald. You're on the way up here. You're the best mechanic in the shop."

"It ain't worth foolin' with, Pete. I'm going to work for the Stanley people."

"Don't do that. Those steam engines they're trying to build won't work in cars. I know a lot of people are going for it, but you wait and see. The gasoline engine will put them out of business pretty soon."

"That may be, but they've offered me more money than I'm getting here, and I can't put up with Pennington's bullying any longer." Ramsey slapped Peter on the shoulder. "Let me put a word in for you. They need good men over there. No sense fooling around with that gorilla."

"No, thanks a lot, Gerald. I think I'll stick it out here."

★ ★ ★ ★

Gerald Ramsey's departure left an empty spot in Peter's life. He had roomed with him ever since he first came to Detroit, and the two got along very well both in and out of the shop. Ramsey was replaced by a dour Scotsman named McCone, who never spoke a cheerful word to anyone. Peter soon grew lonesome, especially during the hours after work. He missed Ramsey a great deal.

Two weeks after Ramsey had left, Peter was busy installing an engine in the framework of Ford's racing car, the *Arrow*, which had run a record ninety-one miles per hour the previous January. It was Ford's pride, and he allowed only his best men to work on it. Sometimes he himself came down and oversaw the innovations he wanted built into it. Scheduled to leave the next morning for New York on a business trip, Ford stopped by late that afternoon to check on the *Arrow* and to talk to Peter. "Hello, Winslow," Ford said. He was a tall, thin man with a narrow face and a pair of intense brown eyes. "Haven't seen you since you got back. Did you have a good vacation?"

"Very fine, Mr. Ford, but I was glad to get back and work on the *Arrow*."

Ford smiled briefly, and the two men talked for some time about the racing car. Finally Ford nodded. "You have a feel for fast cars, Peter. I want you to get the *Arrow* in top shape. Put all your time in on it. I'm going to race it again next month, and I want that engine running smooth."

Peter was enthusiastic. "I'll be glad to, Mr. Ford. I'd like to be there when you drive it in that race."

Ford straightened up. He turned to Peter Winslow and grinned. "You'd like to drive it yourself, wouldn't you?"

"Yes, sir, I sure would. Who wouldn't?"

"Well, maybe we'll see about that. If you're as good a driver as you are a mechanic—well, I'll give it some thought. Take care of the *Arrow*."

"I'll have it purring like a kitten by the time you get back, Mr. Ford." As Ford went to give some instructions to Pennington before he left, Peter turned back to his work and felt better the rest of the day.

The next morning Peter threw himself into renovating the car, forgetting to eat lunch, he was so carried away. It was almost four o'clock when he heard Pennington's voice bellowing, "You've spent enough time on that car, Winslow. Get down there and work on that Model B."

Straightening up, Peter turned to face the muscular foreman. "Mr. Ford told me to stay on this until it's done," he said quietly.

Pennington could not bear to be crossed. "You do what I tell you!" he said, cursed for a moment, then shoved his thumb toward the Model B down the line. "Go down there and pull that engine and get it done before you leave today! You understand?"

"I'll have to do what Mr. Ford said," Peter said tensely, aware that most of the men in the near vicinity were listening carefully to his clash with the foreman. "He told me to stay on the *Arrow* until the changes he wanted were made."

Without warning, Pennington reached out and grabbed Peter's coveralls by the lapels and jerked him around. Caught off balance as he was shoved violently away, Peter stumbled and fell flat on the cement floor. Anger washed over him like a red wave. He was not a violent man, as a rule, but there was a temper in him that once in a while got out of control. He jumped to his feet in one motion and faced Pennington. "Don't ever put your hands on me again, Pennington!" he warned.

"It's *Mr.* Pennington to you, Winslow. And I'll put my hands on you whenever I please!"

Pennington reached out to give Peter another shove. Suddenly, the foreman found his wrists grasped by a steely grip. Despite his weight and heft, he was jerked violently forward. Peter had grabbed Pennington's wrists with both hands and with a grunt now spun the man around. Pennington's feet scrabbled, trying to keep his balance, but he never caught it. With every ounce of his strength, Peter heaved and released Pennington's wrists. The foreman practically turned a flip, landing on his shoulder blades. The explosive *huff* as his breath was driven from him was heard by every man standing around watching.

Silence fell over the shop as Pennington lay for one moment trying to catch his breath. Rolling over he pushed himself up, doubled up his hamlike fists, and advanced toward Peter like an angry bull. "I'm going to bust you up good, Winslow, and then throw you out! You're fired!"

"You can fire me, but I don't think you're man enough to bust me up!" Peter said. He stood where he was, his feet spread wide, his fists clenched and held waist high. He had always been able to defend himself and had a wiry strength that was hidden by the loose coveralls. As Pennington stepped forward and drove a mighty fist toward his face, Peter simply stepped inside it, pushed it aside with his left arm, and with the power coming up from his right leg through his torso with every ounce of his two hundred pounds, he struck the foreman just above the belt buckle. His fist sunk into the doughy stomach, and Pennington doubled over. As he did, Peter brought his forearm down across the foreman's meaty neck. Pennington fell to the floor gasping for breath, and his legs seemed to move helplessly.

Peter Winslow stood looking down at the foreman a moment and then began to collect his tools. When he was through he turned and saw that Pennington had gotten to his feet. The foreman's face was chalky and he was swaying.

"Get out of here! You're fired!" he gasped.

"Mr. Ford will have to hear about this," Peter said.

"Go on! Get out of here!"

Peter shrugged and, picking up his toolbox, left the factory. He went straight to his room, deposited his tools, then stood for a time looking out the window.

"I've done it this time," he muttered. "It'll be me or Pennington, and I'm not an engineer. Mr. Ford likes me, but he'll have to back up the foreman."

It was three days later, after Peter had walked the streets waiting impatiently, when Ford returned from New York. By the time Peter got to him, Ford had heard of the fight and of Peter's firing. He listened quietly while Peter gave his version, then shrugged, a sadness showing in his eyes. "I'm sorry, Winslow," he said finally. "I know Pennington's had trouble with the men before, and good ones, too, but I can't go over my foreman's head."

"Sure, Mr. Ford. I thought it'd be that way."

"Here. I'm going to write you a letter of recommendation. It'll get you a job, I think. Maybe with the Oldsmobile people."

Peter stood while Ford wrote a letter, and then the tall man rose and handed it to him. "I don't write many recommendations like this, Pete. Good luck to you. Maybe someday things will change. I will always be glad to have you back under different circumstances."

"Thank you, Mr. Ford. I'll look forward to that."

Peter left the factory speaking to no one, and as he walked out the door, a sadness settled on him. It was not just the job that bothered him, but the loss of his contact with Henry Ford. He knew that no matter where he went, he would be stepping down, and the usual cheerfulness that was part of him seemed to vanish as the doors closed behind him for the last time.

★ ★ ★ ★

October had come, driving away the heat of summer and bearing the promise of winter soon to come. As Peter Winslow moved along the main street of Detroit, there was no spring in his step nor excitement in his face. He had spent almost a month looking for a job in Detroit that had something to do with automobiles. He had failed, however, and the very best he could do was land a job in a furniture factory. For the past two weeks he had made the same leg to fit a kitchen table all day long. A frown settled on his face as he stepped inside a grocery store and began to pull a few cans off the shelf. He heard a loud, piercing tenor voice singing "I'm a Yankee Doodle Dandy," a song that was sweeping the country. It was from the musical *Little Johnny Jones* written by George M. Cohan, and as Peter brought his small collection of goods to the counter, the singer, a short Italian with curly black hair and olive skin, grinned. "How do you like-a my singing?"

"You ought to be in the show."

"That's-a right. I should be. Here I am clerking in a grocery store when I could be the American Caruso." The clerk added up the items on a pad, then said, "That'll be three dollars and twenty-two cents. Did you hear the other song from that show?"

"I don't guess so."

Immediately the clerk filled his lungs and with great gusto began to sing, "Give My Regards to Broadway." He knew every word of it and performed as though he were in front of an audience of ten thousand people. "Not bad, eh?" he said, grinning broadly when he had finished.

"Not bad," Peter said, smiling briefly. "You ever thought of singing for a career?"

"I never thought of anything else," the clerk said, shrugging his plump shoulders. "I'm-a just doing this until I get my break in the big time. I'm-a going to New York as soon as I get the money. That's where all the big singers get their breaks. You ever been there?"

"Yes. My sister's an actress. She was in a play there. Two of them, as a matter of fact."

At once the clerk became interested and demanded to know all about Peter's sister. When Peter told him that she had gone to Los Angeles to make movies, he shook his head, stating flatly, "That's-a no good. They ain't got no sound. No place for singers, but maybe you could get your sister to recommend me to somebody on the stage in New York."

Peter suddenly found this amusing. "Well, you got a big enough voice for it. I'll give you her address and you can write her." He wrote down Priscilla's Los Angeles address and said, "What's your name?"

"Tony Ameche," the clerk said. "That's-a me." He took the address, stared at it, and then grinned broadly. Sticking his hand out over the counter, he pumped Peter's hand up and down. "One of these days I'm-a gonna say, 'When I was just a grocery clerk, I got my first break when a man called Winslow stopped where I was selling groceries.'"

"Good luck, Tony. I hope you make it."

"I hope you make it, too. What is it you do?"

"I make table legs. Thousands of them. All just exactly alike for twelve hours a day."

The bitterness in his visitor's voice caught Ameche's attention. "What is it you *want* to do?" he said. "Everybody wants to do something."

"I want to race cars, but it doesn't look like I'm going to do it."

"Sure you will. I'll be a big star, and you'll be a race car driver. We'll both be rich and famous."

"I hope so, Tony. Well, good luck."

★　★　★　★

Over the next few weeks, Peter stopped in at the grocery store several times and soon became good friends with Tony Ameche. The two of them ate out, and Tony took Peter to the best Italian places in Detroit. On their third meeting, Tony came in with his cheeks puffed out, his dark eyes glowing with excitement. He was waving a sheet of paper in the air, and he grabbed Peter around the shoulders and hugged him, muttering fiercely in Italian.

"What's the matter with you, Tony? What's going on?"

"Look at this," Ameche said, shaking the paper in front of Peter's eyes.

"Well, hold it still. I can't read it like that." Peter jerked the

paper out of the Italian's hand and read it. "Why, this is from sis."
He scanned it and then grinned broadly. "Well, you can't say anything better than that. I'm surprised she took my recommendation. I'm no musician."

"She's-a saying she'll get me an introduction to Mr. Phil Donner. He's-a gonna do a musical. I'm-a going to New York tomorrow."

"There's no guarantees, Tony," Peter warned.

"Sure. I know that," Tony said airily. "But this Mr. Donner, he ain't never heard no singin' like-a *me!* I'm-a gonna go and be a star!"

Peter tried to talk sensibly to Ameche, but he saw that it was no use. The two ate spaghetti and crisp Italian bread as Tony continuously questioned Peter about New York. His friend was exuberant and full of hope in a way that Winslow had rarely seen. He sat there after the meal listening as Tony outlined his grandiose scheme, and finally when they parted, he shook Tony's hand, saying, "I guess I won't see you for a while."

Ameche grew solemn. He was an emotional man, and tears came to his eyes. "If you hadn't come into the store, I would never have had my chance. Thank you a million times, Pete!"

"Better hold off on the thanks until you're a star," Peter grinned. He reached over and gave the pudgy shoulders of the young man a hug and said, "Leave your address with Priscilla. I don't think I'll be around here long. I'll write to you."

"I'll do that. When you come to New York, I'll get you tickets up on the front row of my show."

"All right. It's a deal. Good luck, Tony."

"Good luck, Pete."

Peter did not see Ameche again, but he did write a short letter to Priscilla. He dated it October 5, 1904.

Dear Priscilla,

    I don't know if you and I have done Tony Ameche a favor. He sounds great to me, but what do I know about singing? In any case, he's leaving for New York to meet with Mr. Donner. It was a little rash of you to do this, not having heard him sing, but it's like you.

    I've been making table legs, and I hope I never see another one again. I'll have to keep on trying for a job in a machine shop or an auto plant, but if it doesn't work out here in Detroit, I may have to go somewhere else. I've got a good recommendation from Mr. Ford, and it ought to help a lot.

I've thought a lot about you lately, sis. I know you had a rough time in New York, but now that you're there in Los Angeles with some family, I feel better about you. I hope you and Serena and Cass and the kids are all doing well. Give my best to Jason. Tell him never to take up making table legs in a factory for a vocation. Better to ride a horse like he's doing.

Putting the pen down, he considered what he had written so far. He tried to think of something cheerful to write but could not. After putting on the stamp and sticking it in his pocket, he rose and went out to mail it.

The job at the furniture factory grew more agonizing each day, and two weeks after Ameche left, Peter had become desperate with frustration. He quit the job and threw all of his energies into finding a better one. Although he had a few opportunities, none seemed to be much of an improvement over making table legs. Finally his money ran low, and he had only enough to pay another week's rent.

After a discouraging day of job hunting, he returned to his room and his landlady met him at the door. "Any luck?"

"Not today, Mrs. Stephens."

"Well, don't be discouraged. A fine young man like you. There's got to be a good job out there for you." She fished in the pocket of her apron and came up with a letter. "This came for you this afternoon."

"Thank you, Mrs. Stephens."

Peter went to his room, sat down on the bed, and opened the letter after seeing on the envelope that it was from Jason. He read,

Dear Pete,

Priscilla told me that you got a job that's not much. Sorry to hear about your bad luck with the Ford plant.

Pete, I don't know if this means anything, but if things get too rough there, you can always come out and work for Imperial Pictures. I've got a job that amounts to being a foreman of a ranch. We have to keep a herd of cattle and move 'em in front of the cameras, and there's always room for another good rider. It won't pay much, but it might be a good place for you to tread water while you're finding your place racing cars. It would be great for me. I'd like mighty well to have you here. Come out anytime. There's always a place.

The letter was simply signed Jason, and Peter stared at it for a long time. The room was dark, but he did not bother to get up and light the gas lamp. He was tired and discouraged at how his luck had run out and nothing promising had happened lately. He looked down at the letter, squinting his eyes to read it again in the growing darkness. As he did so a sudden certainty came to him. "All right, I'll do it! I'm sick of this place," he said aloud. He got up and took several steps around the room, growing more certain that a move to Los Angeles was better than what he had. There was nothing for him in Detroit. He had tried everything he knew. He longed to see Jason, Priscilla, and his brother, Cass, and his family. The more he thought about it, the more the assurance grew within him that he must go.

He slept little that night, and when he rose the next morning, he dressed, packed his suitcase, then went down and met his landlady. "I'm leaving town, Mrs. Stephens."

"Leaving? Where are you going?" the woman asked. She was short and plump with a motherly air about her and had been a good landlady, often feeding Peter some of her excellent cooking.

"I'm going to Los Angeles. I've got a brother and a sister there, and things haven't worked out too well here."

"Well, I hate to see you go, but the good Lord will take care of you."

"I'm sure He will," Peter smiled. "I wonder if I could leave my tools with you. I'll need them sometime, but I don't want to take them with me now. I'll send you enough money to mail them, if you don't mind."

"I'll be glad to, Pete. And I'll be expecting to hear good things from you."

Peter left the house carrying the small suitcase with his few belongings in it. He thought of how his sister and brother were already successful, and here he had done nothing. A great determination rose in him, and his lips grew thin as he thought, *I'll make it! One way or another I'll make it!*

★ ★ ★ ★

The November wind had a sharp bite in it, and as Peter trudged along the highway of the dirt road, he pulled his coat tighter about him. Though it was getting colder, he had no money to spare on a heavier garment. He left Detroit hoping to make good time, but the only rides he had been able to catch were in wagons driven by farmers. A few cars sped by, but none of them stopped to offer him a ride. He had walked all morning and was hungry, and when he saw a bridge up ahead spanning a small river, he paused and then turned aside and made his way under the arch.

"Hello. How you doin', bud?" The speaker was an undersized man of about thirty-five with a thin pale face and sandy hair. He had a hooked nose, and his sharp brown eyes seemed weary as he waved a hand toward a small fire that sent up a curling wreath of white smoke. "Just about to start dinner. Sit down and rest yourself a bit."

"Don't mind if I do," Peter said. He put the suitcase down and advanced to the small fire and held his hands over it. As the heat soaked into him, he shivered and said, "I think we're in for worse weather."

"Probably are," the smaller man shrugged. He had gathered stones and built a small fire inside them and had rigged a stick that now pulled out a small frying pan and a small saucepan. "Beans and bacon sound okay?"

"Yes. Sounds great. I've got some bread and some peaches."

"Just what we need. My name's Easy Devlin."

"Pete Winslow."

"Good to know you, Pete. You come far?"

"All the way from Detroit." He opened his suitcase and pulled out two cans of peaches and half a loaf of bread wrapped in brown paper. Opening the bread, he began to slice it with his pocketknife, saying, "I'm headed for Los Angeles, but I don't think I'm going to get there this year."

"Bad time to be on the road," Devlin said. He began to cough, turning his head aside. The cough seemed to come from deep inside his chest.

"That's a bad cough. Have you had it long?"

"Oh, off and on," Devlin shrugged. He produced some bacon and put it in the frying pan, and it began to sizzle, sending up a delicious aroma. Then he opened two cans of beans and poured them into the saucepan.

"Let me borrow that can opener," Peter said. Taking the instrument, he opened the peaches and set them down carefully, then pulled out a spoon, a knife, and a fork. He had been camping out along the way, for it cost too much to eat at a cafe, and he was practically broke. "You come far?" he asked.

"All the way from the coast." There was a paleness about Devlin's face that spoke either of illness or some sort of indoor confinement. As he stirred the beans and turned the bacon over, he spoke about the conditions of the road in a rather despondent voice. "It's pretty hard this time of the year to get a ride. I been on the road for two weeks now all the way from New York."

"Where are you headed, Easy?"

"Well, somewhere where the sun shines. Get out of the cold. I thought about Florida, then I decided maybe Arizona."

"I hear it's hot enough there, even in the winter."

Each man produced a tin plate, and Devlin dumped the contents of one can into Peter's, then added four slices of bacon. He did the same for himself, then took the bread that Peter offered, and the two men began to eat hungrily. "We'll make some coffee after we get this down," Devlin said, stuffing his mouth eagerly. "Have to make it in the saucepan. I don't have a coffeepot."

"I've got one. Got to have my coffee," Peter grinned. He ate the beans and bacon quickly, then began fishing the peaches out of the open can with a spoon. When they had finished eating he made coffee, and the two men sat drinking it.

"Listen to that. The wind's picking up." He sniffed the air and said, "I don't know this part of the country, but it looks like we might get snow."

"I think so," Peter said. He broke off some more sticks from the small pile that Devlin had gathered and fed them into the fire. "I've never been on the road before. Not like this."

"I have. Not much fun in it," Easy said. He gave Peter a sharp look and said, "What's for you in California?"

"I've got a friend there. We knew each other in Wyoming. He was foreman for my folks on a ranch there."

"You're a cowboy, right?"

"Well, I used to be. I left the ranch to learn about cars."

A light flickered in Easy Devlin's face. "You know about cars? Where have you been working?" He sat back and listened, sipping the coffee as Peter sketched his history. Finally when Peter had finished, Easy said, "I like machinery. Don't know much about cars. I've been out of circulation for a while. You say you couldn't get a job in Detroit?"

"No, not even with a recommendation from Henry Ford."

"That's pretty tough. So now what will you do in Los Angeles?" He listened again as Peter described his sister's profession and the new development of motion pictures.

"My friend, Jason Ballard, he runs the stock and keeps the cowboys in line. I guess I'll ride herd on those critters," he said quietly, draining the last of his coffee. "If I ever get there, that is."

The wind was rising now with a keening sound, and a tense expression crossed Easy's thin face. "Tell you what," he said. "We'll never make it on the road. I made up my mind to hop a freight."

"You mean a train?"

"That's it. There's one of the Union Pacific lines goes across here about a mile away. It's headed west all the way into Arizona—all the way to California, I guess."

"Do you know how to get on one of those things? My uncle works for the Union Pacific, and I know they've gotten pretty tough on people bumming rides."

"I've been a bummer before," Easy shrugged. "You have to be careful of the bulls."

"The bulls?"

"Yeah, the railroad hires men to patrol the cars to throw us bummers off." He grinned then and looked somewhat younger. "They have to catch us first, and if they do, all they do is put us off and we catch the next one."

"How do we get on one?"

"It's not too hard. All we have to do is find a water stop. When the train stops either for coal or water, we find an open boxcar and climb into it. There's always one or two open. Just have to be careful we're not seen."

"Mind if I tag along?"

"This is my lucky day," Easy said. "Always better for two guys than one. That's what the Bible says. Two are better than one."

"You know the Bible?" Peter inquired with interest.

"Know it—don't do it."

"I guess that describes me pretty well," Peter sobered. "When is the best time?"

"As soon as this grub settles, we'll make our way over to Perryville. Union Pacific's tracks go right through there. My guess is they'll have to stop for water. We'll find a place to keep out of sight, and when it stops we'll get on."

★ ★ ★ ★

The wheels of the freight train made a pleasant clickety-clacking sound, and Peter leaned back against the corrugated side of the freight car. "It wasn't too hard," he said, looking over at Easy, who was breathing a little harder. They had hidden behind a shack close to the tracks, and as Easy had prophesied, when the train made a water stop, they had made a run for it. It was not a long run, but it had exhausted the smaller man, and Peter had had to boost him up into the open door of the freight car.

Easy gasped to catch his breath and straightened up, saying, "I'm not much of a runner, but we made it."

"Think I better close the door?"

"Naw. Sometimes they leave a door open a bit and mark the car, then when they see it closed, they know somebody's got on. Just leave it open."

The train made its clacking sound, and Peter stared out the open door. "This sure beats begging rides on a wagon," he said. "And it's starting to snow."

The two men were tired and soon rolled up in their blankets.

Savoring the warmth, Peter spoke in the gloomy darkness that enveloped most of the inside of the car. "Be glad to get away from here."

"Me too," Devlin said.

"What have you been doing, Easy? What's your work?"

A long silence followed, and Peter thought at first that the man had gone to sleep, then the answer came in a thin voice.

"I've been in the lockup."

"You mean . . . in jail?"

"That's right. That scare you to be travelin' with a criminal?"

"Not much. Where were you in jail?"

"Sing Sing."

Peter rolled over and peered through the darkness at his companion. "I've heard that's a rough place."

"It's not a place to spend a vacation," Easy said, a bitterness in his voice. After a while, he went on. "I got out a few months ago and headed straight for New York City. Was in for eight years. It's a long time to be in a grave. That's what Sing Sing is—a big concrete and steel grave."

"They treat you pretty rough there?"

"They treat everybody rough, but three years ago the warden found out I was good with machinery. He had just bought one of these horseless carriages. He called me out and told me I was in charge of it. He said that if it didn't run like a sewing machine, he would put me in the hole. You better believe I kept that thing running."

"Tell me about the automobile," Peter said. "What kind was it?"

"It was an Oldsmobile. I took that thing apart and put it together so many times, I could do it in the dark. He never let me drive it, though."

The two men had a common ground in automobiles and talked for some time about engines and cars. Finally an idea came to Peter. "Look, you need someplace that's warm. Why don't you go with me to California?"

"What would I do there?"

"I could get you a job with the pictures riding a horse."

"Riding a horse? I've never even been on a horse. I don't know anything about horses."

"You must know *something* about horses, don't you?"

"Well, they've got four legs, don't they?"

Peter laughed. "Don't worry about it," he said. "I'll tie you in the saddle so you can't fall off. There's no steering wheel. All you have to do is pull on the reins right to go right, and left to go left. Haul back on both of them to stop the critter."

The silence continued for so long that finally Peter said, "What's the matter? You don't like the idea?"

"I like it fine, Pete. It's just—well, nobody's offered to give me a hand in a long time. It'll take a bit of gettin' used to."

"We'll do it, Easy. You and me. Now let's get some sleep. We've got to ride this train all the way to California."

CHAPTER FIVE

A BIT OF COURAGE

★   ★   ★   ★

By the time Peter and Easy reached Arizona, the weather had improved slightly. There had been no snow, but there was still a nip in the air. Just outside of Phoenix the freight veered off onto a siding, and Easy said instantly, "We've got to get out of here, Pete, and find an outgoing train. They'll be loading this car, and it may be stuck here for a week."

The two left the car, carrying their baggage, and walked out of the yards heading west.

"We've got to stay on the main track. Everything here goes toward California, I think. We'll just find us another car." Pointing to one across some tracks, Easy said, "That one ought to go all the way in, maybe to Los Angeles."

Their food supply was low, and Peter insisted on taking Easy to a small cafe beside the track. It was used mostly by the railroad men, and it was full of brakemen and engineers. As they ate their hamburgers and French fries, Easy listened carefully to the conversation. When they left the cafe, he said, "Did you hear what that engineer said?"

"No, I didn't catch it. What was it?"

"He said he'd be pulling into Los Angeles tomorrow. All we got to do is get on the train behind his engine. We'll wait here until he comes out and see which way he goes."

About thirty minutes later, the engineer, a small, thickset man, sauntered out of the cafe talking in a rapid-fire manner to the brakeman. When he got on an engine drawn up in front of a long line of cars, Easy said quickly, "Come on. This is the big break. One more ride and we're home free!"

The two hurried down the track, keeping their eyes peeled for railroad detectives, but they saw no one. The sound of cars being moved by chuffing locomotives filled the air, and occasionally the shout of a brakeman would come to them faintly from a distance. Fortunately it was a long line of cars, over a hundred, as best as they could tell, but most of them were cattle cars. "I don't want to sleep with no heifer," Easy grinned. "Look, there's some box-cars down the way. One of them is bound to be open." After trying several cars that were locked, they found one with a door slightly ajar. Peter reached up, rolled it back and tossed his suitcase in, and Easy followed.

"Here, let me give you a boost," Peter offered. He leaned over, cupped his hands, and laced his fingers together. Easy grinned as he stepped up, and Peter tossed him high in the air.

"Hey, don't throw me *over* the car!"

Laughing, Peter put his hands on the floor and vaulted, hauling himself up with ease. He rolled and sat down, then grinned at his companion. "All aboard for Los Angeles." At that moment a slight noise caught his attention, and he turned quickly, ready for trouble. Easy had heard the noise also and reached toward his bag, where he carried a short piece of pipe with tape wrapped around the end.

"Who's that?" Easy asked.

Peter's eyes were not yet accustomed to the darkness, but he did see someone standing at the end of the car. "Who are you?" he asked, fearing it might be one of the bulls.

"Just a bummer like you are."

The figure came forward. With astonishment Peter saw that it was a young girl. She was wearing a baggy pair of men's trousers and a bulky plaid Mackinaw coat. From underneath the toboggan cap on her head, black curly hair escaped, with several strands falling down to the girl's shoulders. She had enormous eyes. It was impossible to tell the color of them, but they were dark and wide-set in a rather squarish face. She kept her head turned slightly away, but then she turned to face them fully. A scar ran down from her left temple across her cheek to the corner of her mouth. "I don't want any trouble," she said nervously. "Just leave me alone."

"Why, sure. We'll do that," Easy said. "Where are you headed?"

"Just traveling" was all she said as she moved back into the shadows. "Just don't bother me."

Peter was shocked to find a young girl on a train alone. His sense of propriety shaken, he simply could not imagine a girl traveling as a bummer, roughing it among the hard men who rode the freights. He thought for one moment of how it would be if Priscilla had been forced to do a thing like this, and an impulse came to show kindness to the young girl. "I guess we're all headed the same direction," he said easily and held up the sack in his hand. "We just had our meal, but we got a few extra hamburgers for the road. How about helpin' us eat 'em?"

"No thanks." The answer was brief and unyielding, a hard voice for a young girl.

"Ah, come on," Easy said and smiled at her. "Can't make any coffee, but we've got some orange juice. Might as well pitch in. We can't eat it all," he said encouragingly.

A long silence followed his invitation, and then the girl came forward and stood closer to them. "Well . . . I wouldn't mind something to eat."

"Sure," Peter said. He reached into the bag and handed her a hamburger while Easy fished in his bundle for the bottle of orange juice he had bought the day before. "Not cold," he said, "but pretty good stuff."

"Thanks." The girl took the sandwich and sat down with her back to the side of the car and put the bottle down beside her. She unwrapped the hamburger and then looked at the two men who had sat down across from her, all the while keeping the scarred cheek turned away. "My name's Jolie Devorak," she said, as if in payment for the food. She took a bite and chewed it voraciously. When she'd swallowed that bite, she immediately tore into the rest of the sandwich.

Averting his eyes out of politeness, Peter was aware that she was eating the sandwich with a driving hunger he had come to recognize himself since he had started traveling. There was one more hamburger. He picked it up and looked at it, then said, "I never could stand cold hamburgers. Better eat it while it's hot, Jolie."

The girl shook her head. "I don't want to eat all your food."

"We'll be in Los Angeles tomorrow. Be eating like kings," Peter said, handing her the second hamburger. "My name's Peter Winslow, and this here is Easy Devlin."

The girl said nothing but accepted the hamburger. She was eating as fast as she could, but she stopped halfway through the sandwich to wash it down with long swallows from the bottle. "This is real good," she said. "I was pretty hungry, I guess."

"Been on the road long?" Easy asked.

"Not too long." The answer gave nothing away, and as the girl finished the hamburger, the light that slanted in through the partly open door illuminated her face. Her hair was very black, with some curl to it. She had a European look about her, and her eyes seemed to be a deep blue. She finished the food and wadded up the paper, then rose and threw it out. "Do you want to keep the bottle?" she asked Easy.

"Nope. Chunck it out." He watched as the girl threw the bottle out the door, then as she stood up, leaning her back against the side of the car observing them, he said, "Must be pretty tough for a young lady to be on the road."

"I make out."

"Anybody ever try to bother you?" Peter asked.

The girl's hand flashed inside her jacket and drew out a three-inch blade that glinted in the ray of sunlight shining through the partly open door. "They don't try it but once."

Easy laughed with delight. "I like your spunk, Jolie. Just keep that knife handy and you'll be all right. But you don't have anything to worry about from us."

A look of disbelief washed across the young girl's face. "I've heard *that* before," she said.

"You haven't heard it from me," Peter said testily.

"No, I haven't heard it from you. Thanks for the food." She retired to the far end of the car and sat down, her back against it, her wary eyes on the two men. Ten minutes later they felt the jerking of the cars as the engine lunged against them. An initial jolt almost threw them off balance, and then began the slow, steady pull forward as the sharp shrill of the whistle split the air.

"We're on our way," Easy murmured. "Should be an easy trip."

"I hope so," Peter said. "I've had about enough bumming to do me for a lifetime." The two talked quietly for a while, and finally Easy glanced over at the girl.

"She's asleep," he said. "Hate to see a thing like that. Pretty rough for a girl. How old do you think she is?"

"Hard to say. Maybe sixteen. Seventeen." Peter shook his head sadly. "It's tough. Hard enough on a guy, but for a girl to be out here. I can't even imagine how she's made it this far."

"Guess we better catch a little sleep," Easy said, "so we'll be fresh when we hit the big city." He unrolled his blanket, wrapped it around him, and soon fell asleep.

Peter got his own blanket. It was cold in the car, and he welcomed the warmth of the wool blanket. As he lay down, he glanced at the girl. She was hidden in the shadows, but he had the feeling that if he advanced toward her, he would see the knife appear once again. He closed his eyes, and soon the rhythmic clickety-clack of the wheels over the seams in the track proved to be soporific. He dozed off, thinking of nothing except getting off the freight train and starting a new life in Los Angeles.

★ ★ ★ ★

When the train slowed down, breaking the rhythm of the wheels, Peter awoke and sat up, throwing the blanket aside. "It looks like we're going to have a stop," he said to Easy, who was already awake. "I hope they don't check the cars."

The girl made no comment, but had risen and was now standing, balancing with the sway of the cars. She gave Peter and Easy a cautious look but said nothing as the train pulled to a screeching halt.

"Must be a water stop," Easy said, and then he cocked his head. "Listen to that. Somebody comin'."

Peter heard it also and kept his eye on the door, which had been closed to a six-inch opening. It suddenly was thrust back, and the outline of a man appeared as he heaved himself into the car. He turned and stuck his hand down, and quickly two more men piled in. They sprawled on the floor but got to their feet at once.

"We made it, Satch." The speaker was a big man with yellow hair and pale blue eyes. He appeared to be about twenty-five, and there was a bulkiness in his upper body that spoke of tremendous strength. He was wearing a rumpled pair of trousers, a bulky turtleneck sweater, and a soft felt cap pulled down over his forehead.

"Yeah, we made it, Max. Thanks for the lift." Satch, the speaker, was a small man of about thirty, wearing the same dirty, wrinkled clothes as his companions. He turned and said, "Are you okay, Tony?"

The third man was a tall, thin fellow with a dark complexion and black hair and a pair of shifty eyes. He had spotted Peter and Easy across from him and was instantly on guard. "Hello, bos," he said, which was short for "hobos."

The other two newcomers turned quickly, and the big man named Max said, "You guys got anything to eat?"

Peter recognized at once the threat in the muscular man's voice. They were a rough-looking trio, and he evaluated the chances of turning them down, then decided it would be better to show a little diplomacy. "Got a few cans of beans, some bread, and some bologna." He glanced at Easy, who remained upright, his back against the car, staring at the three. There was a cautious look in his thin face, but he said, "Got a couple cans of fruit, too. Pears, I think, and one of peaches."

"Well, let's have 'em," Max said and advanced on them. He seemed enormous in the shadowy light, and his eyes were a dull blue that appeared to have nothing behind them. He held his massive hands out, and as soon as he had gotten the food, he turned to his companions. "Dinnertime, guys," and the three men proceeded to wolf down the food. They threw the empty cans and papers out the door and began to interrogate the two men.

"Where you headin'?" asked the large man called Max.

"Los Angeles," Peter said, adding nothing to his remark.

Tony, the tall man, said, "You got any money?"

"Not much, and I'm keeping what I've got," Peter said curtly. He was tense and expected an argument, but Tony's white teeth flashed, and he tilted his head back and laughed harshly.

"You're a pretty tough one, but I like that. Keep your check."

"Hey! Who's that back there?" The smaller man named Satch had sharp eyes. He had seen a movement at the back of the car and stepped forward, peering into the gloom. "Come out here! Who are you?" He advanced and then stopped. "Why, it's a girl!"

"A girl?" Tony's eyes narrowed and he moved to stand beside Satch. "Let's have a look at you," he said.

"Leave me alone," Jolie snapped. She reached inside her coat but did not pull out the knife.

Tony saw the movement and laughed. "What you got under that coat, a gun?" He moved forward, and when the girl pulled out the knife and pointed it at him, he laughed with delight.

"Look at that, guys! She's feisty, ain't she?" He reached inside his own coat and drew out a pistol. "Now that ain't much good against a rod," he said. "You better put that knife away." When the girl did not obey, his hand shot out and he twisted her arm. She cried out sharply, and the knife fell to the floor. Tony kicked it over to the back of the car and dragged the girl out. "I said, let's have a look at you!" He put the gun away, his hand shot out, and he jerked the gray toboggan cap off the girl's head. Her black hair cascaded around her shoulders as she struggled to get away from him.

"Well, I always liked pretty black hair. A weakness of mine." He winked at the other two and said, "How do you like my new lady friend?"

"Let me go!"

"Not a chance, sweetheart. What's your name?"

Peter was not afraid of getting a beating, which he had no doubt he would get if he challenged the three, but the sight of the gun had sent a shiver of fear through him. He glanced at Easy, who shook his head quickly, and read in his eyes the message, *Stay out of it!* But it was hard to do, for the three men were gathered around the girl and were all touching her.

"Let's have a kiss. I'll show you what a real man's like," Tony said. He reached forward and took the girl in his arms. She fought against him silently, not asking for help.

Peter could see her face was pale, and her lips were drawn together with determination. She had no chance, of course, and Peter threw caution to the wind. "Let her alone," he demanded, stepping forward.

The three men wheeled around, surprised at the interruption. Max laughed crudely. "We got a hero here, Tony. But I'll sit on him while you have your fun with the girl, then I'll take my turn." He moved toward Peter, his body blocking the light from the half-open door. His hands were stretched out in the manner of a wrestler, his fingers curved like huge claws. There was a cool light in his dull blue eyes, and his lips were open in a sneer.

As the huge man advanced, Peter could only imagine how much the brute enjoyed using his strength on other men. The adrenaline rushed to his head as he heard Satch say, "Bust him up, Max!"

Knowing he had no chance at all in a barroom-style fight with Max, Peter stepped forward and delivered a powerful kick to the man's kneecap. It succeeded, knocking the big man down. Without compunction Peter swung another kick that grazed Max's head and stunned the big man. He did not hit squarely as he had hoped, and before he could recover, the other two men were on him. Fists beat his lips back against his teeth, and a powerful blow caught him in the temple, sending red sparks reeling across his brain. He struck out and hit something and heard a cry of pain, but it did no good. Tony was slashing at him, driving him back against the car. When he raised his hands to protect his face, Satch delivered a blow below his belt that sent unbearable pain through him. Without crying aloud, Peter threw himself forward, and the three went reeling across the car. The fight was a vicious, brutal affair with no quarter asked and none given. He had two fears—that Tony would pull the gun in his belt, and that Max would recover and join in the fray. Peter had little hope as he kicked and fought viciously in a style he had never known. There were no rules, no referee, and he knew that if he fell down, he would be kicked to death.

He bounced off the side of the car, and out of the corner of his eye saw that Max had risen and was reeling toward him, his lips twisted with anger. And then suddenly there was a sound of a clunk, as if someone had struck a melon with a hammer. The huge man fell face forward, rolled over to protect himself, and lay staring up. Easy had come up behind him with the pipe he always carried and hit the big man over the head with it.

"That's all right!" Max growled, his eyes half glazed. He had a thick protection of heavy bone in his skull, and the blow that would have killed an ordinary man had merely stunned him momentarily. He got to his feet and lurched toward Easy, muttering, "That's all right! I'll get you!"

Meanwhile, Tony and Satch, seeing Max getting up and heading for the smaller man, redoubled their efforts. They drove Peter to the floor, and his brain went numb as a kick caught him high on the temple. They grasped his arms, and he felt himself being dragged across the floor. He heard Tony saying, "Open that door wide! We'll give him a toss!"

Across the car, Easy dodged between Max's heavy hands again, but the blow was deflected. With a backhand he caught Max across the temple and saw his eyes dull. As he staggered from the blow, Max was still muttering, "I'll get you!" Easy turned and saw the two men were about to throw Peter out the door of the car. He yelled and advanced toward them.

Seeing the small man come toward him with the uplifted pipe, Tony loosed his hold on Peter and shot his hand under his coat. He came out with the pistol, but just as he did Easy swung the pipe and caught the gun, driving it into the back of the car. Tony yelled, "Get him!" Dodging the pipe, he threw himself on Easy, who collapsed under his weight. Tony and Satch pummeled Easy to the floor, then picked him up and started dragging him toward the door.

"All right! Throw 'em both out! Come on, Max, give us a hand!"

Both Peter and Easy fought back, but the combined strength of the three forced them to the door. They both grabbed at the edges of the car door opening. Seeing the ground rush by, Peter could picture his skull shattering if he were thrown from the car.

"Throw 'em out! Throw 'em out!" Tony yelled as he got a hammerlock on Peter and thrust him forward.

Just as Peter felt one foot slip out and his fingers on the door giving way, a loud shot suddenly rang out, and a yell went up from one of the three hoodlums.

Taking advantage of the moment, Peter struggled back. He managed to get his foot back on the floor and shoved Tony aside. He was dizzy, and when he looked up, he saw Jolie standing there holding the gun with both hands, pointing it straight at Tony.

Tony grinned. "You won't shoot." He started toward the girl, but he took only one step and another shot rang out. Tony stopped and wheeled to one side and grabbed for his shoulder. He held it with his hand, then looked at the blood on his hand, and rage seemed to flow through him. "You won't kill me!" he said. "You ain't got the nerve!" He took another step forward when suddenly the gun rang out again. The shot caught him high in the shoulder and drove him back. With a scream he grasped for the door, but his fingers missed and he disappeared through the opening.

Instantly, Easy jumped toward the girl and whispered, "Give me that gun." She handed it to him, her dark eyes hollows of fear, and Easy said, "All right you two. Out!"

"You can't make us jump! We could get killed!" Satch murmured, but then Easy lifted the gun and put a shot so close to his ear that Satch heard the whirling of the bullet. With a despairing cry, he turned and leaped. Max stood beside the door, dazed. Everything had taken place too fast for his dull brain to grasp.

Quickly Peter reached over, grabbed his arm, and yanked it. Then he lifted his foot and kicked him in the stomach. The big man let out a wild yell, then flipped backward out of the car. Peter stuck his head out the door and saw the man rolling down the side of the slope. Looking back he saw Satch getting up, shaking his fist. He pulled back inside and collapsed against the side of the car. "They're all right," he said.

"Did . . . did I kill him?"

"No, you didn't kill him, Jolie," and then Peter told his lie quickly. "I saw him getting up, holding on to his shoulder. He's okay."

Suddenly the girl began to tremble. Peter came to her side and helped her as she slumped down, then sat beside her. "Don't worry about it, Jolie. You had to do it. If you hadn't, I think they'd have killed all of us. They were a rough bunch." He felt her thin shoulders trembling and saw that she had hidden her face and was weeping. He glanced at Easy, who concealed the weapon under his coat and came over to sit on the other side of the young girl.

"It's okay, kid," he said, patting her shoulder. "You saved our bacon that time. We owe you one for that."

"You . . . you don't think I killed him?" Lifting her hands from her face, Jolie looked up. Her face was stained with tears and tight with strain.

"No," Peter assured her. "He'll make it. They'll patch him up, and those three will probably kill somebody before it's over. He's too mean to die."

Peter gently put his arm around Jolie, but the girl stiffened. Not wanting to confuse her, he quickly pulled it away. "We'll be okay now."

The train rumbled on into the night, but sleep was impossible for Jolie Devorak. She had fought off men before, but never had she shot anybody. In fact, she had never held a gun in her hand. The first shock began to pass away, and finally she glanced up, first at Easy and then at Peter. "I didn't thank you for saving me from that man," she whispered.

"It looks like you saved us," Peter grinned. "Isn't that right, Easy?"

"Dead right! You're all right, kid!" He hesitated, then said, "You got any folks?"

Jolie had learned to keep her own counsel, but the shock of the fight had loosened her restraints. She ducked her head and said, "I'm running away."

"I figured that," Easy said. "Most of us are running away from something. What are you running from?"

She sat up straighter and began to talk. Her voice was low, and the two men had to lean forward to hear her as she said, "I'm running away from my stepfather. My pa left my ma before I was born, and she took real good care of me. But then things got hard, and she married a man called Wilson—and he wasn't any good."

As the girl's voice droned on, telling her sad story, the outside world rushed by. Inside the car they were in their own little world, safe for the moment from men like Max, Satch, and Tony. For a while, at least, they had nothing to fear. Peter listened closely as the girl continued.

She looked up and turned the left side of her face to them. They saw the scar that ran from her temple in a ragged track around her cheek, almost touching her eyelid, then down to the corner of her lips. "He used to beat Ma and me. He gave me this scar." She looked up at them and said wanly, "He fixed me, didn't he? Who would ever look at me with a scar like that?"

"You say your ma died?"

"Yes, and then he started—" She halted, her face flushed, and she dropped her head. "He started touching me. Always trying to get his hands on me. So I ran away."

When Jolie stopped talking, Peter was filled with a pity for her that he had rarely known for anyone. His old life suddenly seemed easy and without problems as he thought of the trouble this young woman had already endured. He was a man of impulse and it showed now. He wanted to put his arm around her, but he knew she was shy and not ready for that. "Look," he said. "Come to Los Angeles with us."

"With you?" Jolie looked up, startled. Her hand went up to cover her scar, a customary gesture with her, and she said, "What would I do there?"

"Why, there are lots of things you could do. I've got a brother there. He's got an orange grove. You could pick oranges. He'd be glad to have you. He's got a fine family. You'd like them, Jolie."

"I couldn't go stay with strangers."

"Well, you could come with us, then. Me and Easy here have got jobs working for a friend of mine in the motion picture business." He went on to explain what they were going to do and then said again, "Come with us."

"I can't even ride a horse."

"Neither can I," Easy said, "but that doesn't matter." The small man sat hunched up, his arms locked around his knees. His face was pale, but there was a light of compassion in his eyes as he said, "Everybody needs somebody, Jolie. Don't try to go it alone. We won't bother you. I know you're afraid of men."

His hand went under his coat, and he pulled out the pistol he had taken from Tony. With a wry smile he reversed it and handed it to her butt first. "If we ever try to hurt you, shoot us."

For the first time a smile touched the girl's lips. They were broad, mobile lips, and she said with just a trace of amusement, "I don't guess I could do that. Just leave me alone. That's all I ask," she said, handing the pistol to Peter.

"Sure, we'll do that," Peter said, stowing the pistol away. "But give it a try. Come on and hitch up with us. We'll be The Three Musketeers."

"The Three Musketeers? What's that?"

"Three characters in a book by Alexander Dumas. They always helped each other when they were in trouble. I guess that's what we've done." He waited, then said, "Come along, Jolie. See how it goes."

The girl dropped her head and stared at the floor. Finally she lifted it again and said quietly, "All right. I'll go with you." She rose quickly, then as if afraid of showing too much emotion, she went back to her blanket at the head of the car. She sat down and closed her eyes, listening in the darkness as the train continued its rhythmic clicking over the steel rails.

CHAPTER SIX

THE THREE MUSKETEERS

★ ★ ★ ★

When the train stopped somewhere at the clearing of the mountains, the three peered out the door, and Easy said, "What kind of trees are those?"

Staring out at the orchard, Peter said, "Orange trees, I think. I've never seen any, but that looks like what they might be." The weather had grown warm, so he took off his heavy coat and tossed it onto his suitcase. "It's warm, isn't it? I guess it's the land of sunshine—like the chamber of commerce says."

Jolie said nothing but stood wide-eyed looking out at the fields that were flanked on one side by rugged mountains rising up behind them. "It's pretty," she said finally, then walked back and sat down on her blanket.

She had moved it up close to the door. Peter was relieved that she had lost some of her fear of them. For a while he stood there, and then the train started up, and he watched the orange grove disappear as the train wound its way around a small town and headed due east. He went back and sat down on his blanket while Easy remained at the door, watching the landscape flow by.

"I'm glad you decided to throw your lot in with us, Jolie," Peter said.

"I don't know about it. It doesn't seem to me like it will work."

He sensed a brokenness in the girl, along with the stubbornness that was part of her character. From what she had shared about her stepfather, Peter knew life had been hard on her. She could not seem to see the pleasant side of anything. "You've had a hard time, I know. I've had a pretty easy life myself."

Easy glanced over and said, "Like I said, I've been in the pen. Whatever you had couldn't have been as bad as Sing Sing."

"It was worse."

Easy's eyes opened wide at the terse statement, and he studied the girl thoughtfully. He had had a rough life himself, but he was a man and, therefore, felt he should be able to take it better. Yet the hardships Jolie Devorak had already suffered in her young life touched him. Though he had hardened in prison, there still was a good side to the man, and he said, "You wait and see. It'll be better when we get to Los Angeles."

Jolie remained silent for a while, then finally lay down on her blanket and closed her eyes.

Peter curled up in his blanket, too, and when he awoke later, he found Jolie staring at him. He grinned at her, but she only stared back at him with a look he didn't understand.

"You don't know anything about me," she said suddenly.

"I know you're young, and life hasn't been fair to you, and you need some friends. That's all I need to know."

There was a streak of doubt and disbelief firmly ingrained in the young woman. She stared at him silently, and he saw that her eyes were a deep blue, a strange color he had never seen before. They were wide and almond shaped, and her lashes were long and as black as her hair that now hung down over her shoulders. She had removed the cap, produced a comb and brush, and had spent some time earlier running it through her hair. Now as she examined him steadily, he sensed that she wanted to believe good things could happen, but all hope had been taken out of her at the loss of her mother and the cruelty of her stepfather. The doubt showed in the set of her face, the wariness in her eyes, and the tenseness of her thin shoulders.

"I hate my stepfather," she said. "There were times when I thought I . . . would kill him if I could."

"I can understand why you would feel that," Peter said quietly. He reached down to his suitcase, flipped it open, and removed three candy bars he had bought at the last stop. He handed one to her, then tossed one over to Easy, who grinned and peeled the paper away at once. The three of them chewed thoughtfully on the candy, and after a time Easy went over and lay down and seemed to go to sleep. The train rumbled on through the countryside, and from time to time Peter would get up and go look out the door. Coming back once, he said, "It looks like desert to me. A lot like Wyoming. I don't see how they can raise oranges in the desert."

Jolie was sitting with her legs crossed, and she gave him a curious look. "Do you ever think about going home again to your folks?" He had told her about the ranch, and now she said wistfully, "If I had a home like that, I'd go to it."

"Well, I guess I'm an ingrate. It's a nice ranch, and my ma and pa . . . well, there's nobody like them. They're great people. But I've got to make my own way, Jolie. A man has to do that to be what he is. I'm going to be a famous race car driver someday." His chin lifted and his firm mouth settled into a line. "I know that sounds stubborn, but it's what I want to do."

"You ain't never been married?"

"Married? Not likely."

"How old are you?"

"I'm twenty-five. How old are you?"

"Sixteen . . . almost seventeen."

"Well, I'm not quite old enough to be your pa, but I'm old enough to be your big brother." There was a rough and craggy handsomeness in Peter Winslow's face, and he smiled at Jolie and ran his hand through his hair. "I always wanted a baby sister."

"I'm not a baby, Peter." The words were curt, and she suddenly raised her hand and touched the scar. "I guess when I got this, that ended some things for me."

"Why, it's just a scar!" Peter protested.

"Nobody would ever want me. Not with this."

Peter was taken aback by the utter finality and deadness in her tone. "Why, sure they will," Peter said with reassurance.

"No, not me." Her words were spoken so quietly he could barely hear them, but he did hear the bitterness and hopelessness in her voice. He wanted to reach out and put his arm around her in a friendly fashion, but he knew she was too wary for that, so he said, "Look, it's going to be better. I know you had a hard time, Jolie, but you've got friends now. You got me, and you got Easy, and you'll like my family. You'll love my sister, Priscilla. She's the sweetest person you could ever meet. And my brother, Cass, he's a fine fellow, and Serena, his wife, there's none better. You're going to be all right."

Suddenly the long, lonesome cry of the engine's whistle rent the air, and somehow the sound seemed to match the sullen mood that had fallen on Jolie Devorak. She had listened carefully to Peter's words, and for a moment hope had flickered in her deep blue eyes, and her lips had grown more relaxed and soft. But the sound of the whistle seemed to draw her back into herself, and she said shortly, "We'll see—but I don't believe it."

Peter said no more but leaned back against the car and closed his eyes. He had never met anyone exactly like this young woman. *She is neither girl nor woman*, he thought. *Somewhere in between, and that's a tough place for any young girl to be.* He remembered Priscilla talking to him when she was at that intermediate stage, and even Priscilla, with all of her gifts and loveliness, had been miserable. He felt the vibration of the wheels as they clicked across the seams of the steel rails and thought, *I'll have to watch out for her. She needs a friend about as bad as anyone I ever knew!*

★　★　★　★

Riding through the pasture to examine the stock that milled around, Jason Ballard said abruptly in a tone of disgust, "They stampede the tallow off these poor critters!" He looked at the short, tubby cowboy riding alongside, whose name was Pudge Jones, and said, "Looks to me, Pudge, that they could just take a picture of one stampede and use it over and over again."

"Good thing they can't." Pudge grinned back at him. He was a freckle-faced individual from Montana. He now stared good-naturedly at his boss and said, "If they could do that, they wouldn't need us, would they, Jase?"

"I guess not." Jason grinned at his companion, then suddenly a movement caught his eye. He pulled his hat forward to shade his eyes better and squinted, then exclaimed, "My sainted aunt! It's Peter Winslow!"

"Who's that?" asked Pudge.

"Miss Priscilla's brother," Jason responded. "It looks like he's picked up a couple of strays. You watch these critters, Pudge." Touching his spurs to the tall, rangy bay's flanks, he held on while the animal shot forward and pulled up in a cloud of dust before the trio that stopped to look up at him.

"Hi, Jason," Peter grinned. "Here I am—ready to take over just like you asked me to."

Jason swung out of his saddle, hung on to the lines, and

thumbed his hat back over his forehead. "I don't seem to recall doin' more than askin' you to come and punch a few cows, but I'm glad to see you, Pete. Does Priscilla know you're here?"

"No, we just got in."

Taking in the ragged, wrinkled clothes of the three, Jason said dryly, "I don't reckon you rode first class." He turned his gaze on the young woman, removed his hat, and said, "I don't know you, miss, but you're sure in powerful bad company with this Peter Winslow."

"This is Jolie Devorak, Jason, and this is Easy Devlin."

"Pleased to know you," Jason said. He whirled the lines of the bay in his hand idly, and his eyes narrowed as he took in Peter's two companions. "Where did you three all hitch up together?"

"Well, to tell the truth," Peter said, "we've been bummin' together. Rode a train halfway across the United States." Quickly he added, "I've got to find jobs for Easy and Jolie, Jason. Can you help us?"

Jolie had stood slightly back, looking up at the tall cowboy. She was entranced by his outfit. He looked exactly like her idea of what a real cowboy should be, all the way from the high-heeled boots to the high-crowned Stetson. There was a friendliness in his eyes, although he looked like he could be hard if necessary, and she waited tensely for his answer.

"Well, we can always put you on a horse, Devlin."

"Got to be honest with you, Ballard. I don't know one end of a horse from the other."

The answer amused Jason. He said, "That'll be up to Pete. He can tie you on, I reckon."

"That's what I told him," Peter said eagerly. "And there's got to be some job around here for Jolie. Don't they need help making these pictures?"

"I reckon they do, but that'll be up to the boss. Come along. We'll go talk to Priscilla about it." He grinned and said, "She's got Porter in the palm of her hand."

"Who's he?" Peter asked as the four walked along with Jason leading his bay.

"Oh, he's the producer. Like I say, Priscilla's got him right where she wants him." He looked down at the young woman and smiled. "Don't worry, miss. Priscilla will fix you up."

It was only a short walk to the set, and Jason said, "Look,

there's Priscilla now. I guess she's just gettin' ready to do a riding scene."

Priscilla Winslow had seen the four coming and had not recognized her brother. Then her eyes flew open, and she squealed, "Peter!" and ran to throw herself into his arms. He held her up, gave her a squeeze and a kiss, and said, "Well, the bad penny's come back. This time we're begging."

"Peter, why didn't you write?"

Peter ignored the question and said, "This is Easy Devlin. He's gonna be ridin' for Jason. Just like me. And this is a friend of mine I want you to be especially nice to, Jolie Devorak. Jolie, this is my sister, Priscilla Winslow."

"How are you, Jolie?" Priscilla smiled, and no trace of the slight shock that ran through her at the sight of the disreputable young girl showed on her face. She put out her hand and saw that the girl hesitated before taking it. "You all look like you could use a bath and a good meal," she said.

"I'll take care of that," Jason said. "For these yahoos, anyhow. If you'd take over Miss Devorak, she wants some kind of a job. You reckon you could talk Mr. Porter into findin' somethin' for her?"

"Why, I'll sure try," Priscilla smiled. "You come along with me, Jolie. You can use the shower in my dressing room to clean up."

As Jolie followed the golden-haired woman, she looked back at Peter almost with fear. He caught the look and said, "Go along. We'll see you in a little while, Jolie."

"Have you known Pete long?" Priscilla asked as she led the girl to her dressing room.

"No, ma'am, not very long."

"Well, he's a handsome thing, isn't he? Even if he is my own brother."

"Yes, ma'am, I guess he is."

When they reached the dressing room and stepped inside, Priscilla grew very busy. "Here's the shower. There's the soap and towels. I'll leave you alone so you can clean up. While you're doing that I'll go talk Mr. Porter into giving you a job."

"Do you . . . think you can, Miss Winslow?"

Priscilla looked at the girl and saw the fear in her blue eyes. "Don't worry," she said gently. "We'll work out something. You just enjoy a good hot shower."

Priscilla left the dressing room and went at once to Mr. Porter's office. She burst in and said, "Mr. Porter, you've got to do me a favor."

Surprised by her intensity, Porter put down the pen he was using and stood up. "What's wrong, Priscilla?"

"It's my brother Peter. He just got here, and he's brought a young woman with him. We've got to help her." She went on to explain what little she knew, and finally she came over and smiled at him. "Just any kind of a job. She could help me with my clothes, and we're always needing someone to carry notes and clean up and, well, there's lots of things she could do."

"How old is she? Eighteen or nineteen?"

"Not that old," Priscilla admitted. "I doubt if she's over seventeen, but it looks like she needs help, and Peter's asked me to do something. Couldn't we please give her some kind of a job? I'd be glad for you to take her pay out of my check."

Porter grinned suddenly. "I bet you always showed up at home with sick kittens, didn't you?"

Priscilla laughed. "As a matter of fact, I did. I was the despair of my mother, but could you please do this, Mr. Porter?"

"I don't see why not, but we won't take her pay out of your check. We do need more help around here, and I suppose you could use her. I suppose Lily could use her, too." Lily was the wardrobe woman and was constantly complaining about being overworked.

"Oh, that's wonderful! I'll go tell her that she's got a job." Priscilla left Porter's office but did not go back to her dressing room right away. She wanted to give the poor girl some privacy and a chance to get cleaned up.

Stan Lem came by, and she told him what she had done. Lem grinned lazily. "Well, that's what we need, some more folks that don't know what they're doing around here."

"You be nice to her, Stan," she said. "It looks like she's had a hard time."

The two stood there talking for some time, and finally Priscilla went back. When she stepped inside she found the girl wearing different clothes. Jolie had on a pair of men's trousers and a shirt, but they were clean, and her dark hair was beautiful as it fell around her shoulders. Priscilla noticed the girl kept her face turned away to hide her scar, but she determinedly ignored that. "You're hired, Jolie. For one thing, you've got to help me keep up with my things, and you can help Lily, our wardrobe lady, too.

There'll be plenty for you to do around here."

Jolie had been waiting nervously, fully expecting Priscilla Winslow to come back and tell her that there was no job available. Now relief washed through her and she suddenly trembled, her hand reaching up to cover the scar. "Thank you very much," she whispered. "I'll do the best I can, Miss Winslow."

★　★　★　★

By the end of the day, Jolie felt much more at home. She had met all the members of the cast and had been able to grasp some of the instructions that Lily Doe, the wardrobe woman, had given her. Priscilla had disappeared to do a riding scene, and she had not seen Peter until late that afternoon.

Priscilla came back and found Jolie, saying with a smile, "Peter and Easy are waiting for you. I'll see you in the morning." She gave the girl a quick hug and said, "It'll be good to have you here, Jolie. You'll be a lot of help to me."

"Thank you, Miss Winslow" was all Jolie could say. She moved outside the set and found Peter waiting for her.

"Follow me," he said.

"Where are we going?"

"Don't ask questions. Just take orders," he laughed. "Did you make out all right? I hear you're working for Imperial now."

"Oh, your sister was wonderful!" Jolie's thin face glowed, and for one moment her lips looked full and vulnerable as she spoke of Priscilla in glowing terms.

Peter listened and helped her into a studio car he had borrowed and shut the door. Getting in beside her, he said, "That's like Priscilla. She's a great one." He started up the engine and drove away from the studio, raising a cloud of dust.

Jolie said nothing, but when he pulled up in front of a store on the edge of town, she looked up and said, "Why are we going in there?"

"Got to get you some working clothes," Peter said cheerfully as he got out.

"But I don't have any money!" Jolie protested.

He opened the door, however, and reached in and took her hand and pulled her out. "I got an advance from sis on our pay. We're going to buy some clothes." He led her into the store and a saleslady came over.

"Yes, sir, may I help you?"

"This young lady wants to buy a couple of outfits. She's right choosy, and so am I. I don't know if you got anything good enough for her," Peter said, raising his eyebrows.

The saleslady, a tall woman dressed in gray, smiled and said, "Oh, I think we can please you, sir. If you'll come along with me, miss."

Jolie never forgot the next hour. She tried on several outfits, and each time Peter would examine them closely. She was terrified at the prices, but he waved that aside. "You can't work for Imperial Pictures dressed like a bummer. You've got to look nice. No more men's clothes," he said, "except when you're on your own." After a while he chose two outfits: one a white cotton blouse with ruffles at the high neck and down the front, a saffron yellow skirt edged with green ribbon, and tan silk stockings; the other was a dress made of a silvery gray cotton trimmed in a white piping around the neck, sleeves, and the bottom of the ankle-length skirt.

Finally they left the store loaded down with bundles, and Jolie said, "I'll never be able to pay for all this."

"Sure you will. You're in the motion picture business now, Jolie," Peter said, helping her into the car.

When he started it up she said, "Where we going now?"

"To the boardinghouse. I'll be staying at the bunkhouse with Easy and Jase, but you've got to have a room. Priscilla told me about this one right around the corner here. It's close, so you can walk to the studio."

He drove to a large Victorian-style house two and a half stories high. The house had wood siding painted a subdued salmon color. It was trimmed in a dark blue-green around the large sash windows, with a steeply pitched black shingle roof. There was a round corner tower at one end of the house that reached high into the sky, with a pinnacle on top of the conical roof. A large veranda wrapped around the front of the house and down both sides, and wide steps led to the front door that had a beautiful stained-glass window in an oval shape. Peter carried the packages for her as they walked up the steps. When they knocked on the door, it was answered by a matronly-looking woman who introduced herself as Mrs. Bell.

"This is Miss Jolie Devorak," Peter said. "She's working for Imperial Pictures. She'll need a room for some time—a nice one."

"Why, of course," the woman said. "I have something that should be just fine. Please follow me."

The room Jolie found herself in on the second floor was beautiful. She waited until Mrs. Bell disappeared and then looked around with apprehension. "It's . . . too nice for me." The large room had two floor-length windows rising high on the walls, almost to the top of the twelve-foot-high ceiling. They were covered with green chintz and had lace overskirtings, which allowed the sunlight to filter through in a muted way. The walls were covered with a shiny white paper, bordered by pink ribbons and bows that gracefully dropped into the corners and encircled the area over the fireplace, and the floor was covered with a pink and green rose-patterned carpet. Pictures in silver antique frames covered the walls and the fireplace mantel. The four-poster bed, with swagged bed draperies of the same fabric, had been covered with a bedspread in a rosette-patterned fabric. A rosewood bureau sat along the wall just inside the door, and a small oak table, with a brass and enamel cloisonné light, took its place beside the bed, both covered with a swatch of antique lace.

"No it's not!" Peter said. He tossed the packages on the bed and looked around the room. "Well, they serve dinner here. I've got to get back to the lot. How about if I come for you in the morning, and you and me and Easy will eat breakfast. Just The Three Musketeers."

"All right, and . . . and thanks, Peter."

"It's all in the lodge," he said. He reached out, and when she put her hand out, he closed his big fingers around hers. "The Three Musketeers, remember?" He laughed and left the room. She could hear him whistling "I'm a Yankee Doodle Dandy" as he went down the hall.

Jolie moved around the room, touching the curtain, the bedspread, stopping to look at the pictures. Never in her life had she seen so many beautiful things. It felt like a dream to her, and she thought fleetingly of the rough life she had had. She went over to the window and looked out, watching as Peter drove off with a roar of the engine. When he disappeared from sight, she suddenly felt weak. She made her way to the bed, sat down on it, lowered her head, and began to weep. A weakness came over her, and she finally rolled over on the bed and buried her face in the pillow as her shoulders shook. She wept as she had not wept since she was a small child.

★　★　★　★

After three days, Jolie had learned to do her job well. There had been much for her to do, and everyone had been kind. She saw Peter and Easy every day, and the three of them went to supper together at different restaurants every night.

Jolie had relaxed considerably. She was quick and picked up things very easily. On the morning of the third day as Priscilla was brushing her hair in her dressing room, she turned to Jolie and said, "Mr. Porter's very pleased with you, and so is Mr. Lem. They both say you are doing a fine job."

"Oh, thank you, Miss Winslow."

"Did Peter tell you about tomorrow?"

A puzzled look crossed Jolie's face. "What about tomorrow?"

"Why, it's Thanksgiving. We're all going to an early service at church, and then we're going out to my brother Cass's house."

"Oh no, I wouldn't want to do that. I'd—"

"We're not asking you," Priscilla smiled. She reached out and tugged at Jolie's lustrous black hair. "You're a part of the family. You've *got* to go, so make up your mind to it."

Jolie said no more, but the next morning she got up and put on the best of the two outfits she had bought. She worked her hair carefully, but as she looked in the mirror, the sight of the scar disturbed her. She turned her head to one side, but the thought came to her, *No matter how nice a dress I wear, I'll always have this scar*. She went outside, and ten minutes later a big car pulled up, with Peter behind the wheel and Priscilla beside him. Easy got out of the backseat and held open the door, saying, "Jump in, Jolie. Time to go to church."

As the car chugged along, Jolie said nothing, nor did Easy. Finally he whispered to her, "Actually, I ain't much on church, Jolie."

"Me either, but we've got to go."

"I reckon so."

★　★　★　★

The service seemed strange to Easy and Jolie. They sat together near the front, with Peter on Jolie's left. Neither of them knew any of the songs that were sung, but both were stunned by the large, opulent auditorium. When the preaching started, Easy said, "I didn't really want to hear no sermon. I heard a few when I was in the pen, but I don't think it's for me."

Jolie did not answer, but when the preacher began to speak, she found herself unable to tear her eyes away from him. His name, she had been told, was Reverend Nolan Cole, and once Peter leaned over and said, "Good-lookin' egg for a preacher. Everybody says he ought to be an actor."

Jolie did not answer. She was listening intently to the sermon. Reverend Cole spoke of a time when Jesus went to Samaria and met a woman at a well. Jolie had not read the story, but she followed the reading from a Bible Peter had produced as the Scripture was read. She had never known such stories were in the Bible. She was ignorant of that book, but the preacher made it come alive for her. She listened entranced as he told of how Jesus spoke to the woman. Jolie was surprised when she found that the woman was not a good woman but had had five husbands. The preacher explained how none of them were really her husband, just men she lived with. Jolie did not take her eyes off of Reverend Cole's face. Somehow the words had a power beyond the magnetism of the speaker's voice.

As they were leaving the church, Peter asked, "Did you like the sermon?"

"I guess I did. Was Jesus really like that?"

Peter was astonished. He had grown up under good preaching, and although he was not a Christian himself, he had a firm conviction that Jesus Christ was the answer. "Why, of course He was. Haven't you ever read that in the Bible?"

"I've never read the Bible."

"You haven't? Do you have one?"

"No."

"Well, take this one," Peter said.

"Oh, I couldn't take your Bible."

"Of course you could. Maybe we could study a little together. Not that I'm a scholar, but Priscilla—now, she is. She's a good Christian."

"Are you a Christian, Peter?"

Peter seemed disturbed by the question. "No. Not really. My folks are, though, and Cass and his wife, Serena, are. I guess I'm the black sheep of the family."

"I guess I'm a black sheep, too, Peter."

"Well, it's something to think about," he said. Then he changed the subject. "You'll love my sister-in-law, Serena, and those kids of theirs are something."

When they finally arrived at the Winslow house, Jolie was received with great courtesy by Cassidy and his wife, Serena. Neither of them asked questions about Jolie's past, and she suspected that Priscilla and Peter had already told them something about her.

They sat down to an enormous dinner of turkey and dressing with giblet gravy, and vegetables, including candied yams, which Jolie had never eaten before. She sat next to Easy, and the two of them did more listening than talking.

In the middle of the meal, Cass suddenly said, "Reverend Cole is a fine preacher, but some of the elders are not sure he's the man for the church."

Priscilla looked up with surprise. "Why, I thought he'd be perfect."

"So did I," Cass shrugged. "But some of the men just aren't sure."

"Well, who do they want, Cass?" Priscilla demanded.

"They don't know, but I made a recommendation to them." He grinned across the table at Priscilla and Peter. "How'd you like to go to a church where the pastor's name was Winslow?"

Peter had raised a forkful of English peas to his lips, but he put it down and stared across the table. "What are you talking about, Cass? A preacher named Winslow?"

"We've already got a preacher in our family, if you'll remember our cousin Andrew Winslow."

"Why, of course, I'd forgotten Andrew," Priscilla said. Andrew was her first cousin, the son of Mark and Lola Winslow. "I've heard him preach a few times. He's a marvelous speaker. As good as Brother Cole, I think."

"Well, he may have his chance. I told the elders about him, and two of them had already heard of him. One of them even heard him preach back east. They fired off an invitation for him to come to the church to try it on for size."

"Do you think he'll do it?" Peter asked. "I thought he was involved with missionary work."

"Well, he is," Cass said, "but I got a letter from his dad not long ago. Uncle Mark says he's getting tired of traveling around and would like to settle down and stay in one place for a time."

"I wish he would come," Priscilla said. "That'd be nice to have more of our family here. I don't know his wife very well. How many children do they have?"

"They've got two. One of them just a baby, a boy," Cass replied. "I don't know his wife, either. I understand that she's an attractive woman, but we just haven't been around them much. They've been on the go with their missionary work."

Jolie took all this in, not understanding much of it. Later she insisted on helping with the dishes, and she found Serena Winslow to be as warm and receptive as Peter had said. Serena stood beside her for a while, washing as Jolie dried, and gently inquired into her background. She listened carefully as Jolie spoke about her life, though the young girl left out much of the suffering her stepfather had caused her. Jolie turned to Serena and said, "I don't know what I'd have done if it hadn't been for Peter and Easy. I was getting pretty low on the limb."

"But you're doing fine now, Jolie," Serena said. "Priscilla and Peter tell me you're doing well at the studio."

Serena's words warmed Jolie, and she continued with the dishes when Serena left to put the children down for a nap. She was standing there drying the last of the dishes when she heard voices floating toward her. She glanced out the window and saw Cass and Peter, who had walked slowly to a point almost beyond her sight. Their voices were clear, however, and she was shocked to hear her own name mentioned. She leaned forward and heard Peter say, "Why, it's all right, Cass. I can handle it."

"Jolie's a nice girl, but you can't adopt her, Peter. You always were quick to jump into things."

Jolie's heart grew heavy as she heard Cass explaining to Peter that the responsibility for a half-grown girl was too much for a bachelor.

"It won't look right. You know it won't, Peter."

"There's nothing wrong. She's just a girl. I'm twenty-five years old, Cass."

"It's not age. It's the fact that she's a young woman, almost, and you're a bachelor."

"Does Serena think this?"

"I haven't talked to her, but I've seen men get into trouble with situations like this. I know she's just a young girl now, but she won't be for long. I'm just saying be careful."

Peter said reluctantly, "All right, Cass."

The two men walked away, and their voices trailed off. But the joy of the day quickly disappeared for Jolie. She was quiet all the rest of the day, and when Peter stopped in front of her boarding-house and said, "I'll see you tomorrow," she had made up her mind.

"No, you won't, Peter."

Peter looked at her, blinking with surprise. "You're not going to work tomorrow? We're shooting, you know. There'll be plenty for you to do."

Suddenly Jolie said, "I'm leaving. I won't be around any-more." She saw the surprise that her statement caused Peter, and he began to protest.

"You just got here. You can't just up and quit like that after Priscilla got you a job. You have to—"

"I heard what your brother said to you," Jolie interrupted him. "And he's right. You can't take on a girl to raise."

"Why . . . why, that's foolish! Cass is wrong," Peter said.

"No, he's not. You're not my father or my brother. We're no kin."

Peter suddenly put his hand out and grasped her arm. "We're The Three Musketeers, you and me and Easy. We're friends, and I'm not raising you. You're making your own way." He spoke earnestly and kept his hand on her arm.

Jolie was very much aware of his grip. His hand was strong and warm, and somehow it gave her comfort, as did his words of encouragement. He urged her to stay, which really was what she wanted to do. Though she felt hurt by Cass's words she had heard, she had nowhere to go. She began to weaken, but turned her face away from him to hide the scar.

"Look," Peter said finally. "This is silly. It's foolish, Jolie. You're not raising me any more than I'm raising you. You've got a job, and I've got a job. I need friends, and I think you do, too."

Jolie turned to look at him and saw the earnestness in his face. "That's sweet of you, Peter," she said. "But I still think I ought to go."

"Sure, when you get a few years older you'll go." He grinned rashly and released his grip. Running his hand over her smooth black hair, he said, "Look, Jolie. In a few years you'll be all grown up, and I'll marry you off to a rich prince."

She reached up and touched the scar and whispered, "No. That'll never happen." But she was glad for his kind words. She turned to him and asked, "Do you really want me to stay?"

"Sure I do." He tugged her hair gently and said, "No more talking of leaving. All right?"

"All right, Peter." She got out of the car, looked at him, and summoned a smile. "I'll see you tomorrow."

"Sure. Tomorrow. Remember, The Three Musketeers."

"Right."

★   ★   ★   ★

When Peter entered the bunkhouse and sat down across from Easy, he looked up and said, "Had a little trouble with Jolie."

Easy was polishing his boots. He halted, looked across at Peter, and asked, "What kind of trouble?" He listened as Peter recounted the conversation, then said, "Well, it could be touchy, Pete. After all, she's a young girl. Almost a young woman."

But Peter was relieved that Jolie had decided to stay. He pulled off his boots, tossed them on the floor, then sat down on the bunk and leaned back, locking his hands behind his head. His eyes were half shut and he murmured, "Oh, come on, Easy. How much trouble can one sixteen-year-old girl be?"

PART TWO

FAITH TEMPLE

★ ★ ★ ★

CHAPTER SEVEN

A SMALL TOWN IN KANSAS

★ ★ ★ ★

Dusk brought with it a gloomy leaden sky in the east, and as Dorothy Hansen Winslow looked out of the window, surveying the flat countryside that stretched out in front of the small cottage, a feeling of weariness swept over her. She had not liked Taylorville from the beginning, although it was no worse than many of the other small towns that had been temporary homes for her. As the sun faded beyond the horizon in the west, a sullen light illuminated the simple frame houses of her neighbors. Somehow they all looked alike to Dorothy, with their white siding and their one-story, monotonous plan. She felt sure that if she entered any of them, they would be no more cheerful than the one she had lived in for the past few weeks. Overhead a flock of blackbirds scored the darkening sky, their raucous cawing striking harshly on her ear. They lit in a barren cornfield two hundred yards from where she sat and began arguing and scuffling among the dried stalks.

Wearily Dorothy turned from the window, and for one moment, she let her eyes run over the living room in her most recent home. Two small windows allowed only minimal sunlight to penetrate the gloom. Stained light brown wallpaper was peeling in many places, and not even one picture decorated the drab walls. The bare wood floor was also covered with stains. Around the stove small holes pitted the floor where hot coals had been dropped. The small couch in the center of the room, once covered in the best silk damask, now showed wear from years of hard use.

The fabric was torn and threadbare, and a broken leg was being leveled by a large, flat rock. An old easy chair with a dirty green woolen covering had the stuffing coming out of the cushion. Next to it was an old walnut tea table, scratched and chipped from years of careless handling. Dorothy had covered it with a piece of cloth to hide the ugliness as best she could. On the table sat an old, tarnished brass oil lamp, which provided barely enough light to read by. As she looked over the dreary room, discontent rose in her so strongly that for a moment she shut her eyes and clenched her teeth. She crossed her arms and stood there trying to blot out the unhappiness that had been steadily growing in her for a long time.

"How many more houses like this will I have to live in?" She spoke the words aloud, and the sound of her voice caught the attention of the three-year-old girl who was sitting on the worn couch looking at a picture book. She was a beautiful child with auburn hair that curled down on her neck, and large, innocent blue eyes, which she now lifted.

"What, Mummy?"

"Nothing, Amelia." Concealing the discontent that ran through her, Dorothy moved over to sit beside the girl and said, "Let me look at your book with you."

"Okay," Amelia said happily.

She was a quiet child and loved picture books more than anything else. Dorothy had obtained a large supply, and the little girl enjoyed pointing at the pictures as her mother turned the pages. Dorothy put her arm around her daughter, drawing her close, and her eyes went over to Phillip, her infant son. He was sitting on the floor, pushing toy cars around, intent on them as he always was. He had black hair and eyes so dark blue that they almost seemed black, a trait that Dorothy knew went back to her own grandfather.

"Daddy home soon?" Amelia asked, looking up suddenly.

"I don't know, dear," Dorothy sighed.

"Daddy gone bye-bye, Mummy?"

"Yes, he has. But he'll be back soon."

"For Christmas? Is Christmas soon?"

"No, Amelia. Christmas isn't soon. It won't be for quite a long while." Aware of Amelia's problem with dates and the passage of time, she smiled and smoothed her daughter's auburn hair down. "Daddy will be home for Christmas."

"We have tree and candy and presents?"

"Yes, of course we will. Now, I've got to fix supper. You look at your book. Maybe you'll get some new ones for Christmas."

Dorothy rose and moved across the room, entering the combined kitchen and dining room. A few hand-built cabinets hung loosely on the wall, some with doors missing. She stared in disgust at the old white wallpaper with faded yellow tulips on it. How she hated that wallpaper! Turning quickly to the icebox, she saw there was only a small chunk of ice, not more than six inches by twelve. *I'll have to get ice tomorrow*, she thought. *Though this house is cold enough without buying ice*. The coal-burning stove in the living room did not throw out enough heat for the kitchen, too. The ancient woodstove that dominated one end of the small kitchen still had hot coals left in it, so she placed several small pieces of kindling inside and carefully fed it until the blaze caught. Then she weighed the firewood in the box beside the stove, selected two medium-sized pieces, and tossed them in. Closing the door to the firebox, she examined her supplies and found two pork chops, half a slice of salami, and the remains of two pounds of bacon. Not knowing when Andrew would be home, she decided to save the chops. As the stove warmed up, she pulled the remains of other meals out of the icebox. She had a small bowl of green beans, another of mashed potatoes, and another containing no more than a cup of English peas.

As Dorothy Winslow stood surveying the meager stores, she thought of her home where she had grown up in Africa. Whole quarters of beef hung in the smokehouse, along with pigs that had been dressed, and wild game. She thought of the vegetables from the fertile garden beside the mission house—the beans, peas, succulent squash, and large cucumbers. The table had always been filled with more food than anyone could possibly eat, and she longed now for those days. Looking around the kitchen, the depressing reality of her situation shook her from her reverie. Shivering in the cold, she reached over and pulled on a worn blue woolen sweater, buttoned it up, and proceeded to heat the food. As it heated, she sat down at the rickety kitchen table, with chairs that were not much better and did not match. *I'll have to get Andrew to nail this thing together or it's going to fall flat!*

She picked up a copy of the *Topeka Journal* and looked listlessly at the front page. The headlines blazoned the news that Teddy Roosevelt had won the presidential election by a landslide.

Dorothy was not overly interested in politics. Her eyes dropped down, and she turned the page and read a story about the death of Frederic Auguste Bartholdi. She had never heard his name, but the article identified him as the French sculptor who had created the Statue of Liberty. With interest, she read how Bartholdi had constructed the steel and copper statue in Paris and then shipped the two hundred twenty-five ton, one hundred fifty-foot statue to New York.

Dorothy read slowly, her mind going back to the time she had visited New York with Andrew shortly after their marriage. She had been stunned at the sight of the best-known statue in the world holding a torch in her outstretched right hand and the Declaration of Independence in her left. Dorothy shut her eyes and remembered how Andrew had held on to her tightly as they ascended up into the torch of the statue. It had been a cold day in December, and they had been alone for a brief time. Her lips grew soft as the pleasant memory flowed back through her of how he had suddenly turned her around. She could see him in her mind's eye as if he were standing before her. He had worn a double-breasted camel's hair wool topcoat with matching hat. She had worn a gray woolen suit-dress with a high neck and a full-pleated coat skirt over a narrower dress skirt. She even remembered that both of them wore spats and soft leather gloves they had bought in a shop in Manhattan. Her memory was very keen, and she could almost feel the silky softness of the brushed beaver tricorn and the fox stole that had been wedding gifts from her parents.

The teakettle on the stove began to send forth a soft, sibilant signal. Opening her eyes with a start, Dorothy rose and went over to make the tea. As she stood before the stove, she remembered how Andrew had wrapped his arms around her and kissed her and then had whispered, "You're the most beautiful woman in the world, and I love you more every day."

A sadness moved across Dorothy's face, making the planes of her cheeks suddenly change as she bit her lip and thought of that happy time. They had been on an extended honeymoon, and Andrew had been appointed Superintendent of Missions for their denomination. She remembered how, as they stood in the torch of the Statue of Liberty after he had kissed her, he had hugged her tight and waved his arms around, saying, "We'll do great things for God, Dorothy. We'll have missionaries flowing out of this country to every nation on the earth. You'll see."

And she had believed him—for a few years. But the glamor of the title Andrew held did not match the lifestyle that followed. His ministry meant traveling all over the country, visiting churches wherever he could get an invitation, speaking to congregations that ranged from ten people in a country church in Mississippi to a congregation of five thousand in Boston. His message was always the same: "God has told us to take the message, 'Go ye into all the world and bear the gospel to every creature.' " He had been highly successful, and the mission volunteers had grown under his leadership until the ranks swelled with men and women willing to go to foreign lands to spread the gospel.

But their life had been hard, and the excitement of travel soon faded for Dorothy. It became a series of long trips on crowded trains pulled by coal-burning engines that stopped at every crossing and every junction that bore a name. The interminable journeys across the land began to wear Dorothy down. She soon tired of being a guest in the home of strangers, and though most of them were kind, after the first year she began to long for a place she could call her own. Her dream for her own home did not happen.

As she set the meal on the table and dragged Phillip's high chair closer, Dorothy thought about her four-year marriage to Andrew. The joy and excitement had dimmed to a dull dissatisfaction. Things had not turned out as she had hoped. And since the children had been born, a monotonous pattern had developed that she had grown to hate. Andrew would find a rental house in some little town like Taylorville, or sometimes an apartment in a larger city, but there was little difference. He would help his family settle in, then say good-bye and leave on a tour, swinging over that section of the country, sometimes being gone for weeks. He was faithful to post letters regularly, but they were always filled with his news of recruiting missionaries, which did little to assuage her unhappiness that had begun years earlier and now was becoming almost unbearable.

Shaking her head, she muttered, "I've got to stop thinking of it." Stepping back into the frigid living room, she shivered and quickly walked over to check the stove. The coal supply was almost gone. She sparingly chose three small chunks of the black fuel, added it to the fire, then shut the door. "Come along. It's time to eat, Amelia." As the girl slid off the couch, Dorothy bent over and picked up Phillip, who began to protest at once. "You've got to eat! Now put your toy down!" she said firmly. Ignoring his protest, she carried him into the kitchen and had the usual struggle of getting his legs into the high chair. He seemed to delight in making it as difficult as possible, and she reached over and slapped his hand, saying, "Stop that, Phillip!" He began to cry, and compunction smote her. "Don't cry. Look what good things we have to eat." When he was securely fastened down, she put some of the vegetables on the plate and watched him scoop them up with his chubby fingers.

"Wait for the blessing," she said, but it was hopeless, for Phillip was more concerned with eating than waiting for a blessing. He reached down, scooped up a handful of mashed potatoes, and clamped it over his mouth.

Dorothy watched as he made a complete mess and shook her head. "Now you and I will say the blessing, Amelia." She bowed her head and said, "God, we thank you for the food. Bless Daddy and bring him back safely. In Jesus' name. Amen."

"Amen," Amelia echoed. After Dorothy had filled her daughter's plate, Amelia began to eat, struggling with her flatware as best she could. She was going to be a very neat person, for already she was showing dexterity with her fork and spoon.

As the children ate their meal, Dorothy merely picked at her own food, eating only a slice of fried bacon and the remains of the English peas. The bread was too old, and the crust was so hard that it crackled beneath her teeth. When the meal was over, she took a towel and cleaned the remains of it from Phillip's face, then went through the same struggle of extricating him from the high chair. Carrying him into the living room, she plumped him down among his toys and said, "There. You can play until bedtime."

"Help do dishes?" Amelia asked.

"Of course. Come along." She went back to the kitchen and pulled a chair over to the stained enamel sink, took heated water, and listened as Amelia chattered happily. When the chores were done, she stood at the entrance to the living room and watched Amelia climb onto the couch with a favorite book in hand. Suddenly a profound sense of loneliness engulfed her. Andrew had been gone this time longer than ever—over a month—and she had grown to despise every inch of the small cottage. The neighbors were polite enough, but it was understood that she would be leaving soon, and there was no time to make lasting friendships. The little church that she attended each Sunday and each Wednesday night was small, and the members had known one another all their lives. She was a visitor, not one of them, and although they were courteous and several of the women had dropped by to pay their dutiful visit, still, it was a lonely existence. She felt like a gypsy, only without the happiness that she sometimes associated with those people.

To distract her mind from the unsettling thoughts that threatened to overwhelm her, she eased herself into the worn arm chair and picked up the copy of *Rebecca of Sunnybrook Farm* she had started to read for the second time earlier that day. It really was a children's book, but it had been the bestseller of the previous year, and her parents had sent her this copy for her birthday. She thought of the library in her childhood home in Africa—shelves lined with big thick books, many with leather bindings, biographies, books of travel, even a great many of the classic novels and works of well-known poets. She had always loved to read, but she and Andrew could not afford to buy books now. She made do with local libraries—when there was one.

Dorothy interrupted her reading only long enough to put the children to bed. Then pulling on a heavy cotton nightgown, two pairs of socks, and a robe that had grown thin with wear, she went back to the living room, pulled the chair up as close as she could to the stove, and tried to soak heat out of the dying fire. There was not enough coal to build a roaring fire, which she longed to do. She read on, hoping to grow sleepy but dreading the loneliness of the cold bed with the thin, lumpy mattress.

She shivered as the cold crept into her bones. She got up and checked the children. Their bedroom was cold, so she put more covers over them, then got her heaviest coat to wrap around herself and went back and sat down before the dying fire.

Finally she nodded and was almost asleep when she heard a knocking at the door. Leaping up she nearly stumbled. Her feet had been tucked under her and had gone to sleep. Stomping them as she went to the door, she cried, "Who is it?"

"It's me—Andrew!"

She flung open the door and saw Andrew standing there in his black wool coat and a soft brown hat pulled down over his face. He stepped forward and opened his arms, and she flew into them, crying, "Andrew!"

Kicking the door shut, Andrew Winslow held his wife in his arms and sensed the relief that washed over her. "It's good to be back," he whispered and then took off his hat with his left arm without releasing her. He tossed the hat on the floor, put his arms back around her, and kissed her. "I've missed you, Dorothy," he whispered tenderly.

"Oh, Andrew!" Tears filled her eyes as the realization of how lonely and miserable she had really been hit her anew. "Why didn't you tell me you were coming?"

He kissed her again, then shook his head. "I didn't plan to be here, but I got canceled out at my next appointment. So I threw it all up and came home."

Dorothy stepped back and dashed the tears from her eyes. Her voice was unsteady as she said, "It's been a long time."

Andrew stared at her for a moment. She was thinner, and he could see the unhappiness in her eyes. He knew she hated for him to be gone, but there was nothing he could do about it. His job demanded it. He made a mental note to spend more time at home, then said, "It's cold as ice in here."

"I know. We're almost out of coal."

"Well, I'll have enough hauled in tomorrow, but we'll use what we have tonight."

"Are you hungry? I have a couple of chops."

"Hungry as a bear. You fix something to eat while I clean up and get that fire going. The children are all right?"

"They're fine. I'll have your dinner ready in a few minutes."

Andrew stepped back outside, picked up the suitcase he had dropped, and brought it in. He took it to the larger of the two bedrooms and deposited it on the bed, then moved into the small bedroom. The light filtered in, and he stood over Amelia, looking down at her face. He touched her hair, leaned over, and kissed her. She stirred but did not awaken. He turned around and bent over the crib, examining his son carefully. He was always fascinated by the sight of his son. A lump came to his throat as he noticed how much the boy had grown in the month he had been gone. Frustrated, he thought, *He's growing up and I'm missing it.* He did not touch Phillip for fear of waking him but stood looking down for a long time, then turned and left, leaving the door slightly ajar.

He sat down at the kitchen table and watched his wife as she fried the pork chops and opened a can of green beans. After making a pot of coffee, she put the meal on the table and sat down. Andrew reached over, took her hand, and bowed his head.

"Thank you, Lord, for bringing me home safely. And, as always, I pray you would bless my dear wife and my children. In the name of Jesus I ask it. Amen." He squeezed her hand, then looked at the two pork chops on his plate. "One of these is yours," he remarked.

"I've already eaten. You go ahead. I know you're hungry, and they're very small."

"Well, if you're sure, but it doesn't seem right."

"No, I've had plenty."

Andrew began to eat hungrily, giving her the details of his trip. Dorothy was not really interested but pretended to be. Long ago she had lost track of the tracings of his journeys of the hundreds of churches he visited. They all seemed to swim together in her mind, and she could not separate them. But her eyes devoured him as he ate, and she filled his coffee cup twice. When he was through, she said, "There's nothing sweet. I'll make a chocolate pie tomorrow."

"That was good, Dorothy. You're a fine cook." The two sat there as Andrew savored another cup of coffee, then he said, "It's cold. A warm bed sounds good to me." He hesitated for a moment and then smiled. "And a warm wife sounds even better." He reached over and took her hand for a minute. He was a big man, an even six feet, but lean. His auburn hair was long and needed cutting, and he had the piercing blue eyes of many of the Winslow men. "Come along," he said. "I've missed you."

Dorothy rose and followed him. She got into the bed, the sheets like cold iron, and when he slid beside her, she turned to him and put her arms around him, whispering, "I've missed you, too, Andrew. . . ."

★ ★ ★ ★

For the first two days after he returned home, Andrew was able to forget some of the tensions of his work. He spent all of his time with Dorothy and the children, but on the third day, all the burdens of his job came flooding back. A stack of mail had arrived, filled with demands for his immediate attention, and he withdrew as he struggled with the problems of the missionary work all over the world. Very few people understood the unrelenting pressures of his job—not even Dorothy. The missionaries who left America and sailed to the far-flung corners of the globe were his responsibility. Some of them who had gone, he well knew, were not qualified to be missionaries. Some of them had left in haste without proper training, and now many of them sent letters complaining of the conditions, as if he could change them. Others grew ill and had to be brought home, and their places had to be filled. It was Andrew Winslow's responsibility to see that these choices were made. He had a board, of course, but none of them worked full time in the missionary service. Most were busy pastors who could come together only at rare intervals to make the overall decisions. For hours Andrew sat at the kitchen table sorting through letters, trying to hold things together in countries that he had never even seen. And there always was the pressure of finding new volunteers to go. Although he was not aware of it, the stress had worn him thin emotionally and robbed him of much of the natural vitality he had had when he assumed the position.

To clear his mind, Andrew left the house and walked for hours to sort out the various demands and needs of all the stations overseas. When he came back he was physically exhausted, as well as mentally and emotionally drained.

★ ★ ★ ★

Dorothy had enjoyed the previous two days, having her husband back, but she had not really grasped all the burdens that weighed Andrew down. She could think of little else but her own needs—her desire to have him home more often, her longing for a place to settle down and call their own. Having come in from his long walk, he was now sitting at the kitchen table sorting through letters again, his brow furrowed, when she said, "What about Christmas, Andrew?"

Andrew had just finished reading a letter from a missionary who blamed him for an exasperating situation in Africa. It irritated Andrew greatly. He had not liked the man from the beginning and had sent him against his better judgment. Now, without even looking up at his wife, he grunted, "I don't have time to think of that, Dorothy! I'm busy!"

For the first time in their marriage, a deep anger and bitterness rose in Dorothy Winslow that overcame her usual respectful and quiet manner. She had been taught to submit to her husband in all things, and she had faithfully tried to do so, always subduing her own thoughts and desires in deference to his. But her anger would be restrained no longer. It welled up in a sudden rush, spilling out in a tone so sharp it startled them both. "You think about Africa and China," she cried, "but not your own family!"

Stung by the biting accusation, Andrew wheeled around and stood to his feet. "That's my *calling*!"

"And what about *my* calling? Am I to be a mother and a father *both* to your children? How can a man rule the house of God if he can't take care of his own family?" Dorothy said, her face pale, her lips drawn together. "You're gone all the time! You're a stranger to your own children! And you're a stranger to me! You spend every moment of your life for someone else, but you have no time for us!"

Harsh words leaped from Andrew's lips, and the once quiet kitchen was now charged with the sudden, violent explosion of feelings that neither had suspected lay within them. The bitter words, both of them knew, would come back to haunt their memories, but they were both gripped with an anger and frustration that had simmered unchecked until now, when it finally had boiled over.

Dorothy began to weep. "You're no husband, and you're no father! Why did you ever marry me if you were never going to have any love for me or your family?" She turned and ran out of the room, slamming the door behind her.

★ ★ ★ ★

The children were asleep, and Andrew hoped that the awful sounds had not awakened them. In a state of shock, he looked down at his trembling hands. "I didn't think anything in the world could do that to me," he muttered aloud. He clasped his hands together and moved to the living room, where he stood staring blindly out the window into the darkness. The suddenness of the quarrel had rocked his foundations. Andrew loved his family deeply and missed them terribly when he was on his lonesome journeys crossing the land. He was a man of dedication and firm opinions, and when he threw himself into any job, whether it be chopping wood, or making a toy for his children, or sending missionaries all over the world, he knew no other way but to give it everything he had. His brother, Barney, a missionary in Africa himself, had once said, "You're a great preacher, Andrew, but you haven't learned to give yourself to other things. It's all or nothing with you."

Pacing the floor with his hands clenched at his sides, Andrew knew an agonizing time that night. He did not go to the bedroom but continued to pace until he grew tired, then sat in a chair pulled up close to the stove. Dorothy's cruel words still burned in his heart. *You're no husband, and you're no father!* He thought of his own happy childhood, his parents, Mark and Lola, and of his sister, Esther—what a close family they had been. He thought, with regret, how he never understood his brother, Barney, when they were growing up, and had kept himself apart from him. That had turned out all right, and now Barney had made a fine life for himself in Africa as a missionary.

Finally he lay down on the couch and tried to sleep, but sleep came only in brief, fitful moments. Just as a gray dawn was beginning to break, he fell into a sound sleep. He awoke with a shock, however, when something struck his stomach with a hard blow. He doubled up defensively, put his hands out, and then he heard, "Daddy!" He opened his eyes to see that Amelia had come and jumped on him. He shook his head until he came to himself. Sitting up, he pulled her onto his lap and held her tightly. "Good morning, sweetheart," he whispered.

"Morning, Daddy. Will you read me a story?"

"Sure I will. As many as you like."

She was toying with the watch chain that he had not taken off and asked, "Can I listen to your watch?" She sat very still as he removed the pocket watch and held it to her ear. With his free hand he stroked her hair and thought how pretty she was. *So much like Dorothy.*

Amelia was still sitting on his lap when Dorothy came in. Andrew looked up quickly and noted the dark circles under her eyes. At that moment, Amelia handed the watch back and said, "Will you be here for Christmas, Daddy?"

Guiltily, Andrew thought of the busy itinerary he had planned and how Christmas at home had been sacrificed to go to a huge church in Kansas City. But as he looked back into the blue eyes of the child, he said, "Yes, I'll be here." He stood to his feet, holding her in his arms, and moved over to Dorothy, who stood stiffly watching him. "I'm sorry, Dorothy," he said quietly. "I was wrong. It was all my fault."

The lines in her face seemed to lessen, and her lips relaxed.

"We were both upset," she said. "I'll fix breakfast."

Breakfast was unusually quick, with Amelia doing most of the talking, and Phillip banging his fists on his high chair and making as much noise as possible. After breakfast Andrew said, "I'm going out for a walk. I have to think. I won't be long."

"All right. Will you stop by the store and get some milk? We're all out."

"Yes. Anything else?"

"No. Just the milk."

He looked at the children and said, "Before I go for my walk, I'll take you out for a while." He dressed them warmly, and carrying Phillip and holding Amelia's hand, he took them outside. There was really nothing to do. He looked around and saw no swings or anything for children to play on, as he saw in other yards. "Come along," he said, scooping up Amelia with his free arm. "We'll just walk, and I'll tell you a story about Christmas."

★ ★ ★ ★

From inside the house Dorothy watched through the window as Andrew made his way down the street holding the two children. The quarrel had sickened her, and she had no inclinations to do anything to the house. She forced herself to clean up the breakfast dishes, then finally went and sat down in front of the stove. Picking up her Bible, she began to read, almost listlessly. There was no spirit nor heart in her. The quarrel seemed to have taken all that away from her. From long habit, she turned to the book of John, her favorite, and began reading in the fourteenth chapter. The familiar words seemed to jump out at her. "Let not your heart be troubled: ye believe in God, believe also in me." She could go no further than that first verse. Tears came to her eyes. It was these chapters that spoke most deeply to her own heart. She loved to read of the acts of Jesus as set forth in the Gospels, and especially this latter part of the book of John when Jesus spoke to His disciples for the last time on earth.

" 'Let not your heart be troubled,' " she read aloud, then began to pray, "Oh, Lord, I have a troubled heart. I've sinned against you so many times with my doubts and my fears, and now I've hurt my husband. Oh, God, I can't stand any more! Do something in my life to make me a better woman. Make me content. Help me to be a better wife to Andrew." She continued to pray for some time, and after a few minutes, a strange sense of well-being and peace settled over her. The Scriptures had this power over her, especially the words of Jesus. Words like "Let not your heart be troubled" came to her again and again. Finally she said, "I can't solve my problems, Lord, but my heart is not troubled now. I put my faith and my trust in you." She sat there for a long time, not really praying but thanking God for the peace He had given her. When she heard the door slam, she closed the Bible quickly and rose to meet Andrew. He was still carrying the children, and she reached over and took Phillip, whose face was cherry red from the cold. "Come over by the stove," she said, taking off his black coat and mittens. "My, your hands are cold." She put them against her cheeks and held them there as he began trying to tell her what they had seen.

Andrew watched Dorothy as she spoke to the children, and finally he said, "I'll go for my walk now."

"All right," Dorothy said, looking up. "It's very cold. Do you have on enough socks to keep your feet warm?"

"Yes, I'm fine. I won't be long."

Dorothy moved to the window again and watched him walk away. He seemed a solitary figure, and she asked again, "Oh, God, help me to be what you want me to be," then she went back to the children.

★　★　★　★

"This letter came for you this morning." Dorothy handed the letter to Andrew, who was sitting at the table, as usual, writing letters.

He took it, stared at the envelope, and said, "It's from the First Church in Kansas City, where I had planned to speak over Christmas. We've gotten some good missionaries out of that church." He opened it, aware that she was watching him. His eyes scanned the lines and he said, "They want us all to come for Christmas service there. Not just me. You and the children, too."

"What are you going to do?"

He fumbled with the letter uncertainly, then looked up at her. "You don't want to go, do you?"

"We don't have any friends there, Andrew." There was a plaintive quality in her voice, although she was quiet, and she said, "I'll do what you say, but it would be a hard time. You can't relax or be yourself when you're visiting in someone else's home during the holidays. I'd rather stay here."

There was no emotion in her voice, and she displayed none of the anger that had leaped out at him earlier, but he had learned from their quarrel that her feelings ran much deeper than he had ever realized before—deeper than she knew how to express openly. Even though she seemed willing once again to accept his decision in this matter, he was certain now that she desperately wanted to have Christmas alone with just the family.

"All right," he said. "I'll write them and say we can't come."

"You do what you must, Andrew."

He did not answer but remained quiet the rest of the day. He spent a great deal of time with the children, but in the afternoon when they were taking their naps, he walked out the door, saying nothing to Dorothy. He was gone for over an hour. When he came back, he took off his coat and hat, stuffed his mittens in his pockets, then came over to sit down beside Dorothy. She had been sitting on the couch mending a shirt and looked up, asking mildly, "Did you have a nice walk?"

"Dorothy, I have something to talk to you about." He got her attention and hesitated only for a moment. He ran his hands with some agitation through his auburn hair, then said quickly, "Last week I got a letter from Faith Temple in Los Angeles."

"Did they want you to come speak?"

"No, it wasn't that. You know my cousin Cassidy has moved there. He's become a farmer, of sorts, raising oranges, and Priscilla's there, too, making those motion pictures." He frowned and said, "I'm not sure that's a good thing for her to be into."

"She'll be all right. Remember the letter we got from your parents last week? Priscilla doesn't seem happy, but she's doing well after that awful affair with that man in New York."

"In any case, there's a very large church there. Their senior pastor has left, and Cass recommended me to the deacons." He saw some interest flicker in her eyes, and he said quietly, "They want me to come and preach for them."

Dorothy could not take this in at once. Andrew had never mentioned any other sort of ministry except his job as Superintendent of Missions. She asked in a puzzled tone, "You mean they want you to come until they find a pastor?"

"No." Andrew reached over and took her hand and held it in his. "I mean they may want me to come *as* their pastor." He held her hand and said quietly, "You've been unhappy, Dorothy, and I'm sorry for it. I feel responsible."

Her love for him rose quickly, and she said, "You've done a fine job. I'm very proud of you, Andrew."

He sat there quietly for a moment, then finally said, "I think we'll go to that church."

"Do you mean just to preach?"

"No." He had thought this out and prayed about it considerably, and now said strongly, "I feel I've done all I can as superintendent. Our quarrel hit me pretty hard."

"I'm sorry I said those things."

"You were right. I haven't been a good husband or a father. This job ought to be done by a single man. I see now what Paul meant when he said it's better not to be married, for a married man cares for his wife. But I've got a wife and children, Dorothy. As I prayed about it, it seems that God is giving me permission, and I'm excited. I'd like to be a pastor, and it's a great church."

Dorothy listened as he described the church, excitement rising in his voice. Finally he said, "And the parsonage, according to what Cass says, is almost a mansion. You'd like it, sweetheart! Your own house, your own garden, your own place."

Dorothy could not control the tears that came to her eyes. She tried to, but her eyes filled, and then the tears ran down her cheeks. "I . . . would like that, Andrew. Very much."

The tears hit Andrew Winslow hard. He had been made aware of Dorothy's loneliness, and now he reached forward and put his arms around her. She began to sob, and he stroked her hair until her body ceased to tremble. He kissed her and said, "This is the right thing. You and the children deserve a home."

"Do you really think it will happen?"

"Yes," Andrew said and smiled. "I think God's in it. It's going to be Faith Temple for us, and we'll do it together."

CHAPTER EIGHT

A PREACHER COMES TO TOWN

★ ★ ★ ★

Although Jason Ballard had been apprehensive about hiring Easy, his fears had proven groundless. True enough, the small man spent as much time falling off a horse as he did getting on, but Easy was quiet and threw his energies into learning his new profession. He was also fiercely superstitious, as was quickly discovered by the crew, and the riders all loved to tease him about it, although they did so often with a straight face. Jason suspected that the small man knew he was being ribbed, but Easy let nothing show on his poker face.

On Tuesday morning at breakfast in the dining room, Jason's riders all made it a point to sit at the same long table. They consumed enormous stacks of pancakes, dozens of eggs, ate biscuits as if they were popcorn, and kept the room ringing with their loud voices and raucous laughter. *They are a fine group*, Jason thought as he slid into his place across from Easy Devlin and Peter Winslow. He pitched into his half a dozen fried eggs, hiding a grin as the hands were all poking fun at Devlin.

Pudge Jones, who was a confirmed hypochondriac by the age of twenty, sat next to Devlin and was complaining about his rheumatism. If it had not been rheumatism, everyone knew it would have been arthritis or some other disease. The more unusual and rare, the better Pudge enjoyed the symptoms of it. But this morning it was rheumatism, and he said mournfully, "I wish old Doc Mortimer were here. He could always cure me up. Always had a pill for whatever ailed me." He glanced at Easy and said, "Devlin, you ever have rheumatism?"

Easy was chewing thoughtfully on one of the fluffy biscuits layered with fresh yellow butter and orange marmalade. "Nope," he said when he swallowed an enormous bite and turned to look at his neighbor. "There ain't no sense in a fellow sufferin' from rheumatism. It's easy enough to cure."

Smiles went around the table. Pudge stared at Devlin and then asked truculently, "Well, what do you do to cure it? I tell you it's killin' me!"

"Why, there ain't nothin' to it," Easy said, shrugging his thin shoulders. "Just carry an Irish potato in your pocket. That'll take care of it."

"Is that right, Easy?" The speaker was Xeno Bruten, a short, muscular man from New Mexico. He had a bald spot with a fringe of brown hair around his head and winked across the table at Jason. "I bet you even know how to cure warts." He held out his hand, and on the back of his wrist was a large brown wart. "None of the doctors been able to do much with this. It's gettin' bigger, too. What do you think, Easy?"

"Well, I reckon if I had that thing on my wrist, I'd take a green pea, cut it, and rub it on the wart." He took another bite of the biscuit, chewed it carefully, then added, "Then I'd take that pea, wrap it in a piece of paper, and throw it away."

"What'll that do?" Xeno demanded.

"The fellow that picks up that piece of paper will get the wart, and it'll fall off your wrist."

Laughter went around the table, but Easy Devlin's face did not break. He had gained color in his brief time in California, and the hacking cough was mostly gone. He finished off his biscuit, drank his coffee down, then said, " 'Course, there's other ways."

"Like what?" Xeno asked.

"Well, you can take a grain of corn, cut out the heart, and cut that wart until it starts bleedin'. Then you take a drop of the blood and put it in the corn where the heart was taken out. Then," he added mildly, putting his brown eyes on Xeno Bruten, "you throw the grain to the chicken. As soon as that chicken eats it, the wart will fall off."

Xeno laughed loudly, but there was affection in it.

Ben Temple had been listening to all this. He was twenty-seven, an even six feet of bull-chested strength. He had black hair, a cavalry mustache to match, and the most unusual eyes. They were violet with heavy black lashes, eyes that any girl would be proud to own. Temple was from Texas and had heard plenty of tall tales. Now he said with a straight face, "I been havin' chills, Easy. Been thinkin' about goin' to the doctor."

"Go on and waste your money," Easy remarked. "What I'd do if was I you, Ben, is I'd get my temperature took when that fever's on you. Tie as many knots in a piece of string as you have chills, then you go out in the woods somewhere and tie the string around a persimmon bush, then turn around and walk away not lookin' back."

"What if there's not a persimmon bush around? I don't think there is any in California. Do I have to go all the way back to Texas? Won't an orange tree do?"

"Nope. Nothing but a persimmon bush," Easy said matter-of-factly.

Peter had finished his meal and sat grinning as the men kept probing at Easy Devlin. He was very glad that he had met the southerner and had grown very fond of him. Looking across at Jason, he asked, "What's on the menu today, Jase? Are we going to be outlaws or heroes?" In the movie business, their job was simply to gallop across the flatlands shooting blanks out of their pistols. Whether they were villains or heroes, only the story line of the motion picture would reveal.

"Ought to be pretty interesting this morning," Jason said. "Gonna do that scene with Priscilla where she gets in front of a stampede and almost gets run down. Then the hero gallops in, scoops her up, and saves her life. Nothing to it."

"Sounds like it could be a bit dangerous, Jason," Peter said. "You take care of Priscilla."

"Don't you go worrying now. I'm never gonna let anything happen to her. You know that," Jason said. Then turning back to the hands at the table, he said, "All right, you yahoos. Let's get movin'. We got a picture to shoot."

★　★　★　★

The scene was shot on a flat plot of ground that looked a great deal like Wyoming's terrain. Jason had the riders holding the herd, but his eyes were on Priscilla as she walked along with her head held high. Then he heard Lem say, "All right, Jason—get them running!"

"Drive 'em!" Jason lifted his voice, then kicked his big buckskin into a run. He gained fifty yards on the herd and saw that
Priscilla had turned to face them, then had started to run. "Come
on, Duke!" Jason shouted and kicked the big horse into a dead
run. As he looked over his shoulder, he saw the herd was closer
than he'd like. *Going to be close. . . !*

Priscilla kept facing the cameras, her mobile face registering
the fear the scene called for—and not all of it was acting. The
horns of the big steers looked suddenly very deadly, and she
paled, then turned to see Jason driving toward her, leaning over.
If he misses me, I'll die! she thought. She lifted her arms, the thunder
of the sharp hooves filling the air. Then he was there, blotting out
the herd. His right arm closed around her waist, and she felt like
a child as he lifted her high and cradled her safe in his strong
arms!

When they were clear of the herd, she smiled at him, excited
by the success of the stunt. "You were wonderful, Jason!" she
cried. Her face was only inches from his, and without warning he
suddenly pulled her tight against his chest and kissed her. Shock
ran through Priscilla at the pressure of his firm lips on hers. His
arms were like iron, and against her better judgment she found
herself responding to his caress. Then she pulled away and whispered, "You must never do that again, Jase!"

"I probably will," he said, then turned his horse toward the
director. He set her down on her feet, then wheeled the buckskin
around and rode back toward the herd.

Priscilla stood there and watched him as he started to round
up the herd. The memory of his lips on hers lingered, and she
knew she would remember it for a long time.

Stan Lem had been more worried about the stampede scene
than he had permitted anyone to see. When Peter Winslow had
come to protest the danger of the scene, he had been within a
hairsbreadth of insisting that one of the smaller cowboys double
for her. He was, however, a stickler for accuracy, and it was difficult for a man to impersonate a woman. A man did not have the
walk, the air, and so he dismissed Peter's concern and let Priscilla
endure the danger. He had heaved a great sigh of relief when Ballard had swept down and hauled her off, and muttered to his
cameraman, "That cowboy is something, isn't he?"

"Sure is, Mr. Lem. I wish he were starring in the picture instead
of Ken Nix. That fella's nothing."

Lem did not permit himself to comment on that. "Get that film ready. I want to be sure it came out right."

"The light was good," the cameraman said. "And we were in close enough, I think, to get a good shot on the expression on Priscilla's face. She didn't forget to show fear, did she?"

"I'm not sure that was acting. When I saw the horns on those beasts thundering toward her, it gave me the shivers." He turned away and returned to the studio to prepare for the next scene, which was to be shot indoors. On his way he stopped at the wardrobe room, where he found Lily Doe and the young girl, Jolie Devorak, busily getting the costumes ready. He smiled at them, asking, "Costumes all ready for the next shot?"

"Yes, they are," Lily said.

"Good," Lem said. "We'll shoot as soon as they get dressed." He turned to go, making his way back to his director's chair. He was sitting there waiting for the actors and the technicians to put things together when he heard a voice behind him.

"I brought your tea, Mr. Lem."

Stan Lem turned and saw Jolie standing there with a cup of tea. His eyes lighted up and he smiled, which made him look much more pleasant. Taking the cup, he sipped it, then looked up at her. "Why . . . I thank you, Jolie. You're the only one I've found around here who knows how to make a real pot of tea."

"I just make it like you told me, Mr. Lem."

Jolie was wearing a light blue cotton dress with pink ribbon trim along the edges of the neck, the short sleeves, and at the bottom of the skirt that came to just above her ankles. She kept her face turned slightly away, concealing the scar, which brought a stab of pity to Lem. He started to tell her there were things that could be done for that but then thought, *I'm sure she's heard that before. Something poignant about the child. I wish she didn't have that scar.* Aloud he said, "You've done a great job, Jolie. You've taken a lot of pressure off of me and the others. I'm very satisfied with your work."

A flush touched Jolie's cheeks, and she gave him a shy smile. "Thank you, Mr. Lem. I'll just leave the pot here in case you want some more."

She went back to the wardrobe room, where she continued to help Lily put the costumes in order and helped some of the actors and actresses get dressed for the next scene. When they had all left, Lily leaned back and said, "That's been a job getting this put together." The scene had been set in a wealthy drawing room with men and women wearing formal costumes. Lily had worked hard to put it all together and now smiled gratefully, saying, "I don't know what I would have done without you, Jolie. You've made life a lot easier for me."

"Oh, it's been fun. It's like playing dress-up, isn't it?" Jolie was sitting across from the older woman, and her black hair framed her face in a most attractive way. She was still thin, the points of her shoulders showing sharply through the cotton dress.

"What about your family?" Lily asked.

"I really don't have one anymore. Just a stepfather."

Something in the way Jolie pronounced the word told Lily that she did not want to talk about it any longer.

Jolie put on a light jacket, although there was little need of it, and left the studio. She was surprised to see the surrey drawn up in front, with Peter sitting loosely on the front seat and Easy lying down in the back.

"Come along, Jolie," Peter said. "We're going out to celebrate."

Glancing up quickly, Jolie climbed into the seat beside Peter, asking, "Celebrate what?"

"Celebrate a good day!" He spoke to the horses, and they moved down the street with a sprightly pace, their hooves clattering against the hard surface of the road.

Looking back, Jolie asked, "What's the matter with you, Easy?"

Easy groaned and said, "I fell off the horse again. I'll never learn to stay on one of them animals."

"I thought you were from Kentucky. Don't they have horses there?"

"Yeah, they got 'em, but I grew up in a poor family, and we couldn't afford such a thing as a horse. I hated them anyway. Got throwed off of one when I was a kid. Nearly killed me. I promised myself I'd stay off as long as I could."

"Well, I bet you got a remedy for sore spots," she teased and waited until he gave his answer.

"Well, there's several things you can do for bruises," he remarked. "But I ain't had time to do none of 'em yet. Besides, there ain't no balm of Gilead here."

"Balm of Gilead? What's that?"

"Plant that grows down south. You boil it in water and dip cloth in it and put it on sore spots. Heals it up almost instant like."

The carriage rumbled on as Jolie carried on a conversation

with Easy concerning some of his folk remedies. She liked the small man very much and smiled as Easy groaned again. Finally she turned to ask Peter about the scene with Jason and Priscilla. "Were you worried?" she asked.

"I sure was, but Jase is a good hand."

Jolie asked abruptly, "Had they known each other before?"

Peter turned to look at her. "Why do you ask that, Jolie?"

"Something about the way he looks at her." She hesitated, then said quietly, "I think he cares for her."

Peter Winslow was surprised at the young girl's quickness. "Yes, he does. He has for a long time. He was foreman of our folks' ranch in Wyoming. Jase has always been in love with Priscilla, I think. When she left to go to New York it just about killed him." He looked at her and smiled. "You're pretty sharp to figure that out."

"It's not hard. He's got a sadness in his eyes when he looks at her."

"I didn't know it was that obvious."

"It is if you look for it."

They said no more about it and soon arrived at a small cafe called "The Green Sombrero." It proved to be a fairly good place to eat, and after putting down a fifteen-ounce sirloin, Easy said, "I reckon that'll heal me up a little bit, but I'd just as soon go back and go to bed."

"So much for our big night out on the town," Peter laughed. "Might be best, though. I think we're gonna have to do some more riding tomorrow." He drove back to the bunkhouse, and after Easy had slowly climbed down and bidden them good night, he turned the horses around and drove them slowly along. It was dark now, and the stars overhead were brilliant. Looking up he said, "I used to try to count the stars when I was a kid. I never did get the job done, though. Too many of them."

At that moment, a falling star scratched its way along the velvet blackness of the night, and Jolie took a deep breath, whispering, "Isn't that pretty?"

"Sure is." Peter turned to look at her, holding the lines idly in his hands. "Did you make a wish?"

"No."

"No wish? That's what you're supposed to do when you see a falling star."

"Is it? Did you make a wish?"

Peter laughed. "I forgot. It's not too late, though. What do you wish for, Jolie?" Out of the corner of his eye, he saw her hand touch her scar, but she removed it quickly.

"It doesn't do any good to make wishes," she said sadly. "They never come true anyway."

Turning more squarely toward her, Peter said quietly, "Sometimes they do. If you work hard enough, sometimes wishes can come true."

"Do you really think so?" There was a plaintive, woeful quality in the young voice that struck Peter powerfully, and he drove on for some time without speaking. When the carriage pulled up in front of her boardinghouse, Jolie said, "You don't have to get down. Thanks for the supper." Her face was thin in the moonlight, and the black hair seemed to frame it as in a picture. She had a wide mouth and her eyes were enormous, and as the moonlight struck her pupils there was a light in them.

Peter said quickly, "I told you it would be better, didn't I?"

"Yes, you did."

Peter reached out slowly and put his hand on her shoulder and squeezed it. She looked at him quickly but said nothing. "You see?" he said gently. "If I had touched your shoulder like that a month ago, you would have pulled that knife on me."

"I guess I would."

"You still have that knife?"

"No, I don't carry it anymore. I have no need for it now." She was very conscious of his strong hand on her thin shoulder, and somehow it made her nervous. She pulled away, saying, "Good night, Peter."

Her voice was abrupt, and she sounded almost angry. When she disappeared, Peter looked at the door for a long time, then turned back to the horses. He spoke aloud, saying, "I hope you fellas understand women better than I do. I'll never understand a girl's moods."

★　★　★　★

The next day at midmorning Priscilla was walking over to a set when she saw Cass coming toward her in a hurry. He was very excited, she saw, and she asked, "What is it? What's happened?"

"Guess who's going to be in the pulpit Sunday at Faith Temple?"

"Is it Andrew? Is he coming?"

"Sure is." Cass's eyes gleamed. He was wearing his working clothes—blue jeans, faded blue shirt, and a pair of light boots. His tawny hair was falling down over his forehead, and his blue-green eyes seemed to sparkle.

Priscilla could never decide whether Cody, Cassidy, or Peter was the best looking of her brothers. They were all big, fine-looking men, and now she said fondly, "Well, that'll be good to have more of the family here, won't it?"

"It sure will," Cass nodded. He frowned suddenly and shrugged his shoulders. "I don't know how Reverend Cole will take it."

"Why, he wouldn't have any trouble finding a church as good a preacher as he is."

"I don't think that's what he had on his mind. There aren't many churches as good as Faith Temple, and I think Reverend Cole was pretty sure he was going to be the next pastor."

Priscilla thought about the dynamic minister and shook her head. "He'll be all right. He can go on as associate pastor, I'm sure."

"Yes, I suppose, but that's not the same thing." He grinned at Priscilla, then reached out and tugged her hair. "We men like to be number one, you know. I'm meeting the train and taking Andrew home. I had to fight the elders over that, but after all, he is my cousin. They can have him after he comes to live here."

"You're pretty sure about it, aren't you, Cass?"

"I heard him preach before. He's even better than Cole. Better than anybody, I think."

★ ★ ★ ★

The train grumbled out of the mountains and across the flats. Dorothy Winslow stared eagerly out the window, and Andrew with only a slighter degree of anticipation. He had been to California before, to San Francisco, but never to Los Angeles. He was excited, however, and put his arm around Dorothy, who was holding Phillip in her lap while Amelia sat quietly looking out the window on Andrew's left. "How does it look, Dorothy?" he asked.

"It's so flat. It looks like a desert."

"It *is* a desert," Andrew said, grinning at her. "You have to irrigate most places. Dry as a bone out here, too. Hardly ever rains.

I'll miss that," he said. "I always did like to lie in bed and listen to rain on a tin roof. Always liked to walk in it, too, but there won't be much of that here."

"Doesn't it ever rain?"

"Well, occasionally, but it's mostly liquid sunshine. Sunshine will have to do for us, I guess." He removed his arm and glanced out the window. "I think we're coming into town."

Almost as he spoke, the conductor entered the car, saying, "Los Angeles—Los Angeles," then disappeared to give the news in the next car.

Andrew arose at once and began to collect the luggage they had. "If you can carry Phillip, I'll take the suitcases."

"I carry something, Daddy," Amelia piped up.

"Sure you can." He handed her a lightweight canvas bag and smiled as she struggled down the aisle with it. "Be careful. The train will be stopping. It will be quite a jerk."

As he had predicted, the train slowed down and stopped with a jerk that forced him to reach down and stop Amelia from falling over.

"All right. That's it. Here we go."

As soon as Andrew stepped off the train and reached back for Dorothy, his eyes swept the station. "Look, there's Cass!" He turned to meet the tall man who had his hand stuck out.

"Hello, cousin Andrew! I haven't seen you in a long time."

"Why, no. You've grown up, Cass. You were just a boy the last time I saw you. At a family reunion, I think."

"That's right." Cass pulled off his hat and said, "This must be Dorothy."

Dorothy took the hand of the tall, handsome man and was relieved at the welcome greeting in his eyes.

"This is Phillip and this is Amelia," she said.

"Let me carry that big fellow," Cass said. He reached out to take Phillip, who, to his parents' surprise, made no protest. Normally he was reluctant to be handled by strangers, but something in Cass's eye made him accept the change without protest. "Come along. I've got another surprise for you."

Andrew followed with Dorothy, who had picked up Amelia. As soon as they got to the driveway, he saw a very tall young man perched in the driver's seat of a huge touring car.

"You remember my brother, Peter," Cass said. "He's the best chauffeur in California."

"Hello, Reverend Winslow." Peter smiled and jumped down from the seat to shake Andrew's hand. He greeted the rest of the family, then directed the loading of the car. As soon as everyone was in, he cranked the machine and leaped in to advance the spark and release the brake, saying, "Hang on!"

"Hey, Peter! Slow down!" Cass protested. "This isn't a racing car, you know!" He turned to Andrew with a smile and said, "Peter's working for Imperial Pictures now, riding a horse mostly, but he's got high ambitions of being a race car driver."

"Looks like he's got a good start," Andrew grinned. He liked his young relatives and turned to face Dorothy, whose face was glowing with excitement. He squeezed her shoulders, then shouted to Peter, "Could we go by and see the church and the parsonage?"

"Sure thing, Andrew!"

Dorothy sat with Andrew's arm around her, holding Phillip in her lap. When they drove by the church, she whispered, "Oh, it's beautiful, Andrew!"

"Not bad, and it's a good church, too, aside from the building. Going to be a bigger one, though, after we've been there awhile, isn't it?"

"Yes." Dorothy turned to smile at him. She had slept little on the train and was more excited than she had been for quite some time.

When they pulled up in front of a big Spanish-style house built like a miniature hacienda, Cass grinned. "There it is. Your future home, Dorothy. How do you like it?"

Dorothy stared at the house and could not speak for a moment. Finally she turned and said in a choked voice, "Maybe we're finally going to have a home to call our own."

"Let's go in and take a look. It's empty," Cass said.

"Could we?" Dorothy asked eagerly.

"I don't see why not," Cass replied. He leaped out of the car and soon the party was touring the inside of the house. The rooms were large and open with curving arches leading to the next room. Only the bedrooms had heavy oak doors on them. Large wide windows were in the rooms to the south side of the house, and narrower floor-length windows were throughout the rest of the rooms, all with black iron rods running vertically on the outside of each window. The walls were a pastel pink stucco, and the floors were a brown-red clay tile. Bright area rugs covered a large portion of the floor in the living room, dining room, and bed-rooms. The kitchen was the brightest room in the house with its stucco walls painted white. The area surrounding the sink was covered with small squares of ceramic tile in a white, yellow, and red mosaic pattern.

Dorothy moved from room to room, exclaiming over each one. "Why, it's already furnished," she said.

"Sure. The furniture goes with the parsonage. Of course, you can get rid of any you don't like," Cass said hurriedly.

"Oh no! It's beautiful just like it is!" She ran her hand across an ornately carved walnut corner cabinet and seemed to shiver with delight. She turned to Andrew and whispered, "It's the most beautiful house I've ever seen. We're going to be so happy here."

It took some persuasion to get Dorothy out of the house, but finally they did. Cass made arrangements to take them to his house, and after they had all gone in and Cass introduced them to Serena and the children, he walked outside with Peter.

"Thanks for being our chauffeur, Peter. The big car came in handy."

Peter climbed in the car and looked quizzically back toward the house. "I reckon Andrew's wife, Dorothy, really wants to stay. Did you see her face when she walked through that house?"

"Sure did," Cass said. He shrugged his trim shoulders, saying, "I suppose it's been hard on her having to move all over the country."

"She'll be disappointed if the church doesn't invite him to be the pastor."

"I reckon she will, but I don't think that will happen. When the church hears him preach, they'll snap him up. Good night, Peter."

"Good night, Cass."

CHAPTER NINE

A New Year for the Winslows

★ ★ ★ ★

The elders of Faith Temple gathered on Christmas morning for a combination business and prayer meeting. It was sometimes difficult, as Paul Sears said wryly, to tell the difference between the two when the elders met. He sat watching as the others filed in and took their seats in the conference room off the main auditorium, wondering what these four men would have to say. Although he would not have claimed it for himself, Sears was by far the most spiritual man on the church board. He was a plumber who worked for himself, and his appointment to the board by the congregation had been a surprise to many. He was a quiet man who rarely spoke in the public meetings. But it was Paul Sears who was most often sent for when there was sickness, and it was Sears to whom men came—and women also—bringing their troubles, for he had the Spirit of Christ about him in an unusual fashion. Now as he watched Cyrus Tompkins, the chairman, come to stand at the head of the table, he kept his own counsel and listened. At least three members of the board had been in favor of asking Nolan Cole to serve as full-time pastor, but Sears and Dr. Maurice Gunn had opposed that, and Tompkins had declared they would not ask any man to fill their pulpit until the vote was unanimous.

Cyrus Tompkins was a tall, rawboned man of sixty with faded blue eyes and white hair. He was enjoying his retirement after a successful career as a stockbroker in New York. He had tired of the big city in the East and had come to Los Angeles for peace and quiet. When he lifted his voice, there was the tinge of old Alabama in him, where he had been born and spent the early years of his life.

"Well, brethren," he said, "I suppose before we pray we ought to say what we think."

Harold Parsley, a short man of forty with black hair and blacker eyes, spoke up. "I think we all know what we think, Cy," he said. Parsley was the head banker of the First National Bank in Los Angeles. He was accustomed to having his own way and now shot a sharp glance at Sears and Dr. Gunn, saying, "We wouldn't even be meeting like this if you two fellows weren't so quarrelsome!"

Dr. Maurice Gunn was the youngest man on the board, at the age of twenty-eight. He was no more than medium height, but his erect posture made him seem taller. Now he turned a set of level brown eyes on Parsley and said with a trace of Boston in his speech, "Harold, it's not a thing we can decide so easily. It's not like electing a man to the board of your bank. We've got to have the man that God wants us to have."

Parsley hated to be challenged, especially in front of others. Suddenly he shrugged and said, "I think I know the mind of God as well as you do, doctor. We'll not find a better preacher than Nolan Cole if we turn this country upside down!"

Franklin Simmington suddenly spoke up. He was a thick man, bulky and heavy, and his big hands that were folded in the front of him were scarred with rope burns after half a century as the owner of one of the largest ranches in the area. He still didn't know how many acres it covered. Looking across the room, there was a gentleness in him as he said, "Now, Harold, that's what we're here for. To seek the mind of God on this."

At once Cyrus Tompkins nodded. He wanted Cole to be the pastor very badly, but he had great confidence in Paul Sears and in Dr. Gunn, having seen their wisdom in situations in the past. "I think we'll not discuss it any longer, brethren. Let us go to God in prayer. As you know, I was in favor of Reverend Cole serving as pastor, but if that's not God's will it would be a tragedy. Let's just pray and seek the Lord." They all knelt down and for fifteen minutes prayed quietly, the silence broken only occasionally by a short petition uttered aloud. Finally, Tompkins rose to his feet and the others followed suit. He cast his eyes over them carefully, saying, "Somehow I feel this is the most important decision this church will ever make. We must be right about it, so we'll meet again after the service to share our feelings about Brother Winslow and his suitability."

As Tompkins turned and left the room, followed by the others, Harold Parsley whispered audibly, "Bunch of foolishness! We have God's man right in our hands, and we're likely to let him get away!"

★ ★ ★ ★

The auditorium was full to overflowing, and extra chairs had been brought in. Cass and his family had come early, knowing that the Christmas morning service would be packed out. And now he looked about with satisfaction and said, "Well, it looks like we've got this whole pew filled up with Winslows and friends."

Serena glanced down the row and saw that it was filled with their children. Priscilla and Dorothy and her children were there. Peter had brought Easy Devlin and Jolie Devorak with him. "I think it's working out fine with Jolie," Serena said. "She's making her own way, and everyone is pleased with her work at Imperial."

Cass nodded reluctantly. "I guess you were right about that. I didn't have to worry about old Peter."

Even as he spoke, the choir filed in, led by a silver-haired director, and began to sing "Joy to the World!" Without pause, they sang a number of familiar Christmas hymns. The joyous sound of five thousand voices filled the large auditorium.

Jolie Devorak had never heard anything like it. She pressed closer to Easy and said, "It's beautiful, isn't it?"

"Prettiest thing I ever heard," Easy admitted. He had heard her singing and said, "You sure got a pretty voice, Jolie. I can't sing a lick myself."

Jolie turned around and saw that Peter was smiling at her and flushed. She had positioned herself so that her scarred face would be opposite him, knowing all the time that it was foolish to try to hide it. He held the songbook out, and they sang "O Little Town of Bethlehem," their voices blending together with the others.

"We do pretty well," Peter said. "I didn't know you could sing so good."

Jolie did not answer. Somehow it saddened her. She could remember the few Christmases when her mother had taken her to church, but as time had gone on that had become rarer. She knew that she had missed something in life, and there was no way to go back and make it up.

While the choir was singing, the elders came in and took their seats on the large platform. Every eye in the auditorium was fixed on the two men who took seats together over to the right of the pulpit. They were accustomed to Reverend Nolan Cole, but Reverend Andrew Winslow was the man they had come to hear. He was wearing a light tan suit with a burgundy tie, and the suit fit his lean body perfectly. He sat quietly facing the auditorium, the lights overhead catching the auburn tints of his hair and his electric blue eyes sweeping over the congregation. From time to time he would drop his head for a while, and then he would look up with a smile on his lips.

Finally Reverend Cole came to the pulpit. He seemed sober and not as dynamic as usual, but he smiled as he said, "It is my privilege and joy to introduce Reverend Andrew Winslow, his wife, Dorothy, and their two children, Amelia and Phillip. As you know, Reverend Winslow has served as Superintendent of Missions for our denomination for the past few years, and I need not add to those of you who keep up with mission work that under his leadership the gospel has gone out in greater force to foreign fields than we have ever known."

As he continued speaking in glowing terms of the visiting preacher, Dr. Gunn leaned over and whispered to Paul Sears, "He's laying it on pretty thick, isn't he, Paul?"

But no one seemed to mind the flowery introduction, and when Cole turned to say, "Come and preach to us, Brother Winslow," the crowd settled back with anticipation.

Andrew Winslow rose and walked to the pulpit, a worn black Bible in his right hand. Placing it on the pulpit, he glanced at Reverend Cole and grinned a boyish grin. "I wish my mother could've heard all those nice things Reverend Cole had to say about me," he remarked, and a slight laughter went over the congregation. "Brother Cole was very generous, and somehow I feel like a waffle that's had syrup poured all over it." This time the laughter was louder, and for a few moments Andrew spoke of how happy he was when he had received the invitation to come and preach. He told how he and his wife had heard such marvelous things about Faith Temple, and now he had seen with his own eyes the spirit of the church.

Finally he ended his preliminary remarks and let a silence fall over the congregation. Without opening his Bible he began to quote the Christmas story from the second chapter of Luke. " 'And it came to pass in those days,' " he said in a clear, ringing voice, " 'that there went out a decree from Caesar Augustus, that all the world should be taxed. . . .' " Somehow the quoting of the old story was effective in a way that the reading never could be. The minister's voice rose like a trumpet from time to time, and at other moments he spoke in what was little more than a whisper. He was a magnificent reader, this Andrew Winslow. His strong voice was like an instrument that could strike any chord, and by the time he had quoted the first twenty verses, every person in the auditorium sat stock still waiting for the application.

Suddenly Andrew asked, "When is Christmas?"

He looked around, and every person in the large crowd seemed to feel he was looking directly into them. Jolie felt the electric blue eyes touch her, and she blinked, certain that he knew everything in her heart.

"I suppose the answer is December the twenty-fifth," Andrew said slowly. "That's the logical answer, but somehow I feel in our day, in this age, in this country, it is not answer enough. Oh, it's easy to set a day and call it Christmas. It's very simple to go out and buy presents and wrap them in colorful paper with red and green ribbons, then put them under a tree and call that Christmas. But that," he said firmly with a slight shake of his head, "is *not* Christmas."

Leaning forward, Andrew Winslow placed both hands on the pulpit. An electric energy seemed to flow out of him as he went on, sometimes rapidly, sometimes slowly, quoting from both the Old Testament and the New Testament, bringing in history to reinforce his points. He wove humorous and sad stories into his message. But again and again he would pause and say, "When is Christmas?" He did this more than twenty times during the hour in which he spoke, and finally when he came to his conclusion, he said, "I want to tell you *my* concept of when Christmas is. Christmas," he said, "is when we exalt the Lord Jesus Christ not only in our hearts but in our acts and in our words. No matter what day it is, when we love the man, or the woman, or the young person next to us and let them have the best that's in us for the sake of the Lord Jesus. That is Christmas."

His strong voice rolled out across the congregation as he spoke on about the necessity of worshiping God in spirit and in truth and in deed. "Only when all three of those are one," he said, "is it Christmas. And now let me introduce to you Jesus Christ who *is* Christmas. He is the meaning of peace on earth. He is light— He is love—He is mercy and goodness and splendor. Without Him this world would be nothing, but *with* Him each man and woman, each boy and girl, can have that peace on earth that we have sung about in our hymns. We can know that what happened in that little town of Bethlehem can happen in our own lives, and that's why on this day I bring you not a new and strange and complicated doctrine." He paused, and the tears in his eyes rolled down his cheeks. "I bring you the Lord Jesus Christ, Lord of heaven and earth, and this morning He is asking one thing from each one of us. *Make Christmas happen every day!* On Monday, Tuesday, Wednesday. Every day of the week. Every month of the year. Every year of our lives. When Jesus reigns in our hearts, when we have made Him Lord of all, it will truly be Christmas."

All over the church handkerchiefs were being pulled from women's purses, while the men struggled valiantly to control their emotions. Then he said, "I want us to stand to our feet and I want us, this day, each one of us, to bow before the Lord of lords and the King of kings. Will you join me at this altar as I kneel and ask the Lord Jesus to let Christmas be my life? Not just one day in the year, but every single day for the rest of our lives. We will find the truth of the Scripture only in the Lord Jesus Christ."

The choir began to sing, and Andrew Winslow walked down off the platform and knelt simply and bowed his head. For a moment the church was stunned. It was not something they were accustomed to. Suddenly Paul Sears left his place on the platform and joined the kneeling man, and then Dr. Gunn did the same. The other elders quickly joined them and knelt around Andrew. Soon a crowd began to pour out of the pews into the aisles. They came weeping, but with a note of victory, and soon the altar was filled so that there was no more room. The choir continued to sing, and the members of Faith Temple fell on their knees before the Lord.

Cass and Serena had gone down to the altar with their children, as had Dorothy with Amelia in her arms. Peter wanted to go, but he knew he would be a hypocrite. He watched Priscilla go forward. He glanced over at Jolie and saw tears running down her cheeks. Leaning forward he saw that Easy was moved, too.

His eyes were shut and his teeth seemed tightly clenched. The three of them stood there until the service was over.

As they filed out, Easy grabbed Peter's arm and said, "I guess you and me and Jolie are just too hardhearted. Too late for me, but not for you, Jolie."

Jolie suddenly turned and stared at Easy. "It's not too late for anybody," she whispered. Then she whirled around and walked rapidly away, her face filled with emotion.

The two men looked at each other, then silently filed out after her.

★　★　★　★

The elders somehow made their way back to the meeting room, bringing Andrew with them. When the door was closed, Cyrus turned to the elders and said, "After a meeting like that, there's no doubt in my mind. I move that we extend an invitation to Brother Winslow to come as our pastor."

Every elder, including Harold Parsley, spoke up with an "Amen," or a "Yes," or a "Bless God."

Cyrus Tompkins turned to Andrew and said, "We feel that it's the will of God for you to come, but I know you'll want to talk with your wife and pray about it."

Andrew was somewhat overcome at the openness and the instant quality of the invitation. His eyes fell on Nolan Cole, who had also come in with the elders. Cole said nothing but stood with his back against the wall, his eyes turned down.

"Yes, of course, I will talk to my wife at once."

"We don't want to rush you," Cyrus Tompkins said, "but we'd like your answer as soon as you hear from God."

"You will have it," Andrew said. "And now I must go find Dorothy."

He turned and left the room, and Cyrus turned to Nolan Cole, who was standing silent. "Brother Cole, I think we're all agreed that you've done a fine job as associate pastor, and I know that the board would like you to stay on in that position if Brother Winslow accepts the call."

Cole looked up and seemed to have trouble speaking for a moment, then he cleared his throat and nodded. "I appreciate your invitation and will certainly pray about it."

He turned quickly and left the room. Harold Parsley shook his head. "He's not too happy, is he? He expected to take the pulpit himself."

"I wouldn't be surprised if he didn't go to another church," Dr. Gunn said. "He'd be a good senior pastor."

Sears had been watching as Cole left, and he said nothing, but there was a strange look on his face as he left the room with the other elders.

★ ★ ★ ★

Andrew said nothing to Dorothy during dinner. They had gone out together with the children, although they had received many invitations for dinner from members of the church. Every one of the elders had asked them out, but Andrew had graciously refused, saying, "My wife and I need some time alone."

Now they sat in a quiet restaurant only a few blocks from the church. Both of them had been too excited to eat much. They had spent most of the time at the table trying to prevent Phillip from destroying everything in sight and seeing that Amelia was fed. Finally, Andrew said without preamble, "The elders have asked us to come to the church."

"They want you as pastor?"

"Yes. It was unanimous." His eyes glowed, and he reached over and took her hand. "We will pray about it, but what's your impression?"

Dorothy squeezed his hand as hard as she could and started to speak, then something came to her and she closed her lips and dropped her head.

"What's wrong, Dorothy? Don't you like the church?"

Lifting her eyes, Dorothy said, "I like it too much. I'm afraid to make a decision, Andrew. I'm afraid I want you to say yes because it's a lovely house, and you'll be with us instead of on the road all the time. You'll have to decide. My judgment is no good. I can't even pray about it." She smiled humorously for a moment, then said, "I tell God that I want His will to be done, but all the time He knows I'm saying behind His back, 'Let your will be for us to come to Faith Temple.' "

Andrew squeezed her hand and laughed aloud. "I don't see anything wrong with a preacher's wife and a preacher having a little comfort. This is a fine church. It can do a mighty work for God. We'll pray about it." He looked at her with one eyebrow lifted and said, "I'm almost as bad as you are. I want to come here as pastor, and I can't decide whether it's because I'm tired of being on the road and tired of the responsibilities of being superintendent, or because it's something I want to do for the Lord."

"Your sermon was magnificent this morning. God was surely in it." Dorothy looked very pretty as she sat across the table from him. She had bought a new outfit, a salmon-colored dress, with matching short bolero, trimmed in a dark gray. The neckline had a tiered lace trim and the dress had decorative seams with fine pleated inserts of gray. Her face, which had been so tired and worn when Andrew had returned to Kansas from his last recruiting trip, was now fresh looking.

"You look like the girl I courted in Africa," he whispered. He was rewarded by her smile, then he said, "I think we'll get an answer soon."

The answer came on December 31. There was a watch service at the church, and Andrew and Dorothy attended, leaving the children with Cass and Serena. They joined the prayer group gathered there, and when midnight came there was a time of rejoicing and thanksgiving for the past year and the year to come. Andrew was filled with joy at the sight of the large crowd that filled the church. He could sense their spirit of prayer and was moved by the warm acceptance he felt from the people. He turned to Dorothy, put his arm around her, ignoring those who were smiling at them, and whispered in her ear, "God is in this, Dorothy. I'm going to accept the call to this church."

"Oh, Andrew! Are you sure?"

"Very sure!"

"Then I'm sure, too," she said and without thinking kissed him. She heard a muffled giggle and looked around to see many of the church members grinning widely at them. "Well, a woman can kiss her husband if she wants to on New Year's Eve, can't she?"

"Certainly can," Dr. Gunn grinned. His own wife, a petite brunette named Marilyn, sat beside him, and he suddenly turned and kissed her, saying, "I think it's a good habit."

It was a night that the church remembered, and the next day, January 1, 1905, Andrew came to the pulpit. There was a serious look on his face, and he said, "Before I preach, I must tell you that my wife and I have been much in prayer about the matter of your church." He waited until the silence was complete. As he looked out across the auditorium, he saw the people were holding their breath. He had not told anyone about his decision, and he saw Cass and Serena looking up, waiting anxiously for his words. After a brief pause he said, "It is my joyous duty to announce that Dorothy and I feel God has called us to join your fellowship—"

Someone cried, "Hallelujah!" and a spontaneous applause broke out all over the congregation. Without any urging, everyone stood, and as they applauded loudly, Andrew left the pulpit, went down to where Dorothy sat, and reached out his hand. He pulled her to him, and as they turned to face the congregation, they felt closer than they had in years.

Serena saw that Dorothy was struggling to keep back the tears, and she whispered to her husband, "Cass, we'll have a fine pastor, and a fine pastor's wife."

CHAPTER TEN

A TOUCH OF LONELINESS

★ ★ ★ ★

"... and I think if I have to make one more of these motion pictures dashing around on a horse and firing blanks I will go mad!"

Priscilla Winslow looked down at the last line she had written in her journal, and with a grimace of distaste she shook her head and lifted her eyes to stare out of the window of her apartment. A light rain was falling, and the sun shone feebly through the thick clouds. Some of the leaves that had fallen from the trees were very large, and a gusty wind tossed them about. As they began to make colorful shapes on the ground, some of them glittered like diamonds, their wet surfaces reflecting the electric streetlights.

Leaning back in her chair, Priscilla leafed idly through her journal for the past year. She noted the world events that she had commented on throughout the months since she had been in California: men had started digging like moles to create a canal in Panama; a scientist named Albert Einstein had put forward a theory that he called relativity, which the world seemed excited about, but which Priscilla did not fathom in the slightest.

She noted on January 17 of that year that Russian troops had killed more than one hundred unarmed protesters at the Winter Palace in St. Petersburg, setting off terrible unrest and bloodshed throughout Russia, and in the Far East the Japanese army and navy had thoroughly defeated the Russians, slaying over two hundred thousand Russians in one battle and destroying the Russian navy at Tsushima.

As she turned the pages, she read the note she had made when the body of John Paul Jones, long buried in an unknown graveyard in France, had been recovered and brought back to the United States. The largest diamond in the world, over three thousand one hundred and six carats, had been found in the Transvaal and had been named the Cullinan Diamond. She smiled as she remembered what Peter had said: "If I had just a chunk out of that, I could build the best race car the world ever saw." She read on, remembering that Peter had attended the annual automobile show in Madison Square Garden and had come back raving about the motorcars he had seen there. She leaned back and thought of what had happened in the world of the theater. *Peter Pan*, starring Maude Adams, was still a big hit.

But death had taken its toll, for in that year Henry Irving, the first actor to be knighted, had died, as had Maurice Barrymore, another great actor who had left his heritage in his children— John, Ethel, and Lionel, who were beginning to dominate the stage themselves. In the realm of literature, the world had lost Jules Verne, the popular French novelist, and the Russian writer Anton Chekhov had also passed away from the scene.

Somewhere outside her window a dog barked sharply, and she looked out to see a large mustard-colored dog charting purposely across, leaving his footprints in the carpet of leaves. He appeared to be following after something and determinedly plowed on through the heavy wind.

The year had been rich in music; especially popular were the contributions of George M. Cohan. Two songs from his *Forty-Five Minutes From Broadway* had swept the country. One bore the title of the play, and the other was "Mary's a Grand Old Name." America had also been singing "Wait 'Til the Sun Shines, Nellie," "My Gal Sal," "In the Shade of the Old Apple Tree," and "Come Away With Me, Lucille, in My Merry Oldsmobile."

With a sigh, Priscilla picked up her pen and began to make another entry in her journal.

> Here it is December 15, 1905. In two more weeks we will celebrate Andrew's first year as pastor at Faith Temple. The church has grown unbelievably, far more than any of us ever dreamed. Andrew is such a marvelous preacher, and people in the countryside are coming for miles to hear him preach.

The church has been forced to go to three services on Sunday to accommodate everyone. The decision to build a huge new building was difficult. Most people were afraid of the move, even the elders, but Andrew has a way of pushing his way through difficulties, and now the architects have done their work, and the cornerstone will be laid on December 25, Christmas Day, the anniversary of Andrew's acceptance by the church.

Tired of writing, Priscilla put her pen down, threw on a woolen coat, and left her apartment. Peter had urged her to learn to drive a car, but she had no desire to ride in such a noisy contraption. Women were not drivers, for the most part. She hailed a cab that was moving slowly down the street and gave the driver Andrew Winslow's address. The cabby, a short, rotund man with rosy cheeks and bushy black eyebrows, grinned. "That's the preacher's house, is it now?"

"Yes, Brother Winslow's home."

"Sure, and I know it well, miss. I'll have you there in no time."

The sun came out and the wind ceased to blow as Priscilla made the short trip to the parsonage. By the time she paid the driver, giving him a generous tip and taking his hearty thanks, the day had brightened to its usual California splendor, although it remained chilly. Dorothy met her at the door, greeted her with an embrace, and the two women went at once into the large living area on the southern side. The sun shone through the windows, and as they sat down and Dorothy served hot chocolate and small tea cakes, they chatted steadily.

"How is the picture going?" Dorothy wanted to know.

"Oh, it's over. We finished yesterday." Priscilla took a bite of the cake, sipped the hot chocolate, and drew her lips back quickly. "That's hot!" she exclaimed. "But very good." She sipped more cautiously, then cocked her head and said, "I'm glad it's over. I like to ride a horse, but one picture after another is too many."

"You have made a lot of them this year, haven't you? Almost nonstop." Dorothy's voice was sympathetic, and she leaned back in her chair, studying her actress friend carefully. Dorothy was wearing a light blue cotton dress with a scooped neckline edged with delicately embroidered white flowers. The short, puffy sleeves had the same flowers, and her waist was cinched in by a wide white belt. When Priscilla commented on how pretty her dress was, she shrugged her shoulders. "I got it a week ago. It is rather nice, but tell me more about the pictures. Are you going to do another one?"

Priscilla hesitated. She toyed with the cup of hot chocolate, turning it nervously in her hands. She was unhappy, or perhaps uncertain, and her manner showed it. "I'm tired of doing the same old thing, Dorothy."

"But didn't you do the same old thing in New York? I mean, every night you put on the same play."

"Plays don't last forever. Every one of these westerns is just like every other one. I couldn't tell you the last five we made."

"But they're successful, aren't they?"

"Oh yes. Very much so. I can't complain about that. Imperial's been very generous, but it's so boring."

The children came in at that moment and demanded Priscilla's attention. Climbing up in her lap, Phillip began playing with a string of beads she had about her neck, and Amelia stood on the couch and touched her earrings softly with an inquiring hand.

"I can't believe they've grown so much in a year. Phillip's almost two, and Amelia's going on four."

"I know. They grow up so fast. Amelia, don't pull on that earring. You'll hurt Miss Priscilla."

"I wasn't pulling, Mama!" Amelia protested. "I didn't hurt you, did I, Priscilla?"

"No you didn't, sweetheart. Would you like to try these on?" She grinned at the child, who nodded enthusiastically. Unscrewing the earrings, Priscilla carefully put them on the girl's tiny lobes and laughed as Amelia ran away to view herself in the mirror. "I don't have any earrings for you, Phillip."

"Let's go see the birdies," he begged, tugging at Priscilla's beads.

"I just may do that. Would you like to go, Dorothy?"

"Yes, I would," Dorothy said quickly. "You run along, Phillip. We'll walk down to the park after Priscilla and I finish our cocoa." She watched as he left the room protesting and finally shook her head. "He'd argue with a signpost, that child! I don't know who he gets it from. Maybe my father. He was pretty much like that."

For the next few minutes, as they finished their cocoa and cake, they talked about the children. But then Priscilla said, "You had a wonderful year. In two weeks it will be a full year since you've been here. I know you're pleased and happy with the way the church has grown."

A shadow seemed to cross Dorothy's face. She put her cup down, laced her fingers together, and said in a rather flat voice, "Yes, the church has grown wonderfully."

Something in the other woman's tone struck Priscilla, and she inquired gently, "Is something wrong, Dorothy? I thought things were going so well."

"Oh, there's nothing wrong. I'm just being foolish." Dorothy put her cup down and moved nervously around the room. "This is such a beautiful home. The most beautiful I've ever had, and after traveling around, living in dingy apartments and little crack-erbox houses in out-of-the-way places like Kansas, it's just heaven. I even have a maid come in three times a week to help."

"It is a beautiful home," Priscilla said.

"I know. I'm not complaining. It's just that—"

When the other woman broke off abruptly, Priscilla rose, put her cup down, and came over to her. Putting her arm around Dorothy, she asked gently, "What is it? Is there trouble?"

Turning to face Priscilla, Dorothy hesitated, then said in a low voice, "It's just that—well, Andrew's never here, Priscilla. And the church takes all of his time." She saw Priscilla starting to answer and shook her head, saying, "Oh, I know. It's a big job he's taken on, and the church has nearly doubled under his leadership. And with getting the new building program through, and all of the programs he started for young people, he's done a marvelous job, but . . ." She bit her lip nervously and shook her head again. "I hardly see him at all, Priscilla, and I get lonely."

"But you do a lot of church work. You're on a lot of the committees."

"Oh, that. That goes with being a pastor's wife, but I mean the nights he's gone to a meeting and I come home and take care of the children, and he doesn't come home sometimes until after midnight." Abruptly she looked up and gave a halfhearted laugh. "I shouldn't complain. I've never had such pleasant surroundings in my life. Come. Let's go to the park."

Their visit to the park was pleasant, although the wind was gusting again, but there was a lack of ease in Dorothy that troubled Priscilla. She said no more about the problem, but after she left to go to the studio, she said to herself, "I've got to do something, but I don't know what. It wouldn't be right for me to go tell Andrew that he's not paying enough attention to his family." Then a thought came to her and she nodded. "I'll ask Cass to do it. They've gotten really close over the past year. I think Andrew would take it from another man."

★ ★ ★ ★

Jolie had been wandering around the waterfront fascinated by the beautiful yachts and smaller boats that came sailing in and out over the emerald green water. The last reel had been shot on *Western Sunset*, the last western produced by Imperial, and she was taking a forced vacation. It gave her a greedy, rich feeling to have money in her pocket. Aside from her room and board, and a few clothes, she had spent practically nothing but saved all of her wages. Now as she walked along the beach enjoying the brilliance of the sun glittering on the water and the white-capped waves crashing on the shore, she suddenly felt a pang of loneliness. For the past year she had been so busy helping as Imperial cranked out one "odor"—as the pictures came to be called because of their use of horses—after another, she had had little time to relax. After her years of hardship and even brutality at the hands of her stepfather, just to be able to wake up in the morning and know that she had a warm room, money for food and clothes, and a job at which she had become quite proficient was truly satisfying.

Leaving the beach, she wandered among the shops that lined the streets. Most of them were one-story buildings. The large office buildings were farther south. She stopped in front of a dress shop and studied the latest fashions. Moved by a sudden impulse, she went inside, where she was met by a white-haired woman with a pleasant smile.

"May I help you, miss?"

"Would it be all right if I tried on that dress in the window? The blue one with the striped skirt?"

"Why, of course it would. I think we would have it in your size. What size do you wear?"

"I . . . don't know."

The woman's eyebrows rose, but she smiled even more broadly. "Well, come along and we'll soon find out. The blue one, you say?"

"Yes, and the hat, too, please."

The clerk soon brought the garment and left Jolie alone to put it on. She quickly removed her dress, beneath which she was wearing a knitted cotton chemise with cotton hose, and slipped on the garment. She stepped outside to look at herself in the full-length mirror, and the clerk came over to make a few adjustments.

"Why, that looks lovely," the woman said. It was a two-piece outfit consisting of a muslin shirtwaist of dark blue and a printed striped skirt with alternating blue and white stripes. The skirt came down six inches above the ankles, and the clerk watched as Jolie fingered the wide white collar, then placed the straw hat with a matching band of blue and white stripes on her head.

"Tilt it just a little bit this way," the clerk said. She tightened the white belt and pushed the sleeves up, saying, "They wear them like this usually." Stepping back, admiration came to her eyes. "You look very nice in that. It's made for a young woman with a figure like yours."

Jolie flushed at the woman's words. Her figure had filled out over the past year, and as she turned she saw that the garment followed the contours of her body in a very pleasing manner. She was somewhat shocked but also delighted at the difference the dress made to her appearance. Her other dresses were rather shapeless, but this one showed off her figure to the best advantage.

"Now, if you just wore some white stockings and a pair of white low-heeled shoes, you would be ready for any outdoor exercise," the clerk smiled.

"How much would the shoes be?" Jolie asked.

"Let's try them on, and we'll see the whole outfit together." Jolie loved the dress, and when she had donned the white stockings and a pair of low-quarter, lace-up shoes, she knew she had to have it.

"I'll take it," she said, opening her reticule to pay for the outfit.

"Fine. You're lucky to be just the right size. Some young girls are too short or too tall, or too heavy or too thin, but you look like you were made for a dress like this. It fits you perfectly."

Ten minutes later, Jolie walked out of the shop wearing her new outfit and carrying a bundle with her old clothes. Jolie felt strange. She had never bought anything for herself in the way of clothing except underwear and stockings. Now as she walked in the sunshine, she suddenly became aware of a young man leaning against the corner lamppost who had fastened his eyes on her. As she passed by, he let loose a low whistle and said, "Hello. Going my way?"

A thrill went through Jolie, although she had been approached before by young men. She ignored him and proceeded down the boulevard. Wanting Peter to see her new outfit, Jolie walked to the movie lot, which took the better part of an hour. A cool breeze made the walk pleasant and kept her from getting hot. When she got there, she went around to the back of the house. As she had suspected, Peter was underneath the beginnings of a car, banging away loudly. She stood watching for a moment, then called out, "Peter?"

The banging stopped, and Peter came skidding out from under the car. After he stood to his feet, he paused abruptly. His eyes flew open and he whistled on a low note. "Well," he said with approval, "I see you've been shopping. Turn around. Let me see you." He watched with admiration as Jolie pirouetted back and forth, noting that whenever possible she kept her scarred cheek turned away from him. "You look beautiful, Jolie," he said. "You're absolutely a knockout."

His words brought a pleased expression to Jolie's blue eyes, and she said, "Why, thank you. I thought it was pretty. It's the first dress I ever bought by myself," she confessed, smiling at him. He was wearing a pair of greasy overalls worn thin by much wear and had an oil smear over his right eyebrow. "How's the car coming?" she asked. "I thought Easy would be here working with you."

"He's gone to try to find a piston for the engine, but I doubt if he will."

Jolie came closer and suddenly stooped low and looked underneath the car. It was rough looking with a boxy body and four large balloon tires. The engine sat directly on the frame in front of the seat, which was large enough for two drivers. "What are you doing to the engine?" she asked.

"Well, nothing really," Peter said. "But you see, most cars transmit the power from the engine to the wheels with a chain and sprocket."

"You mean like on bicycles?"

"That's right!" Peter nodded. "But a few years ago a fellow named Louis Renault found a way to get rid of the chain drive. He put a shaft in and a gearbox, and that's what we've done here. You see that long rod running there? That's the prop shaft. The engine turns over, which turns the shaft, and that's what turns the wheel."

"But I don't see how it works," Jolie said. She turned her head half upside down to stare underneath, and her hat fell off. She snatched it up but continued to stare. "The shaft is turning round and round this way, and the wheels go this way in a different direction."

Peter glanced at her with surprise. "That's right, Jolie. That's why we have to have a gearbox that changes the direction of the power. It's pretty new, but soon all cars are going to be made like this."

"I expect Mr. Renault made a lot of money from this invention."

"Well, he would have, but he was killed. He and his mechanic ran into a tree in the Paris-Madrid Race. They were driving a car made something like this one, but they had a streak of bad luck."

A shudder seemed to come to Jolie's deep blue eyes, and she gave Peter a sudden strange look. "I wish you wouldn't take chances when you get the car going, but I know you will. That's the way you are, Peter."

"I'll be all right," he said. "Come on." He picked up a cloth, wiped his hands off, and said, "Let's go get one of those newfangled drinks. What do they call 'em—Coca-Colas?"

He led her to a soda fountain two blocks away, chatting all the time about the car he was working on. When they got to the drugstore, they seated themselves on chairs made out of wire and propped their elbows on a marble-topped table. He ordered two Cokes, and they sat there and sipped the strange-tasting concoction. "These things will never go over," he said. "I don't like them."

Jolie sipped her drink, and finally after a time she said, "Peter, there's something I want to do."

"Like what, Jolie?"

"I'm so ignorant. I only went to school through the fifth grade, and I don't know anything." She looked up at him with a longing in her eyes that moved him. "I don't want to be ignorant. Somehow I want to learn, but I don't know how."

Peter shifted on the chair, his brow wrinkled. Finally he said, "Well, we'll find something. Let me think about it."

"All right, Peter."

They finished their drinks and started walking back toward the bunkhouse, and he cut his eyes around, taking in her trim figure in the new dress. "You've grown up." He smiled and touched her arm. "I've been watching Harley Potter chase around after you. He really thinks you're something."

Harley Potter was one of the many workhands employed by Imperial Pictures. He was a sturdy young man who moved heavy furniture and large props around with apparent ease.

"Is he going to be your steady fella, Jolie?"

"He doesn't like me," Jolie shrugged. "He just wants to use me."

The blunt statement uttered so matter-of-factly sent a shock through Peter. It came to him suddenly that this young woman had had a much rougher life than he had and she had learned to fend for herself. He cleared his throat and said, "Well, you shouldn't be going out with fellows like him, anyway."

Jolie did not answer but began at once to talk of something else. Before long she decided she needed to get back and left just before Easy returned, without the part he had gone in search of. Both men watched Jolie disappearing down the street.

"Good-looking girl, ain't she?" Easy said. "If only she didn't have that scar. She thinks about that all the time."

"Yes, she does," Peter said. "We're going to have to see a doctor or something, Easy, and get that taken care of. She deserves a break in life."

★ ★ ★ ★

It was late afternoon and Cass was walking with Priscilla between two rows of orange trees. The wind had shifted, and he was enthusiastic as he showed her how the trees were growing in the grove. "I'm going to buy two more fields and put in young trees," he said.

"Do you have the money?"

"Well, no, but I've been in to talk to Harold Parsley at the bank. It won't be any trouble to get a loan. I'll have to put the place up for security, though."

"I hate to see you do that. I don't have much, but I think Uncle Mark would be glad to lend it to you."

"I hate to ask the favor," Cass shrugged. He was an independent young man, wanting to stand on his own two feet. His move to Los Angeles to own and operate an orange grove had been a gamble, but Cass Winslow was determined to succeed, and he was not about to change his mind.

"I wanted to talk to you about Dorothy, Cass."

"Dorothy? What about her?"

"She's not happy. I visited her this morning, and she didn't complain, you understand, but I could tell that she's troubled." She hesitated, not knowing how to put the matter, and finally stopped and looked at her brother. He turned around to face her, and she said quietly, "It's Andrew. He's so caught up with the church work that he's neglecting her and the children. She's lonely, Cass. I wanted to go and talk to him, but I don't think it would be right for a woman. But I think he'd listen to you. Would you go talk to him?"

Cass removed his cap and ran his hand through his hair. His face turned into a grimace, and he said, "I'd feel odd doing that, sis. After all, he's my pastor. *I'm* the one who needs looking after."

"I think pastors need looking after, too, and he *is* our cousin. Anyway, you think about it. I think it's serious. Andrew's a wonderful pastor—but he gets so caught up with the ministry that he forgets the more important things."

Cass nodded abruptly. "Okay, I'll do it. I don't know how he'll take it, though. Most men don't like to be corrected on the way they carry on their lives, but I'll try it, sis."

"Thanks, Cass."

"What about you? Are you happy with what you're doing?"

"Not really. I'm about ready to give it up." When she saw his look of surprise, she added, "It's just the same thing every day. Don't worry about it, though. I can always go back to New York and get a job in a play."

"I hate to see you do that, sis." He put his arm around her and squeezed her. A smile caused a dimple to appear on the right side of his cheek. "I need you around here. Don't be running off. Something will come up."

★ ★ ★ ★

Three days after Priscilla's conversation with Cass, Dorothy came to the church. She found Nolan Cole lounging in the outer office and said, "Hello, Reverend Cole. Is my husband here?"

"Yes, but he's in a meeting with the building contractors." He made a face and shook his head. "They've been at it now for two hours, and it looks like they might be in there two more. You know your husband. He doesn't think anybody knows as much as he does about anything."

Suddenly Dorothy laughed. "That's about the best description of Andrew I've ever heard," she said.

"You're looking very nice. Is that a new dress?"

It was indeed a new dress, one which Andrew had not noticed. It was a light tan linen day dress with a low neckline surrounded by a narrow notched collar. It had light brown ribbon running horizontally on the bodice, short sleeves, and a long skirt with a wide sash at the waist. She appreciated the attention of the man who had come to stand beside her. As she looked up at him, she thought again how attractive he was and wondered why he had never married. *At thirty*, she thought, *he must've had many chances.* Aloud she said, "I'll just wait awhile."

"Come into my office. I've been wanting to talk to you about this new young people's program that I want to start over on the south side of town."

"All right, Reverend Cole."

"You make me feel like a hundred when you call me that. When we're alone, couldn't it be Nolan?"

"Of course, and I'm Dorothy." She flashed a smile at him and entered his office.

"Here," he said, "have a seat, and I'll show you what I've done." For over an hour the two pored over the plans for the new youth program.

Finally Dorothy glanced at her watch and said, "I've got to go. My baby-sitter will go off and leave the kids if I don't get back soon."

"What about Brother Winslow?"

"Just tell him I waited as long as I could."

When she rose to her feet, he came over to ask, "Do you have a way home?"

"Oh, I'll catch a cab."

"No need of that. I've got my car outside. I've got to make several calls, anyway."

"Well, if it wouldn't be too much trouble. . . ."

The two left the building, and Nolan led her to an automobile she had never seen.

"What kind of a car is this?" she asked as he sat down beside her after starting the engine.

"It's a Rambler Touring Car," he said. "It's got a two-cylinder motor. It gets up to thirty miles an hour."

The heavy car moved off, and Dorothy grabbed at her hat, her red-blond hair blowing behind her. "I need a driving bonnet of some kind," she laughed.

"I've always liked that color of hair. My mother had it," he remarked as he steered around the wagons and buggies and other cars that confronted him.

"Did she really? Where are your people from?"

"Originally from Indiana. We left there when I was younger, though, and moved to Albany in New York State."

He told her about himself until they reached the house, and when he stopped the car, he leaped out at once and came around to help her down. His hands were warm and strong, and he held hers for a moment, smiling at her. "We'll have to work some more on the youth program. Maybe you could go over there to that part of town and look the situation over if you're going to be in the program."

"All right, Nolan. I'd be glad to. Thanks for the ride." She went into the house and closed the door behind her. On a sudden impulse, she peeked out the beveled window in the front door to catch a glimpse of Nolan as he sped away. Noticing the sun glinting on his blond hair, she wondered again why he had never married. *Maybe he's just one of those natural bachelors*, she thought. But he was far too masculine and attentive to women for that. She had observed many of the women in the congregation make it a point to speak to the handsome young assistant pastor, but he seemed not to be drawn to any of them. *He'll marry one day*, she thought. *But he'll be hard to please.*

★ ★ ★ ★

Andrew's meeting lasted until almost seven. He had fought over the details of the new sanctuary with the contractor, convincing him to change his view on several points in a way that did not alienate the man. Afterward Andrew rushed immediately to a meeting of the elders and found them impatiently waiting for him. "Sorry to be late," he said. "I've been talking to the contractor. This won't take long, but I want us to start an inner-city program to try to reach those who don't attend church. I would also like us to begin planning for a school to train young pastors in the area."

Harold Parsley stared at his pastor and shook his head. "Pastor, we've got more than we can do now! I don't see how we can take on any new programs!"

Andrew smiled at Parsley and began explaining what he wanted to do. He was a persuasive speaker, and though he sensed resistance in the elders, he spoke for an hour and answered all their arguments. Finally he said, "Look. Attendance is booming, and so are the offerings. God is moving in our midst. This is no time to sit around and wait! We must launch out and reach the unsaved and the unchurched."

Cyrus Tompkins had been carried along by the electric personality of his pastor for a year. He had been supportive, but now he said cautiously, "There's one problem with all this, Pastor."

"What's that, Cyrus?"

"It's you. You're spread pretty thin, Brother Winslow. You need to take it easier."

Andrew laughed. There was an exhilaration in him that overflowed. He had always been a man to throw himself into everything with all he had, and the spectacular growth of the church had spurred him on. "God's given me strength, and I'm going to use it for Him," he announced. "Don't worry, brethren. I'll be fine."

After the meeting was adjourned with a short prayer, Cyrus and Paul Sears stayed to talk for a moment. Sears said at once, "I think you're right, Brother Tompkins. The pastor's working too hard. He can't keep it up."

Cyrus shook his head. "I've seen men like that before. They work themselves into an early grave. Work to them is like whiskey to some men. They just have to have it."

"I'm concerned about him. He's lost weight," Sears remarked. "And his family. It's hard on them, too. We've got to do something to help him."

"Maybe hire another pastor."

"That wouldn't help," Sears said, shaking his head. "He would just find more programs. We've got to pray that he'll learn to pace himself so he won't burn out before he's forty."

"We'll pray about it," the elder nodded, and the two men left looking sober and troubled.

★　★　★　★

As Andrew left the meeting, he was surprised to find his cousin Cassidy Winslow waiting for him.

"Why, hello, Cass. I didn't know you were here. Why didn't you let the secretary know?"

"She said you were in a meeting with the elders," Cass shrugged. "I didn't want to bother you, but I do need to talk to you for a minute."

"Why, of course. Let's go to my office." Turning, he made his way down the hallway and opened a door. "Come on in, Cass." He waited for his cousin to step inside, then closed the door and said, "Sit down and let's talk." As Cass took a seat, Andrew pulled up a chair across from him. "Some kind of problem?"

"Yes. I guess you get a lot of that. People coming in with problems."

"It happens pretty often," Andrew smiled. "What's the trouble? Is it financial?"

Cass shifted uncomfortably. He had rehearsed a little speech, but now he was not certain that it was what he ought to say, but he plunged ahead, stating, "It's not my problem I've come to you about, Pastor. It's yours."

Surprise caused Andrew to blink. "My problem? I didn't know I had one."

Cass began to speak, commending Andrew for the fine work he had done. He spoke simply and plainly, adding up the triumphs of the church over the year, but finally said, "Serena and I are worried about how hard you've been working."

"Oh, is that all? The elders have just been talking to me about that. But I'm all right."

"You may be, but . . ." Cass hesitated, afraid to take the plunge, then said quietly, "I don't think you're spending enough time with your family."

Andrew stared at the man across from him. Anger rose in him, for he was a proud man, but he waited until it passed. "You think so, Cass?"

"Well, no man can do as much as you've done with the church, and at the same time pay enough attention to his family. I'd just like to see you show a little bit more balance."

Andrew hesitated, then suddenly smiled. "You know, I'm glad you came, Cass. I need to be reminded. I get so carried away with programs and all there is to be done that I can't think of anything else. But I think you have a point, and I'm going to spend more time with Dorothy and the kids."

Cass somehow sensed the insincerity behind Andrew's words. Not that he was lying purposely, but Cass knew Andrew well enough to realize that this was a promise lightly made. He rose quickly, saying, "Well, Serena and I will be praying for you as we always do."

He left the church and drove home, and when he went inside, he found Serena at once and told her what he had done. "But he won't do it," he said, shaking his head in frustration. "He doesn't know how to quit work. I wish he'd break his leg or something."

"That wouldn't help," Serena said quietly. She stood, considering what Cass had told her, and then said, "Maybe you did more good than you thought. He took it well, didn't he?"

"He listened and he agreed, but it didn't mean anything," he said ruefully. "That man will work until something forces him to stop."

CHAPTER ELEVEN

AMELIA'S BIRTHDAY PARTY

★ ★ ★ ★

The note came as a surprise to Jolie, and she stared at it for a moment, wondering what it could mean. It said simply, "We have some work to do on the upcoming two-reeler. Please come to the studio at ten o'clock."

Jolie stared at the note, which had been brought by one of the young men who worked for the studio, but he left before she could question him about it. It was already nine o'clock, and she dressed hurriedly, had a quick breakfast with the landlady, then made her way to the studio. She was surprised to see several cars and buggies pulled up outside. There was no shooting today that she knew of. They were between films, and she moved quickly, curious as to what the next film would be.

She stepped inside the studio, then, seeing nobody in the roof-less section, moved to where the meetings usually took place. As soon as she stepped into the darkened room, she almost turned and left. Suddenly loud cries of "Happy Birthday, Jolie!" broke out, and the lights came on. Jolie stood speechless as she looked around the room crowded with people. Peter came over to her and said, "We caught you that time, didn't we? Did you ever have a surprise birthday party?"

Jolie almost said, "No, nor any other kind," but she was speechless. Looking around she saw most of the riders standing beside Jason, all of them grinning broadly. Shifting her glance, she noticed Priscilla. Even Stan Lem was there.

Priscilla came over and kissed her on the cheek. "Happy Birthday!"

At that moment Lily Doe came in carrying a white cake with nineteen candles burning brightly. The group broke out singing "Happy Birthday." When they had finished, someone said, "Blow them out and make your wish!"

Jolie was so overcome it took her three tries, but when everyone laughed, she turned and said with tears in her eyes, "I never had such a thing before. Thank you all. Thank you so much!"

The rest of the party was like a dream for Jolie. She received many small presents, but strangely enough, none from Peter. After the cake and the ice cream were eaten, and she had opened her presents, and they had played several silly games, Peter said, "Okay, that's enough birthday party. Come along. I'll help you get these presents back to your place."

Jolie thanked everyone again and then followed Peter outside. They had plenty of help to load the gifts in the car, then they were on their way. Peter's hair blew in the wind as he grinned at her from time to time. "Did you notice I didn't get you a present?"

For a second Jolie was embarrassed. She had noticed and had felt a twinge of disappointment. "You don't have to get me anything, Peter. You've done so much for me already, and I know it was you who got the party together."

"Well, I'm not quite the villain you think I am. I do have a present for you."

She turned to him eagerly, her eyes brilliant in the morning sun. "What is it?"

"I won't tell. You'll have to wait until we get to your place. It's waiting for you there."

Jolie could not imagine what sort of a present could not have been brought to the party, and she began to interrogate him. But he only laughed at her, shaking his head.

"You can wait until we get there. I think you'll like it, though."

When they reached her boardinghouse, Peter climbed out of the Oldsmobile that belonged to the studio and came around and helped her out. "You ready for your present?"

"Yes. Is it in the house?"

"No, it's outside," Peter remarked.

Quickly Jolie scanned the front porch but saw no packages. She saw nothing, as a matter of fact, except a thin young man who was sitting in the porch swing watching them. "I don't see any present," she said.

With a laugh Peter took her arm and steered her up the steps. When they were at the top, the young man stood up. Peter turned and said, "Here's your present. His name's Tom Ziegler. Happy Birthday, Jolie."

Confusion swept over Jolie, and she looked at the young man. He was very tall, a couple of inches over six feet. He had a lanky build, mild gray eyes, and fine brown hair worn rather long. He appeared to be about twenty, and after meeting Jolie's gaze, he dropped his eyes and put his hands behind his back.

"What are you talking about, Peter?" Jolie demanded.

"I mean Tom here is your present. He's a college student, and he's going to be your tutor. He's all paid up for three months. We'll see how much he can cram into your head in that time."

Still somewhat confused, Jolie looked at the young man as he lifted his eyes. He smiled shyly and said, "I don't know if I'm much of a teacher, Miss Devorak. I've never tried it before. All I've ever been is a student."

"Why, he knows about everything," Peter said. "I went to the dean of the college and asked for the brightest young fellow they had to do some tutoring. This fellow never made anything but an *A* in his life. Isn't that right, Tom?"

A flush came to the young man's rather gaunt face. He was not handsome in the least, but there was a pleasing look in his features. He looked, Jolie thought, like the pictures of a young Abraham Lincoln.

Jolie turned to Peter. "It's the sweetest thing you could've done for me, Peter. How did you ever think of it?" She suddenly reached up, pulled his head down, and kissed his cheek, something she had never done before. A flush came to her own cheeks, and she dropped her eyes, then heard Peter laugh.

"Well, at least I got the ice broke between us. You two can start right now. Is that all right, Tom?"

"That's fine, sir."

Peter leaned over and gave Jolie a hug. "Happy Birthday, Jolie. Now, you go right ahead and get educated."

Jolie stood there feeling awkward as Peter took the steps in one leap, climbed into the car, then departed with a wave of his hand and a roar of the engine. Turning to the young man she said, "I'm awfully ignorant, Mr. Ziegler."

"Don't call me that," he said quickly. "Tom's fine."

"That's all right then, but you'll have to call me Jolie or I won't know who you're talking to." She smiled and said, "What do we do first?"

"Well, I brought some books. Maybe we can just sit in the swing and talk about what you might like to study for the next few weeks. We've got to start somewhere."

Jolie sat down in the swing, and Tom joined her, then reached down and pulled out a satchel of books between his feet. "Would you like to study history, or maybe arithmetic?"

"I don't know anything about any of them. I'm so ashamed, Tom, but you'll soon find out how ignorant I really am."

A shy smile touched his broad lips. "I doubt that, Jolie," he said. "Well, let's start with a little arithmetic and see how you do with the basics."

★　★　★　★

" . . . So that's what I've come to tell you, Mr. Porter. I'm sick to death of these westerns, and I just can't do another one." Priscilla had come to Edwin Porter's office, and after greeting him, she had proceeded to tell him that she could not do any more of the two-reelers.

To Priscilla's surprise Porter did not seem disturbed. She had expected him to try to argue her out of leaving because the short western films had been very successful. But he shrugged his beefy shoulders and said quietly, "I'm pretty tired of them myself, if you want to know the truth, Priscilla. We've about rung all we can out of them. Several other companies have started making them, and pretty soon there's going to be a glut of them on the market."

Priscilla was relieved and said quickly, "I don't want to seem ungrateful, but—"

Waving his hand, Porter said, "Don't worry about it." He grinned then and leaned forward, excitement touching his gray eyes. "I've got something else, though, that you're going to like."

"Another kind of motion picture?"

"Something altogether different. It's not my idea. One of my assistants came and told me about it. It's the first time anybody ever gave me a good idea like this. Sit down and let me tell you about it, Priscilla."

The two of them sat down, and he began to talk rapidly. "What

I want to do is make a series of short films that all tie together."

"I don't understand," Priscilla said, a puzzled look on her face. "What do you mean all tied together?"

"Each film will last only about ten to twelve minutes, and the story will stop there. Then it will take up again in the next reel where that one left off. But here's the thing. It will be an adventure film. At the end of the first reel you'll be the heroine, and you'll be about to be killed, or something awful will happen. Like in the stampede. We'll cut the film off right when the cattle are about to run over you. Or we could have a scene where you're about to be shoved off a cliff by the villain, or run over by a train. Something like that."

Instantly Priscilla caught the notion. "And at the beginning of the next reel, the audience will see how I get saved from death?"

"Right! I think we'll get people interested. They come to see the first one where you are about to die, then they'll come back a week later to see the next episode." He got up and began walking around the room, waving his arms with excitement. He was a volatile man, this Edwin Porter, a genius in his field, and now he felt that he'd come onto something new. He came over and reached out and grabbed Priscilla's arm, squeezing it hard. "And listen to this. Guess who I signed to be the hero in this project? Todd Blakely!"

"Why, I'm surprised at that! He's doing so well on Broadway."

"He's wanted to try the movies for some time, but he's been waiting for his big chance. And I've convinced him that this will give him more exposure. It'll be great. Todd as the hero, and you as the beautiful heroine."

"What will you call it?"

"I'd like to call it *The Dangers of Darlene*. All the people like to see a beautiful, helpless woman in trouble, and then a dashing hero come galloping out of nowhere to save her."

"Will it be all horses again?"

"It'll have some horses, but there'll be cars, too. It'll be up-to-date."

"If you need help with the cars, my brother Peter can help you. He knows all about them."

"I'll remember that," Porter nodded. "Now, what about it? Are you willing to think about it, Priscilla?"

"It sounds like fun," Priscilla said. "Something different from bouncing around on a horse."

"It'll make you a star, kid," Porter said. He patted her shoulder and said, "I'll get the contracts drawn up at once."

★　★　★　★

Nolan Cole had waited outside of Andrew Winslow's office for half an hour looking at his watch nervously. When Winslow appeared, walking rapidly and followed by three men, Nolan stepped forward, saying, "Pastor, I've got to see you."

With an impatient look, Winslow said, "Can't it wait? I've got an important meeting here. It's taken a lot of work to get the architect, the building superintendent, and the banker here to tie this new building altogether."

"I know you're busy, but this is important."

"All right. Would you gentlemen please step into my office?" Opening the door for them, he said, "I'll be right with you." He closed it again and turned to Nolan Cole. "What is it, Nolan?"

"I know you just got back from Sacramento, but have you been home?"

"No, I just got in this morning. What is it? Is someone sick?"

Cole stared at him in dismay. "Have you forgotten it's Amelia's birthday?"

A shock leaped into Andrew's eyes, and his lips drew wide in a grimace. "Oh no! I did forget it! I didn't sleep a wink last night! I haven't even gotten her a present!"

"Well, the party's starting in thirty minutes. Can't you get through with this meeting, or at least let me handle it?"

"Thanks, Nolan, but I have to be here." Andrew paused and said, "Look, go buy a present for Amelia and go on to the party. Tell them I'll be there just as soon as I can."

Nolan shook his head. "That's not the same thing, Andrew. You know what kids want better than I do. Amelia's been looking forward to this for a long time."

"I know, I know, but I just can't go now. I couldn't get these three together again for three weeks. You go on. Buy her something nice." Andrew reached into his pocket, pulled out some bills, and handed several of them to Nolan. "Get anything you can find. Don't worry about the cost, and I'll be there as soon as I can."

"All right, but—" Nolan started to protest, but Andrew wheeled and disappeared into the office, closing the door behind him.

Nolan's lips tightened and he shook his head. He left the church and drove rapidly to a department store. After looking through the whole toy department, he finally picked out a doll that he thought the girl might like, then went on to the party. As he parked his car, he noticed several others in front of the parsonage, and when he went inside, Helen, the maid, greeted him.

"The party's in the big drawing room, Reverend Cole."

"Thank you, Helen."

As he made his way down the hall, he heard the sound of high-pitched giggling and laughing. Turning into the drawing room, he saw that it was decorated with balloons and streamers, and that eight or nine children about Amelia's age were there with their mothers. He felt like a fool.

Dorothy excused herself from one of the women and came over to him and asked, "Where's Andrew?"

"He's . . . on his way," he said briefly with some embarrassment. "He sent Amelia's gift with me and said to tell you that he'd be here as soon as he could."

All delight and pleasure drained from Dorothy Winslow's face. She took the doll and studied the face of the assistant pastor, then said so quietly that no one but he could hear, "He forgot, didn't he, Nolan?"

"Well, he just got in this morning from his trip, and there was a meeting—"

"There's always a meeting," Dorothy said, a harshness in her tone. "Amelia will be heartbroken. Did he pick the gift out himself?"

"Well, no. I'm afraid I did, and I'm not sure she'll like it. It's a doll."

"She won't like it unless her father is here to give it to her," Dorothy said bitterly.

"I'm sorry, Dorothy," Nolan said. He reached out and touched her hand briefly. She looked up, and he added, "It's not right, and I'm terribly sorry."

"It's not your fault." Dorothy managed a smile and said, "Thank God you came. You can tell Amelia that her daddy is on the way."

It was a fine birthday party with all that children like—cake and ice cream and games—but Nolan saw Amelia looking at the door from time to time. Finally the party was over and the children left, and Nolan went over and said, "I'm sorry your daddy didn't make it. He was held up, Amelia, but he'll make it up to you."

"He didn't come," Amelia said, and tears welled up in her eyes and ran down her cheeks. She turned and ran out of the room.

As Nolan started to leave, Dorothy said, "Wait here, Nolan. I want to talk to you." Turning, she met the eyes of Serena, who had brought her children to the party, and quickly looked away as sympathy showed on Serena's face. Leaving the room, she went after Amelia to try to console her.

Nolan Cole wandered around the room, watching as the maid cleaned up, and fifteen minutes later Dorothy came back, her face puffy, and he knew she had been crying.

"Come into the library," she said, casting a look at Helen and leading Nolan out of the large drawing room. When they were inside she shut the door and said, "Tell me about it." She stood there listening as Nolan tried lamely to explain, but her lips hardened and she said, "He couldn't even come to his own child's birthday party." Then she drew her shoulders together and tried to smile. "Come along. There's some coffee in the kitchen. Can you stay?"

"Well, for a while, I suppose." He followed her out of the room down to the kitchen, and soon the two were sitting at a table as the bright sunlight filtered in on them. Nolan said little, but Dorothy unburdened herself. She was angry to the bone at Andrew's inexcusable thoughtlessness. He had terribly disappointed and hurt Amelia.

"I shouldn't be complaining like this to you," she finally said.

"It's all right." Nolan smiled and said, "I hear a lot of complaints from wives about how their husbands neglect them."

"I bet you do," she said. Curiosity came to her and she said, "Do any of these women ever—" She did not know how to finish, and her cheeks flushed with embarrassment. "I didn't mean to pry," she said.

Nolan Cole leaned back in his chair and laughed and smiled. "Some of them do," he said. "They're lonely."

"That's no excuse."

"No, it's not."

"Why have you never married, Nolan?"

The question caught him off guard, and he blinked with surprise. "That's coming right out with it," he said, then he began to trace a figure on the table with his forefinger. He was a man who was good with words, but confronted with this direct question, he seemed to be uncertain. The long pause of silence seemed to go on forever.

"You don't have to tell me," she said.

"I don't mind, but, you see, I don't really understand myself." He looked up, and there was a vulnerable quality in his face. He was a strong man, active, able, but now somehow, there was a troubled light in his blue eyes. "I never found a woman that I loved."

"That's strange. You're attractive and intelligent. Many women would love to have you, I'm sure."

"But I've never found one that I wanted. Some have attracted me for a while, but nothing ever came of it." He looked up and smiled briefly. "I don't know how to explain it, Dorothy."

"What do you want in a woman?" she asked, curious.

"Beauty, charm, intelligence, a sympathetic ear, and a lot more."

Dorothy suddenly laughed. "No wonder you haven't found one! There are no women that have all those qualities."

"Certainly there are. You have them all."

Dorothy was taken aback. "Why, Nolan! What a thing to say!"

Nolan suddenly stood to his feet. "I didn't mean to say that, but it's true enough." He seemed disturbed and said, "I'll have to go now, Dorothy. I'm sorry the party turned out badly for Amelia."

She rose and came to him, putting out her hands. He took them both and stared at her with an odd expression in his eyes. She did not speak for a moment, then finally she whispered, "You made it bearable. Thank you for coming."

He held her hands and studied her face for a moment. He seemed about to speak, then put his lips together as if to cut the words off. "I must go," he said hurriedly. He turned and left the room without another word.

Dorothy sat down at the table and thought about how strangely he had behaved. Her cheeks grew warm as she remembered his words, *You have all those qualities.* She was starved for affection, and the warmth of his gaze and the sincerity of his words had driven away some of the anger she had felt at Andrew's absence. She sat there for a long time, then finally rose and left the kitchen.

★ ★ ★ ★

Todd Blakely proved to be a real charmer as Priscilla had suspected. She arrived at Edwin Porter's office to meet with them, and she found the young actor to be as handsome as she remembered. "I saw you once on the stage when you played Hamlet," she said. "You were marvelous. I always wanted to tell you."

Blakely was not a tall man, but he was well built and had the classic handsome features demanded by the stage. He had an English nose, high forehead, and his hair was dark, as was the thin mustache on his upper lip. He smiled at Priscilla with perfect teeth and took her hand, gripping it firmly. "Thank you so much. It's a compliment I appreciate from one of the profession."

"Have you been in Los Angeles before?"

"No, it's my first trip," Blakely said. "I understand you've been here for a year."

"Yes, I think you'll like it."

"Perhaps you'd show me around. I never do well in a strange town by myself."

"Why, of course. I'd be happy to, Mr. Blakely."

"Todd," he corrected her. Then he said, "Perhaps we could go out and have dinner. You know the best places. We could talk about the new project."

Familiar with actors and their ways, Priscilla knew she was being approached in a more than businesslike way. She smiled and said, "I'd be happy to, Todd. Come by about seven tonight."

"That will be wonderful," he said. He turned to the producer and said, "We're going to have a hit, Edwin."

"I believe we will. Want me to come along tonight? If you're going to talk about the project, I'm sure I could give you some insight." With a wicked light of humor in his eyes, he laughed at Todd's expression. "Don't worry. I was just kidding. Go out and have a good time with Priscilla."

★ ★ ★ ★

Blakely arrived precisely at seven, chauffeured in one of the studio's new cars. He took her to the restaurant she recommended, where they enjoyed a fine meal and exchanged the usual pleasantries about their careers. Afterward they went to the theater for a rousing production of the latest Cohan musical. After the play, they were driven back to Priscilla's place. When the car pulled up in front, Todd got out to walk Priscilla to her front door. As they came to the doorway, Todd asked, "May I come in for a while?"

"No, Todd," Priscilla said. "I'm going to bed. We'll probably have a hard day tomorrow. Edwin's a real hard-driving man."

He leaned forward and put his hands on her arms and attempted to draw her forward to kiss her, but she resisted. His eyes opened wide with surprise. "What's wrong?" he asked.

"Nothing's wrong. It's been a nice evening." Priscilla pulled back, put her hand out, and when he took it rather stunned, she laughed. "A nice try, Todd, but you'll have to find your female companionship elsewhere. I don't play the game."

He knew exactly what she was saying, and his handsome face made a picture of puzzlement as he stared at her. "Well, that will be different," he murmured.

"Are you angry?"

"No, of course not." He smiled again, squeezed her hand, and said, "There's always another day. Good night, Priscilla. Thank you for going out with me."

"Good night, Todd."

As Blakely left, he was amused by his own reaction. He was so accustomed to easy successes with women that Priscilla Winslow's refusal had taken him completely by surprise. He leaned back in the seat and thought about her for a moment, finally murmuring, "A beautiful woman, and chaste as well. That might be a challenge, but I've always liked challenges." He smiled in the darkness and began to whistle as the car made its way down the streets of Los Angeles.

★　★　★　★

Todd Blakely persisted in his attempts to form a close relationship with Priscilla. They went out several times the next week, but each time the ending of the evening was the same. She presented him a cool demeanor, and there was amusement in her eyes as she firmly resisted his attempts to come inside each time he took her home.

Stanislas Lem had observed Todd's attempts to win over Priscilla at work. Lem knew the type of man Blakely was and decided to talk to Priscilla about it. He found her at work one day and said, "Are you going to be able to handle Blakely? He's used to having women fall all over him."

"He's sure been making his try, but that's the way Todd is. No, Stan. I won't have any trouble with him. His pride might be hurt a little bit, but perhaps we can get the picture finished before he loses his temper."

That same day Jason Ballard was standing close by when he heard Todd Blakely make a remark about Priscilla. The actor implied in his speech to one of the cameramen that he had been having some success with Miss Priscilla Winslow. "She's not as cold as she seems," Todd laughed. Actually, the man could not stand for anyone to think that he was ever unsuccessful in his single-minded pursuit of women.

The words had struck Jason hard, and he had stepped in front of Blakely and said loud enough for everyone in the vicinity to hear, "You're a liar, Blakely!"

Todd Blakely had never been challenged so abruptly, especially not by a lowly member of the crew. He knew Jason only as a cowboy who rode a horse and drove cattle, and now he exploded bitterly with a curse. Before he could say another word, he suddenly found himself flat on his back with a cut on his lips. He had been pulled to his feet by the cameramen and the assistant director, who apologized for Jason, but Jason had turned and walked coldly away.

Todd Blakely's ego was enormous. He went immediately to Edwin Porter and demanded that the man be fired. Porter argued that Jason was a valuable man, but he saw the futility of it.

"All right," Porter said wearily. "I'll see that he leaves the lot." Leaving his office, he went to Jason and said, "Jase, I'm sorry, but you shouldn't have hit him."

"I know," Jason said. "I suppose you have to fire me."

"I have no choice," Edwin said grimly. "I can't go against the star."

"It's okay, Mr. Porter. It's not your fault."

As soon as Priscilla heard of the incident and Jason's firing, she went at once to Porter, who shook his head grimly, saying, "I can't go against the star, Priscilla. You know that. Jason should have held his temper."

Priscilla stared at Porter for a moment and then said, "I'll talk to Todd."

"It won't do any good. His pride's hurt. That's a lot worse than the busted lip he got. I'm glad Jason didn't break his teeth out," he said. "That would have spoiled him for the camera."

Priscilla turned and went straight to Todd's dressing room. She knocked briefly, and when his voice bade her to come in, she opened the door. He rose and said, "Why, Priscilla—"

"Todd, I don't want Jason Ballard fired."

"Why are you interested in him?" Todd asked suspiciously.

"He's an old friend of mine. He was the foreman on my parents' ranch in Wyoming for years. He's a good man."

"No, he can't stay," Todd said stubbornly.

"Why did he hit you, Todd?" she asked, already knowing the answer. "It was because you made a remark about me, wasn't it? How successful you were with me—isn't that right?"

Todd Blakely's face flushed. He could not find an answer for this beautiful woman who stood in front of him. Her blue-green eyes seemed to flash fire, and at last he mumbled, "Well, I'm afraid that's true, Priscilla. I always did have a big mouth, and I apologize to you."

"It doesn't matter, Todd, although for your own sake I think you ought to be more careful. I'm afraid I'm going to have to ask that you let Jason stay on, no matter if it does hurt your pride. It wouldn't be fair to do it any other way."

Todd Blakely started to argue, but he saw the determination in Priscilla's eyes. "All right, Priscilla," he said quietly. "I was out of line. You can tell your friend he can stay."

"Thank you, Todd. I was sure you'd see it my way."

Leaving the star's dressing room, she passed by her own door, where there was a large silver star. She stopped and looked at it for a moment and muttered, "The silver star. That's what I thought I wanted, and now look what kind of people I'm working with." Angry and disturbed, she went to the bunkhouse and found Easy and Peter sitting on the front porch. "Is Jason inside?"

"Yeah. He's packing his clothes," Peter said bitterly. "And I'll be next. I'm going to black both of Blakely's eyes when I see him!"

"Save a part for me!" Easy said.

Seeing they were both angry, Priscilla said quickly, "It's all right. I've talked to Blakely."

Peter brightened up. "You mean Jase isn't fired?"

"Go tell him to come outside," Priscilla said. She waited while Peter dodged inside, and when Jason came outside with a stormy look on his face, she went up to him at once. "I'm sorry about what happened. It was nice of you to defend me."

"I should have busted his head!" Jason muttered. "Or shot him!"

"You've got to understand," Priscilla said quickly. "That's just the kind of man he is. He doesn't mean anything by it."

"Then he ought to change his ways."

"I doubt if he'll do that, but he has agreed to let you stay on."

Jason stared at her suspiciously. "You didn't go begging him, did you?"

"No, I didn't beg him! I told him he'd have to agree or I'd give him a black eye."

Suddenly Jason laughed, and Priscilla reached out her hand. "Please stay, Jase. I know it's hard for you, but I don't think you'll have any more trouble with him."

Jason Ballard stood there looking at this girl he loved so deeply. He had been ready to leave and now said quietly, "It might be better if I left anyway, Priscilla. It's hard being around you all the time and never being able to be with you."

Priscilla dropped her eyes. He was holding her hand, and she said finally, "I wish you'd stay, Jason. I really do. Will you?"

He could refuse this woman nothing. "All right, Priscilla. I'll stay," he said. He was still holding her hands and said, "How about we go get a hamburger?"

She threw her head back, and her honey-colored hair swung around her back as she laughed up at him. "All right. That sounds fine to me."

CHAPTER TWELVE

A KISS IN THE DARK

★ ★ ★ ★

At the end of February, work began on *The Dangers of Darlene*. No one was more delighted than Peter Winslow. He was hired by the studio to be in charge of any filming that required the use of automobiles. Since there would be several crashes and daring rescues, Peter walked around on a cloud just thinking about it.

Jolie was happy for Peter. She stayed busy doing the costume work but took on the additional job of a new position called a "Script Girl," in which she was required to see that all the actors had the final edition of the script in their hands the day before shooting. The new job kept her very busy, but she was pleased with her promotion and the extra earnings it provided. She was even more pleased with the tutoring sessions that she had three times a week with Tom Ziegler.

Ziegler appeared regularly at Mrs. Bell's boardinghouse, and Jolie easily retained permission to use the small library room for a schoolroom. There were only four boarders at the present time, and all of them went to their jobs during the day, so at three o'clock in the afternoons on Mondays, Wednesdays, and Fridays Ziegler showed up promptly. He came a little early on Friday, and when Jolie greeted him, he said, "I brought some new books that I think you might like."

"Come in, Tom," Jolie said. She led him into the library and watched as he upended the canvas book bag that he carried and began to pull them out.

Selecting one, he said, "I think it's time you started on some literature."

"Literature?" Jolie assumed a doubtful look and shook her head. She was wearing a yellow dress with green polka dots and a high neckline with a small collar of white. The short, puffy sleeves also had a small band of white just above the elbow, and the waist had a wide green belt cinched in tightly. She had just combed her hair out so that it hung in ringlets over her forehead and swept the back of her collar. She looked fresh and clean, but at the word "literature," she appeared to balk. "I don't see any point in studying things like that. They're just silly stories!"

"Well, I thought we might begin with poetry," Tom said.

"That's even worse!" Jolie answered. "Why don't we just do math? I'm good at that."

"Well, there's more to the world than a column of figures."

Ziegler had grown a little more comfortable in Jolie's presence, but still there was a shyness in him. Though he was reticent to talk about himself, Jolie had found out much about his life by questioning him a lot. Ziegler had been raised by his widowed mother in a sheltered world. He attended a small college while still living at home. He had never been away from home, nor had he much experience in the world.

When she had asked him what he wanted to do in life, he had replied, "I want to be a lawyer." And when she asked why, he said, "Well, I think I could help people."

Jolie had little experience with legal affairs, but she had shaken her head and said, "I don't see that lawyers can help people much. Maybe a doctor might be better."

Now she watched as he opened a thin blue volume and settled back to listen. He had a pleasant baritone voice, which sounded a little strange coming out of such a thin, lanky body, but he read well.

He thumbed through the slender volume, and finally his eyes lit up with a pleasant glow. "Here's one I've always liked," he said. "It was written by a man called Thomas Campion, who lived back in the sixteenth century. The name of it is 'There Is a Garden in Her Face.'" He began to read the poem with obvious pleasure.

There is a garden in her face,
Where roses and white lilies grow;
A heavenly paradise is that place,

Wherein all pleasant fruits do flow.
There cherries grow, which none may buy
Till "Cherry Ripe!" themselves do cry.

Those cherries fairly do enclose
Of orient pearl a double row;
Which when her lovely laughter shows,
They look like rosebuds filled with snow.
Yet them nor peer nor prince can buy,
Till "Cherry ripe!" themselves do cry.

Her eyes like angels watch them still;
Her brows like bended bows do stand,
Threatening with piercing frowns to kill
All that attempt with eye or hand
Those sacred cherries to come nigh,
Till "Cherry ripe!" themselves do cry.

Looking up he seemed to have been caught by the rhythms of his own voice. "Did you like that, Jolie?"

"It's pretty, but I don't understand a word of it. What does it mean?"

"Why, it's about a lovely young girl. There is a flower garden in her face where roses and white lilies grow. That simply means she had a lovely, fair complexion with rosy lips. And then the poet says, 'A heavenly paradise is that place, wherein all pleasant fruits do grow.' You have to remember that this isn't a vegetable garden, but a beautiful flower garden. And notice the last two lines, which are what we call a refrain. 'There cherries grow.' What do you suppose that would be, Jolie?" He watched her as she thought hard.

Finally she said, "Cherries? I suppose that would be her lips."

"Exactly right. And you have to know one thing about this poem. The street-sellers used to wander through the streets of London selling cherries, and everywhere they went they would call out at the top of their lungs, 'Cherry ripe!' which meant they had cherries for sale. Now look at these two lines. 'There cherries grow, which none may buy, till "Cherry ripe!" themselves do cry.' "

Leaning forward, Jolie placed her elbow on the table and her chin in her palm. She stared at the words for a long moment, reading them over silently, moving her lips. Then abruptly she straightened up and said, "Oh, I know! 'Till "Cherry ripe!" themselves do cry.' No one can kiss her until she says it's all right."

"That's very good! Very good, indeed! Now look at the next stanza. It just simply describes the beauty of the young woman. 'Those cherries fairly do enclose, of orient pearl a double row . . .' "

"That's her teeth, isn't it, Tom?" She read the next line. " 'Which when her lovely laughter shows, they look like rosebuds filled with snow.' Oh, that's pretty!" she said. " 'Like rosebuds filled with snow.' I can just see it."

"Well, that's what poetry's supposed to do," Tom said. "It is a lovely image, isn't it? What do you make of the last stanza?"

Again Jolie read in a whisper the lines of the last stanza. " 'Her eyes like angels watched them still.' That's her lips, isn't it? 'Her brows like bended bows do stand, threatening with piercing frowns to kill all that attempt with eye or hand those sacred cherries to come nigh, till "Cherry ripe!" themselves do cry.' " She looked up and laughed. "Why, that's easy! Her eyes are guarding her lips, and her brows are like a bow with an arrow, and she'll shoot anybody who tries to kiss her until she says it's all right."

Tom Ziegler nodded his approval. "It's going to be easy to teach you literature. You have a flair for it. Most people wouldn't make anything of that poem."

"Why, it's real pretty. I didn't think any poetry could be like that. Do you think he was in love with the girl?"

"I don't doubt it a minute," Tom said, looking at Jolie. "They were real lovers back in those days."

"Teach me some more, Tom," she said. "Find another one about a beautiful young girl."

"That shouldn't be hard," Ziegler smiled. "Seems like poets like to write about pretty young girls."

For over an hour Tom moved back and forth through the book, reading and then explaining several poems. Jolie was delighted by how much she liked it. "Can I keep the book and see if I can figure out some for myself?"

"That's why I brought it," Ziegler said. He handed it over to her and opened the front page. At the top, in strong script, was written, "To Jolie, with warm regards. Tom Ziegler."

"Oh, it's a present!"

"Yes, you just had a birthday, so this is a belated birthday gift."

"Why . . . thank you, Tom. Come on. I'll buy you a chocolate soda down at the drugstore to reward you for being such a good teacher." She stood up and Ziegler stood also, looking a little flustered. She hesitated, then stared at him. "What's the matter?"

"Well, I don't know. Mr. Winslow might not like it. He just hired me to teach you."

Cocking her head to one side, Jolie studied the young man carefully. She had been forced to become a student of men to protect herself, and she had been somewhat puzzled by Tom Ziegler. In the long hours that they had spent together, not once had he tried to hold her hand, or kiss her, or even say anything that could be construed as improper. He had been a perfect gentleman. Though he was not as dashing as some of the actors she had seen at Imperial Pictures, he was pleasant looking, tall, well dressed, and highly educated. She sensed an uncertainty in him, and she stepped closer and put her hand on his arm. "Are you afraid of me, Tom?"

Ziegler, acutely aware of her grip on his arm, flushed. "Why do you ask that?"

"You seem to be. Have you ever had a girlfriend?"

The flush on his cheeks grew brighter, and Ziegler said, "Well, no, I haven't."

"That's odd. How old are you? Twenty? Haven't you ever even kissed a girl?"

Ziegler cleared his throat and shifted his feet with embarrassment. When she saw that he did not need to answer, she laughed and tugged at his arm. "Well, come on. I promise I won't bite you." He picked up some of the books, stuffed them into the satchel, and as the two left the house, she said, "You need a few lessons if you're ever going to romance a young lady. Maybe if you can teach me poetry, I can give you some lessons in that."

Tom Ziegler was stunned by the young woman's outgoing manner. He muttered, "I guess I could use it." He turned to smile at her and shrugged, saying, "I guess I'm as far behind in love and courtship as you are in algebra and geometry."

She laughed and said, "Well, we'll teach each other then, Tom.

★ ★ ★ ★

"No, it won't do. We'll have to shoot the scene again!"

Priscilla had just gone through a romantic scene with Blakely that called for him to embrace her in a half-reclining position. He had kissed her thoroughly and gone even further than Lem, the director, had told him, but for the third time he had shook his head and frowned, saying that it wasn't good enough.

Priscilla glanced around at the cameraman and the light man, who were grinning broadly, and shoved Blakely away. "It's good enough for me, Todd." Looking toward the director for help, Priscilla said, "What do you think, Stan?"

Lem, who was a perfectionist, had been satisfied with the first take. He was well aware, as were all the onlookers, what Todd Blakely was doing. "I think that'll do fine, Todd. It was a good scene."

"Well, I could do better, I think." He turned with a slight smile toward Priscilla and said, "By the time we get through with this picture, there are enough romantic scenes that we'll be able to do it much better."

"I'm sure we will," Priscilla said dryly, glancing at Lem.

"Let's take a break," Lem said, nodding to the crew. "Be back in thirty minutes."

Leaving the set, Priscilla started to make her way to her dressing room when she saw Jason Ballard, who had been watching. For some reason this troubled her, and she could feel the blush creep into her cheeks. However, she walked up to him and said, "Hello, Jason."

"Hello, Priscilla." He stood there looking down at her from his great height, and his eyes were unhappy. He spoke quietly so that no one could hear except her. "I can't stand seeing that man maul you. Why do you let him do it?"

"It's part of the making of a picture. It doesn't mean anything, Jason."

"Then why did he have to do it three times? You're crazy, Priscilla, if you think he's just doing it for his art's sake!"

"Jason, you don't know what you're talking about," Priscilla snapped. She was angry because she knew that Ballard was exactly right, and she herself had felt uncomfortable and disgusted. "You take care of your horses, and I'll take care of Todd Blakely."

"I can see how you were taking care of it. It seems to me you rather like it."

"Jason, don't say anything more!"

Grabbing her arms, he pulled her forward. "I'm going to say a lot more!" He began to speak plainly and bluntly, telling her, "You've got to stop letting this sort of thing happen to you, Priscilla."

"I'm not the director! I didn't write this plot! It's in the script!"

"So anything that's in the script, you'll do? Is that it?"

"Yes. As long as I'm an actress, I have to do what the director tells me to do, and what the script calls for."

"Well, suppose the script calls for you to get into bed with him? Would you do that, too?"

Before she could think, Priscilla's anger flared up and she slapped Jason's face. At once remorse struck her, and she said in a horrified tone, "Jason, I'm . . . I'm sorry. . . ." But he had turned and stalked away, his back stiffly upright.

Priscilla looked around and saw that people were pointedly ignoring the little scene, but they were aware of what had gone on. Todd Blakely was watching also. He smiled at her and walked across the set toward her.

"A little trouble with your old friend? Too bad. I suppose he was upset about the scene between us."

"Yes, he was." Priscilla hesitated, then added, "And so was I, Todd. Those other two takes weren't necessary."

He ran a well-manicured hand through his meticulously groomed hair, then said, "I suppose not, but I make chances wherever I can. You won't have anything to do with me off the set, so I'll have to convince you on the set that I'm the right man for you."

Priscilla gave Blakely a disgusted look, shook her head, and then left. She walked out of the studio feeling discouraged. Hailing a cab, she went directly home. The work at the studio had left her so tired that she decided not to go out for supper.

She had already dressed for bed when a loud knock on her door startled her. Pulling on a pink silk robe, she went to the door and cracked it open. "Who is it? Oh, it's you, Peter." She opened the door and stepped aside. Seeing her brother's troubled face, she asked, "What's wrong?"

"It's Jase," Peter said with disgust. "After he left the set today, he went out and got drunk and punched a fellow out. He caused such a ruckus they threw him in jail."

"Jail? Oh no, Peter!"

"He wouldn't talk about it, but I heard how you had a fight with him on the set. What's it all about, sis?"

Unwilling to explain, Priscilla said, "You wait here. I'm going to get dressed."

"Where we going?"

"We're going to get Jason out of jail, of course. We can't leave him there."

An hour and a half later, Priscilla, Jason, and Peter emerged from the city jail. Jason was sullen, and one side of his face was swollen. Priscilla turned to Peter and said, "Go get in the car, Peter. I want to talk to Jason alone for a minute."

"Okay, sis."

As soon as Peter was out of hearing distance, Priscilla said, "I'm sorry this all happened. It was really my fault, Jason." She put her hand on his arm to turn him around, and she saw an infinite sadness in his eyes. "I'm really sorry," she whispered. "I guess there was enough truth in what you said to make me angry. It wasn't you as much as myself."

"You been having second thoughts about acting?"

Priscilla hesitated. "I think I can handle it. I won't do those scenes over again with Blakely, or anybody else, and I won't take a script that has anything in it that will offend me. I've been struggling with fitting my faith into my profession ever since I was saved. Now I'm seeing that I must put my relationship with Christ first and live as He would want. My life, including my acting, will have to line up with that."

"You can't do that, Priscilla," Jason said slowly. "You've been around actors and directors long enough to know that you have to give the public what it wants, and evidently that's what it wants."

"Let's not talk about it anymore tonight."

"No, I guess not, or tomorrow either." Jason hesitated, then shook his head. "I've decided to leave. I can't take it anymore. Watching you every day and not being able to put my arms around you."

Priscilla felt a sudden jolt. "But, Jason, you can't leave."

"Yes I can, and I will. You think you can handle this, Priscilla, but I don't. I've been watching actors now for about a year. Something about it gets into people's blood. It sucks out what they really are and makes them into something different up on a screen." He had thought a great deal about this, and though he was not a philosophical person, Jason had arrived at some definite conclusions. "After a while, you'll become what's up there, and you'll lose that sweetness and purity and . . . goodness that's always been what I loved about you. You can't handle it, Priscilla, but I know you won't leave. So I'm going back to Wyoming. I have to get away from all this." He waved his hand toward the studio in disgust.

Priscilla knew that Jason Ballard was not a man easily swayed. "Don't leave right away. Wait a while. We'll talk," she pleaded.

She leaned against him, and as she touched him, Jason wavered. He could never refuse her anything, and now he said, "Well, maybe not tomorrow, but I can't stand this anymore. I feel like a starving man outside a glass window with a restaurant inside and people eating food. When I look at you, that's how I feel, Priscilla. I want to marry you so much, and I can't have you. Not like you are."

Priscilla did not know what to say. She had a deep affection for Jason Ballard, but she did not know how deep it went. Her experiences with Eddie Rich had been so painfully humiliating and terrible that she was still struggling with it. Now she merely said, "Come on, Jase, we're both tired. Let's get some sleep. Tomorrow night just you and I will go out for a ride in the country. Maybe drive out to see Cass and Serena. I'm tired of the studio, too."

"I'd like that. Come on, I'll see you home," Jason said quietly. He took her arm, and they turned and made their way down to the car.

★ ★ ★ ★

"Hey! It's ready, Easy! I never thought it would be."

Peter Winslow stood back and admired the car that stood before the pair, proud of what they had accomplished. "We didn't have much to start with, and now look what we've got," he said.

Easy wiped his hands on a greasy rag and nodded. "It looks good, but how will she run?"

"I'm gonna take her out right now for a spin and try her out. Do you want to go?"

"Naw, I like to work on 'em, but you're liable to break my neck." He added thoughtfully, "Why don't you go ask Jolie. Didn't you promise her a ride?"

"Hey, that's right. I'll zip right over and pick her up."

"Well, don't break her neck. You know what you did this morning?"

"What do you mean?"

"You went in the front door of the house and came out the side door. Don't you know that's the worse kind of thing to do? It breaks your luck for a long time."

"Oh, baloney! There's no such thing as luck. A man makes his own way."

"You watch what I tell you. You're in for a hard time. A person always ought to go in and out the same door. I thought everybody knowed that!" Easy said, shaking his head.

Peter ran inside the bunkhouse, washed, shaved, and put on some new clothes he had been saving. He pulled on a pair of brown striped pants with cuffs on the bottom, a plain white shirt, and a short, brown single-breasted jacket with patch pockets. Leaving the house, he leaped into the car and gunned it out of the yard, yelling at Easy. "I'll be back to give you a report as soon as I've tried her out in the open!"

He held the speed down until he got to Mrs. Bell's boarding-house. Seeing Jolie up on the porch with young Ziegler, Peter left the engine running, locked the brakes, and jumped out without opening the door. Taking the steps two at a time, he said, "Hey, Jolie, I've got a surprise for you!" He waved his arm toward the car that he and Easy had painted a brilliant fire-engine red. "The car's ready!"

"I see it!" Jolie looked up from her books with interest. "It looks fine. How does it run?"

"That's what we're going to find out. Come on. You get to take the first ride."

Jolie blinked and said with an apologetic tone, "I can't do that. We haven't finished our lesson yet."

Peter's jaw dropped. He had thought that Jolie would be ec-static over the race car, as happy as he was. She had been inter-ested in the construction of it, and more than once had asked him to take her out when it was finished. Now, however, she merely sat there with a book open before her, saying only, "I wish I could go, but we're right in the middle of a lesson."

Peter wanted to say, "Forget the lessons! Come on and let's go!" He gave Ziegler a hard look, and the young man dropped his eyes. Then Peter said, "Okay. Keep your nose in the book!"

He whirled and headed down the steps toward the car.

"You really ought to go with him, Jolie," Ziegler said, urging her quietly.

"Oh, I know I was wrong." Jolie jumped up and whispered, "We'll have our lesson day after tomorrow, Tom."

"All right."

Jolie caught up with Peter when he was even with the car.

When he turned around, his face was cloudy and he did not speak.

"I don't know what was the matter with me, Peter. I was right in the middle of a hard part of arithmetic. I would like to go with you if you still want me to."

Her face was turned up, and as usual, she kept the scarred side away from him. However, the rest of her complexion was clear and pure, and her lips trembled a little. He saw that she was near tears. "Aw, sure. You can go. Come on. Get in."

Jolie quickly got in the car, and when Peter seated himself, he turned and smiled at her. "Look. Don't get too smart. You won't want to ride around in a heap with a dummy like me."

His smile was warm, and Jolie took a deep breath of relief. Some people kept grudges forever, but Peter Winslow did not. She smiled at him and said, "I'd never do that, Pete. Now, let's see what this thing will do."

★　★　★　★

Dorothy looked at the elephant and then smiled at Phillip. "What do you think about that beast?" she asked.

Phillip's eyes seemed as large as half-dollars. He whispered, "He's so big." He moved back behind his mother's skirts and peered out fearfully at the monstrous animal.

Amelia, on the other hand, was standing right up beside Nolan Cole. Nolan had bought a small bag of peanuts and was handing them to Amelia, who fed them in turn to the inquiring trunk of the elephant.

"Look! His nose is all hairy!" Amelia cried with delight. Fearlessly she reached over and ran her hand on the rough hide of the elephant. "Feel it, Mr. Cole."

Obediently, Nolan touched the trunk and laughed. "Pretty rough, all right. Do you like him?"

"Sure, I'd like to ride on him."

"Well, I think they offer elephant rides. Maybe you and I could do it."

"Could we?"

"Don't see why not." He turned and called back, "Amelia wants to ride the elephant. Would that be all right?"

Dorothy smiled a little nervously. "Do you think it's safe?"

"Well, if he falls on us, he won't do it but once," Nolan laughed. "Sure, it'll be all right."

"Well, go ahead." She watched as Nolan spoke to the trainer. The man nodded and then led the elephant to a platform. A smile turned the corners of her mouth up as she saw Nolan take Amelia's hand, and the two of them settled into the basket that was tied on the elephant's back. The elephant trainer walked slowly in front, leading the beast on. Amelia laughed and giggled as they went around and around.

As soon as they got off, some of the other youngsters from the group that Dorothy and Cole had brought along clambered for rides, but Dorothy was firm. "You can't ride an elephant without your parents' permission. Next time you bring a note, and we'll see."

Cole came back laughing. "First time I ever rode an elephant. It's quite an education, this ministry you've gotten me into."

Dorothy had started up a program for the younger children to give some of the working mothers half a day off, and even those who didn't work. It had been a tremendous success, but she could not have done it without Nolan Cole's aid. He planned the trips, arranged for the transportation, and chaperoned the children with a patience and fondness that Dorothy admired.

"I don't know how you're so knowledgeable about children," she said, shaking her head as they made their way back to the carriage. "You're so wonderful with them."

"Well, I was a kid once myself, you know." Nolan was wearing a dark gray woolen single-breasted suit with fine stripes, a white shirt, a dark blue tie, a pearl gray fedora, and a short topcoat of black cloth. He grinned at her and said, "You're not bad yourself. We make a pretty good team."

"Yes, we do. The youth work is going wonderfully. I wish the church appreciated all you do, Nolan. You never speak of it."

"Want me to toot my own horn? Hey, look at me! Nolan Cole the Wonder Boy!"

"Oh, don't be silly," she laughed. "But you might let me say a word."

"No, don't bother. The Lord knows about it, and that's enough."

Dorothy gave him an approving look, and all the way back to the church, where they delivered the children to their parents, they talked about the next outing they would have with the children.

After all the children had gone home with their parents, and her own had been taken home by Helen, their part-time maid, the two went into Nolan's office, where they made more detailed plans. Finally looking up with surprise, Nolan said, "Why, it's seven o'clock, and we haven't had a bite to eat. Are you hungry?"

"Oh, I could eat a sandwich, I suppose."

"Well, let's go and get something."

"That would be nice, Nolan," Dorothy said.

Opening the door for her, he waited until she was seated, then went around and got in on the driver's side of his oversized car. He drove a short distance to an elite restaurant. Going inside, the head waiter led them to a table. Instead of a sandwich they both ordered a full meal. As they waited for their dinners to arrive, they discussed how much they enjoyed working together on the youth ministry. It was a pleasant time, and Dorothy's cheeks glowed. "It's hard work," she said, "but it's good for me."

"It's good for the kids, and good for the church," Nolan said, smiling at her.

The waiter arrived with their dinners then, and Nolan asked a short blessing. As they ate, they continued to speak, but suddenly Dorothy lifted her eyes and started. She was facing Mrs. Harriet Simmons, a widow who faithfully attended their church. Mrs. Simmons was a straight-laced lady of sixty who spent a great deal of her time surveying the lives of the church members with great care. Dorothy saw now the woman's brows furrowed with suspicion, and her eyes were staring at her almost harshly. She met the woman's gaze defiantly, then turned to see that Nolan Cole had seen her also.

"That old biddy watches everybody like a hawk," he sighed. "Well, are you ready to be gossiped about?"

"It's ridiculous!" Dorothy snapped.

"Yes, it is. The poor old woman hasn't had much of a life of her own, so she tries to mind everybody else's business."

Dorothy was ready to leave then, and Nolan paid the bill and escorted her to the door. One last glance showed that Harriet Simmons was still staring at them and already talking to another woman who had come to join her.

By the time they reached the parsonage, it was dark outside.

"I suppose Andrew is home by now," she said.

"No, don't you remember he had a meeting with the executive committee?"

"Oh yes, he did." Dorothy's voice was flat.

Nolan said, "Well, it was a wonderful day, wasn't it? I hate to see it end."

Dorothy put her hand on the door handle, reluctant to open the door and say good-night. Before she could make up her mind to thank him and go inside, Nolan looked up suddenly and said, "What a beautiful night. Look! There's Orion!"

"Orion? Where?" Dorothy asked as she stepped closer to him and searched the sky. "The only thing I know is the Big Dipper."

"Right over there. See? It looks kind of like a dressmaker's dummy—the stars, that is. The shoulders, and the skirt out at the bottom, and the waist nipped in. See?" He turned her around and put his arm over her shoulder and pointed at the sky.

Following his gesture, she whispered with delight, "I see it! I never knew that! Now I know the names of two constellations and where to find them!" She started to move away, but he put his other arm on her shoulder, and they found themselves standing in a half embrace, the moonlight filtering down over them as they turned and faced each other.

Strange sensations ran through Dorothy Winslow. One side of her mind and heart was saying, "Move away," but the strength of his arms, and the approving light in his bright blue eyes seemed to hold her. She was a woman who needed attention, who longed to be told she was pretty and desirable—something Andrew had not done in a long time. She stood there waiting, transfixed by the moment, her face tipped up expectantly. He leaned slowly forward, hesitantly at first, and kissed her lips. He did not grab at her but merely increased the pressure, drawing her against him. He was the first man she had kissed in years except for Andrew, and she found herself yielding to him without even thinking about what she was doing.

Nolan stepped back and laughed. "Well, there's one kiss Reverend Winslow won't get."

"You . . . you shouldn't have done that!" Dorothy said, suddenly coming to her senses.

"I know I shouldn't, but you're such an attractive woman, Mrs. Winslow. So pretty and sweet. I just couldn't help it. Blame it on the moon up there, or on Orion's gentle persuasion."

Dorothy fumbled for the door handle and said abruptly, "Good night, Nolan. I . . . I really must go in now."

Seeing the look of anguish on her face, he tried to make light of the situation and soothed, "Don't worry, Dorothy. It was just a kiss. It won't happen again."

"It *mustn't* happen again!"

Nolan Cole grew serious. He studied her face for a long moment, then shrugged. "I can't guarantee that. Good night, Dorothy." He turned quickly and walked back to the car.

She stood and watched him as he drove away, and even then she did not move. Slowly she lifted her eyes overhead, found Orion, and studied it for a moment. She was more disturbed than she had been in a long time. Something in him had reached out to her, and aside from the kiss itself, she felt his admiration. "It mustn't happen again," she whispered, then turned and entered the house.

PART THREE

A FORK IN THE ROAD

★ ★ ★ ★

CHAPTER THIRTEEN

JOLIE FAILS THE TEST

★ ★ ★ ★

"Hey, Pete! I think I'll run down to the store and get us some red soda pops," Easy said.

Peter Winslow was stretched full-length under a graciously curving palm tree, his hat pulled down over his face. The July sun had baked him a golden brown, and sweat stained the faded cotton shirt that he wore open to the waist to catch the breeze. Thumbing his bill cap back, he cracked one eye open and muttered, "Get a quarter's worth of bologna and a box of soda crackers—and get some cheese, too."

"Right."

As Easy sauntered away, Peter turned his head lazily and viewed the car, thinking how much of his hard work and sweat had gone into its creation. "You've got more different breeds of car in you than a yard dog has ancestors," he muttered. He and Easy had robbed parts from every conceivable make and model of automobile so that the original ancestry of the vehicle was impossible to determine. Now as it sat there gleaming, its fire-engine red radiating a color that almost hurt the eyes, the racing car looked fast even standing still—at least to Peter. He eyed the machine with satisfaction. "Wish we could've found a redder paint. It just doesn't stand out enough as it is."

"Doesn't stand out enough?"

Peter, startled by the sound of another voice so nearby, sat bolt upright. Jolie had silently walked up and was looking down on him. "If it got any redder, it'd look like it was straight out of the infernal pit." She smiled, her eyes laughing at his expression. "What's the matter? You got a guilty conscience? I never saw a man jump up so quick."

Peter's hand shot out and grabbed Jolie's ankles, and as she uttered a muffled scream, he jerked her so that she sat down abruptly on the sandy earth. "Learn to be respectful of your elders!" he said, hanging on to her ankle firmly as she squirmed.

Kicking at him with her free foot, Jolie cried furiously, "Let me go!"

Peter kept his hand clamped down on the slender ankle, a wide grin spreading across his lips. Just then her lightweight cotton skirt started to fly up as a breeze gusted, and he reached out with his free hand and pulled it down. "You ought to be more modest, Jolie. What would Brother Winslow think?"

Jolie managed to kick free and gathered her skirt as she stood up, her face flaming. "You're a beast!" she announced, her lip pouted in a rather attractive fashion. "You have no manners! You're . . . you're uncouth!"

"Uncouth? You've been reading the dictionary again, Jolie," Peter teased.

"Never mind if I have! You are uncouth!"

"I'm as couth as you are. Now, if you'll sit down here, I'll explain how I'm going to win the great race down in San Diego."

Almost instantly Jolie forgot her irritation. She sat down cautiously beside Peter, her eyes wary. "You keep your big meat hooks off me!" she said. "What about this race? When are you leaving?"

"It's the July the Fourth Race. Easy and I'll pull out tomorrow. I'll have to nurse that baby along." Here he nodded at the gleaming red vehicle and smiled with satisfaction. "I'm going to take first place and come back with a pocket full of cash."

"Take me with you, Peter!" Jolie begged.

"Why, I can't do that!" Peter protested. "You've got your lessons to take from your tutor."

"Oh, I'm way ahead on that," she shrugged. "You know what I learned yesterday?"

"What?"

"I learned that Columbus discovered America and didn't even know it. He was trying to find a route to the Indies. When he landed on the islands of the Caribbean he thought he had found the Indies. That's why we call them the West Indies today."

"I always thought that fellow wasn't very bright," Peter grinned. "What are you studying things like that for? Why don't you study something useful like baking cakes or diapering babies?"

Jolie shook her head, her black hair catching the breeze, and the sun glinting in it. "I already know how to bake cakes. I need to learn about other things." She turned to him, her lips growing soft and her voice wheedling. "Please take me with you, Peter. I won't be any trouble."

"Maybe not, but it would be awful crowded with three of us in the car."

The argument went on until Easy returned with a paper sack filled with bologna, crackers, and cheese. He sat down and divided it all among the three of them. "We'll have to share this here red soda pop," he said. The trio sat munching crackers while Jolie transferred the brunt of her argument to Easy. She could always get anything she wanted out of the small man, and finally Devlin turned and said, "Ah, we can squeeze up, I reckon. It ain't that far to San Diego." He took a huge bite of bologna sandwich, washed it down with pop, then brightened up as an idea broke in on him. "Hey, why don't we get a truck and a trailer from Imperial? We could haul the car down and not run any danger of bustin' the tires or blowing the engine on the car."

"Now, that's a swell idea," Peter nodded. "What's the use of having a sister who's a big star if I can't use her once in a while for my own selfish purposes?"

"She'll do it, Peter." Jolie nodded with an air of certainty. "She thinks you're the greatest—but I don't know why."

Peter lifted an eyebrow lazily. "You never appreciated my manly virtues," he said, winking at her. "When you get older you'll learn what a rare specimen I am."

Jolie reached over and took his hand and looked up at him pleadingly. "I'll recognize it right now if you'll take me with you, Peter. Please?" Her lips pursed, and she fluttered her eyelids.

Peter stared at her, then shook his head in disgust. "You're learning all the wiles of womanhood too quick—but I guess it'll be all right if I can finagle a trailer and a truck out of the company. You'll have to get a little bit dirty. We don't have room for a lot of luggage. Tell you what." He grinned. "You can be our mechanic.

Get yourself a suit of white overalls, and we'll have the name of the team put on the back."

"What's the name of the team?" Easy asked. "I didn't know we had one."

"We'll just choose the name of the car."

"And what's that?" Jolie demanded. "The Red Devil?"

"Nope," Peter said. He winked at Easy and said, "The name of the car is—the *Jolie Blonde*."

Jolie stared at him and could not believe what she was hearing. "You're naming the car after me?"

"Why not? The rules say we've got to name it something." Peter came to his feet and walked over to the car. "We'll get one of the artists that works on the sets to paint it right here in great big yellow paint. *Jolie Blonde*. And we'll put it on our shirts and your coveralls."

Jolie flushed and suddenly appeared to be very embarrassed. "Thank you, Peter. That's so sweet of you." Her eyes brightened and she whirled, calling back, "I'm going to get my coveralls right now and embroider the name on the back myself!"

As Jolie went dashing off, Easy grinned. "You just think of that? The *Jolie Blonde*?"

"Sure. It makes the kid feel good. Why not? It's a pretty good name."

"I guess so. It's better than *The Square Donut*, or *The Uncooked Frog*." Easy smiled. He swallowed the last of his red drink and said, "We better go get one of those artists to do the name on the car so the paint will have time to dry if we're leaving tomorrow."

★   ★   ★   ★

The meet at San Diego was a combination car show and race. They pulled in late on the afternoon of July 3. After a supper at a small restaurant near the meet, they walked back to the track, rolled up in bedrolls beside the trailer and the truck, and fell asleep almost immediately.

The next morning they were up early. "Come on. Let's get something to eat," Easy said. "My stomach thinks my throat's been cut." He led the way back to the same place where they had eaten the day before. The place was already crowded with people who had come for the race. The three of them sat down to a breakfast of pancakes, eggs, bacon, and scalding black coffee.

After Peter paid the bill and they left the restaurant, they strolled down toward the lines of cars already being eagerly viewed by spectators. Glancing at Jolie, Peter said, "You look nice in your coveralls, Jolie."

Jolie responded to the compliment with a quick smile. The coveralls were snow white and clung to her youthful, trim figure. On her back, in a fancy, curling script, was the title, *Jolie Blonde.* "I had to stay up half the night getting the name on the back," she confessed. "Does it look all right?"

"It's spelled right, I reckon," Easy grinned. "I hope it brings us good luck."

Jolie suddenly remarked, "Oh, I forgot! I got this rabbit's foot just before I left. It ought to bring us good luck." Plunging her hand into her pocket, she pulled out the furry object and handed it to Easy.

Staring at the object, Easy shook his head in disgust. "This ain't no good!"

"What's wrong with it?" Jolie demanded. "It's a real rabbit's foot!"

"I can see your education has certainly been neglected. I thought everybody knowed that the only rabbit's foot with any luck at all in it is the left hind foot. This one here is the front right foot. You might as well chuck this thing away!" he said in disgust.

Peter laughed out loud. "We don't need any rabbit's foot. All we need is to get in that car and step on the gas, but first let's look at some of these little beauties to see what we're up against."

They moved to the first car in the line, which was an imposing Franklin. It had a strange-looking round grill, and Easy nodded at it. "That thing's got an air-cooled engine. I ain't got no confidence in them."

They moved to the next car, and Peter said, "Now, this is something light."

"What is it, Peter?" Jolie asked.

"Why, it's a Packard Roadster. It's got a T-head engine, a magneto jump-spark ignition, and it displaces 349.9 cubic inches. A real go-getter!"

All this meant nothing to Jolie, but inwardly she vowed to learn more about cars as soon as they got back.

They moved along the line examining Ramblers, a Cadillac Model K Runabout, and a Buick Turtleback Roadster, which had a tilt steering column. They stopped to admire the large Model H

Buick, and the four-cylinder Cadillac.

"How much would this cost, Peter?" Jolie inquired.

"This one? About two thousand dollars."

Jolie was shocked. "I'll never be able to drive one of those," she said wistfully.

"What do you need with that when you got the *Jolie Blonde*?" Peter asked lazily.

"Peter, can I drive it sometime? I don't mean now at the race, but I mean when we're back home?"

"Why, sure. We'll get out there in the desert. That way, if you hit something, it'll be a cactus and not an innocent bystander."

Jolie started to say something, but right then a loudspeaker blared, "All racing drivers report to the stand immediately!"

"Guess we better get going," Peter muttered. "Easy, you and Jolie unload the *Jolie Blonde*. I'll go sign us up."

Jolie hurriedly returned to the car, guided by Easy, and helped as best she could while Easy backed the car off the trailer. He started the engine, then got out and listened to it with a practiced ear, his thin face intent. "Sounds good, don't she?"

To Jolie it sounded loud, but she nodded enthusiastically. "Do you think we'll win, Easy?"

Easy pulled his cap off and racked his sandy hair, then jammed the cap back on. "Well," he said, "I put a four-leaf clover in my shoe the first thing this morning. That's always worked pretty good for me."

Jolie stared at the small man cautiously. "Do you really believe all those things about luck?"

"Believe 'em? 'Course I do!" He stared at her lustrous black hair and said, "Tell you a secret, Jolie. Next time you braid your hair, leave out a strand."

"Whatever for?"

"Well, that means you'll marry within the year," Easy grinned.

"I'm not studying getting married," she said, her face growing pink.

Easy grinned at her skeptically, then shrugged. "Well, we got a race to win. We'll take this matter up later."

He moved over, lowered himself behind the wheel, and Jolie quickly got in beside him. Carefully avoiding spectators, he drove the car slowly to the track, where they were met by Peter.

"Right over there, Easy. We're fourth in line."

"What's the competition look like?" Easy demanded.

"Pretty stiff," Peter admitted. He was wearing a pair of charcoal gray slacks, a royal blue shirt with the sleeves buttoned down, and a soft checkered cap on backward, with goggles to be lowered during the race. He waved toward the line of cars and said, "That's Albert Dingley there in the Pope-Toledo. See that Locomobile Joe Tracey's driving? That's a ninety-horsepower job."

"There's a steam-powered White Roadster—don't know the driver. But the ones to beat are those French fellows. Don't know what they're doing here, but that Renault has won lots of races."

The loudspeaker blared, "All drivers prepare for the start!"

"Come out of there, Jolie." Peter smiled and reached out and put his hands under her arms, lifting her clear easily. Setting her down, he said, "You got a hug for good luck?"

At once Jolie came forward, put her arms around him, and squeezed as hard as she could. "Beat everybody, Peter," she whispered, then stepped back and caught his wink. "I'll be waiting at the finish line," she said.

Peter turned then and said, "Well, climb aboard, Easy. Here's where they separate the men from the boys." The two men got into the car. The roar of the racing engines and the smell of burning oil filled the air. The cars painted all the colors of the rainbow gave a festive look to the race. Peter pulled his goggles down and gripped the wheel.

Easy shook his head and said, "I hope you get the jump on these birds," he muttered and then pulled down his own goggles.

The gun sounded so abruptly that Peter was almost caught off guard. He shoved his foot down and the *Jolie Blonde*'s rear wheels spun and leaped forward. Albert Dingley, in his Pope-Toledo, took the lead and held it for the first two laps. Peter managed to hold on to fourth place, and then good fortune rather than good driving came to his aid. The second-place driver, Joe Tracey in his Locomobile, rammed the Pope-Toledo, and both cars spun off the track and out of the race.

"We got a chance," Easy yelled. "This four-leaf clover's working. Pour on the gas, Pete!"

The race seesawed back and forth among the French team, the speedy Renault, and the *Jolie Blonde*. For the last three laps, none of the cars could make a definitive gain. Finally, as they headed into the last lap, the Renault went into a spin, and by the time it had recovered, Peter and Easy were only yards away from the finish line. The Renault picked up speed but was four lengths behind as the *Jolie Blonde* sailed by the man with the checkered flag, who waved it enthusiastically as they shot by. The crowd yelled and hollered, and Peter screamed, "That's the sweetest music I ever heard, Easy!"

"It is nice, ain't it!" Easy said, pulling off his goggles.

When they got the car stopped, the large crowd mobbed them instantly.

They clambered out, and someone shoved a large trophy at Peter. Grabbing it, he held it high in the air with one hand. Suddenly Jolie squeezed through, and he reached out and hugged her with the other arm.

"I'm Adams with the *San Diego Star*. . . ." The speaker was a slightly freckle-faced reporter with a pad and pencil in his hand. "How do you feel about winning the race?"

"I feel better than losin'," Peter said, grinning. He fielded the questions the reporter shot at him, and the crowd all listened.

Finally Adams glanced at Jolie, who was still resting under Peter's arm. "Is this your wife?"

Peter smiled somewhat awkwardly at Jolie, then looked back at Adams, feeling rather foolish. "Why, no."

"Your lady friend, then?" Adams pursued.

"Well, she's a lady, and she's a friend." Peter suddenly grinned. He gave Jolie a squeeze and said, "This is the real Jolie. Easy and me named the car after her."

After the excitement was over, and the car was loaded for the trip back to Los Angeles, Easy went to the back of the trailer to check on the tie-downs. Jolie, who was sitting close to Peter to make room for Easy, looked up at him. "I'm so glad you won, Peter. It was wonderful."

"It's a lucky car, as Easy would say." He looked down at her face, her blue eyes shining and catching the gleam of the setting sun. "Glad you came?"

"Oh yes!"

"Better than studying algebra, huh?"

Jolie thought for a minute. "It's more fun," she said. "I'm going to go to all your races from now on."

"Pretty sure of that, are you?"

"I can, can't I, Peter?" Jolie pleaded.

Easy came and plopped down just at that moment. He slammed the door of the truck and said, "Time to go. The fun's over. Back to work."

But Jolie persisted. "Can I, Peter? Go to your races?"

"We'll see."

Jolie nodded confidently. "All right, we'll see." But as she sat there squeezed between the two men, thinking of the future, she thought, *He'll let me go. I know he will.* . . .

★　★　★　★

For two days after they returned home, Jolie was in a glow over the trip to the race in San Diego. When Tom Ziegler came to give her her next lesson, for the first time she gave him no time for study. She described every inch of the journey, and then portrayed the race itself in vivid detail. She ended by saying, ". . . and Peter and Easy are going to take me to *all* their races. It's going to be such fun."

Ziegler had been listening quietly, noting the excitement of the young woman. "I'm glad you had a good time, Jolie."

"You should have seen me when they crossed the finish line. I was so excited. I wish you could go sometime, Tom. Have you ever been to a race?"

"No, I never have."

"Next time there's one close by you can come."

"Well, I'm pretty busy." He hesitated for a long moment, then said, "My mother sent you an invitation. She wants you to come and have supper with us tonight."

It was the first such invitation, and Jolie was somewhat surprised. Tom rarely mentioned his mother, and Jolie was curious about his family. "Oh, that would be nice," she said.

"I'll come by and get you around five," he said. "That's a little early, but you can visit with Mother for a while before we eat."

Jolie opened her books, but her mind was not on the lesson. Half of her imagination was still running over the events of the race. The other was thinking about going to the dinner with Tom and his mother. *It'll be enjoyable*, she thought as she studied Tom's thin, studious face. She wondered if he resembled his mother or his father. *Well, I guess I'll find out tonight*, she decided.

Later that afternoon as Jolie was getting ready, she took more care than usual, putting on a new dress she had just purchased. It was made of a heather gray lightweight fabric and had a high neckline, loose-fitting bodice, and elbow-length sleeves trimmed with pink. She smiled at her reflection in the mirror, satisfied with the results. A soft knock sounded on her door, and when she opened it, her landlady smiled and said, "Mr. Ziegler is here."

"Thank you, Mrs. Bell." Grabbing up a bag, she rushed out of her room and went downstairs to meet him. "I'm ready," she said.

"I got us a carriage," Tom said. "You look very nice, Jolie. Is that a new dress?"

"Yes, more or less. I've worn it only once. Do you like it?" She turned around for his approval.

"Real pretty, Jolie."

The two went out to the carriage that was waiting in front of the boardinghouse, and Tom gave the address to the cab driver. With a flick of the lines, the horses started a slow trot down the road. Tom seemed strangely silent on the way. Jolie wondered at this, and she herself was affected by his rather quiet mood.

The cab pulled up in front of a low bungalow in a residential area a few miles from Jolie's boardinghouse. Tom helped her down, and she waited until Tom paid the cab driver. Then as he turned to her, she said, "I'm anxious to meet your mother."

"I hope you'll like her," he said, then hesitated. "My mother's rather a direct person."

"Why, you must get your shyness from your father," Jolie remarked.

The remark caught Tom Ziegler's attention, and he faltered as they passed down the path lined with flowers. "I suppose that's true. He was very quiet. He was like me—or rather I'm like him."

When they reached the door he opened it and allowed her to go in. He stepped inside and called out, "Mother, we're here."

Jolie waited expectantly, and a woman appeared out of a door down a rather narrow hallway. As she came closer, Jolie saw that the woman was older than she had expected.

"Mother, this is Miss Jolie Devorak. Jolie, I'd like you to meet my mother."

"How do you do, Mrs. Ziegler?"

"Very well. I'm glad that you could come." Dora Ziegler was a tall and rather formidable woman, apparently very strong physically. She had iron gray hair, a squarish face, and appeared to be in her fifties. To Jolie's surprise she looked nothing at all like Tom, and her suspicions were confirmed that Tom got his looks, as well as his mannerisms, from his father.

"Come and sit in the parlor, Miss Devorak."

"Oh, please call me Jolie. Everyone does."

"Very well." Mrs. Ziegler led the way into the parlor, and Jolie took her seat on a stiff, hard horsehair couch. Tom did not sit beside her but moved to an ancient-looking straight-backed chair, which he sat on nervously, locking his fingers in front of him.

Mrs. Ziegler seated herself on an oak Eastwood easy chair upholstered in chintz of a very drab brown print, and put her small, but intense, brown eyes on her guest. "My son tells me that you work with a group of actors and actresses."

"Yes, ma'am. I work for Imperial Pictures," Jolie said. She felt intimidated by the woman's heavy stare and stirred nervously.

"What is your age, if I may ask?"

"I'm nineteen."

"What about your family?"

There was a steely edge to the woman's voice, and Jolie sensed the disapproval in her stolid gaze. "I . . . don't really have any family."

"You're an orphan?"

"Yes, only a stepfather, and we . . . didn't get along." Then she added quickly, "But I'm doing very well. I make enough money to have a nice place to live, and Tom here is helping me a lot with his tutoring."

"I'm sure he is."

Tom Ziegler sat quietly, offering only a word here and there. His face was drawn, and Jolie noticed a nervous tick in his right eye. *What's he so nervous about?* she wondered. She glanced back at the large woman sitting across from her and thought suddenly, *Why, he's afraid of her!* She said nothing aloud of her observations but continued to answer the questions that Mrs. Ziegler fired at her one after another.

Finally the interrogation appeared to be over. Mrs. Ziegler said, "I think dinner is ready. If you will give me a few moments, I will go set the table."

"Let me help you," Jolie offered eagerly.

"That won't be necessary. Everything is ready. I'll come for you when it's time."

Tom stood up as his mother left the room and fidgeted, seemingly not certain of what to say. After a long moment of silence, he asked, "Well, what do you think of my mother?"

"She seems to be a very . . . strong woman."

"Yes, she is."

For the life of her, Jolie could not think of another remark to make. Finally she said in a rather inane fashion, "I'm sure she did her best for you after your father passed away."

"Oh yes!" Tom nodded eagerly. "She did everything for me. It was hard, too. She had little money. But she always saw I got the best education possible under the circumstances."

Jolie looked up and said, "Is that your father?" nodding toward an oval portrait behind glass. "I see it is. You look very much like him."

"So they say. I didn't actually know him very well. He died when I was only eight, but I remember he used to take me out to the beach. He would make boats, and we would race them." He hesitated, seemingly lost in thought. "I missed him so much. Life wasn't the same after he died."

"It's hard for a mother to raise a son alone, I suppose." Then she added quickly, "But I'm sure your mother did the best she could."

"Yes, of course she did."

At that moment Mrs. Ziegler appeared and said, "You may come into the dining room now."

Quickly Jolie arose and walked before Tom out of the parlor, down the hall, and to the left into the dining room.

The dining room was a medium-sized room with two small windows covered with heavy dark blue curtains. Jolie's eyes scanned the room, taking in the carpet of green, black, pink, and red rose patterns. Pictures of landscapes and gardens hung on the pale blue-and-green wallpapered walls. Her eyes opened wide at the sight of the table. It was the most elegant setting she had ever seen. It was more beautiful than even one of the expensive restaurants where Priscilla had taken her to eat one time.

The large oval-shaped table was surrounded by four late Victorian balloon-back chairs and was covered with a white, stiffly ironed cloth with the crease placed directly in the middle of the table, dividing it in half. In the center of the table was a small white lace centerpiece cloth, where a cut-glass vase of fresh flowers had been placed. At the corners of the centerpiece were four highly polished silver candlesticks with candles burning. Fancy dishes of appetizers and salted nuts sat between the burning candles. And each place setting had a white cloth napkin, three forks of varying sizes, a china plate, two knives, one spoon, a small glass dish of salt with a tiny spoon in it, and a water goblet. Close to each place setting was another small glass bowl, a finger bowl, half filled with water and a small slice of lemon floating on top.

"You may sit there, Miss Devorak," Tom's mother said, ignoring the first name of the girl. She herself sat at the head of the table, and Tom, as if on cue, walked around and sat down across from Jolie.

Though the setting was elegant, it was a strange and uncomfortable meal. When Jolie looked down, she saw an array of knives and forks and had not the slightest idea of what to use them all for. She survived from committing any faux pas mainly by waiting until Tom or Mrs. Ziegler used one of them, and then she followed. The food was good, she supposed, but she was so tense that she could not enjoy it.

Almost at once, Mrs. Ziegler began talking about Tom and the struggle she had had to educate him. She put great stress on how she had to sacrifice everything. "Now he's halfway through his college career," she ended finally, "and he has a brilliant future ahead of him."

"Oh, Mother!" Tom protested. "Not all that brilliant."

"Don't say that, Tom! You're going to be a fine attorney, and who knows, attorneys often go into politics. You'd do well, I think, running for office someday."

Tom shifted nervously. "I don't think I'd be very good at begging for votes."

Ignoring this, Mrs. Ziegler said, "And, of course, he will marry well. That's so important for a young man who's on his way upward in the social and business world. Don't you think, Miss Devorak."

Jolie nodded, murmuring, "I'm sure it is."

"We've talked about it, Tom and I," Mrs. Ziegler said, and her eyes fell on Jolie in a strange fashion. "It would be terrible if he threw himself away on some young woman who could not help his career. One reads about these things in the newspapers. Men who should know better than to marry chorus girls—actresses."

Instantly Jolie recognized that the entire evening was a red-flag warning. *Keep your hands off my son!* Jolie's face grew pale, and she had very little to say for the rest of the meal.

After the meal, they returned to the parlor, where Jolie spent as miserable an hour as she could ever remember. Finally the ordeal was over, and as Jolie moved to the door, she turned to say, "Thank you very much. It was a very fine dinner, Mrs. Ziegler."

"You're very welcome, I'm sure." Mrs. Ziegler did not add the customary, "You must come again." Instead she turned to Tom and said, "I wish you would hurry back, Tom. There are some things we need to discuss."

Tom coughed and then muttered, "Very well, Mother."

Neither Tom nor Jolie said much on the way back to her boardinghouse. When he left her at the door, he said nervously, "I'd better get back."

"Thank you for asking me, Tom," Jolie said quietly. She saw something like pain in his eyes and said quickly, "I'll see you day after tomorrow for my lessons."

"Of course. Good night, Jolie."

Jolie entered the house, going directly to her room. Closing the door, she went to sit on the bed. A heavy sadness settled in her heart—not for herself or for the coldness of Mrs. Ziegler's treatment. She had borne worse than that. She grieved for Tom Ziegler, perceiving very clearly that he was the prisoner of his mother's lofty and selfish ambitions. She sat there and sighed, "Oh, Tom. . . !" She shook her head, got up, and began to get ready for bed, wondering what Mrs. Ziegler wanted to talk to Tom about that was so urgent. *Probably*, she thought as she brushed her hair after putting on her gown, *she wants to warn him against young girls who work with actresses and other lowlife people. . . .*

CHAPTER FOURTEEN

FRENCH PERFUME

★ ★ ★ ★

The August sun was still high in the sky as Dorothy Winslow stopped abruptly outside Parson's Department Store. The financial problems of life had finally disappeared when she and Andrew had moved to Los Angeles. Faith Temple paid a more than adequate salary. The years of near poverty, however, had brought habits that died hard, and Parson's was *the* store in Los Angeles. It was an imposing four-story building built of cement, brick, and glass that gleamed in the yellow sunlight, but there was only a small black marble sign on the cornerstone. Everyone knew Parson's as the store where the well-to-do shopped. Wealthy people came from all over southern California to shop here, but Dorothy had never done more than pay a quick visit. The price tags had taken her breath away, and she had gone to stores with more reasonably priced merchandise.

Somehow, as she stood looking at the mannequins in the window, all marble faced and haughty, a strange idea began to take shape within her. At first she ignored it and once almost walked on down the pavement, but then she turned squarely to stare at the display. One was a sheer peach-colored nightgown underneath a lacy black negligee. She was transfixed by the daring combination, unable to tear her eyes away. The gown itself was low-cut and nipped in at the waist, and she knew instinctively that only a woman with an excellent figure could wear it.

Finally Dorothy straightened up, her lips grew tight, and she marched into the store with determination. The lingerie department was on the second floor, and she took the wide, curving stairs up, noting that there were no poorly dressed people in Parson's. When she reached the top step, she was intimidated by the richness of the oriental carpet and the displays of clothes that she knew were frightfully expensive. For a time she wandered about hesitantly, hoping that no salesclerk would approach her. For a while she looked around undisturbed, but then a tall woman wearing a simple but well-tailored dress and a string of enormous pearls around her neck came, saying in a voice that was almost a purr, "May I help you make a selection?"

"Oh, I really don't know what I want." This was not true, for Dorothy knew *exactly* what she wanted. Somehow it seemed almost *immoral* to buy the lingerie she had seen in the window.

"Would it be a gown or a frock?" the lady asked. Seeing Dorothy's hesitation, she said, "My name is Miss Hampton. I'd be glad to help you with anything that might interest you."

"I . . . I thought the peach gown and negligee in the window were very pretty."

"Oh, you have fine taste! Come along," Miss Hampton said. As she moved away, Dorothy followed her. Soon the two women were in front of a rack from which the saleslady pulled the gown down. "I think this would be perfect for you with your coloring, and you're a size eight, I think?" Miss Hampton removed the gown and held it up and nodded with admiration. "A perfect fit, I'm certain. But why don't you go try it on? It's hard to tell about these things—and lingerie is so important, don't you think?"

Dorothy had had few thoughts on the subject, but she found herself nodding, taking the gown, and soon she was in a dressing room. She looked around nervously, checked the lock on the door, and removing her clothes, she slipped into the gown, then pulled the negligee on over it. There was a full-length mirror in the room, and as she looked at it she gasped. The silk clung to her figure, outlining every curve, and the low cut of the bodice was more daring than anything she had ever worn. She stood for a long time staring at herself, turning to every possible angle. There was even a mirror on the other side of the room so that she could see how the outfit looked from the back.

"Does it fit?" Miss Hampton's voice came through the door.

"Oh yes, it does! It's very nice. I'll just be a moment." Hastily Dorothy removed the negligee and donned her street clothes.

Gathering the lingerie, she unlocked the door and stepped outside.

"I know you looked lovely in it," Miss Hampton smiled. "I'm sure you'll want to take it home with you."

"Well, I don't know. It's so . . . well, it's a little more exotic than anything I've ever bought."

Miss Hampton suddenly smiled. She had a wealth of auburn hair done up in the latest fashion, and she winked slyly, saying, "Well, your husband will like it—and that's who a woman really buys her clothes for. Not for herself, but for her husband, don't you agree?"

"I suppose that's true. But I'm not sure my husband will like anything quite this . . . daring."

"Why, of course he will! Men like that sort of thing." She urged no more but stood waiting, and soon Dorothy made the response Miss Hampton expected.

"Well, all right. How much is it?"

Dorothy, by sure force of will, did not gasp when she heard the price. *I'll have to make it up with my housekeeping budget*, she thought. But aloud she said, "I'll take it with me."

"One more thing. Would you step over this way, please?" Miss Hampton moved along the counter, holding the gown and negligee, and stopped before a glass case. She opened it and took out a small bottle in a curiously wrought cut-glass fashion. "This is the latest perfume. It is called 'Love at Night.' It came all the way from Paris. Here, let me put a little on your wrist." She pulled the stopper out, moistened a finger, then touched Dorothy's wrist. As Dorothy breathed the fragrance of the perfume, Miss Hampton's lips curled upward. "When your husband gets one hint of that, I think you'll see it's worth the money. After all, that's a woman's job to make herself attractive for her husband."

By this time Dorothy was not quite so inhibited. "It is very lovely," she said. Without even asking the price, she said, "I'll take a bottle of it, but a very small one."

"Of course. Now let me wrap these for you."

Soon Dorothy was paying for her purchases, barely managing to keep her face straight at the amount. She handed the money to the saleslady, took the package, and said, "Thank you very much."

"Thank you!" Miss Hampton beamed, her eyebrow arched as she leaned forward. "I wish you'd come back soon and tell me how your husband liked it."

Dorothy flushed and nodded, then turned and left the store. All the way home she was building a dream of how she would surprise Andrew with the lingerie and the perfume. She was frightened that her plan would not work, but the thoughts came floating to her, *I can make him want me! I know I can!*

★ ★ ★ ★

Dorothy concealed the lingerie in a drawer in her chest and placed the perfume under it.

When she shut the drawer she thought defensively, *I don't know why I'm hiding it like it was some sort of sinful thing. It isn't, really.* She took a deep breath, then went downstairs and began cooking supper. The children were playing noisily in the drawing room, and from time to time she would go check on them, but her mind was on Andrew.

At five o'clock the door opened, and when Andrew came through calling out, "I'm home!" Dorothy's face brightened. She went to him at once and said, "You came home early! I'm so glad! I'm fixing your favorite supper. Shrimp and snapper."

Andrew leaned over and kissed her cheek. "That's fine," he said. "I'm pretty hungry." He turned and went to the children. Sitting on the floor beside them, he began to ask them about their day.

Dorothy happily went about the final touches of the meal. The perfume and the lingerie were on her mind, and she hurriedly set the meal on the table. Andrew ate well, but she saw that he was tired.

"You're working too hard," she murmured. "I can tell you're exhausted."

"I'm all right," Andrew shrugged.

He did not comment on the meal, much to Dorothy's disappointment, but she put that from her mind. After supper she washed the dishes while Andrew read stories to the children. When she was finished cleaning up, she went in and sat quietly across from him, studying the face of her husband. It was a strong face, thinner now than it should be, but he was still one of the handsomest men she had ever seen. She thought back to when Andrew and his brother, Barney, had first come to Africa to her father's mission station. At that time it was Barney who had attracted her.

Barney had been a prizefighter and a rough fellow indeed, with none of Andrew's smoothness. But that had come to nothing, and Barney had married Katie Sullivan. Now they had two lovely children. Dorothy had married Andrew, and it had been a storybook romance for the first six months. But then when they'd returned to America and Andrew had begun his busy life as Superintendent of Missions, everything had changed. As she sat there thinking, she could tell he was tired.

Finally he got up and said, "It must be your bedtime, children. Isn't that right, Dorothy?"

Dorothy got up quickly and, ignoring the inevitable protests, took the children at once up to their bedroom. She scrubbed them down, had them brush their teeth, put their pajamas on them, and saw them into their respective beds, saying a prayer over each, a ritual they had come to enjoy each night.

When she closed the door to the bedroom they shared, she returned to the living room and saw that Andrew was half asleep in his chair.

"You're tired," she said. "Why don't you take a bath, and we'll go to bed early."

Andrew shook himself and stood to his feet. He yawned hugely, saying, "I think I will." He made his way out of the living room and disappeared down the hall.

Nervously Dorothy waited, giving him time to take his bath, then she moved to the bedroom. He was just coming out of the bath wearing his pajamas. "I'll wash up," she said rather breathlessly.

"All right, I want to go over these figures." He picked up a loose-leaf book and got into bed, snapped the bed light on, and began to read.

Dorothy hesitated for a moment, then moved over to the chest and removed the lingerie and the perfume. She carried it into the bathroom, concealing it, although she saw that he was deep in his study of the figures. Quickly she bathed, dried with a fluffy towel, and then put on the nightgown. It once again made her feel strange, and she wondered if she could go through with it. It had all seemed so logical when she had bought it, and now she had to summon up all of her courage to put the perfume behind her ears and just a touch on her neck. Capping the perfume she put it in the medicine cabinet and stepped to the door. She put her hand on the knob, and suddenly a pang of terror seized her.

I can't do this! she thought and stood there unable to move. But her other gowns were in the chest, and she thought, *It'll be all right.* She opened the door and stepped into the bedroom, the silk caressing her body. She imagined she heard a swishing sound as she moved across the room.

"I have to get up early in the morning. I've got a big day," Andrew said without looking up.

"I'll set the clock." She picked up the clock on the bedside table and set it, then glanced at him. "Do you want a drink of water, or anything, before I get into bed?"

Somewhat surprised, Andrew looked up. "Why, no. I don't think so," he said. He started to look back, then put his glance back on her. "That's new, isn't it?"

"Yes, do you like it?"

"Pretty," he said and then closed his book.

He did not inquire as to where she had bought it, and Dorothy's spirit flagged as he said no more. He settled down on the pillow and closed his eyes after shutting off his light.

Dorothy quickly switched off her light, pulled off the negligee, and got into bed beside him. He did not move for a time, and Dorothy shyly moved toward him. She put her arm across him, and he stirred for a moment. Then he put his hand over hers and squeezed her wrist, but that was all. Dorothy moved closer, pressing against him, and when he did not respond, she whispered in desperation, "Do you like my new perfume?"

Andrew was half asleep. "What?" he asked, his voice fuzzy.

"I asked if you liked my new perfume?" Dorothy said distinctly.

He turned his head and sniffed. "Oh yes. It smells good."

Dorothy was bitterly disappointed. She lay there for a moment, and then she did something she had never done before. Putting her hand on his neck, she pulled him around and, raising up, put herself against him and lowered her head. She kissed him with a longing and a fervency that expressed her deep loneliness. She practically prayed for some kind of response.

Andrew was somewhat shocked. "What is it?" he said. "What are you doing?"

"I . . . want you to love me, Andrew." The words came hard, for she had never been a woman to speak in such a manner. Andrew had always been the one who made the advances toward lovemaking, and Dorothy felt her face flushing in the dark.

Suddenly Andrew pushed her back and raised himself up on one elbow. He stared at her in the moonlight that came through the window and said, "You're behaving strangely, Dorothy."

Dorothy whispered, "Is it strange for a woman to want love?"

Andrew had had a difficult day. Ordinarily he would never have said such a thing, but things had gone wrong at every turn, and he had come home with the burden of failure in the building program that disturbed him greatly. Now he grunted, "I don't know what's wrong with you! I expect you get loved enough! Do you want a man to follow you around quoting poetry to you?"

His words hit her like a physical blow. As she lay there, tears of frustration rose in her eyes.

"All this you're doing now. What's it supposed to mean with this perfume and nightgown?"

"Nothing." Dorothy's voice was flat. "It doesn't mean anything." She rolled over and pressed her fist against her lips and kept her eyes shut tight. She wept silently, and sleep eluded her. She felt cheap and knew that it was not her fault—and at the same time she felt humiliated and rejected. For the first time in her married life, she had reached out for love, speaking words that had been hard and difficult for her. Andrew had turned from her and now slept heavily, not knowing that he had destroyed something sweet and precious in the woman that lay beside him silently weeping.

★　★　★　★

"What's the matter? You look pale."

Dorothy had put breakfast on the table and fed the children but had eaten practically nothing. She glanced up at Andrew, who was looking at her with a puzzled expression. "Nothing," she said. "I'm fine."

Andrew hesitated. He took a bite of toast, chewed it slowly, then shook his head. "You look tired. Why don't you have Helen come in and keep the children and take a day off?"

"No, I wouldn't want to do that." Dorothy's voice was toneless, and there was a deadness in her eyes as she looked at Andrew. She got up, saying, "You'd better hurry to your meetings."

"I guess I had." Andrew got up and went and kissed the children. "You be good now. Don't give your mother any trouble today." He put on his coat and hat, then turned at the door, briefcase in hand, saying, "I've got to go to Sacramento tomorrow. Did you remember?"

"Yes, I remembered. You'll be gone for three days."

Andrew hesitated still. "It's an important meeting. Pastors from all over the country will be there, and I'm the keynote speaker. Quite an honor."

"Quite an honor." Dorothy's words were an echo of Andrew's, but there was no excitement in her voice.

Andrew stared at her for a moment, then shrugged and said, "I'll try to get home early tonight." Still he hesitated, as if something was troubling him. "When I get back, why don't we take a little vacation? Two or three days out at that little resort up north on the coast. The one that you like so much."

"That would be nice." Dorothy had heard this before many times. It was a catch phrase, almost, that Andrew offered her. A bait or a reward for enduring his long absences.

"Well, we'll do it then. I'll see you early tonight."

All morning long Dorothy moved mechanically about the house. The children demanded her time, and so she read to them, then took them for a walk. She smiled without anything reaching her eyes. When they got back, she cooked their lunch but ate nothing herself. After they were in bed for their nap, she went upstairs, removed the gown and negligee from her dresser, and the perfume from the bathroom cabinet. She went downstairs and wrapped them in a paper sack, her lips drawn in a straight line. Stepping out the back door, she yanked open the lid of the garbage can and violently threw the sack inside. It struck with a dull thud, and she slammed the lid back, then walked inside, her shoulders drooping. She lay down but did not sleep. A restlessness and an unhappiness enveloped her like a dull gray cloud. Once she raised her hands over her temples, squeezed them, and tried to hold back the sharp bite of tears that threatened to spill out. She dashed them away, got up, and walked around the room wringing her hands. She felt embarrassed and humiliated, and most of all rejected. Her heart felt heavy. She did not know what to do to gain Andrew's affection, or at least the expression of it. "I wonder if he still loves me," she whispered. "He did once, but now he never tells me that I'm pretty. He doesn't hold my hand as he used to, or surprise me with a kiss. It's like I'm a stranger here."

Finally she could not bear the confines of the house any longer. While the children were still asleep, she went outside and began working in the garden. It had been one of the pleasures to have a home of her own and plant flowers that she knew she would get to harvest and make into fragrant bouquets. She had donned canvas gloves and was working with her roses when she looked up to see a small black car without a top pull up with *Western Union* painted on the side. Straightening up she had a moment's dread as the delivery man leaped out and started up the front steps. Telegrams came for Andrew on rare occasions, but somehow she felt oddly fearful.

"I'm over here!" she said.

"Oh, there you are." The man came over and asked, "Mrs. Winslow?" He had on a white shirt with a bow tie and a pair of dark gray pants. His hat was set on top of thick red curls.

"Yes."

"Telegram, Mrs. Winslow. Sign right here, please."

Nervously Dorothy took the pencil, signed the pad, and then nodded as the young man said, "Thank you very much!" and went back jauntily toward his car. He roared off, and she stood holding the yellow envelope with the window. Removing her gloves and putting them down, she slowly tore open the envelope and unfolded the single sheet of paper. Her eyes flew to the name of the person who had sent it, and she saw her mother's name. Lifting her eyes, she read the words: *Your father died this morning of a heart attack. You cannot come, of course, for the funeral, but I wanted you to know his last words were of you. Pray for me, for I will be lost without him.*

The world suddenly grew dim for Dorothy Winslow. She closed her eyes and swayed, and then with a shaky motion made her way over to the wooden chair she had painted apple green. She sat down, and all her strength drained from her. She felt as if someone had struck her in the pit of the stomach, and she was unable to breathe for a moment. She could only think of her father and the thousand memories of his kindness.

★　★　★　★

As soon as Andrew walked in the door, he took one look at Dorothy's face. "What's wrong? Is it one of the children?"

"No." Dorothy could say no more. She handed him the telegram and watched him as he read it. He looked up and compassion shone from his grief-stricken face. It was real, for he had had a great affection for Dorothy's father. "I'm sorry," he said and stepped forward. He put his arms around her and held her, but Dorothy did not respond. The grief that pierced her heart was too sharp and overwhelming, and the rejection of the previous night was still a bitter taste in her mouth.

"I wish we could go to the funeral," he said slowly. "But it would take weeks to get there."

"It's impossible," Dorothy said. She pulled away from him and turned, then walked across the room and stared out into the twilight as it fell over Los Angeles. She watched the lights of the city begin to illuminate the sky as the sun went down, dragging the light with it and leaving the murkiness of the night.

Andrew came over and stood beside her. He did not touch her but said, "He was a fine man. A wonderful missionary."

Dorothy did not answer. She stood there thinking of her father. She felt totally alone in the world, but she could not say a word to break the silence that seemed to lock her inside a dark cell.

The rest of the evening seemed like a terrible nightmare for her. Andrew hovered over her, tried to get her to eat, and when she would not, he said, "You need to sleep. Perhaps we ought to get Dr. Gunn over. He could give you something."

"No. I wouldn't want to do that," Dorothy said wearily. She was sitting in the chair in the living room and closed her eyes. She knew Andrew was watching her, but somehow she could not respond, and then suddenly she shook her shoulders. "I'm sorry, Andrew. It's just such a shock." She stood up, and he came to her and put his arm around her. He held her, and she began to feel a comfort that she desperately needed.

"Come along," he said finally. "It's late. I'll fix you a glass of warm milk. Maybe you'll sleep. We'll talk about it in the morning."

Dorothy obeyed, and that night he did hold her in his arms, and a surge of hope within her heart began to grow. The grief at the loss of her father somehow was eased as Andrew held his arms around her and kissed her on the temple, whispering, "It'll be better. It'll be all right."

But when Dorothy rose the next morning feeling somewhat better and went down to breakfast, she found him there with his coat on looking harassed. "I got a phone call. I tried to call and cancel, but they insist that I come to Sacramento." He looked at her shamefacedly and said, "I know it's a horrible time to leave, and if it were any other meeting, I'd stay. But, Dorothy, this means so much to the church. There'll be leaders from all over the United States." He continued to speak, making a case that he knew was weak and feeble.

Dorothy stared at him, not believing what she was hearing. He was going to leave her at the most critical hour of her life. At a time when she needed him the most. A protest leaped to her lips, but then she pressed them together, shutting it off. "All right, Andrew. There's nothing you can do here."

He stared at her for a moment and then shook his head. "If it were any other meeting . . ."

Dorothy did not answer. He came over and kissed her and said, "I need to go to the church for some things, but I'll be back to check on you before I leave. Get someone to take care of the children. It'll be too much for you now, and I'll be back in three days, and we'll take that little vacation."

"All right, Andrew." Her voice was wooden, and her eyes were dull as he turned and left the room. The shutting of the door had a sound of finality that sent a chill through her as if something had ended in her life.

CHAPTER FIFTEEN

A DAY WITH NOLAN COLE

★ ★ ★ ★

As Dorothy awoke on the second day of Andrew's absence, she realized dully that no one had come to console her. Not even one church member had called on her. *Andrew must not have told anyone about my father.* She was shocked at the sudden realization. *I suppose he thought I would let them know.*

She put on a dress, picked almost at random, and left her bedroom. The children were already awake, and as they clambered over her, she realized she did not have the strength to cope with them. After feeding them breakfast, she went to the phone and called their part-time maid and baby-sitter, Helen Teague.

Helen was a widow who loved children and had proved to be a faithful and dependable attendant for Phillip and Amelia. A tenderhearted and compassionate person, she was distraught herself at the news of Dorothy's father's death. Hearing that Dorothy was there all alone with the children, she said, "Don't you worry. I'll come over right away and stay just as long as you need me. I can take care of everything while you get some rest or do whatever you have to do."

"Thank you so much, Helen. You don't know how much this means to me."

By the time Helen arrived and took over the children in a thoroughly competent manner, Dorothy was ready to leave the house. She needed to get outside. "I may be late, Helen," she said as she left.

"That doesn't matter. I can stay all night in the guest room like I did before."

"Oh, I don't think that will be necessary. I should be back by suppertime."

Leaving the house, Dorothy turned and walked slowly down the sidewalk. She had no destination in mind and passed by several neighbors, greeting them with a false smile. She walked for over two hours, simply moving from street to street, not really paying attention to anything except her own thoughts and the precious memories of her father. He had been a man of deep faith and one who had lived life to the fullest, and she could not picture him being gone. He had been a true friend and companion to his wife, and Dorothy knew that her mother must now feel lost. She formed a scheme in her mind to send for her mother. *She can't stay there at the mission station by herself,* she thought as she turned and walked down a residential street, noting absently the arrangement of flower beds and the blooms on the trees. She did not know how her mother would adjust to life in America, but somehow she must. For years Africa had been the only home her mother had known.

Dorothy finally noticed with a start that she had wandered almost as far as the church. She did not want to go there, because she did not want to talk to anyone. So she made an abrupt about-face and started home, but at that moment she heard her name.

"Dorothy!"

Quickly Dorothy turned toward the street as Nolan Cole pulled up in his car. He left the engine running but put the brake on, leaped out, and came to stand before her. "I'm surprised to see you here." He removed his hat, and when he smiled, his teeth gleamed whitely against his tan. "Can I give you a ride somewhere?"

"I . . . I don't think so."

Her hesitation caught Nolan's attention. He blinked and studied her face for a moment, then asked abruptly, "What's wrong? Something wrong with the family?"

She did not answer right away but then slowly said, "It's my father. He died at his post at the mission station in Africa."

"Oh, Dorothy, I'm so sorry!" The words came quickly, and when he put out his hand, she put both of hers in it. He held them for a moment and said, "You shouldn't be alone. What are you doing out wandering the streets?" Then his brow furrowed and he asked with a look of deep concern—almost disbelief, "Andrew *didn't* go to Sacramento, did he?"

Dorothy nodded without speaking. Her throat had choked up, and she could not say a word.

Now Nolan sounded irritated as he said quickly, "Well, come along. We'll find someplace to talk."

Dorothy knew she should not, but she did not resist as he led her to the car, helped her in, closed the door, then walked around and got in beside her. Without a word he drove to the beach, a fairly empty stretch with only two or three figures farther down the shore taking their morning walk.

Dorothy got out as he came around to help her, and they made their way down a narrow pathway to the beach. They walked along in silence, watching the waves crash onto the shore, feeling the salty tang of the wind whipping off the water. Fleecy clouds scudded across a hard blue sky, and the raucous cries of sea gulls wheeling overhead punctuated the soothing sounds of water and wind.

Finally they reached a large log turned gray by the passage of time and smoothed by the continual lapping of the waves. "Here. Sit down, Dorothy." She sat down numbly, and Nolan sat beside her. "Tell me about it," he said gently.

At first she spoke haltingly. Sensing his genuine care, she began to speak more freely, even recounting some of her fond memories of her father. She did not look at him, but he was there, and he listened. As she spoke, she saw a school of dolphins arching their backs, their fins outlined against the sky. She paused and watched until they had made their way across the horizon, and then she turned and attempted a smile. "Thank you, Nolan."

Nolan shrugged his shoulders. "Andrew shouldn't have left you alone." Then, as if realizing that was the wrong thing to say, he suddenly stood up. "Come along. Let's walk some more."

"I'll get sand in my shoes."

"Well, we'll take our shoes off, then."

"We can't do that."

"Why can't we?" He reached down, pulled off his shoes and socks, knotted the strings, and tossed them over his shoulder. "Here. Give me yours. I can carry them in my hip pocket."

Dorothy stared at him, then hesitantly she took off her shoes. She wore stockings that came below her knees and took those off, too. She stood up, and they began to walk down the beach. The surf came crashing in, and at times they had to scamper away to keep from getting their clothing wet.

Finally, after they turned and made their way back to the car, Nolan said, "Do you need to be back right away?"

"No. Not until suppertime. Helen Teague is caring for the children."

"I want to show you something you might like."

Curiously she followed. They put their socks and shoes back on, got in the car, and he drove down the shoreline to a marina. When they got out, he led her to a small skiff with a single mast moored at the end of a dock. "This is mine. Do you like boat rides?" he asked.

"I've never been in a sailing boat," Dorothy said as she looked at the small boat rocking gently in the water.

Grabbing her arm, Nolan smiled and said, "Climb aboard and let me have the privilege of giving you your first ride."

She gladly took his hand and allowed him to help her into the skiff. And for the next two hours Dorothy Winslow enjoyed herself immensely. The gentle warmth of the sunshine and the cool ocean breezes provided the balm she needed to soothe the hurt of long-pent-up feelings and her immediate grief, and she felt enormous gratitude for Nolan's kindness. She sat in the prow while Nolan sat in the stern, holding the tiller in one hand and shifting the sail from time to time as he brought the small craft about. The wind caught her hair and tossed it wildly. She laughed with abandon at her futile attempts to hold it in place.

"Forget about that! Real sailors don't mind wind in their hair."

The sea was fairly smooth, and the gentle rocking motion of the boat over the swells was a delight.

"So, tell me, Nolan, where did you learn to sail?" Dorothy asked as she leaned forward, turning her head and gazing at the distant shoreline.

Nolan sighed deeply and watched Dorothy, her silky hair now resting gently on her shoulders. "When I was about ten years old, I visited with my uncle who owned a small orchard near San Francisco. The current up there is similar to here, and we would spend as much free time as possible on his small sailing boat. My uncle at one time served with the merchant marines, and the tales he would tell of far-off lands brought out the adventurer in me. Before the summer was up he had me sailing on my own, and I have loved it ever since."

Dorothy was completely relaxed now. Finally she sighed, "I'd better be getting back, Nolan."

"All right." He swung the tiller about and expertly brought the small craft in. As it approached the shore, he judged the distance accurately and loosed the sail so that the boat headed back to the dock at the marina. Leaping out, he pulled the prow up and held out his hand. After he helped Dorothy onto the dock, he tied the boat up and fastened the sails down.

They were quiet on the drive back to the parsonage. Dorothy wondered at just how comfortable she felt in Nolan Cole's presence, even when neither of them were saying a word. Finally, as they pulled up in front of her home, Dorothy said, "I'm glad you found me, Nolan. I needed someone to talk to. You've been a great help."

He didn't answer for a moment, then said, "Have you remembered the meeting of the youth committee at the church this evening?"

"Yes, but I'm not going. I don't think I could handle that just now."

"Oh, but I think you should. You need to keep busy. It'll just be a short one, and early enough that we could take the kids out afterward and buy them hamburgers. What do you say?"

"Oh no, Nolan, I couldn't do that!"

"Of course you could!" he said firmly, jumping out of the car and running around to Dorothy's side. He said no more, simply helped her out of the car and escorted her up the front walk.

Helen met them as they came through the front door, and she greeted Nolan respectfully. She had known him for a long time, since she was also a faithful member of Faith Temple. "Well, you two look like you've been blown about by the wind."

"So we have, Helen. Have the children behaved for you?" Dorothy asked.

"With a little help from me they did," Helen said, smiling. "Do you want me to stay and fix supper?"

"No, that won't be necessary. Thank you so much for your help today."

As Helen got her coat on, Dorothy pulled some bills out of her purse and handed them to her, saying again, "Thank you, Helen, for coming so quickly."

But Helen refused the offer of payment. "Not this time,

Dorothy. I really wanted to be here for you today—simply as a friend."

Dorothy gave the dear lady a hug and thanked her again; then Nolan offered to drive Helen home. "I'll be right with you," he said as the older lady stepped out the door and headed down the front walk. Speaking quietly, he told Dorothy, "You get the kids ready, and soon as I take Helen home I'll come back in time to get you all to the church. Then we'll go out after the meeting and find a good spot to eat unhealthy hamburgers and greasy fries." He flashed a quick smile.

Another weight that had burdened her heart lifted from Dorothy. She had been dreading spending the evening alone, and now she smiled. "All right. I'll get them ready."

An hour later, Nolan returned and the four of them drove to the church. The children went to the nursery while Dorothy and Nolan took part in a brief meeting of the youth committee. It was only six-thirty when the meeting dismissed, and half an hour later they were perched on stools in a small diner. Phillip loudly ordered his "hang-ga-ber," drawing smiles from a number of nearby patrons, and Amelia asked for hot dogs. They smeared mustard liberally on them and downed them with gusto.

"I think those kids would eat anything," Nolan grinned. He reached over and tousled Phillip's hair and said, "Don't eat so fast. Nobody's going to take it away from you."

"These are good hamburgers," Dorothy said. "They make them better at a cafe than I can make them at home."

"That's the old stale grease they use," Nolan said and winked.

"Oh, don't be silly."

When they had finished their meal, they walked down one of the streets for a time looking in all the windows, then they got in the car and drove back to the parsonage. Dorothy started to say good-night, but it was early and she still dreaded being alone. "Come in and have a cup of coffee, Nolan."

"I think I could use it, and these kids have demanded a story."

Dorothy led the way in, and soon they were all in the living room. Nolan sat cross-legged on the floor and began telling the children a story. After a time, his eye lit on the gramophone, and he said, "Do you know how that thing got invented?"

Dorothy looked up with surprise. "Why, Edison invented it, didn't he?"

"Well, more or less. He made a machine that would record

some kind of sound, but actually it was all on cylinders, inconvenient and expensive. A fellow named Emile Berliner should have gotten the credit. He was the one who invented that flat disk and a way to duplicate them." He went into a long explanation of how the master record was made on a disk of zinc, and finally said, "Not everybody likes gramophones."

"Why, I think they're wonderful. My favorite is Enrico Caruso."

"Well, I suppose Caruso liked it. He made a fortune off of making records, but did you ever hear of John Philip Sousa?"

"You mean the man who wrote all those marches?"

"That's him. He wrote 'Stars and Stripes Forever.' I think that brought him about three hundred thousand dollars, but he thought phonograph records were awful."

"Why would he think that?"

"He thought music should come from the soul, and a machine doesn't have a soul. I remember he got pretty rabid about it. He said mothers would be recording their lullabies on a record and making babies listen to them."

"That's foolish!"

"Sure is! Myself, I've got quite a collection. Maybe you'd like to borrow some of them." He began to name off the records he had.

"I love music," Dorothy commented.

They talked about all kinds of music, until the children grew cranky. Dorothy picked up Phillip and said, "I'd forgotten the time. I've got to put them to bed." The children were so sleepy they went without protest.

When she came back she found Nolan standing beside the gramophone, going through the flat disks reading the labels. "You have a good selection, Dorothy."

Turning from the gramophone, he said, "I guess I'd better get going." He stepped over to Dorothy and took her hands in his. "Dorothy, I can tell you loved your father greatly. I'm so sorry about your loss."

Their day together had helped Dorothy keep her mind off of her father's death, but Nolan's words spoken so gently, and the compassion in his eyes, brought her loss back to her with a keenness she could not deny. She dropped her head, struggling against the sudden emotion, but the tears began to flow, and she found herself weeping uncontrollably.

Nolan Cole put his arms around her as the wave of grief overwhelmed her. There was a fierce quality to her weeping, and she no longer cared if someone saw her or heard her. She held on to the lapels of his coat and pressed her face against his chest. His arms around her were strong and warm, and he said nothing, but she could feel his sympathy.

Finally the storm passed. Nolan released her, and when she looked up, he suddenly leaned forward and kissed her tears-tained cheek and whispered, "I'll be thinking of you. Call me if you need me." He released her and quietly left the house.

Dorothy heard the front door close, and in the sudden silence of the room, the sense of loss and loneliness threatened to overwhelm her again. She quickly turned out the lights and fled down the hallway to the bedroom. After she had bathed, put on her gown, and lay down in the darkness, she let the events of the day flow through her mind. She remembered how miserable she was when she had left the house that morning, and how Nolan had lifted her spirits with his tender concern.

"He took it all away—all my grief," she whispered. A thought came to her very clearly, which she did not speak aloud. *Nolan Cole is more aware of a woman's needs than Andrew. How strange! A man who's never had a wife but who knows what a woman craves and needs. . . .*

CHAPTER SIXTEEN

A LITTLE PEACE OF MIND

★ ★ ★ ★

Priscilla straightened the hat on her head and examined it critically in the mirror. Her thoughts suddenly flashed back to the days when she was an unhappy girl at her home in Wyoming. She had plastered her walls with pictures of famous actors and actresses and read every scrap of news about them she could get. She had been so desperately certain that if she could become an actress, then all the world would be bright and exciting, and her happiness would be complete.

"Well, I've got it. The thing I always wanted," she muttered, pushing the hat around. It had cost more than any outfit she had ever bought while she was growing up, but somehow she took no pleasure in it. It was a yellow and white taffeta hat with a broad brim and white ostrich plumes, and it matched her dress perfectly. Still, she found herself feeling slightly depressed and listless as she applied a little powder to her cheeks. She wondered, as she often had, if she had missed something in life, but could not determine what it was. As she thought of her future, she tried to picture more success on the stage, which meant more money and more hats. Any hats she wanted—but the thought brought no thrill with it.

Disturbed by her thoughts, she rose, put on a light cream-colored jacket, and left the house feeling strangely deflated. When she arrived at the studio, she went through the scenes that Lem had planned, performing mechanically without feeling greatly excited by it.

Right after the last scene, Todd came to her and said, "Come along. We're going to celebrate."

"Celebrate what?" Todd was always finding something to celebrate, and she had told him once that he would celebrate the birth of a groundhog if nothing else offered itself.

This time, however, he was practically glowing with excitement, but he said only, "I'll tell you after dinner if you're a good girl."

"All right, Todd."

They went to the Silver Slipper, one of the most expensive restaurants in Los Angeles, and Todd ordered an entree for the two of them with an exotic foreign name. The waiter brought it out on a silver platter, carefully setting it on a stand by their table, and with a practiced hand, he poured a clear liquid over the entree, then lit a match to it. The whole dish flared with a beautiful blue flame.

Priscilla watched this little drama with delight as the flame died and the waiter began to lay the portions out on their plates. "If my dad were here," she laughed, "he would have jumped up and thrown a bucket of water over that thing."

"He must be quite a man, your dad."

"The best man I ever knew," Priscilla said quietly. "He and Mother have had the happiest marriage I've ever known. They would do anything for each other. Not a selfish bone in either one of them. Not like me," she ended glumly.

"Hey! Stop putting yourself down!" Blakely protested. He reached over and squeezed her hand. "Enjoy your meal first," he said. "Then I'll tell your fortune."

Smiling briefly, Priscilla shook her head. "I don't believe in fortune-telling."

"You'll believe this one," Todd said confidently. "Now, eat hearty."

Priscilla enjoyed her meal but could not work up any intense curiosity about Todd's surprise. It was probably a trip to Sacramento or San Diego. He was constantly pressuring her to accompany him on one of these trips—which she never did.

Finally, as she leaned back and sipped her cup of coffee, she said, "Well, let's have it."

"All right, here it is, Priscilla. I've had an offer from Carl Maxwell."

Despite herself, Priscilla was impressed. Carl Maxwell was one of the two or three producers on Broadway who could make a star out of a waitress or a mechanic. Leaning forward, she asked, "What sort of a play is it?"

"That's another surprise. It's by Terrence Block." Todd grinned broadly when he saw her reaction. "I thought that would interest you. Block's written three hit plays in a row, and Maxwell tells me this one is better than any of them."

"I'm glad for you, Todd. I suppose you'll be leaving for New York as soon as the serial is completed."

"Not quite. I have another serial to finish, but you haven't heard the real surprise yet. I'll tell you that when I get you home, if you treat me right, that is."

"Don't bank on that," Priscilla said dryly. Blakely had tried every possible means to get himself invited into her apartment with no success whatsoever. Now Priscilla leaned back and shook her head. "Why do you keep after me, Todd? Women flock all around you. You could have almost anyone you want, and most of them are prettier than I am."

Blakely smiled and shook his head. "I guess it's the case of wanting what you can't have. When I was a boy, all my parents had to do to make me do something was to tell me I *couldn't* do it."

"Sounds just like you," Priscilla laughed. "But when I say you can't come into my apartment, I mean it. And you might as well make up your mind to it."

"Well, maybe that's part of the surprise," Blakely said.

He was a fine-looking man, his face not even lined by the dissipation she knew characterized his lifestyle. His features were smooth, and he had an attractive cast to his long lips. He was one of those men whose features fit together perfectly. *Almost too perfectly*, she thought.

They left the restaurant shortly after, and she asked him twice what the surprise was, but he waited until they were at her front door, then said, "Now, ask me in, and I'll tell you."

He stepped forward, but she put her hand on his chest and smiled, shaking her head. "A good try, but no cigar, Todd. I'll just have to do without the surprise."

She turned to go inside, but he took her arm and shrugged.

"All right. I didn't really expect to get inside your citadel there. But here's the surprise. Maxwell has agreed to give you a contract to do the lead lady's role in Block's new play."

Priscilla blinked. "Well," she whispered, "that *is* a surprise!"

"I'd think so. Any actress in the world would jump at the opportunity to star in anything written by Block and produced by Maxwell. Well, I guess my surprise did catch you off guard." He pulled her forward, and she knew he was going to kiss her, and she permitted it. When he moved his head back, he said, "I've never met a woman like you, Priscilla."

"You said that before," Priscilla said, but she noticed a certain seriousness about him that was unusual.

"I might have. But I mean it, Priscilla. I suppose it's your innocence. There's not much of that admirable quality left in our world, is there? And some women put it on like a costume and take it off when it suits them, but you really *are* innocent."

"I'm not all that innocent, Todd. You know about me."

"Eddie Rich? That doesn't count. You were trapped into that relationship by that swine. He deceived you!"

"Nevertheless, I'm sort of shop-worn goods," she said with a slight strain of bitterness in her tone.

"Don't think of it like that!" He reached up, stroked her hair, and they stood silently for a minute. When he kissed her again, Priscilla felt her heart flutter in a way she never had before. He seemed different tonight. He stepped back and kissed her hands, saying, "Good night. We'll talk about this later." Then he wheeled and left, leaving her staring after him.

Priscilla was surprised at his capitulation. Usually it was a battle to keep him out, but as she turned and entered her apartment, she stopped and thought, *What do I really feel for Todd?* She stood there pondering the question, thinking of all the times they had spent together. This last caress had been somehow different. "Am I falling in love with him?" she asked aloud, then her mouth twisted with a wry expression. "If I start talking to myself, they'll lock me up," she muttered under her breath.

★ ★ ★ ★

The next week was difficult for Priscilla. She could not put her mind on her work. The offer to do a play with Carl Maxwell back in the East was a big decision. Blakely was surprised that she was even considering *not* doing it. "How can you even think of doing anything else, Priscilla? You'll never get another big chance like this!"

"I know, but I'd have to move back to New York, and I'm not sure I'm ready for that."

"It'll be different," Blakely said. "I'll be there with you. We'll set that town on its ear. You'll have Broadway at your feet, and the whole city!"

Priscilla listened to him, but at the same time she was being pressured by Porter to sign a contract for another serial. She knew she had grown tired of the movie business and longed to be back on the stage, but Porter's offer would allow her to stay in California close to her family. Never had she felt so confused.

Finally, two days before the last scenes were shot, Peter came and took her out for dinner to Carlo's, a small Italian restaurant near the studio. As he sat across from her, expertly rolling his spaghetti up on a fork, he talked cheerfully about his racing car, his eyes bright with excitement.

"I'm glad you named it after Jolie. That was sweet."

"Well, she liked it. You know," he said with some surprise, "she's actually pretty good at mechanics. Nothing big, but she knows how to change oil and spark plugs, and she likes to fool around with a car. And she's a pretty good driver, too, for a woman."

"For a woman!" Priscilla said. "I don't like the sound of that."

A humorous glint appeared in Peter's eyes, and he stopped eating his spaghetti long enough to reach into his pocket. "I've given a lot of thought to women, and now I've found out that I've been pretty well right all along."

"What do you mean by that?"

"Well, I always felt they were a little bit savage. Not quite civilized, you know."

Priscilla found his foolishness amusing. "You're the savage, Peter," she said. "Not me."

As they talked and enjoyed their meal, Peter's quick eyes saw that Priscilla was not herself. "You're getting stale, aren't you, sis?"

Looking up with surprise, Priscilla smiled wryly. "You're pretty sharp, Peter." She told him about the two offers, adding, "My head's going around in a whirl. Sometimes I just want to leave it all and go someplace and do something I've never done before—anything to get away for a while."

Peter leaned back and studied her carefully for a moment. Then he said, "Let's do it, then!"

Startled, Priscilla said, "Do what?"

Peter leaned forward and took her hand and held it. "Let's go home for a visit. We haven't seen the folks in a long time. I'm sort of tired myself. I could use a little vacation."

"Why, we can't do that!"

"Why can't we? The serial will be over tomorrow or the next day, and you've got plenty of money, and I've got a good car."

The more Peter spoke, the more Priscilla was intrigued with the idea. "How long would it take?" she asked.

"What difference does it make? We'll stop when we get tired, eat when we get hungry, drink when we get dry. It'll be a big surprise for the folks, and I'd like to smell some of that fresh Wyoming air. Let's do it!"

Impulsively, Priscilla agreed with her brother. "All right," she said. "We'll go as soon as the serial's over. Maybe Thursday." She leaned forward and patted his cheek. "You're good medicine, Peter. This savage woman needs someone like you!"

★ ★ ★ ★

The next day Peter told Easy he was going home and asked him to come along. Easy shook his head firmly. "Nope. I reckon I'll head up to Frisco. I've got a friend there I haven't seen in a long time, if he's out of jail. You go and have a good time."

Later that day Peter stopped Jolie as she was walking across the set with an armload of scripts. "Priscilla and I are going home to Wyoming to see our folks day after tomorrow. I'd like to have you come along, Jolie."

Jolie was taken aback. "Why, I couldn't do that."

"Why not?"

"Why, I'm right in the middle of my studies. I'm afraid if I quit, I'll lose what little learning I got."

"Well, I think that's wrong," Peter said. "You don't learn everything out of a book. You've never been on a cattle ranch, have you?"

"No. You know I haven't."

"We'll call it a field trip. I'll show you how cattle are raised and how a ranch operates. That could come in handy if you marry a wealthy rancher someday, or if you marry a poor one, for that matter."

Jolie pursed her lips and thought rapidly. "If you really want me to go, Peter, I will. I'll tell Tom we'll be gone for—how long?"

"Oh, probably a few weeks. When we get there, we'll relax and put you on a horse and go packing. It'll be a lot of fun."

"It sounds wonderful, Peter. Thank you." As he turned and walked away, Jolie watched him go, thinking of how much this tall young man had brought into her life. *I may have saved his life when he was about to get thrown off that train*, she thought, *but he's paid it all back a hundred times.*

★ ★ ★ ★

The trip from Los Angeles to the ranch was a delight to all three of them. Some of the roads were practically nonexistent, and Priscilla had commandeered a large Maxwell touring car instead of the race car that Peter proposed to drive. "I'm not going to be packed in that little old car, the three of us, all the way to Wyoming," she had stated flatly. And Porter, still anxious to sign her to another contract, had been glad to furnish the transportation.

It was the middle of June 1906, and unseasonably hot, especially after they left the coast. The heat beat down unrelentingly, and dust clouds rose behind them as they headed into the mountains. Overhead the bright blue skies were cloudless. At night they stopped wherever they could find an inn or hotel in some of the small towns, avoiding the large cities.

It was a time of release for Priscilla. As soon as they left Los Angeles, she immediately put all the problems of decision making behind her. She and Jolie became very close, laughing at Peter's foolishness, and sharing the same room when they stopped each night.

They arrived at the ranch at dusk, and Peter stopped the car a short distance from the house. "Look! Mom and Dad are on the front porch. Bet they think we're traveling salesmen," Peter grinned. Then he pulled up in front of the porch with a great clashing of brakes, stood up, and yelled, "Hey! Is supper ready?"

Dan and Hope Winslow leaped to their feet and ran out to the car. Dan threw his arms around Priscilla, lifting her clear off the ground, and whirled her around. "I ought to paddle you for springing this on me!" he growled. "Why didn't you tell us you were coming?"

"We wanted to surprise you!" Priscilla laughed. She hugged her father, then turned to her mother and exchanged embraces. "Mom, you're looking younger."

"Now, don't try to pull that theater talk on an old woman!" Hope said in a sprightly fashion. Then she turned and said, "And who is this you brought with you?"

Peter said at once, "Oh, this is a good friend of ours, Jolie Devorak. Jolie, these are my parents, Dan and Hope Winslow."

"Well, it's real nice that you came with the children," Hope said. She went forward and kissed Jolie's cheek impulsively, not seeming to notice the scar on the young woman's face. "Have you ever been on a ranch before?"

"No, ma'am," Jolie said shyly, embarrassed by the kiss, and yet pleased at Hope's warm acceptance. She was not at all sure of herself in this strange world, but as Peter took her arm and guided her inside, she began to feel better.

As the rest bounded up the front porch, Priscilla and Hope held back for a moment. Arm in arm, they turned and looked out over the front yard of the ranch. The rose bushes near the porch were in full bloom this time of year and Priscilla noticed the barn was almost packed with hay. A herd of beef cattle were grazing in a nearby field. Sighing, she turned toward her mother. "You have no idea how much I needed this trip."

Without uttering a word, Hope patted Priscilla's arm and gently kissed her cheek.

★　★　★　★

That night as the two young women prepared for bed, Jolie looked around the room at all the pictures of actors and actresses, all of the mementos of childhood, even some dresses that Priscilla must have worn when she was no more than ten or twelve. "It must've been wonderful growing up in the same place with fine parents like you have. I bet you had a happy time here."

Priscilla turned and studied the younger woman. "I should have," she said quietly, "but I made quite a pest out of myself. I never realized how good I had it back then. All I could talk about were all of these actors and actresses. I guess because I always wanted to go east and see them, nothing seemed good enough here. At the time, Jason was the foreman, and I treated him shamefully," she added quietly. "I wish he'd come with us, but he couldn't get away."

The two girls slipped into their nightgowns and crawled into bed. Jolie lay awake for a long time, enjoying the sense of enormous space all around her. As they had driven onto the ranch, she had seen the mountains in the distance and the flat tableland that stretched all the way to the horizon. Finally she went to sleep thinking of how nice it was to be a part of a family . . . in a way.

*　*　*　*

"But I'm afraid, Peter. That horse looks mean."

Two days after they arrived, Peter had brought Jolie out after breakfast to the corral and saddled a buckskin mare. "Don't worry. Princess won't do anything to disturb you. She won't do more than a slow walk. Here, put your foot right in the stirrup." He had shortened the stirrups for Jolie and had held on to her arm while she gingerly put her foot in, then he boosted her up. "Throw your leg over, and you're there. You see?"

Jolie looked down from her perch and held on to the saddle horn grimly. "I'd rather ride in the car, Peter."

"Ah, cars are nice, too. Here, these are the reins. Hang on to them while I get mounted."

"But she may run away!" Jolie said.

"Not Princess!" Peter insisted. He swung easily into the saddle with a grace that Jolie had always admired and pulled the bay up close. "Come along," he said.

"How do I make her go?"

"Kick her in the sides, shake the reins, and say, 'Giddy up!' "

Apprehensively, Jolie gave the mare a minor sort of kick, and to her surprise Princess stepped out slowly. She hung on to the reins with one hand and the saddle horn in the other.

Peter laughed, saying, "Settle back. Princess is a lady."

For the next hour, Jolie grew accustomed to the sedate pace of the mare and was able to look around. Peter took her on a tour of the ranch, explaining the various aspects of ranching. As they headed back, he grinned and said, "You're doing fine. You want to try a little trot?"

"I guess not," Jolie said cautiously. "Not today."

"All right," Peter said. He slouched in the saddle, his eyes constantly searching the horizon. His flat-crowned gray hat was pulled down over his eyes, shading them from the August sun, and he seemed almost a part of the handsome bay. He looked like he belonged to the land.

"Peter," Jolie said, "I love your parents."

"Well, so do I," he grinned at her. "They like you, too."

Jolie's hand went to the scar, as it frequently did, and Peter suddenly said, "Jolie, have you ever been to a doctor to see about that scar?"

"No, I haven't." The girl's answer was curt. She did not like to be reminded of it and now turned her face fully away.

"Don't turn away from me, Jolie," Peter said quietly. "I don't know much about such things, but I know doctors can do a lot."

"They can't help me."

"How do you know that? You've never been to one to find out," Peter argued reasonably. "As soon as we get back to Los Angeles, we're going to go have an expert surgeon take a look at it."

"What good would it do? It would cost too much even if something could be done."

"I know what my mom would say."

"What would she say? She wouldn't talk about my scar."

"She'd say, 'The Lord owns every doctor's office in the world, and if He wants Jolie Devorak to get treated by one, it'll happen.' " He smiled gently and said, "Mom's always one to believe that God will do what has to be done."

Jolie turned to glance at him. She truly admired him, with his easygoing nature and handsome, masculine features. "Do you believe that, Peter?" she asked quietly.

"I believe it because Mom and Dad do, but I think it's something you have to try for yourself before it's any good." He did not speak for a while and seemed troubled. "Sis is a Christian, and so is Cass and Cody. I'm the black sheep."

"I'm a black sheep, too."

He looked over, pulled his horse closer to hers, and slapped Jolie lightly on the back. "Then we'll form a flock of the black sheep of Wyoming," he said, smiling.

"It's all right as long as we're both together. Sheep aren't so bad."

"You don't know 'em like I do," Peter said with a cynical twist to his lips. "Dumbest animal on the face of the earth."

"But the little ones are cute, aren't they?"

"Yes, they're cute—they're delicious, too."

"Peter, don't talk like that!"

"Well, why are you so holy? I noticed you bucked into that bacon this morning. Those little pigs were cute, just like lambs."

He teased her all the way back to the ranch, and as she stepped down, he said, "Tomorrow we'll take a longer trip. Go out to the river and maybe have a picnic."

★   ★   ★   ★

"What about this young friend you brought along, Priscilla?" Dan inquired. "Where did you say she was from?" He had walked out to the edge of the corrals with his daughter, and the two had leaned against the bars studying the horizon. The sun was starting to dip low in the sky, casting Priscilla's eyes into the deeper shadows. She turned to face her father, and after a moment's pause, she said, "It's hard to say, Dad. It's rather strange the way Peter picked her up." She had already told him of how Peter had found Easy and Jolie, and now she said thoughtfully, "She seemed almost like a little girl then, but this last year she's matured into a lovely young woman, except for that scar. Too bad about that."

"Peter's told me he's going to take her to a surgeon to have him look at it."

"I imagine she's pretty sensitive. Any young woman would be."

"Yes, she always keeps her face turned away. I hope it works out for her."

The two talked on and after a while walked on down to the tiny creek that wound its way in a serpentine fashion around a group of cottonwoods. They stood looking down, and Priscilla said, "I remember how I used to come out and try to swim in this creek when it was up. Nearly drowned a few times."

"I remember that," he said. Dan Winslow was sixty-two, but still strong and hale and intensely masculine. He looked over at this daughter of his and had long thoughts that marked the creases of his mouth as he moved his lips slightly. "You were quite a handful to raise," he smiled. "But you've turned out real well, daughter."

"I was just *awful*, Dad," she said emphatically. "I don't know why you didn't throw me in the well."

"Wanted to a few times," Dan grinned, then reached over and passed his hand over her thick, lustrous hair that caught the last glows of the sun. "But I'm glad I didn't now. Are you happy?" he asked abruptly.

Priscilla was almost ready to give a quick, easy answer, but her conscience prodded her to be completely honest. This was not always easy for her. She dreaded opening herself up to anyone. But she knew her father loved her and would always be there for her, as he had been in the past. During her rebellious years, they had had some rather fierce disputes, but after they were over, her father had always come over and put his arms around her and kissed her, saying, "We can fuss and fight all we want to, but after it's over, you're still my little girl." He had been the rock of stability in her life, and now as Priscilla turned away from him slightly, a troubled expression clouded her eyes. Finally she turned around and said frankly, "I don't know, Dad. I've got everything I ever wanted, but somehow it just doesn't seem like enough."

Dan studied his daughter's face carefully, admiring the clean sweep of her jawline and the depth of her gaze. "You want to tell me about it?"

Priscilla told him about the decision that confronted her and how confused it made her. Finally, she gave a halfhearted laugh and said, "I haven't been a Christian all that long, Dad. But I thought Christians were supposed to have peace."

"You're right about that. Jesus said, 'My peace I give unto you,' and Jesus never told anything but the truth."

"Why don't I have it, then?" Priscilla frowned.

Dan hesitated, not wanting to preach a sermon. He said simply, "I think peace is a little bit harder to come by than most people think."

"Even after we've become followers of Christ?"

"Even then. You see, daughter, our peace is not *ours*. It comes directly from God, and Jesus said, 'My peace I *give* unto you.' We can't trick Him into giving to us. And sometimes there are things in our heart, I think, that keep us from taking the best God has for us."

"Why wouldn't anyone want peace? If it's there for the taking, I want it."

Dan Winslow's heart ached for his daughter. It had for a long time. He put his arm around her, saying gently, "Well, daughter, I know one thing, the peace that the world offers will never satisfy. Jesus longs for you to accept His peace."

Priscilla looked long and questioningly at her father. Her trembling lips tightened as she blinked away a tiny tear.

CHAPTER SEVENTEEN

"YOU'RE NOT MY FATHER!"

★   ★   ★   ★

The summer of 1906 was a happy one for Jolie Devorak. The stability that had come into her life sank deep down into her, and her face glowed with satisfaction. All summer long she worked for Imperial Pictures, went to automobile races with Peter and Easy, and continued her studies with Tom Ziegler. She grew very fond of that young man who was so very serious, but all during that summer, and even into fall, she never went back to his house. The one visit with his mother had intimidated her.

"You need to learn about what's going on in the world," Tom told her one day.

"What for?" she asked. "I don't live in China. Why should I know what's going on there?"

Tom looked up from the book he was holding and gave Jolie an astonished and sorrowful look. Somehow the emotions mixed together. His lean face seemed to stretch as he said, "You live in the world. We all do. There's a part of a sermon that I'd like for you to read. It's from a man named John Donne who lived back in the seventeenth century." He leaned back and quoted, " 'No man is an island entire of itself. We are all part of the continent, so that if a piece is broken off, the whole continent suffers.' " He shrugged and said, "That's not exact, but you see what he means, don't you?"

Jolie had become quite adept at interpreting the intricacies of literature and poetry. She was wearing her white coveralls that she wore to the races with *Jolie Blonde* on the back and looked very pretty. She had washed her hair the night before, and it was always extremely curly after that. Now she pushed her hair aside and said, "I think I see that. Somehow we're all together, even though we're far apart." She smiled brilliantly, her teeth gleaming against the golden tan she had from going to the races and being out in the sun. "I guess it's like we're all in a big boat, isn't it? Even if we don't know everyone on the boat, we're all together on the same journey."

Tom was delighted. "That's exactly right! I think that's as good a metaphor as Donne's," he said.

Ever since that time, Jolie had taken more of an interest in newspapers and periodicals. That year, of course, the San Francisco earthquake had been the big story in America. Five hundred people died suddenly in the catastrophe of April 18. And tens of thousands of people had been left homeless in the aftermath. The damage was enormous, destroying three thousand acres in the center of the city. On an international scale, the war between Japan and Russia had finally ground to a halt the year before, with President Theodore Roosevelt acting as the negotiator of the peace. This year he had been awarded the Nobel Peace Prize for his contribution. The more Tom encouraged her, the more Jolie read. She grew interested in the labor struggles and finally came to understand the charges against Standard Oil, who were attacked in a hearing before the Interstate Commerce Commission. It was difficult for her, but she kept at it until finally she had a good grasp of the labor situation.

In August of that year, King Edward of England had traveled to Germany, where he spoke with Kaiser Wilhelm II. Tom told her how the political tensions were significant, and that all the nations of Europe were building up huge armies and navies. "Someday," he said, "there'll be a war over there."

"Will it come over here, do you think, Tom?"

"I don't think so, but it'll be terrible over there. And with all the trouble in Russia," he added, "there's no telling how many people will be killed."

She became aware of the great men and women who had died that year, including the great Norwegian dramatist Henrik Ibsen and the French painter Paul Cézanne, and read an article concerning a German professor named Arthur Korn who used a telegraph late that spring to send a photographic image more than a thousand miles. She had spoken about this to Priscilla, asking her, "Do you think one day they can take pictures of a play and send it into people's houses?"

"Oh no! That's not possible!" Priscilla had said. "Radios and telephones work, but they'll never be able to send pictures like they do messages."

Early one morning in August Jolie had brought a newspaper to her lesson. "Look here, Tom." She handed him the paper with a grin on her lips, and he read it aloud.

" 'Enrico Caruso survived his day in court. Vocal chords, if not honor, intact. The world-famous operatic tenor was charged with annoying a Miss Hannah Graham in the Central Park Zoo monkey house in New York City. Caruso protested his innocence in low, soft tones, preserving his voice for an approaching production of *La Bohème*. Some fellow admirers surrounded the singer and expressed their faith in him. A police officer present called him "curs and dogs," inviting hisses from the assembly.' "

Tom looked up with puzzlement. "Why did you mark this item?"

"Because it shows how silly people are," Jolie said, her eyes sparkling with indignation. "There he is the most famous tenor in the world, I suppose, making thousands of dollars, and he has to pick on a young woman in a monkey house. I think *he* deserves to be behind the bars instead of the monkeys!"

Tom smiled at her. "I think you're a little bit hard on the fellow. Maybe she was a very pretty young woman. Perhaps he only spoke to her. The paper doesn't say, and then again, maybe the woman was too touchy. He may have meant nothing at all, except being pleasant."

Two thin lines appeared between Jolie's dark eyebrows, and a frown brought the corners of her lips down. "I know all about men being *nice* and *attentive* to women," she said bitterly. "I've had to fight them off since I was thirteen years old."

Tom stirred uneasily in the swing. They were sitting together, books balanced on their laps. Tom did not answer for a moment. He had no easy solutions for the hardships Jolie had already suffered in her young life. His life had been so sheltered by his mother that he did not even know about things like this. From far away came the lonesome wail of the one-fifteen freight coming in from the east. When it died down, Tom turned to face her, saying simply, "You've had more experience in life than I have, although

I'm older and should have had experience with girls. When I was very young, I went straight home from school and started doing homework. Mother always demanded that I do more than the teacher assigned, so that I would always be first in the class." An odd light touched his gray eyes, and he said softly, "I guess I've missed a lot."

Jolie had long been puzzled about this side of Tom's life. All the young men she knew had been aggressive, except for Peter and Easy. From the first time they had met her, they had treated her kindly. She trusted them, but no other men. She had a guarded air about her whenever a young man began to talk to her, as if she had retired behind a high wall.

"You know, I guess I'm a little bit like that woman in the monkey house. Every time a man takes a strong interest in me, I throw my guard up because I figure he's just the same as my stepfather."

"You never thought that about me, I hope!" Tom was startled and turned to face her.

"No, of course not!" Suddenly Jolie broke out into delightful laughter. Her eyes seemed to crinkle until she could barely see, and she said, "I never thought of such a thing, Tom!" The idea amused her, and she shook her head, sending the curls cascading around her shoulders. "Why, you've never even tried to hold my hand!"

"I guess I wouldn't know how," Tom admitted bashfully.

"You really ought to pay more attention to girls," Jolie said. "Most men need to pay less, but I think you need to pay more."

Tom sat there silent for a moment, looking down at his long fingers holding the book. He closed it suddenly and put the book down, then looked up at her. "There is a young woman I admire, but I don't have any idea of how to go about telling her so."

"Who is she, Tom?"

He smiled but shook his head. "I wouldn't be telling that," he said. "It won't come to anything anyway."

Suddenly Jolie grew determined. "No reason why it can't," she said. "You're not a bad-looking fellow. You wear nice clothes, and you've got good manners. Why, lots of girls would be glad to have you come courting."

"I . . . I don't know how to start," Tom said nervously.

Jolie said, "Well, you can practice on me." His mouth opened with shock, and she laughed and reached over and patted his hand. "Just for practice. I'll tell you what. You know lots of poetry.

I bet you write some sometimes."

"Yes, I do. But it's not very good."

"Well, the next time you come, you write a pretty poem like some of those romantic poets you've been trying to get into my head. Then you talk to me just like I was a young woman you were calling on."

Tom looked at her strangely. "I suppose I could try."

"Go on. Try it now. You've got enough of that poetry in your head, I know. You must've memorized a truckload of it."

"I'd feel like a fool!"

"It's just practice," Jolie urged. "Go ahead. Recite me some poetry and then tell me how pretty I look."

Tom hesitated for a moment, then turned to her and began quoting a poem:

How do I love thee? Let me count the ways.
I love thee to the depth and height
My soul can reach, when feeling out of sight
For the ends of Being and ideal Grace.
I love thee to the level of everyday's
Most quiet need, by sun and candlelight.
I love thee freely, as men strive for Right;
I love thee purely, as they turn from Praise.
I love thee with the passion put to use
In my old griefs, and with my childhood's faith.
I love thee with a love I seemed to lose
With my lost saints—I love thee with the breath,
Smiles, tears, of all my life!—and, if God choose,
I shall but love thee better after death!

Jolie sat very still while he spoke, and when he finished, she breathed, "Oh, Tom! That's *beautiful!*"

Clearing his throat, Tom smiled shyly, then said, "Jolie, you . . . look very pretty today. You have the prettiest hair I ever saw." Abruptly, without warning, he reached over and took her hand, kissed it, then released it quickly, his face flaming with embarrassment.

Jolie, taken aback by the gesture, stared at him. Seeing his intense embarrassment, she said quickly, "That was wonderful, Tom." She reached over and grabbed the lapel of his coat and tugged it gently until he looked at her. "You don't need much practice," she teased. "Try it again next time."

"All right," Tom said, managing a smile. "I will."

The two had not noticed Peter who had walked up and paused at the foot of the steps. Suddenly Jolie caught a motion and turned to see him standing there. "Why, Peter, come on up and sit down." She laughed and said, "Tom's giving me lessons."

"I see he is." Peter's voice was cold and hard, and he came up on the steps and stood before them, his hands shoved deep into the pocket of his trousers. "Are your *lessons* about over?"

Tom Ziegler was aware that Peter had seen him kiss Jolie's hand, and he got up hastily and began stuffing books into the canvas bag he always brought them in. He muttered, "Yes, we're all through. I'll see you day after tomorrow, Jolie."

"All right, Tom. I'll finish that history book you wanted me to read." She watched as he scurried away, not looking back. His head was bent over, and his shoulders were slumped.

"Is this the kind of lesson you two have? Hand kissing?"

Jolie was astounded. "Why, Peter," she said, "that didn't mean anything!"

"What else is going on besides hand kissing?"

Jolie looked up and saw that Peter's face was tense. "Do you think I've been doing something wrong with Tom?" she demanded.

"I don't know. Have you?"

"If you think that, then there's no point in answering you! You've already got your mind made up!"

"If he kisses your hand, then I wouldn't be surprised if he did even more. And you didn't appear to be outraged."

"Tom Ziegler's a very sweet young man!" Jolie said, an anger growing in her. She was resentful of his accusations. "If you want to be jealous, then you ought to put your mind on Kenny French." French was one of the members of the crew who was constantly finding an excuse to put his hands on Jolie and beleaguered her to go out with him. "He's the one that's always finding some way to get his hands on me!"

"I'm not jealous!" Peter snapped. "I'm . . . I'm just *worried* about you. You're just a kid, and you don't know how easy it is to get in trouble!"

"It's none of your business! You're not my father!" Jolie snapped.

"It's a good thing for you I'm not!" Peter was furious and sorely upset by what he had seen. "If you were my daughter, I'd give you a lickin' so bad you wouldn't be able to sit down for a week!"

"That's what my stepfather did! Do you want to see the scar?" Jolie turned her face and pulled her hair back so that the scar was plainly visible.

Suddenly Peter realized what his angry words had just done. Jolie was trembling and staring at him with a hard look in her eyes that he had not seen since the first time he had met her in the boxcar. A wave of remorse washed over him, and he licked his lips trying to think of something to say.

"Good-bye, Peter!" Jolie turned and started to leave, but he caught her arm as she passed by. "Let go of me!"

Instantly Peter did. "Wait a minute, Jolie," Peter said quickly. He ducked his head and then shook it in a futile gesture. "I don't know what's the matter with me. I'm . . . I'm sorry, Jolie. I didn't mean to say those things. It's just—well, you are an attractive young woman, and I've seen some of them get into trouble. I just don't want anything to happen that would hurt you."

Jolie's anger instantly fled. "I'm sorry I lost my temper, Peter. But really, you don't understand about Tom. Do you know he's never had a girlfriend?" She went ahead to tell him how innocent and naive Tom Ziegler was, and Peter listened attentively. Finally she said, "So I just told him to read me some poetry and tell me I looked nice so that he would get used to talking to a girl. Then he'll find somebody. There's some young woman he's interested in, but he's too shy to talk to her."

"I wish I'd known that," Peter said, shaking his head ruefully. "I made a fool out of myself." He reached out his hand, and she put hers into it. He squeezed it and grinned crookedly. "I know you're straight as an arrow, Jolie. Just don't pay any attention to what I said." He hesitated, then said, "Don't guess you'd care to go for an ice cream soda?"

"Sure I would." Snatching up her straw hat, she tied it under her chin and took his arm. "Let's go. Maybe I'll have two sodas."

"Have three if you want," Peter said, and the two left the porch and proceeded down the street.

The incident was not forgotten, however, by either of them, and Jolie especially thought of it often. *He seems almost jealous. But he just didn't understand.*

★   ★   ★   ★

The scene was simple enough, at least from Priscilla's point of view. All she had to do was hang by a rope suspended from a beam overhead. A stagehand placed a short ladder under the rope. After she had climbed it and grasped the thick, rough strand, he pulled it away.

"All right, let's see some real terror on your face, Priscilla!" Lem shouted. He was only five feet away, but he had formed the habit of shouting commands so that he could be heard all over the set.

As the rope slowly unwound, Priscilla let it get her even with the camera and then opened her eyes wide and formed the words, "Help! Please help me!" with her lips. She did not even say them aloud, but had learned to overdo the words so that the viewers could read her lips.

She held on tightly as Lem called out more directions to the cameramen and lighting crew. Turning back to Priscilla, he said, "All right. Give us a nice scream and then let go of the rope!"

Priscilla tried to maintain the look of absolute terror, opened her lips and screamed, although she made no actual noise, and then let go of the rope. She dropped to a mattress that the tall stagehand had placed beneath her and let herself sprawl out to get out of range of the camera.

"Okay! That's it!" Lem said. "We'll call it a day here." He came over and stood beside her and helped her up. "That was fine, Priscilla. You looked scared out of your wits. We'll take it up tomorrow where you fall down into a pit of snakes."

Priscilla stared at him. "Real snakes?"

"They're real, but they're not poisonous," Lem assured her.

"I hate snakes!" Priscilla muttered.

"Well, we'll take a few shots of some big rattlers beforehand. The ones near you will just be bull snakes. At least that's what the fellow from the zoo promised me." He stared at her more closely. "I hate snakes myself. I wouldn't want to touch 'em. Are you sure you can do it?"

"I can do it as long as they're not poisonous." She shuddered and said, "I just don't care much for them."

Lem laughed and suddenly put his arm around her. "You've done a great job, Priscilla. I didn't believe there was an actress on earth without temperament, but I believe I've found one."

"Well, I'll probably dream about snakes tonight." Priscilla smiled, then turned and moved to her dressing room. She removed her boots and the riding jodhpurs and white silk blouse that were her standard costume for the serial. It was growing cold outside, so she put on a heavy cotton combination corset cover and knickers over black hose, then slipped into a green wool suit-dress. Grabbing up a hat that matched the dress, she left the dressing room. As she moved outside and headed for the door, she was surprised to see Dorothy Winslow waiting for her. The two had become fairly close. Dorothy had stopped by the studio several times during the summer to take her out to lunch. It had seemed to Priscilla that Dorothy was lonely, and now she moved forward with a smile, saying, "Why, Dorothy, how nice! I hope you've come to take me out to lunch."

"If you have time," Dorothy said. She was wearing a woolen suit-dress with a high neck and a pleated coat skirt over the narrow dress skirt. She had on high spats that matched the dress over black patent shoes and a tricorn hat of brushed beaver.

"I wish we knew someplace to get chili. I miss that from Wyoming."

Stan Lem was nearby and instantly replied, "Have you ever been to The Diner?"

"No, but I've seen it," Dorothy said. "It's that little restaurant they put into a railroad car, isn't it?"

"Yes, one of the Union Pacific's old dining cars. I've been there several times, and I had a bowl of chili there not long ago. I was surprised to find it was pretty good. Watch out if you go there, though. They'll put so many chili peppers in it, it'll take all the fur off your tongue." He grinned and left them, and the two women headed out of the studio.

"I wish one of us could drive," Dorothy said, "but we'll just have to go in a hansom, I guess."

"Someday they'll make a car that'll start just by pushing a button. I'm afraid those cranks are too hard to work, and besides, a lot of people have gotten their arms broken when it pops back." Priscilla got into the hansom cab, and Dorothy gave the instructions to the driver. They chatted on the way to the restaurant, mostly Dorothy listening as Priscilla gave her humorous version of the latest ending of the episode. ". . . So I dropped off the rope. To the audience it looked like I'm dropping twenty feet down into a pit. Tomorrow morning I'll get on a box, which will be out of the range of the camera, jump down, and they'll see me hit the bottom."

"That sounds like fun," Dorothy smiled. "I always enjoy watching you make these things. They're more fun than seeing the serials themselves."

"They're calling them *cliffhangers* now," Priscilla said. "Other studios are starting to produce them, too. I imagine, as is always the case, the market will soon be flooded with serials like *The Dangers of Darlene*."

When they arrived at the restaurant and went inside, they were delighted to find it unchanged and as charming as Lem had described it. It was broken up into tables with white tablecloths and glass vases with flowers. A waiter dressed in black with a white shirt came to take their order. He lifted his eyebrows when they both ordered chili. "With hot peppers or without?" he asked.

"With for me," Priscilla said. "You'd better not, Dorothy, if you're not used to western chili."

The two women sat there sipping iced tea, and finally when the chili came, Priscilla tasted it tentatively. "Oh, this is good!" she said. "Nice and hot. Just the way I like it."

Dorothy tried her bowl cautiously and said, "It is good, but I don't think I could take it with the chili peppers like you do. You must have a mouth like leather."

Priscilla took another spoonful and nodded. "We had chili all the time on the ranch. It was just like beans and bread, especially in the wintertime."

The two women enjoyed their meal and afterward tried some of the home-baked pies. Dorothy tried the lemon, while Priscilla had the chocolate. It was Priscilla who brought up the subject of the church, and for a time they talked about the new building.

"I suppose Andrew's as busy as he has ever been since the construction started," Priscilla said and was surprised to see the sudden disturbed look that came over her friend's face. "What's wrong, Dorothy?" she asked.

Dorothy had put the subject off as long as she could. She began to speak in a low voice, relating all that had happened since the death of her father. "I don't know what to do, Priscilla," she concluded miserably.

Priscilla listened intently, and after a moment's hesitation, said, "I know you're lonely, Dorothy, and you miss Andrew terribly. But I want to tell you something, and you mustn't take offense."

"What is it?" Dorothy sat up straighter, and a look of apprehension etched her features.

"It's about Reverend Cole," Priscilla said carefully. "There's been some talk that you're seeing too much of him."

Instantly Dorothy became defensive. "We work together with the youth program. It requires that we spend a great deal of time together."

Priscilla reached over and put her hand over Dorothy's and squeezed it. She smiled gently, saying, "I know there's nothing wrong, but you know better than I how careful a minister's wife has to be. People put you and the pastor up on a pedestal."

The words struck Dorothy Winslow hard, and her lips grew tight. She did not answer for a moment, but there was a rebellious cast to her lips as she said, "I don't want to be on a pedestal!"

"You can't help it. As Andrew's wife, it's only natural that people in the church are going to look up to you, Dorothy!"

"Well, they shouldn't!" Dorothy said abruptly, and then she realized how sharply she had spoken. "I'm sorry. I didn't mean to snap at you, but it's so unfair."

Priscilla hesitated, then said, "Dorothy, you know about what happened to me when I was younger, and how I made a bad mistake about a man back in New York. I think women have to be very careful."

"Why? Are they more responsible than men?"

"I think we're more emotional. We get lonely easily, and we get discouraged quickly. I think it's worse for us than for most men. A man can go out and bat a golf ball around or shout at a baseball game. Women can't take their frustrations and problems out that easily—at least *I* can't."

The truth of Priscilla's words struck Dorothy, and she sat there for a time quietly thinking about it. "What are they saying? What have you heard about me and Nolan?"

"Oh, nothing really bad! Just that he's come to your house when Andrew wasn't there."

"He took the children and me out for a meal after I got the news of my father's death. Andrew wasn't here then. He had just gone to a conference in Sacramento."

"That was kind of Nolan, I'm sure, but . . ." Priscilla hesitated, then said, "Nolan Cole is one of the most attractive men I've ever seen. More than any movie star, really, that I've met, or any actor. You're lonely, and—well, that's a bad combination, Dorothy."

"Are you telling me I shouldn't see him anymore?"

"Oh, I can't make your decision for you, Dorothy, but I do want to ask you to be careful."

Dorothy struggled between intemperance and affection for this beautiful woman who could have any friend she wanted but had taken the time to be with her. "There's nothing between Nolan and me," she said finally. "We're just friends. But I'll be more careful."

"I think that's wise."

They changed the subject then, and after leaving the restaurant, Dorothy had the cab take Priscilla to her apartment. They embraced and Dorothy kissed Priscilla on the cheek, saying, "Thanks for having lunch with me. It helps to have a good friend like you to talk to."

Afterward, in the carriage going home, Dorothy thought long and hard, and with some trepidation, about what Priscilla had said about her relationship with Nolan Cole. She knew she hadn't been completely honest with Priscilla about Nolan being simply a friend. She remembered his kiss on the porch, and the way he held her hands, and the intensity of his gaze. She knew in her heart that Priscilla was right. She could deny no longer that her feelings for Nolan were indeed improper. "I'll have to break it off and leave the youth program," she told herself with resolve.

In the days that followed, Dorothy thought about Priscilla's words. Yet each time Nolan asked her to get involved or go on an outing with the youth, his charming smile and enjoyable companionship was more than she could resist. She finally decided to continue with her work with Nolan, but admonished herself to be very careful. As the days passed, Priscilla's warning slipped away from Dorothy, and she found herself looking more and more forward to her youth work. And she would no longer admit to herself that it was not the young people she thought of so much as Nolan Cole himself.

CHAPTER EIGHTEEN

A MINOR ACCIDENT

★　★　★　★

At the end of the first week of December, Priscilla was restless. There had been no shooting for over a week that involved the cowboys, and she had not seen Jason for several days. Going to the stable, she saddled up a small iron gray mare and rode out to the open pastures where the herd was kept.

Jason heard the sound of a horse approaching at a fast gallop and looked up. When he saw it was Priscilla, a subtle change took place in his expression. By the time she rode up, he was able to simply smile and take his hat off. "Hello," he said as she pulled her horse up beside him. "No shooting today?"

"No, and I'm glad. I'm getting tired of it." Priscilla was wearing riding jodhpurs that she often wore in the serial, but the weather was cool, so she had donned a green and white wool mackinaw coat. A toboggan cap held her honey-colored hair in place except for a stray ringlet that had escaped and was exposed at her neck. The ride had brightened her cheeks and her eyes, and she slapped the mare on the neck and looked around at the milling herd. "They're getting fat, aren't they?"

"Be going to market soon, I expect," Jason said, looking at the grazing herd.

Surprised at Jason's reply, Priscilla quickly turned around. "The herd's going to be sold?"

"I reckon so. Most of it anyway. Porter talked to me about it a couple of days ago. The western thing is kind of running its course. He said he wanted to keep a fourth of the herd, and maybe just me and one more puncher to take care of 'em."

"What will he do when he needs a bunch of outlaws for a shot?"

"Don't guess there'll be much more of that," Jason drawled. He replaced his hat, shoved it back on his head, and examined her thoughtfully. "Not much for me to do around here when that happens."

Jason had mentioned leaving several times. He was unhappy, and Priscilla knew that she was the cause of it. Still, she could not help saying, "I wish you wouldn't leave, Jason. It would be lonely around here without you."

Jason smiled briefly, but there was no real warmth in it. "I don't reckon you'd miss me too much, Priscilla," he said finally. "Your time is pretty well taken up."

"I've tried to explain, Jason. I'm not really involved with Todd."

"I thought seeing someone on a regular basis was 'involved'!"

"I told him that our relationship will never go anywhere."

"Then why do you keep seeing him?"

"I . . . I don't know. I guess because he asks." It sounded foolish even to Priscilla's ears, and she laughed with a certain degree of embarrassment and her cheeks grew rosy. "I know that sounds silly."

Jason leaned forward, placing his hands on the horn of his saddle, and stood up on his stirrups and stretched. He had thought of little else but Priscilla lately, and many times had given her up for lost, as far as he was concerned. He felt a heavy grief at the thought of losing her, which he never expressed to anyone, not even his best friends on the crew. To himself he had been more honest, and as he looked at Priscilla, he thought, *I don't know why I stay around here tormenting myself with something I can't have, like a kid with his nose pressed against a candy store and no money in his pocket. I'd be better off back in Wyoming, or anywhere else for that matter.* Now he rocked back in the saddle and said, "Priscilla, I hate to say anything more about you and Blakely. But I think you're making a sad mistake. Oh, I know he's rich, and a famous star, and all that." He hesitated, then shook his head.

"What is it?" Priscilla asked, seeing a shadowed look in his eyes that troubled her. "What's the matter, Jason?"

"I think you're headed for a fall, Priscilla. You had one bad one, and I'll never rebuke you for it. It's all over as far as I'm concerned about Eddie Rich, but you were partly innocent in that. You didn't know about that man, but Todd Blakely is what he is."

"You think he's deceitful?"

"I think he's spoiled, used to his own way as far as women are concerned . . . and you're a challenge to his talents in that direction. Once he gets you, you won't be any more to him than any of the other women he's had."

Priscilla flushed at the implication, but she could not refute it. Lately, the same thought had occurred to her. Finally, unable to reply, she lifted her head and met his eyes. "I'm all mixed up, Jason. I had a long talk with Dad when I went for a visit. Some of the things he said—well . . . I've been thinking them over."

"Smart man your dad," Jason nodded. "Whatever he told you, you pay attention to it. Well, I'll be staying for a while. How about a race?" he said and grinned as she instantly lifted her head, and her eyes flashed. "You always did crave to beat me. Well, here's your chance. That's a pretty fast mare you got. What about that grove of cottonwoods over there by the road?"

"All right," she said. "There and back." She poised in the saddle as Jason wheeled his mount around, then said, "Go!" The two horses shot off, and Priscilla lost her cap before she had gone twenty yards. Her honey-colored hair flew out behind her as the mare galloped. She leaned forward in the saddle, and at least for the moment she managed to put all of her problems out of her mind.

Though Jason beat her only by a few yards, she still enjoyed her ride with him. Afterward the two of them went out and had lunch together. She took him to The Diner for good chili. For two hours they laughed and talked—very much like old times. When he took her back to her apartment, she turned to him and said, "Thanks for putting up with me, Jason. You're good medicine for me." She looked at him fondly and said, "Good old solid Jason. You never change."

"Cowboys never change. They just die," he grinned. He reached out, pulled her forward, and kissed her cheek. When she did not object, he kissed her on the lips. She responded for a moment, then when she pulled away, he shook his head. "You're very special to me," he whispered. "Good night, Priscilla."

Priscilla thought about those kisses for a long time. They were light, and yet she knew that behind them lay a deep love and passion that Jason Ballard kept tightly within proper bounds. She dreamed of him that night, but the next morning she could not remember what the dream was about. After eating breakfast, she picked up her Bible and read for a long time in the book of Proverbs, a book that had always fascinated her. The short, pithy sayings somehow caught in her mind, and she could not forget them. One of them that she read was, "A fair woman without discretion is like a jewel of gold in a swine's snout." At first the phrasing of the proverb amused her, and she murmured aloud, "I'd like to see Sue, our big old sow back home, with a diamond ring in her snout!"

The incongruity of it amused her, but later on that morning, after she was cleaning the apartment and sorting out her clothes, the proverb came back. *Without discretion.* She wasn't at all certain of the meaning of that word and looked it up in the dictionary. She read the definition aloud. "The freedom or authority to make decisions and choices. Power to judge or act." Another definition said, "Careful of what one does and says." She closed the dictionary and leaned back thoughtfully. "The power to choose or act," she mused. "I guess I've been without discretion, all right. But I don't want to be anymore." She closed her lips firmly and put the dictionary down. She knelt for a time of prayer with her heavenly Father, asking Him to help her become the woman *He* wanted her to be.

Finally she left the house, and after walking for a time, she decided to go talk to Andrew Winslow. She knew he was not aware of his failings as a husband—as least she didn't think so—but she knew he had a lot of experience and wisdom that might help her. And besides, he was family to her.

She went directly to the church, but the secretary, Mrs. Goodson, said, "I'm sorry, Miss Winslow, but the pastor's gone out to the new building. It's in the last stage, you know, and he stays there almost every day, and then half the night he spends with the contractor. Would you like to see Reverend Cole? I think he's in."

"No, I'll see Brother Winslow some other time." Priscilla left the church and went at once to the new building. It was located on highly valued property right in the middle of Los Angeles. Though the structural work was complete, workmen were still swarming all over it doing all the countless finishing jobs, outside and inside. She saw Andrew high up on a scaffold with three men and stood and watched for a while. He was gesticulating eloquently, and she could see the other two were listening as he talked. "He's too busy now," she murmured, so she turned and walked away.

She had dinner alone, then went back to her apartment and spent a quiet evening reading and stopping to pray for guidance from time to time. She had been impressed how many times the book of Proverbs mentioned wisdom, and she finally knelt down before she went to bed, buried her face on the bed covers, and sought God earnestly for a long time.

★ ★ ★ ★

Dorothy arose early, dressed, and paused to look at Andrew, who was still sleeping soundly. He had come in after eleven and had tried to be quiet to keep from waking her. She had not been asleep, however, but had pretended to be. Even in sleep, his face was tense, and he seemed to be having a disturbing dream. One hand opened and closed spasmodically.

Leaving the bedroom, she went to the kitchen and began to fix breakfast. Soon the children were up, which meant the usual struggle to get them dressed and fed and keep them occupied.

Andrew came into the kitchen wearing his favorite robe that was so old it was patched in several places. He had two new robes that had been given to him for gifts, one of them by Dorothy herself, but he always went back to this old one. She said now as he sat down, "What would you like for breakfast?"

"Oh, eggs, I guess, and some sausage if you have any."

"Yes, I think we have plenty." Dorothy went about cooking the sausages, and Andrew slumped in a chair at the table and read the front page of the paper. When she brought his plate of food, he tossed the paper aside and said, "You've already eaten?"

"Yes, I ate with the children."

"Well, sit down and talk to me while I eat, then."

He began to eat and listened as Dorothy told him about the new tooth that Phillip was getting, and other small things, all of it about the children.

Andrew listened and made a few small comments. After he had finished his breakfast, he sat back and sipped his coffee. "The building is almost finished." He saw how tired she looked and said, "You're not as excited about it as I thought you would be."

"It's going to be a fine building," Dorothy commented flatly.

She did not care in the least for the building and had wished many times that the project had never been started. She saw it as the enemy that had taken her husband away from her and wrecked her family. But she dared say none of this to Andrew.

Seeing that she was indifferent, Andrew said, "You and Nolan are working on the Christmas program, aren't you?"

"Yes, it's well underway."

"Does it look good?"

"Oh yes. There's plenty of talent, and Nolan's an excellent musician." She went ahead briefly to describe her part in the program, which was mostly helping with the costumes and prompting for the speaking parts.

Andrew picked up another piece of toast, nibbled at it without appetite, then put it down. Shaking his head, he said, "I've got to go to Sacramento with the building committee. We had to spend more money than we thought, and First National here says we need to get the loan elsewhere. We've got too much wrapped up. I was a little surprised at Brother Parsley. I thought he could swing it for us."

"When do you have to go, Andrew?"

"Day after tomorrow."

He looked at her and saw her disappointment. "I won't be gone long. Only a couple of days." He saw her lips grow tight and suddenly felt a surge of irritation. "Dorothy, sometimes I don't think you care anything about the church or the work we do here!"

Dorothy looked up quickly, and an answer leaped to her lips, but she knew he would never accept it. For days she had been growing more and more withdrawn. The only things she had any enthusiasm for were the children and the Christmas program. She said quietly, "I'm grateful that the church is doing well."

"Well, why don't you show it more, then?"

Before she could think, the bitter words she had held in for so long escaped. "Why don't you show yourself to be more of a husband than you have, then?" She mocked his tone and got up angrily, distressed that she had spoken out so.

Andrew rose at once, caught her, and turned her around. "Why would you say a thing like that? I've explained a hundred times how this building project is not a thing that can be put off! It's not something I can delegate! It's what God has given me to do!"

"And God didn't give you a family to take care of?"

Though there was a stinging truth in her words that Andrew had kept in the back of his mind, he shook his head and denied the charge. "We all have to make sacrifices. Do you think it's easy on me being away from you and the children all the time?"

Suddenly Dorothy gave up. She saw that his lips were set with determination, and his eyes had that certain glint that revealed the stubbornness she knew lay deep within him. She had always admired it, because he was a man who was firm in his duty, but now she felt so far away from him that she said slowly, in a voice that was hollow and with eyes that seemed to be dead, "Andrew, I don't feel like a wife anymore." She turned and pulled away from him.

Andrew stood stock still for a moment and watched as Dorothy left the room. He loved his wife dearly. Yet her words were so filled with grief that he suddenly realized he could not let them stand. Quickly he moved forward and caught her as she was going toward the bedroom. "Come back and let's talk about it, Dorothy. I can't put off my trip to Sacramento, but as soon as I get back—"

"Oh yes, we'll go to that little camp out on the beach. Just you and me and the children, and we'll have time just for each other." Dorothy saw his face color in shame. They both knew he had said this to her not once but many times.

For one moment Andrew could not speak, then he said, "Dorothy, I think you ought to see Dr. Gunn. You're tired and run-down. Maybe he can give you a tonic."

"What I need isn't a tonic," she said wearily and turned again, pulling away from his hand.

"Well, what do you want, then?" he said angrily.

Dorothy Winslow stopped and turned to him. "I want," she said deliberately, "to have a husband who cares for me. I want a husband sitting in front of the fire with me at nights after the children have gone to bed so that I can talk to him and tell him what's in my heart, and I want him to tell me what's in his. I want a husband to take me to a place out on the beach where we can walk and feel the wind and the sun, and enjoy being together as a husband and wife should. I want to look out the window and see my children playing with my husband and know that they feel secure with their father."

Andrew listened and the words cut him. "Is there anything

else you want?" he asked harshly.

Dorothy looked him full in the face. "I want a husband who knows how to love me intimately—which you don't, Andrew. You haven't the slightest idea about what a woman needs in that way!" She waited for him to speak, but instead his face suddenly stretched with an emotion she could not identify. He turned and walked away, and she heard the door slam outside. For a moment she stood there. Then she went to her bedroom and sat down on the bed. Her mind felt numb. The scene had drawn every last resource of emotion she had left in her. She had said things to him that she never thought she would hear herself say, and now she could not feel sorrow for it, only a great sense of emptiness. It was as if her heart and mind and spirit had been removed, and there was nothing left but an empty, lonely shell. She tried to pray to her heavenly Father, but her prayers seemed to stop at the ceiling. Even God seemed to have left her alone. She wanted to cry, but no tears would come, only the ache of loneliness that never went away.

★ ★ ★ ★

Andrew did not come home the day after the quarrel until late, and then he slept in the spare bedroom. The next morning he and Dorothy said nothing to each other except the bare amenities when he left for Sacramento. He stood at the front door and said in tones as stark as she had ever heard, "I'll be back in two days. We'll talk then."

He had an odd expression on his face, and for one moment Dorothy thought he intended to say more. He even moved forward half a step, and her heart leaped when she thought, *He's coming to me.* But then he turned and left the house without saying another word.

All that day it was cloudy, and the wind blew out of the north. The next morning Dorothy called the baby-sitter and asked her to come, but Mrs. Teague had her married children there with a house full of grandchildren and said, "Oh, I just can't, Mrs. Winslow! I'm so sorry."

"That's all right, Helen," Dorothy said. "You need to be with your family." Finally she remembered Serena asking her more than once to bring the children out to the orange grove and let them stay for a few days. Dorothy had promised Serena that she would do that, and now she went into the living room where the children were playing and said, "You're going to go on a little vacation with Serena and Cass. Would you like that?"

Naturally the two children were excited about a change, and for the next hour she packed up everything they would need for a three-day visit. She left the house with the children, piling their baggage into a cab. She made the trip out to the grove and found Serena ecstatic about the children's visit.

"Are you sure they won't be any trouble?"

"Of course they'll be trouble, but Benjamin and Elizabeth need company, and so do Amelia and Phillip. They need to be together more," Serena said.

"I thought I'd go into the city and work on the Christmas play full time, but I'll come back if you want me to."

"No, it'll be a little rest for you. I know how it is with children." Serena spoke calmly and obviously was pleased with the unexpected visit. "Leave them here as long as you want to. A week if you'd like."

"No, just two or maybe three days. Andrew's gone to Sacramento with the men on the building committee, and I thought I could get caught up on the work I need to do and take a little rest, too."

"You do that, and don't worry for a minute about Amelia and Phillip. They'll have the time of their lives."

★　★　★　★

The house seemed strangely lonely, and Dorothy wandered around aimlessly after returning. It was too early to go to the rehearsals for the program, so she put on her coat and went out and ate at a seafood restaurant on the beach. Afterward she walked for a while along the beach. She had her head down, mostly thinking about her life and how dissatisfying it had become. She looked up once and saw a young couple in their late teens moving toward her. They seemed to be unaware of the world. The girl was looking up into his face, and he was returning her glance. Dorothy could not help overhearing them speak as they passed, but neither gave her a nod. The girl was saying, "And after we get married . . ."

The sight of the two, which ordinarily would have been amusing, depressed Dorothy. Their obvious infatuation with each other painfully reminded Dorothy of what she longed for in her marriage. She left the beach hurriedly and went to the church. Nolan was waiting with the participants, singers, and actors who were beginning to gather for the rehearsal. He left off speaking to the young man who was directing the small orchestra they had put together and came to her.

"Hello, Dorothy," he said. "Are you dreading this?"

"No," she answered, taking off her coat. "Not at all. Why, are you?"

"Well, we've got a lot of work to do. If it comes off, I'll be pretty well the most surprised man in California." He smiled at her, and his eyes crinkled at the corners in a most attractive way. "Some of these kids can't sing a lick, but they've got to be in the play anyway."

"We'll use whatever talent we have," she smiled. "It'll be a good experience for them."

Both of them threw themselves into the rehearsal. It was rough at times and would require a few extra rehearsals. Dorothy admired Nolan's energy and the way he had of encouraging people. She wished Andrew could be like that. When the rehearsal was over, Nolan drove several people home, including Dorothy.

"You'd better get a good night's sleep. It'll be another hard rehearsal tomorrow," Nolan said as she got out of the car.

"Thanks for the ride, Nolan."

The next day Dorothy got up early and did a little housecleaning. She felt a twinge of loneliness with the children gone that she had not anticipated, so she went out and did a little shopping to fill the time. She was actually glad when the time for rehearsal came for the Christmas program.

Dorothy lost herself in the work, and when it was over, she got into the car with Nolan and two of the workers, a young man and a middle-aged woman, Mrs. Wofford. After they had dropped Mrs. Wofford off at her home, Dorothy found herself chatting with Charlie Boyington, who directed the music. "Are you happy with that third number, the one about the star?"

Boyington spoke eagerly about the play until Nolan pulled up in front of his house. He got out, saying, "Good night, sir. Good night, Mrs. Winslow."

Nolan pulled away from the curb and looked across at Dorothy. "Are you as tired as I am?"

"I don't think so," she said. "I like all the activity, and they're so anxious. It's one of the church programs I think is worthwhile. I enjoy putting our lives into the young people and the children."

Nolan turned to his left, and Dorothy said in surprise, "This isn't the way to the parsonage."

"I've got your Christmas present, and I can't wait until Christmas to give it to you. I'll just run out to my place and get it."

"What is it?" Dorothy asked.

"No fair asking, and no use, either."

Nolan seemed extremely happy, and Dorothy smiled at the liveliness in him that she always admired. She sat there quietly as he drove out to his small house on the beach. She had been there before with other members of the youth group for a meeting and had admired his taste. It was only a small cottage, but it was decorated in a fashion that pleased her, with seashells and nets, and a mounted sailfish that Nolan had caught himself.

Pulling up in front of the house, Nolan shut off the engine, then immediately said, "Why did I do that?" He shook his head in disgust. "Now I'll just have to crank this thing again!" He got out of the car, calling, "I'll be right back."

Dorothy sat in the car and watched as he ran up to the front door. He unlocked it, disappeared, then almost at once was back. He ran back to the car and held up a gaily wrapped package with a green ribbon. He leaned in on the driver's side, put the present down, and said sternly, "Now, don't touch that until I get back in! You can open it on the way back to your house!" He reached in and set the spark, then moved to the front of the automobile. Dorothy watched as he spun the engine and it didn't catch. She heard him muttering to himself, and he tried twice more. Finally he came back and made an adjustment to the controls on the steering wheel and shook his head. "Someday they'll invent something to get these things started without all this nonsense!"

Dorothy shook her head in sympathy, and although it was dark, a bright moon bathed the beach in silver beams. She saw him bend over, heard him grunt, and then suddenly there was a high-pitched whine. But more than this, she heard Nolan cry out with pain.

"Nolan, what is it?" she cried. There was no answer, and she could not see him. Fear gripped her heart. She knew cranks were dangerous things. She had heard how people had broken their arms when the crank caught. It had such power that it could spin around and break the forearm of the person if they weren't careful.

Dorothy ran around to the front of the car, and her heart seemed to skip a beat as she saw Nolan lying sprawled on his back with blood on his face. He lay so still that she thought, with a sudden frantic fear, he was dead. When she ran and knelt beside him, she saw that he was breathing heavily and his eyelids were fluttering.

"Nolan, are you all right—?"

She pulled his head up and saw blood flowing down over his right eye onto his cheek, and there were spatters of it on the light gray coat that he wore. *The crank must have somehow flown out and caught him in the temple.*

Nolan began to stir, and his eyes fluttered again.

Dorothy leaned forward and heard him saying, "What's—" He reached up and touched the cut, and his hand came away with blood on it.

"Nolan, I've got to go get some help—a doctor."

He slowly opened his eyes more and his mind seemed to clear a little better. "No," he protested and struggled to a sitting position. He touched his head again, saw the blood, then said, "I don't know what happened. The crank came flying out, and I guess the tip of it caught me across the head."

"I've got to get a doctor for you," Dorothy insisted.

"There's not one closer than five miles, and he's asleep. Let me up. I think I'm all right."

Dorothy saw that he was still a bit befuddled, and his legs were unsteady.

She helped him up, and he grabbed her shoulders, muttering, "The whole world's spinning around."

"Come on. Can you walk as far as the house? We can call a doctor from there." She heard him mutter, "Guess so—" and they started for the house. He stumbled along, and she bore most of his weight as he shuffled awkwardly. When they reached the door, he fumbled into his pocket, and she took the key from him. Unlocking it, she pushed the door open, reached inside, and switched on the light. "Be careful of the step," she said. His arm was around her, and she led him into the living room. "You're still bleeding. It's going to get blood on the furniture."

"Get a towel from the bathroom," he muttered. He leaned over against the wall, and she ran to the bathroom and got a large towel. She also grabbed a washcloth and wet it with cold water. Running back, she draped the huge bath towel over the couch and said, "Lie down. You might be going into shock." She helped him over to the couch and made sure his head was on the towel, then she lifted his feet up. Fearfully she held the washcloth tightly on the cut. He winced under her hands, and she whispered, "I'm sorry if it hurts—but it's got to be done if we're going to get it to stop bleeding." She drew a sigh of relief when she saw that the bleeding began to slow. Lifting the cloth a bit, she said, "It's not as bad as I thought, Nolan, but I think a doctor ought to see it."

He shook his head briefly and said, "No, I don't want a doctor. I just want to lie here and rest a minute."

"Do you have any bandages and tape? Maybe some iodine?"

"All in the medicine kit—in the bathroom."

Dorothy rose and went to the bathroom, found the medicine kit, then came back. "Lie still," she said. "I think I can dress it. I don't think it needs stitches. Hold this until I heat some water."

"All right. The teakettle's on the stove."

She went to the kitchen and heated water over the gas flame. She found a basin, filled it, then got more clean washcloths and returned to the living room. Putting the basin down on the coffee table, she began to wash away the blood. When she had cleaned the wound, she examined it carefully. "It's not deep. Just wide, and the bleeding's almost stopped."

"It hurts something fierce, but I guess that's to be expected. Can you put a bandage on it?"

"Yes, you have plenty of tape and gauze." She pulled out a bottle of iodine and looked at the skull and crossbones. "This is going to hurt, Nolan," she said.

"Go ahead. Hold me down if I kick," he said, smiling up at her.

Dorothy removed the stopper and began to apply the fiery disinfectant to the wound. He flinched several times, and she took her free hand and held it gently against his head. "I'm sorry to hurt you," she whispered.

He did not answer, and she continued until the cut was treated. She made a bandage and taped it to his head, then said, "How do you feel?"

Nolan said, "A lot better." He got up slowly and swung his feet off the couch. She sat down beside him and said, "Be careful with this bandage. It's hard to fix a bandage there with your hair so close."

"I feel all right now," Nolan said, and indeed strength had come back to him. His eyes were clear, and he reached up gingerly and touched the bandage. "It caught me off guard. I never heard of a thing like that before."

"If it had been just a little bit over to one side, it could have killed you, or put your eye out."

"I guess I was lucky, then."

When he turned to her, Dorothy saw the gentle look in his eyes. The suddenness of it all had knocked all of the confidence out of him. He seemed younger somehow, and Dorothy reached up and touched the bandage again. "Does it hurt?" she whispered.

Nolan caught her hand, and to her shock, opened it and kissed her palm, then held the hand tightly. "No, it doesn't hurt at all now," he said in a voice that suddenly became unsteady. "You're a good nurse, Dorothy."

Dorothy sat there, and her palm seemed to burn where he had planted the kiss. His hands were growing warmer now, and she made no attempt to remove her own. He said nothing for a time but gazed intently at her face. She dropped her eyes at first, and when the silence ran on, she looked up and saw the compassion and the admiration she had so longed for but had not received.

Nolan put his free arm around her, and Dorothy wanted to protest, but she said nothing. He turned to face her and gently drew her closer. Her heart started to flutter, and she was aware of the lean masculinity and the strength of his arms and chest. Almost in a daze, she saw his face and then felt his lips on hers. She tried to break away, whispering, "Don't, Nolan—" but then as he kissed her again, she felt her resolve weaken and her arms went up and around his neck. As she sensed him demanding more, she pulled her lips away and made one last effort to protest. "Don't let me do this! Make me stop, Nolan! Make me stop. . . !"

"I love you, Dorothy. I have for a long time."

And at those words, whispered in her ear with such fervent longing, Dorothy Winslow succumbed. She knew she needed to flee, to run, to never look back. But she did none of these things. . . .

PART FOUR

VICTORS

★ ★ ★ ★

CHAPTER NINETEEN

THE END OF IT

★ ★ ★ ★

Edwin Porter was two men. On the set he could be a terror, driving the director, the crews, the cameramen, and even the carpenters who worked on the set like a madman. At times his language would become abusive, and his face would glow a ruby red. Priscilla had heard one actor say, "He's going to have apoplexy and die one of these days while he's having that kind of fit."

But there was another side to the man. He could be charming and persuasive when he chose to be—and he usually chose to let this side of his personality show when he wanted something from someone. More than once Priscilla had seen him turn on the charm and persuade people to do things they had vowed *never* to do. As she entered his office one rainy February morning, Porter rose from his desk smiling and came over to take her hand. She knew at once that he wanted something from her.

"Come in, Priscilla," Porter beamed. His sharp gray eyes glowed with warmth, and he held her hands for a moment, saying, "Why, you're cold! Come over here and sit down and I'll get you a drink. What would you like?"

"Why, nothing, thanks." She smiled and shook her head as she took her seat in the modernistic chair that looked to be nothing but bent stainless steel wires and two pads of leather. "You never give up, do you, Edwin? You know I never drink."

A look of chagrin swept across Porter's round face, and he shook his head, laughing ruefully. "Well, you're about the only person in this business who doesn't drink. How about some coffee, then?" Without waiting for her reply, he moved to the door, opened it, and bellowed in a stentorian tone, "Effie! Fix some fresh coffee for Priscilla, and make it strong and black like she likes it!" Wheeling, he came back filled with energy and marched to his desk. Snatching a sheaf of papers, he sat down across from her, drawing his chair up until their knees almost touched. "Look at these, Priscilla—reviews. All good, and here's the report on attendance."

Taking the papers, Priscilla leafed through them and was pleased with the reviews. The last sheet she studied even more carefully, then looked up, her eyebrows arched with surprise. "Well, they're very good, but for a serial that comes out in twelve episodes, I don't see how you can attach the number of people in the theater to them. They come to see the main feature, don't they?"

"These are very accurate. All we have to do is compare them with features that show without the serial to boost them up." He spoke decisively and crisply, running his hand through his thinning gray hair at times. Sometimes when he grew excited he grabbed hold of his hair and appeared to lift himself out of his chair with it, a sight that never failed to amuse Priscilla. "I'm very proud of you," he said, reaching over to pat her hand.

"Oh, I'm very proud of you, too, Edwin." Priscilla returned his smile. She had to be on her guard against most of the men in the theater, but Edwin Porter had been married to the same woman for thirty-one years. He had four children and seven grandchildren, and his inordinate pride in his clan was manifested by the portraits that completely decorated one wall. She also knew that he had made motion pictures of all of his family, and now she said suddenly, "You've been very good for me, Edwin. I appreciate all the times you've had to put up with me when I was cranky and hard to live with."

"Never a time! Never a single time!" he protested. He got up and began to pace the floor, a restless energy driving him. Effie returned with the coffee. Porter thanked her and poured Priscilla a cup, then one for himself. As he sipped the brew, he talked all the time as rapidly as possible. Finally he cocked his head to one side and set his coffee cup down. "You're probably wondering why I called you here this morning, Priscilla."

"Let me guess," she said with a smile. "You want me to do something, don't you?"

Taken aback, Edwin stared at her for a moment, his jaw dropping slightly, then he slapped his meaty thighs and roared with laughter. "You're too smart for me, Priscilla! Women are like that . . . they somehow have the gift of knowing what's going on in a man's mind." He shook his head with admiration, then grew more serious. "Only two more episodes, and we're through with this cliff-hanging business. I expect you've got enough bruises, scars, and contusions to do you for a while, don't you?" he asked wryly.

"It's been fun. It's been much more interesting than doing a Broadway play, but you're right. We've done three of them, and I think I've earned that silver star on my dressing room door."

"You certainly have, and I don't blame you for wanting to try something new."

"You know about the play that Maxwell wants Todd and me to do on Broadway?"

"Yes, Maxwell called me, as a matter of fact. He wanted to know if I could recommend you. In other words, did you have a temperament?"

"What did you tell him, Edwin?"

"I told him I wanted to adopt you. You're the kind of girl I'd like to have for my daughter, and that you're the most untemperamental star I've ever had working for me." She started to thank him, and he held up his hand, saying quickly, "It's all true. Every word of it." Then he drew his chair even closer, and his face became more animated. "I have a script I want you to read. It'll be something different from these cliff-hangers, all right." He got up at once, went to his desk, and opened a drawer. Pulling out a thick manuscript, he brought it back and said, "Here. Take this home and read it—and read it seeing yourself as the star. It's different from anything that's been done." He grew very serious, then said in a quieter but still intense voice, "It could be good for everybody. Good for Imperial Pictures, good for me as a producer, and good for Stan as a director. Most of all, it could make a star out of you. You could be as big as Eleanor Glyn."

Alarm bells suddenly sounded as Priscilla listened to him. The film that had become very big recently in just a short time was entitled *Three Weeks*. It was an English film, and the first review that Priscilla had read of it had the word of warning: "Not for young ladies!" Though she had doubts, she had convinced herself that as an actress she needed to be informed on the popular films. She had gone to see the film and had been shocked by the blatant, raw sensuality that had flashed upon the screen. She had sat there uneasy and uncomfortable. More than once she was tempted to get up and leave the theater. The story itself concerned a queen of a mythical Balkan land who, forgetting her husband, had a torrid romance with a handsome young man.

As Priscilla sat there holding the manuscript, flashes of memory came to her, and she recognized that the scenes from the movie had been burned into her mind. She had left the theater feeling soiled, the vivid images troubling her deeply. The movie was titillating audiences everywhere and making the producer extremely rich.

Running her hand over the top sheet of the manuscript, Priscilla hesitated for just a moment, then looked Porter full in the eye. "Is this like *Three Weeks*? I mean, is it based on seduction and illicit sex?"

For once Porter was flustered and lost his normal poise. He stuttered for a moment. "Well . . . uh . . . in a way, I suppose, it has that element in it."

"Come now, be honest, Edwin. It is that sort of film, isn't it? You want to cash in on the popularity of Eleanor Glyn's work."

Porter shifted uncomfortably and pulled his hair with both hands again. If it had not been such a serious moment, Priscilla would have been amused at the sight. Porter cleared his throat and began to speak rapidly. "We've got to face reality, Priscilla. You and I know these things are in the world. All we're doing is showing the world as it really is."

"There are things that shouldn't be shown on the screen," Priscilla said firmly, knowing that it would get a rise out of Porter, which it did.

"You're talking about censorship now, but I'm not going to let a bunch of Puritans dictate what sort of movies I put on the screen! They're nothing but a bunch of blue noses, anyhow!"

Instantly, Priscilla challenged him. "The Puritans who came on the *Mayflower*, and their immediate descendants, gave this country more than any other group. They brought a sense of mission with them, and they gave their lives, over half of them, that first year to found a community where men could worship God freely."

Priscilla admired the Puritans greatly. She had read everything available on their lives and their heroic attempts to cross the sea to a place where they could worship freely. She had heard the stories of how one of her own ancestors, Gilbert Winslow, had come from England and founded the House of Winslow in America. "And furthermore, if you knew your history, you'd remember that all of the Ivy League Colleges were founded by the Puritans, as you call them. I mean Dartmouth, Yale, and Harvard. All of these institutions of higher education were founded by men who believed there was a right and a wrong and chose to face danger rather than give in to it." She sighed and shook her head. "I don't see how I could do this thing, Edwin."

"You're an actress, Priscilla! You won't *become* the woman in the play—and furthermore the story reveals how this woman has to pay for her sin. That's what you Christians believe, isn't it?"

"Well . . . yes . . ."

Eagerly Porter hammered his point home. "People need to see that wrongdoing brings retribution. The woman in this play, true, is a wicked and sinful woman, but you have women like that in the Bible, don't you? What about Delilah? What about Salome? The Bible doesn't try to cover up such things. From the little I've read, it doesn't hide people's wrongs."

Priscilla could not answer, because she knew he was right. Slowly she said, "I'll have to think a great deal about it—and pray about it, too."

Porter felt he had gained a victory. "That's fine! Fine!" He reached out, pulled her to her feet, and patted her shoulders. "You can have some input into the story. We could work it out where we could make a good thing out of this." He hustled her to the door smoothly, saying as he opened it, "Go home right now. Read it as quick as you can. Get back to me as soon as you have finished it, and we'll go out and talk about it some more."

Priscilla went home disturbed by the problem the script was sure to bring. Changing into a pair of rose-colored lounging pajamas and a robe, she made herself some coffee and then sat down to read the play. She stopped only for a sandwich and a glass of milk at noon. By two o'clock she turned the last page of the manuscript over. Setting it down, she sat back in the lounge chair she had curled up in and closed her eyes. The script was not as blatant as she had feared. True enough, it starred a woman who was immoral, and who was the cause of ruin of several men. She had even caused a breakup of a family. But as Porter had said, at the end of the movie retribution overtook her, and she paid a terrible price for her wrongdoing.

Slowly Priscilla got up and walked around the room, running over the script in her mind. She thought about the elements in the plot that she disliked and wondered if Porter had been speaking truthfully when he had indicated that she could have some control over the script. His offer was unusual. As far as she knew, only the giants in the entertainment world enjoyed this privilege. Going to the window, she stared outside at the trees. Some of them seemed to hold their limbs up as if in prayer to the damp, gray, leaden sky. She turned quickly and went to take a bath. She had washed her hair and was wrapping a towel around it when the telephone rang. She hurried to pick up the receiver. "Hello, this is Priscilla."

"Priscilla, this is Todd. I'll be by in about two hours. We'll have an early dinner. All right?"

"All right, Todd."

The two talked a few moments, then Priscilla hung the receiver up and went to sit before her dressing table mirror. She wished it were sunny so she could dry her hair outside. But the sun was a thin, pale disk almost hidden behind skeins of dark, low-flying clouds. Instead, she toweled her hair dry and spent some time trying a new hairstyle. When she was satisfied with how it looked, she dressed.

Since Todd Blakely was not to arrive for another hour, Priscilla sat in an overstuffed chair by the window and watched the clouds score the sky, drifting along driven by the high winds. Picking up her Bible she began to read the Scriptures. Once she let the Bible fall open, and it opened at the book of Proverbs. Her eyes flew to the verse she had underlined, *"As a jewel of gold in a swine's snout, so is a fair woman without discretion."* She stared at that verse for a long time thinking about its meaning, then quietly she closed the Bible and prayed, "Oh, God, please show me the way! Don't let me get out of your will!" Priscilla had discovered that sometimes it was possible to talk too much to God. Once she had heard Cass remark, "If we're talking all the time when we're praying, how can God speak back to us? That would be impolite of Him, wouldn't it?" She had smiled at the time, but she had learned there was something to this and had run across many Scriptures indicating the importance of waiting on God. *"They that wait upon the Lord shall renew their strength."* This verse had become a favorite of hers. She had, therefore, learned to present her prayers to God and then to simply sit quietly, waiting for any impression that God would give her. It had been a revealing experience for her. She had often heard her parents speak about God talking to them. She had discovered this was the way God spoke to her in the stillness of the night sometimes. She simply thought about the Lord Jesus upon the cross, dwelling on the meaning of His death—and out of that meditation oftentimes an impression would come. It would become stronger until finally she recognized that it did not come from her own imagination, but that God had definitely put it there.

Todd arrived on time, and the two went out to Miro's, a popular restaurant. The dance floor was crowded with young couples, and an eight-piece band played constantly as they had their dinner—filet mignon, crisp, fresh white bread, and a salad with an unusually spicy dressing. The food was very good, and Todd was in an excited mood. His cheeks glowed from a fresh shave, and a faint odor of lotion lingered in the air as he leaned closer to Priscilla and whispered, "You look lovely tonight, Priscilla. I'll have to be sure no one runs off with you."

"You just can't turn it off, can you, Todd? Paying compliments to women."

"I suppose not, but I mean that one. You do look beautiful," he said, once again impressed at the freshness of the woman who sat across from him. The slightly oval symmetry of Priscilla's face gracefully accented her eyes, which matched the green of the dress that she wore. Her lips were well formed, long, with the lower lip slightly protruding, giving an alluring effect to those who noted it. She had small ears laid flat against her head, and her small jade earrings caught the light from the chandeliers overhead.

Priscilla grew nervous as he studied her, not liking such attention, and said, "Todd, Porter gave me a script to read today." She sat quietly, twirling the glass of water nervously as she described it and spoke of her apprehensions. "It's just not the sort of thing for me."

"Well," Todd said quickly, "of course, I hope you don't do it. I want you to go with me to New York and star in Maxwell's play. But, to be truthful about it, Maxwell's play has some of those same elements that you're afraid of." He saw disappointment sweep across her face and then shook his head, saying firmly, "You're not seeing this thing right, Priscilla. It's the actor's job to present the world as it is. You remember what Dr. Johnson said about Shakespeare's plays? They held the mirror up to life. That's all these plays are doing. They're showing that there's evil in the world."

"But there's good in the world, too," Priscilla argued. "At the same time a holdup is taking place in New York, right down the street a fireman's risking his life to save some helpless people. Why dwell only on the ugly side of it?"

"Because it's there, and art needs to show it."

"I think I'm beginning to see what's happening, Todd. Unfortunately people are more thrilled at seeing the bad things. That's why some people rush over to view the bodies after a bad accident." Her shoulders twitched with distaste, and her lips formed a grimace. "I don't know why, but there's something in us that is drawn to the ugly things of the world. To be truthful, I think it's the devil."

"The devil? You don't believe in that old myth, do you?"

"Yes, I do."

Todd was somewhat surprised and stared at her with clinical interest. "I don't believe the Bible is literal. I think it's all just a myth to teach us something about ourselves."

"I don't agree with you, Todd, which is precisely why you and I would never make it in any type of serious relationship. We're too far apart in what we believe."

"You can go your way, and I can go mine in religious matters of opinion."

"I don't think so, Todd. I can't imagine not being able to share the most important part of my life with my husband!" Priscilla shook her head and wearily listened as he continued to argue. When they got back to her apartment, he put his arms around her, and she submitted to his kiss as usual. As she did so, she suddenly had a thought, *It's getting too easy for me. I wouldn't have let him kiss me whenever he wanted to a few months ago, but now I think nothing of it.* A fear took her, and she gently put her hand on his chest and drew back, saying, "Good night, Todd. I'll see you tomorrow." She saw the disappointment in his eyes, but she remembered her prayer from before. Deep inside she knew she had to make some important choices. If she wanted to walk in discretion, then she knew that her relationship with Todd had to stop.

"All right. Tomorrow, Priscilla," he said, then shrugged and left.

When she closed the door of her apartment, she leaned against the doorframe and suddenly felt utterly exhausted. It was not a physical fatigue, since she had done nothing demanding on the set recently. The emotional strain of making the decision to return to the stage in New York, and the constant pressure from Todd, she had found, were as debilitating and tiring as spending all day cleaning house. She went to bed almost at once. Kneeling, as had become her custom for a few moments each night, she said, "Oh, God, you know my heart, and you know how I'm capable of ruining my life. Don't let me take the wrong road. I don't want to be like a jewel of gold in a swine's snout. So, I ask, Lord Jesus, that you keep me free from anything that would displease you."

She got into bed, and somehow the prayer seemed to help. As she lay there thinking about what the future held for her, a sense of peace began to calm her thoughts, and she drifted off into a dreamless sleep.

★　★　★　★

Andrew Winslow stood in the entrance of the new church building he had practically built with his own hands—or so he felt. He walked out of the foyer and into the large sanctuary that sloped upward into a cathedral-like ceiling. Looking up he was disappointed he did not feel more excited at the impressive sight. He walked around studying the freshness and newness of the structure. He ran his hand along the smooth, polished walnut pews and felt the velvety softness of the plush royal blue cushions. Going up onto the rostrum, he looked back and visualized the choir, three hundred singers in glistening white robes, their voices soaring over the congregation. Stepping behind the pulpit, a masterpiece of carpentry, he ran his hands over the polished, bleached walnut, admiring the work. He looked out across the rows of empty pews and imagined every one of them filled to capacity, seven thousand people attentively waiting for him to bring them the Word of God.

A heavy and oppressive silence seemed to hang over the enormous room. Sunlight slanted down from skylights that had been strategically placed in rows, eliminating the need to use electric lights for morning services. But today it was cloudy out; the feeble rays barely penetrated the frosted glass, and the dimness depressed him. His eyes wandered up to the six enormous crystal chandeliers suspended far above. Suddenly his conscience smote him. *The price of just one of those chandeliers would pay for a missionary's work in Africa for a year.*

He thought of Barney, his brother whom he loved so well, who was working hard on the African mission field, and for a moment Andrew smiled. His brother was not at all like him. Barney was a jewel, but in the rough. He had been a prizefighter in his youth and had experienced a terrible life on the Lower East Side of New York City as a drunk. Then he had been converted at a rescue mission. Barney had matured in his faith rapidly, and it had been he who had first surrendered to the call to go to Africa as a missionary. Andrew remembered with fondness how Barney had convinced others, including himself, to go and preach the gospel across the sea.

As Andrew thought back over those challenging but fulfilling times, a dissatisfaction settled on him as he looked around at the ornate woodwork and the spectacular stained-glass windows that threw glittering reds and greens and yellows across the church as they portrayed the lives of the saints. He felt the thick pale beige carpeting under his feet and said aloud, "Barney would be lost in all of this." He thought about how he himself had gone out to the villages of Africa, and suddenly it all came back to him—the stench, the dirt, the filth, the fear and poverty, and the blind obsession with the witch doctors who led the people into horrible practices. *Am I happier now than I was then?* In all honesty, he could not say that he was. He realized that even as Superintendent of Missions, he had lost touch with the men and women who were risking their lives every day for the Lord Jesus Christ on foreign fields. He had once been a part of that adventurous life, and though it was tiring and exhausting, he had felt a deep sense of purpose knowing he was serving God in a meaningful way.

Abruptly he looked up, and the glitter of the chandeliers caught his eye, and again he thought of their immense cost. He shook his head as a man tries to shake off an angry bee, but the nagging thoughts would not leave him. Quickly he left the rostrum and walked down the aisle, but he was not content nor pleased with himself.

"What do you want, Winslow?" he demanded of himself angrily. "You've built a fine church here, doubled the attendance, quadrupled the offerings, and here's this wonderful, beautiful building all to the glory of God."

But as he left the building, he had a gnawing fear that he had built on sand—that not all of this had been God's plan for his life. It was a terrifying thought for him. He had not felt it for years, since the time when he was a young man groping to find God's will. The realization that he had made a wrong turn, that he had invested these last years in something that was man's pursuit and not of God, shook him with a cold fright that left him almost physically weak. Suddenly he felt a need to be with Dorothy and the children. A pang of guilt reminded him just how much he had neglected them lately. He ran quickly to the black Maxwell touring car and anxiously cranked it up, then leaped behind the wheel and headed for home.

When he reached the house, he shut the engine off and went inside. The children ran to meet him. He picked up Phillip with his right arm and Amelia with his left and grinned at them. "How are you fellas today?"

"I'm not a fellow, Daddy!" Amelia protested. "I'm a girl."

"That's right, you are. Well, no one could mistake that." He kissed her smooth cheek.

"Daddy, can we go out to Uncle Cass's orange grove and ride the horses again?"

"Sure, sometime. Where's your mother?" He lifted his eyes expectantly. Usually Dorothy was right behind the children.

"She went out," Amelia said. "Mrs. Kennedy's keeping us today."

Her words deflated Andrew, and he carried the children into the kitchen. Mrs. Kennedy, who lived two doors down, was sitting at the table busily peeling potatoes. She was a matronly woman with a cheerful red face and greeted Andrew at once. "Well, pastor. You're home early."

"Yes, I thought I'd take a little time off. Where did Mrs. Winslow go?"

"She said she had some errands to do and would be back by five o'clock."

"Oh, I see. Well, fix a good supper tonight, Mrs. Kennedy. I'm hungry enough to eat a pair of shoes."

Amelia giggled. "That's silly, Daddy! Could you really eat shoes?" She looked at him with inquisitive eyes. "No," she announced, shaking her head. "You're just teasing."

"That's right. I am. Well, suppose the three of us go play a game until supper is ready."

"What kind of a game?" Amelia asked excitedly.

"Any game you want."

"Horsey," Phillip cried immediately. "Get me on your back."

Andrew grinned but uttered a sorrowful groan. "I should've chosen the game myself. Maybe checkers."

They all went into the large room that had been made into a playroom for the children, and at once Amelia pulled a small table over.

"We're going to have a tea party."

She began arranging her dolls in two of the chairs while Phillip protested. "No tea party. I want to play horsey!"

"First the tea party, then the horsey," Andrew announced. He looked at his children and thought how handsome and alert they were, then breathed a quick prayer of thankfulness to God for their health. He had seen children who did not have such a blessing, and he realized he had forgotten how terrible it could be to have a child who was sick. "Come on now. Let's have this tea party," he said and sat on the floor across from Amelia and next to Phillip.

★ ★ ★ ★

Dorothy was sitting beside Nolan Cole clenching her hands tightly together. He had called her earlier, begging to see her, and had said, "I'll have to come to the house if you won't meet me." Terrified at his threat, she had agreed to meet him. She had called Mrs. Kennedy to watch the children and begin supper. As soon as the older woman had arrived, Dorothy had thrown on a raincoat and hat and walked out into the cool air. Nolan had been waiting a block away from the house. She looked around nervously and then got in the car. "Nolan, we've got to stop meeting," she said, looking straight ahead. "It's not right."

Nolan did not answer. He got out and started the car, then climbed back in and drove to a road along a deserted stretch of beach. Pulling the automobile up in the sand, he shut the engine off and reached for her, drawing her close. "I've missed you, Dorothy," he whispered. He kissed her then, his arms holding her tightly.

Dorothy resisted for only a moment. She had been a different woman since that night in his house when she had first surrendered to his desires. Since then the affair had driven her to the depths of despair. She knew full well the enormity of the heinous wrong she was committing against her husband and children—and against God. Time and again she had wept and prayed that God would forgive her—but in her loneliness she had not found the strength to break off the affair. Nolan had at first been so gentle, but now his lips seemed more demanding. Yet she could not resist him when he began to stroke her back as he was doing now. It always stirred her for some reason. He knew how to make her happy; he knew how to say the sweet things she had wanted to hear for so long.

But this time was different. She pulled back abruptly and placed her hand on his chest. "Nolan," she whispered, her voice almost frantic, "we can't keep on like this! We've been terribly wrong! You know we have!"

"I love you. Can that be wrong?"

"I have a husband," she said, looking down.

"He's not been a husband to you."

"I . . . I know, but he hasn't been as wrong as I have. He's been faithful to me, at least." Bitterness choked her voice, and she turned her head away, tears rising in her eyes. "I never thought I could do a horrible thing like this. Since I was a little girl I've tried to follow the Lord, and now . . . now I've made my loneliness and disappointment an excuse to break God's law. And . . . and it's wrong!"

She started to cry, and suddenly Nolan's hands drew her around. He held her face between his broad, strong hands and kissed her lips gently, then whispered, "I want you to marry me. I love you. But you're right. We can't keep on like this. I know it's wrong, but I've got to have you, Dorothy! I've never loved a woman before, not really, but I love you."

"Marry? What are you talking about?" she said, startled.

"I'm talking about a divorce, of course."

Dorothy had been caught up in the affair through a series of tragic blunders. A great weakness in her had taken her unawares, but she had not tried to excuse herself. She had confessed in her heart that her adulterous behavior was an abomination to God, and her own conscience tormented her almost every waking hour. But not once in all this time had she thought of divorce. It was not a thing talked about among the people she knew. A divorced woman was little better in the sight of many than a prostitute.

Nolan was watching as she struggled with what he had said. "We both sinned against God, but you deserve some happiness, and Andrew's not going to give it to you. He never will. He's caught up with his work and this building project. He's a good man, but he never should have married. He should've been like Paul, who didn't have a wife. As a matter of fact, he's mentioned that several times in his sermons, hasn't he?"

Mutely Dorothy nodded, but her mind was spinning in a whirlwind of emotions. "Why, it would ruin your ministry," she said. "And think of what it would do to the children. And Andrew, too. We can't ruin their lives. Take me home," she cried frantically.

For a while Nolan argued with her, but finally seeing she was adamant, he got out and started the car. He got back in slowly, almost like an old man, discouragement and a look of emptiness lining his face. The affair had worn him down, too. He had been trapped by his own foolishness and self-conceit, and he well knew the price he would have to pay if he ran away with a minister's wife. The effect of his sin had already taken its toll on his ministry. He no longer displayed the same love and patience with the children in the youth program. In fact, one family had made a formal complaint to the church elders about his harshness with their son on an outing. And when Andrew had asked him to preach one Sunday, Nolan had declined, making some lame excuse.

They were both silent until they got to within a few blocks of the parsonage. When Dorothy got out she said, "Please don't call anymore, and don't write notes. I can't go on like this. It's over, Nolan."

Nolan did not answer but stepped on the accelerator, and the car moved away down the street.

Dorothy turned and walked home, feeling the weight of the world on her shoulders. The shame and guilt sliced like keen knives inside her, cutting her to pieces. When she reached the house and stepped inside, she did not see how she could bear to look her children in the face. She slowly removed her coat and hung it in the coat closet. Hearing voices coming from the playroom, she walked to the door. She was shocked to see Andrew on his hands and knees with Phillip on his back screaming in delight. "Get up, Daddy! Get up!"

Andrew turned and looked up startled, then got to his feet,

pulling Phillip off his back. "Hello, Dorothy. I came home early."

Dorothy could not say anything for a moment. It had been so long since Andrew had played with the children. From the look on his face, she knew he had still not forgiven her for their quarrel. Ever since then, they had been sleeping in separate bedrooms. Avoiding his eyes, she turned to leave, murmuring to herself. Leaving the playroom, she went to her bedroom. When she closed the door behind her, her hands were shaking. She had the tremendous urge to throw herself on the bed and give way to mindless weeping, but somehow she held a tighter rein than that on herself. *I can't face him,* she thought miserably. *How can I look him in the eye—knowing what I've done?*

The rest of the evening was abject misery for Dorothy Winslow. She said very little during the meal and excused herself to clear the table. As they sat in the living room afterward with the children, she was silent most of the time. The children were loud and noisy, and Andrew paid more attention to them than was customary. Occasionally he glanced at her.

Finally, when the children were in bed and Dorothy started down the hall, he stopped her. "You're looking pale," he said. "Are you sick?"

"No, I'm fine," Dorothy said briefly. She saw that he was looking at her in a peculiar fashion, and once again the sickening guilt rose in her throat, burning, and she quickly left, saying, "Good night." She closed the door and stood there waiting. Part of her hoped that Andrew would come to her, but if he did, she didn't know what she would do. She stood listening and heard his footsteps as they approached. Her breath caught, and she bit her lower lip as the footsteps stopped outside of her door. For a long moment she knew he was going to come in, but she did not know what she would say. A yearning rose in her to find some sort of peace with him—and with God. Then the footsteps moved away, and she heard the sound of the spare bedroom door closing gently.

She rose late the next morning, deliberately staying in bed until she heard Andrew leave his bedroom. She dressed slowly and went to the kitchen just as he was leaving. He was kissing the children and turned to look at her. He looked haggard and tired. He had lost his vitality, and she wondered how much of his strength had gone into the stones and brick and mortar of the church building. He looked at her for one moment, and she could not meet his eyes but heard him say, "Good-bye, Dorothy. I'll see you this evening."

"All right." The answer had been barely audible, she knew, but she could say no more. Her heart ached from the burden of her sin. She hurt with an indescribable pain such as she had never known before.

All morning long she felt like an animal in a trap. Again and again she thought of Nolan Cole telling her, *"I love you, and I want to marry you. . . ."* The words repeated themselves in her mind, and she worked frantically around the house trying to occupy herself.

Midafternoon, while the children were taking their nap, the telephone rang. She almost didn't answer it but finally picked it up. In the back of the house she could hear Mrs. Kennedy, who had come to help with the laundry as she sometimes did. Quietly Dorothy said, "Hello?"

It was Nolan. "I've got to see you, Dorothy."

"No, we mustn't!"

"Either you come to my house, or I'll come to yours. We've got to tell Andrew what's going on."

Terror flooded Dorothy Winslow. She had a sudden picture of herself being pinioned by Andrew's penetrating eyes and knew that she could not bear the shame. "No, don't do that!"

"Then come and we'll talk."

Dorothy hesitated for a moment, then said, "All right, but we'll have to go where we're not seen."

"Nobody ever comes by my house. I'll pick you up at the old place and bring you here."

Dorothy steeled herself. "It's all over! I've been wrong, but I'm not going to do this anymore!"

A silence seemed louder than words, and then he said, "Come to my house and we'll talk. If that's your decision, then that's the way it will be. But I love you, and I'm not giving up easily."

Dorothy felt another wave of fear and futility, but she knew she had to see him one more time. "All right. I'll come, but I can't stay long, and I won't change my mind." She put the telephone receiver on its hook with trembling hands. Her knees were weak, too, but she knew she had to go. Quickly, she told Mrs. Kennedy she would be gone for an hour or two, then left the house. When Nolan came by, she got into the car silently and said nothing as he drove along the back roads and finally stopped in front of his house. She stepped out and walked stiffly to the door. As soon as they were inside, she turned around and faced him squarely. Her eyes were enormous, her voice as firm as she could make it. "It's all over, Nolan. . . ."

CHAPTER TWENTY

NERO

★ ★ ★ ★

Jolie's twentieth birthday was not what she had hoped. Peter and Easy had gone off to a car race, and she felt lonely. It had been too far for her to make the trip. When she got up that morning, the first thing she thought of was the wonderful surprise party she had enjoyed so much the previous year. A smile spread across her face at the fond memories. She got up, washed her face, and dressed, but the day held no similar promise of surprise. By the time Tom Ziegler came by at two o'clock for her lesson, Jolie was tired of her own company and glad to see him. "Come on, Tom," she said. "Teach me something wonderful today."

Ziegler smiled and said, "Happy birthday, Jolie. How does it feel to have been on planet earth for twenty years?"

She laughed. "I don't feel much different. Somehow I thought I would. Come and sit on the swing."

When they reached the swing on the porch, Tom stopped in surprise and said, "That's a new cover for the swing, isn't it?"

"Isn't it awful?" Jolie said. "My landlady thought it was wonderful, but somehow it makes me nervous to sit on George Washington."

The cover for the swing had a large embroidered portrait of George Washington that ran long ways. Jolie laughed, saying, "You can sit on his chin, and I'll sit on the top of his head."

As they sat down, Tom shook his head. "It doesn't feel right sitting on George Washington's chin." He reached into his bag and pulled out a small package with gaily wrapped paper and handed it to her. "Happy birthday!" he said again.

"Oh, Tom, you shouldn't have! But I'm glad you did," Jolie said. She tore open the package and stopped abruptly as her eyes fell on the beautifully designed broach with small green stones set in gold. "Oh, it's . . . it's beautiful, Tom!" she whispered. Picking it up she stared at it and then immediately pinned it on her blouse. "There. How does it look?"

"It sets off your eyes beautifully," he said. "It makes them look just like the sea."

"Now, you stop that, Tom Ziegler! You've practiced enough on me. What about that girl you're interested in? You've been quoting poetry and kissing my hand and spouting pretty speeches for a long time. Have you said anything to her yet?"

Tom grew strangely silent. He sat tensely in the swing, then suddenly he turned toward Jolie. His brow was furrowed, and his mouth drew tight as he said, "I have a confession to make, Jolie."

"You, a confession? You couldn't have! You've never done anything wrong!" she teased him.

"No, I'm serious. I have done something wrong, and I've got to tell you about it."

Jolie paused, somewhat taken aback by his solemn expression. She saw something like fear in his eyes, and she said quickly, "What is it, Tom? What's wrong? What have you done?"

Ziegler swallowed hard and then said hoarsely, "I've lied to you."

"Lied to me? About what?"

"About . . . about that girl I told you I liked." He hesitated, then shook his head. "It was a foolish thing to do."

"It's not foolish for you to admire a girl. I think it's what you should do, a young man like you."

"You don't understand, Jolie. I just made up that story about a girl." Suddenly he reached out, took her hands, and held them tightly. "The truth is," he said, his voice slightly above a whisper and his face contorted with an emotion she could not understand, "you're the girl, Jolie."

Jolie stared at him, unable to speak for a moment. She liked Tom Ziegler immensely, but to her he was a friend, and she had never once thought of him as having romantic inclinations. "Why, that's not possible, Tom," she said.

"Why isn't it?" He kept her hands locked tightly in his and

then began to speak more freely. "You know what my life's been like. I've been shut up in the house with my mother for most of my life, and I've been spending all of my time at my studies. There's never been any time for me for anything else, but since I started coming over here, it's been different. I can talk to you in a way I can't talk to other girls. I hope you'll think of me as the man you might marry in two or three years when I'm out of school and have established myself in my profession enough to be able to take care of you as you should be."

"Marry you?" Jolie was astonished, and her face grew pale as she stared wide-eyed into Tom's eyes. "Why, Tom—!"

"You don't have to say anything right now except one thing. Do you like me at all, Jolie?"

"Why, of course I do, Tom. But that's not the same thing."

"It's enough for me—for now." He suddenly leaned forward, giving her time to draw back. When she didn't move, he kissed her gently on the lips. It was a light caress, and he drew back almost frightened. "Well," he said, blinking with surprise. "That's out of the way."

"What? What's out of the way?" Jolie asked.

He smiled suddenly, looking almost handsome. "Why, the first kiss. That can never happen again. It can come only once. And . . . and I wanted it to be with you." He straightened up and picked up a book and stared at it for a moment. Then looking at her he said, "I won't bother you in any way, of course, but I thought you ought to know how I feel."

Jolie could not for the life of her think of a thing to say. His kiss had left her in a daze. When she knew he was going to kiss her, a slight shiver had run through her. Other than Peter and Easy, never in her whole life had a man treated her with such respect and tenderness. Normally they had made demands, leaving her afraid. But Tom was so different.

As Tom began to talk about the history of Greece, she understood not one word that he said, so confused was her mind. For the rest of the lesson she could not give an intelligent answer to any of his questions. Finally when he left, she threw on her hat and coat and went out for a walk, trying to still the swirl of thoughts in her mind. *Marry him!* she thought. *Tom Ziegler?* Why, it was so sudden, so unexpected, that it was a thing to wonder at and to marvel about. *Why would someone so educated be interested in me? I barely know anything, and this scar . . .* Jolie stopped in the middle of her thought and reached up to touch the ugly red scar. She shook her head and knew that for weeks she would not be able to face him without seeing his earnest face and hearing the plea in his voice as he had spoken to her of his love on the swing. It was the first time a man had spoken to her of honorable love, although many had spoken to her of another kind. She could not help but have a tender and good feeling about the fact that this young man, so strange and shy, had offered to share his life with her.

★ ★ ★ ★

Jason Ballard stood staring at the huge black-maned lion as if hypnotized. A trainer named Charlie Paddock had been working for several days with the crew creating the setting for the last stunt in the serial. Jason had known that there would be a lion involved. Now, however, as he stood there beside Peter and Easy, an uneasiness stirred in him, and he muttered, "That's a terrible-looking beast!"

Peter shook his head. He was also shocked at the size and apparent ferociousness of the animal. "I don't like this one bit, Jason. How is it supposed to work, anyway?" He had come onto the set for the first time, having taken two days off to go to a race with Easy, and now the two men had returned, along with the rest of the crew who were fascinated by what they had heard.

Jason swung his arm around. "Well, here's the way it's supposed to work. They made this set to look like part of a jungle. Most of it's potted plants, I guess, and artificial vines. That over there looks like a rock face, but it's not. It's artificial, too. What happens is that Priscilla falls down from what is supposed to be the top of a cliff and lands on this flat spot. Then that lion comes out of the jungle, sees her, and she sees him and screams. She can't escape because the rock behind her is too steep to climb, so the lion comes and makes a jump at her."

"And the episode stops with that?" Peter questioned. "How does she get out of it?"

"I don't know," Jason said. He locked his lips together and would say no more, listening with half an ear as Easy began to speak.

"That's an awful-looking critter. Why, look at the size of those teeth! And here it is Friday the thirteenth! Sure is a bad day to try to do a thing like this."

"It's a bad day any day!" Peter said. "What idiot thought up this idea?"

"Who knows?" Jason shrugged. "Of course, it'll be filmed in segments. Part of it will show Priscilla falling off, when she'll only fall a couple of feet. Then they'll cut to the floor, and she'll fall down sprawled on the ground. They'll get a scene of the lion coming closer, and then they'll take the picture when she's supposed to see the lion and scream. She'll get out of there then, and they'll take the footage of the lion."

"Well, as long as she won't actually be in there with that beast, I suppose it's all right," Peter said.

"I guess so," Jason said grudgingly. He moved over to Paddock, whom he had met earlier, and asked, "You're sure you'll have that lion under control, Paddock? If he got loose, I hate to think what could happen to Priscilla."

Charlie Paddock was a short, well-built man. He traveled with a circus doing his wild animal act. He had black curly hair, sparkling black eyes, and was rather handsome. He looked over toward the lion pacing back and forth in the cage and grinned. "You're not afraid of Nero, are you?"

"I'll tell the world I am!" Jason said frankly. "I had a tangle with a grizzly bear once and just barely got away, but this beast looks worse than any bear I've seen."

"Nero is a pretty bad actor," Charlie said, "but he knows who the boss is." He picked up the whip and cracked it at Nero, who had been staring out of his cage with brilliant green eyes. Suddenly he opened his mouth, exposing tremendous white teeth and a red tongue, and let out an ear-splitting roar, which made everyone around jump.

Paddock laughed. "It's all right, Jason. Relax. I'll be there all the time. Look, let me show you again how it works." He took them around through the set and showed them a wire cage of heavy steel that led into the jungle. "There's a gate on the other end of this," he said. "It's wired to a switch. Can't open until somebody pulls that switch. What we do is pull Nero's cage around here"—he pointed at the end of the runway—"lock it in, then I pull the door here on Nero's cage. He's trained to do that. He'll go out, someone will open the door, and he emerges out on the floor of what's supposed to be the jungle. Of course, Miss Winslow won't be out there. Nobody will be. They'll already have shot the scenes with her. She goes out the door right over there." He led them back, turned a key and opened it, then shut it and locked it again. Turning to them, he said, "Don't worry. Nothing can go wrong."

Paddock went about checking on some details, and Jason looked up to see that Priscilla had come onto the set. She was wearing a pair of black jodhpurs with her customary white long-sleeved silk shirt. It was a man's shirt, and two of the buttons at the top were unbuttoned. She wore a sun helmet, and her honey-colored hair caught the lights overhead as she walked toward them.

"Hi there, fellas," she said. She gave a look at the lion and seemed as impressed as the others. "He's huge, isn't he? And look at those teeth! I don't see how Mr. Paddock gets in the cage with him. Have you ever seen his act?"

"Not me, but I wouldn't get in a cage with a beast like that for a million dollars!" Peter said.

"It's not just him. He gets in the cage full of lions and tigers, about ten or fifteen of them."

"You mean he turns his back on some of them?" Jason asked. He shook his head. "He must be crazy! It's a wonder he's not clawed all to bits."

"Oh, he's been clawed several times! Look at his right forearm sometime. He's got a terrible scar there, and he said he had others, too." Her eyes sparkled, and she looked at Peter. "I told him you'd be nervous about me getting close to that lion, and that you wouldn't get in a cage with a ferocious beast like that."

Peter shook his head and said, "Charlie just said he takes more risks than when I drive those race cars as fast as I do."

"Well, I guess we're ready to start." Stan Lem had come over and nodded. "You ready, Priscilla?"

"All ready, Stan."

"Paddock, we're ready to do Priscilla's segment. You can get the lion in place, but unlock the door and let Priscilla in so we can film her scenes first."

"Sure, Mr. Lem." Paddock struggled for a moment with the catch and muttered, "This thing needs some work." He yanked it open finally, and when it gave, the door swung open, creaking with an eerie sound.

"There you go, Miss Winslow. If some of you fellows will help me," he said to the stagehands, "we'll pull Nero back and join his cage to the runway."

Priscilla stepped inside, and the cameraman moved in to get the shots. The first was a simple shot made at the top of the cliff, then they cut away as she teetered and seemed to fall. Next, they cut away to the floor, and Priscilla came down into the artificial pit and glanced apprehensively at the green leaves, trying to ignore Nero's loud roar that came to her through the scenery. Following Lem's directions, she made a slight jump and sprawled on the hard surface.

"That's it!" Lem said. "Just right. Now, while you're still pushing up with your hands, look over toward the jungle. You hear the lion, and you're suddenly afraid. That's it! Hold it! More! Now jump to your feet and throw your hand up over your mouth to show you're holding back a scream. This is where you've seen the lion. You've actually seen that beast! Let's have lots of terror here—great! Great! That's perfect! Now, back up toward the wall—that's it! Your back right against it. Now, hold your hands out as if you could hold that lion away with them. That's it! One more! Hang on now! Look as scared as you can, Priscilla!" Finally he was satisfied and said, "Cut! That's a take! Okay, Paddock!" he hollered, signaling that the scene with Priscilla was finished and Paddock could get ready to help them get the shots of Nero.

Paddock was standing with a stagehand, and he was out of sight of the action. He turned to Jim Wilson, who had been his assistant on building the set, and said, "Okay, here we go, Jim." Paddock threw up the cage and reached through and punched Nero's flank. "I guess they're rolling the cameras. They wanted to get one of him coming out of the jungle."

"Are you sure we're ready?" Wilson asked nervously.

Paddock was accustomed to people being frightened of his wild animals. He reached over and said, "It'll be okay. Here, this is the button that releases the inner cage door and lets Nero into the set." He reached out and threw a toggle switch, which started a slight humming. "We'll have to do this several times, and I'll need to be out front. So I'll put him back in here, and he'll come right into the cage. You drop that cage right here that I just opened, and that's all there is to it." Paddock turned to leave, thinking about the best ways to make Nero react and get good shots for the cameramen.

Priscilla had strolled casually over to the caged door through which she had entered, behind which the cameras had been stationed. She turned and looked up at Jason, who was watching the scene from the top of the artificial rock wall. "Now, are you satisfied?" she said. "That wasn't so bad, was it?"

Paddock appeared right then and suddenly his face turned pale. He gasped, "Miss Winslow—" He ran over, shouldering men aside, and made a grab at the latch that held the door shut. At the same moment Priscilla heard a sound, a low, guttural rumbling behind her. She thought it was from Nero, who was locked safely away, but when she turned, the huge black-maned lion suddenly stepped out into the open and paused.

"Priscilla! The lion!" Peter yelled.

Priscilla's blood seemed to freeze. The lion was standing in the middle of the set, confused by the lights, and she could not move.

Charlie Paddock shouted, "Miss Winslow—through here!" He grabbed the latch and heaved, but nothing happened! Paddock let out a short utterance, a mixture of fear and anger, and yanked at the latch again. "It's jammed!" he said. He yanked one more time and racked the skin from his palms. Turning, he saw Nero slowly advancing.

"Paddock! Do something!" Lem cried out in an agonized voice. He was watching the lion move forward slowly, and his heart seemed to stop when the lion swung his head around and roared.

"Got to go through the chute!" Paddock yelled. He pushed men aside, knocking one of them down in a mad dash to get around and come through the other way. He could not seem to move fast enough. When he reached the cage he saw Wilson standing there befuddled. "The lion's in with the woman!" he shouted. "Help me get this cage out of the way!" The two men fought to open the cage, and both of them feared the terrible mauling that would happen to Priscilla Winslow if he did not get there in time.

Priscilla backed up slowly, her eyes never leaving the lion. Her movement caught the lion's eyes, and his head suddenly fixed. Priscilla's back touched the wall, and she tore her eyes from the huge animal long enough to sweep around the set. Paddock had disappeared, and Peter was desperately tearing and beating at the jammed lock.

Priscilla stood against the wall frozen, not able to speak or to cry out. Nero suddenly went into a crouch as she had seen cats do many times. He tensed his legs down under him, and she saw the huge muscles ripple on the sides and legs of the lion. His eyes seemed to glitter, and his mouth opened slightly, revealing two rows of sharp, ferocious teeth. She could almost feel them tearing into her flesh, and all she could do was stand there and pray. It was not a prayer of words, but a desperate plea from her heart. A wordless, almost mindless, cry that seemed to echo in her spirit for God to do something.

She watched as the lion gathered himself and knew that he was about to spring. There was no place to run, no place to hide, and she knew she was no match for the speed of the fierce animal.

Somebody—she thought it was Easy—said, "He's going to jump! Somebody get a gun!"

Nero was not more than seven or eight feet away from her now and could not miss. She tried to close her eyes but could not. Then the lion twitched his tail, and she knew she was lost. . . .

She thought with regret of all the things she would never do, but at the same time she was conscious that despite her fear of being mauled, she was not afraid to die. It was only the sense of things lost that grieved her. She drew back, prepared to feel the tearing jaws and claws of the wild beast.

Suddenly Priscilla heard a yell, and something struck the lion directly on the back. Nero had been prepared to spring but was knocked off balance.

Priscilla did cry out then when she saw that Jason had leaped from his perch on the fake cliff and had struck the beast, knocking Nero off balance, and sprawled directly in front of him.

"Jason!" she cried, and a shout went up from the onlookers. For a moment Nero was confused, then he gained his equilibrium and spotted the man lying in front of him. With a roar he leaped, and Jason lay helpless in his path. Jason did not try to rise but rolled on his back. As Nero reached him, Jason unleashed a tremendous kangaroo-like kick that caught the lion in the chest. The lion clawed quicker than the eye could follow. His mighty claw swung out and caught Jason's leg, ripping the trousers and tearing into flesh. Crimson blood immediately stained Jason's pants.

The lion crouched to spring again as Jason lay curled in pain. Suddenly a voice broke from behind him. "Nero!" and then there was a sharp cracking sound. The lion whirled, and Charlie Paddock emerged from the trap carrying nothing but a whip in his hand. Nero immediately advanced, crouching toward the man who stood still and met his eye with a steely look of command. "Nero!" he said in a hard voice. "Back, Nero!" Paddock lowered his voice and said in a different tone, "He's going to follow me, Miss Winslow. You stay right there until I get him back into the chute."

Jason lay sprawled on the floor and watched as Paddock slowly moved to the lion's right. Nero followed, and at several points seemed about to spring. Paddock spoke constantly, and several times, just as the lion was about to attack, Paddock would crack the whip with a single motion of his wrist, causing the lion to flinch and stop. Looking down, Jason saw the blood that had stained his torn trousers dripping onto the floor. Ignoring the pain, he glanced at Priscilla. She was not watching the action between Paddock and Nero. Her eyes were fixed on him. Suddenly he smiled and winked at her and saw her react in shock. Despite Paddock's instructions, she stepped to his side and knelt, putting her arms around him. They both turned to watch as Paddock maneuvered the beast, putting himself between Nero and the two people who were crouched on the floor behind him. Nero roared and prepared to spring, but Paddock's whip cracked again, and the small, trim trainer leaped forward. "Back, Nero! Into the cage!" he shouted.

Nero swung his head uncertainly, dropped it, and with a disgruntled roar entered the cage.

"Throw that switch, Wilson!" Paddock yelled. He heard a whirling sound, and the cage door slammed with a thud behind the lion. Paddock immediately ran over and knelt down beside Priscilla. "Did he get you bad, Jason?"

"Not too bad," Jason said.

Paddock pulled the pant leg up and shook his head. "Those claws are dirty. We've got to get you disinfectant and maybe a few stitches." He looked over and said, "Break that door down!"

Within minutes Peter appeared back on the set with a sledgehammer, gave one mighty swing, and the door creaked open. He came rushing over, his eyes wide with fear. "Are you all right, sis?"

"I'm all right." Priscilla had her arms around Jason, and she looked down and whispered, "How could you do it, Jason?"

Jason Ballard nestled in her arms, aware of her soft figure pressing against him. He looked up, and despite the pain in his leg, he grinned. "Never was a lion couldn't be had," he muttered. It was part of the old refrain he had often said, "Never was a horse couldn't be rode. Never was a rider couldn't be throwed."

She suddenly leaned forward and kissed him full on the lips.

Tears filled her eyes, and then she hugged him fiercely as the people on the set crowded around. Jason's face was pressed against her, but she could understand his muffled words.

"I'd have jumped in with the lion sooner if I'd have known it would get me this kind of response!"

CHAPTER TWENTY-ONE

BITTER FRUIT

★ ★ ★ ★

"I'm not sure we ought to bother Nolan at home," Dr. Gunn said. He shifted uneasily behind the wheel of the small car that sped through the growing darkness. "Why couldn't we talk about it tomorrow at church?"

Harold Parsley turned to face the doctor, saying, "If we're going to hire another pastor, we need to get his feelings on it. It was a pretty big disappointment for Nolan when the church chose Brother Winslow. Now, we've settled it, haven't we? We need a third man to come on to take some of the load off of Andrew and Nolan, too."

"I don't see what the rush is," the doctor said.

"I don't want talk to get around to Nolan that we're looking for another associate pastor. He might feel threatened by it. If he's not home, we'll just talk to him tomorrow, but he probably is."

"All right. You win, Harold, but I can't stay long. I've got to make some calls at the hospital."

"It won't take long." The two men had been in a meeting with the elders, which had lasted past eight o'clock. They had decided to call a third man onto the pastoral staff. After considerable talk, Parsley had convinced Dr. Gunn that they should inform Nolan that night, and Gunn had finally given in. Now the two men sped along, and Parsley remarked, "His house is right down on that old road. It isn't too far from here. It's just off Elm Street going to the beach. . . ."

★ ★ ★ ★

Dorothy had never felt so washed out and emotionally drained. For an hour she listened as Nolan tried to persuade her to leave and marry him. At first she answered with arguments, but soon she saw that he was past listening to reason. She finally sat down in a chair and closed her eyes, putting her head back. He came over, knelt beside her, and whispered of his love for her. But there was no response in her heart now, nothing but bitterness and ashes. She looked up once and said, "Nolan, I never loved you—never!"

"I think you did. I think you do now," he said.

"No, I was lonely, and I allowed myself to be drawn away from Andrew. I liked the things you said. Every woman likes to be told that she's admired, that she's pretty—but I should never have allowed myself to get involved with you. I knew it was terribly wrong all the time." She rose and wrung her hands, saying, "Why did I ever do it? Things can never be the same again! There's no going back from a thing like this!"

"Then let's go on," Nolan urged. He caught her in his arms, but she struggled free.

"Nolan, you're never going to touch me again."

Her face was pale, but Nolan Cole saw the fierce determination in her eyes and slumped. "I guess I've always known it would end like this. I'll have to leave the church."

"No, don't do that," Dorothy cried. "What we did was very wrong, but it's not the end of life."

"No, I'll have to leave. I do love you no matter what you feel about me. It would be torment for me to stay around."

For some time she tried to persuade him, but he was adamant. Finally she looked at the clock on the mantel and started. "Look, it's nearly nine o'clock! I've got to get home! They don't know where I am!"

She hurriedly grabbed her coat, and Nolan helped her put it on. He did not attempt to touch her, and as she settled her hat, he said only, "I know it's over, but I'll never forget you, Dorothy."

Without answering, Dorothy stepped outside the door. Nolan followed her and almost ran into her when she stopped abruptly. He looked up, and a shock ran through him as he saw Dr. Gunn and Harold Parsley. Their car was parked out in the street, but neither of them had heard it stop. The two men were almost on the porch, not five feet away from the couple, and now a sense of doom filled Nolan Cole. He stood there silently staring at the two men.

Dorothy was as stunned as Cole at the sight of the two elders from the church. Her lips moved, yet she was unable to speak a word. Fear tore through her as she stood there, and her knees trembled as a wave of guilt washed over her.

★ ★ ★ ★

Gunn and Parsley were as shocked as the startled pair they faced. The silence ran on, and finally Dr. Gunn said quietly, "I'm sorry to see this. I'm sorry for both of you—and sorry for Brother Winslow. Come along, Parsley."

Parsley started to speak angrily, but Gunn grabbed his arm and pulled him toward the car. When they were back inside the car and seated, Gunn started the vehicle and drove away in silence. Parsley looked back toward the house, then turned and said furiously, "Are you just going to let it go like that, Gunn?"

Gunn's face was stiff and fixed as he stared ahead at the road. He had always had an affection and admiration for Dorothy Winslow, and he'd always trusted Nolan Cole as a man of God. The sight of them coming out of Nolan's house had been one of the worst shocks he had felt in his entire life. He drove on silently, saying nothing as he thought about the pain and devastation this would cause.

Parsley looked at him, peering into the darkness, and said bitterly, "It wasn't innocent. Did you see the look on their faces? They're guilty! Both of them! It was written all over them!"

"Yes, it was," Gunn said slowly.

"Well, what are we going to do about it?"

Gunn was a compassionate man, but he had a great deal of wisdom, too. "It'll have to come out, Harold," he said, "but we'll do it as quietly as possible."

"You mean we won't denounce them publicly?"

"What good would that do? It would just shake the faith of some, and it would destroy both of them."

"Well, don't they deserve it after what they've done?"

"Do you want to get your just desserts, Harold?" Gunn asked quietly. He turned quickly and held Parsley's eyes with a penetrating stare. "You've never done anything wrong? You'd be glad to have every action of your life scrutinized and put before the eyes of men?"

The doctor's sharp tone caused Parsley to flinch. He settled down in his seat and pulled his head between his shoulders as the car rumbled along. Finally he said gloomily, "All right. I won't throw the first stone. I guess that's what you're saying, but we've got to do *something*, Gunn."

"Yes, we have to go to Andrew and tell him what is happening." He drove on silently for a while, then he said, "And I'd rather die a thousand deaths than to tell Andrew Winslow that his wife has been unfaithful with his friend. . . !"

★　★　★　★

"Stop the car, Nolan. Don't drive up in front of the house. I'll get out here."

"What difference does it make? Harold Parsley will make sure everyone knows before twenty-four hours have gone by."

Dorothy did not argue. She feared the same thing. As she opened the door, her mind was numb from dread with what lay ahead. She got out, and when Nolan said, "Dorothy . . ." she ignored him and walked stiffly down the walk. The car roared by after a moment, but she forced her eyes away from it, not even wanting to see the car that Nolan owned.

As she walked toward the parsonage, she thought of a story about a man going before a firing squad. At the last moment, he had been reprieved, but the condemned man had written graphically about the fear, the shame, and the guilt that had gripped him as he made those last steps. Now she knew exactly how that man felt. When she reached the front door and put her hand on the knob, she seemed to be paralyzed. She could not move for a moment, neither could she pray, although she tried. "How can I pray to God," she whispered, "after the horrible way I have sinned against Him? How can I face Andrew and the children?" She stood there hesitating, overwhelmed by despair, and then somehow she summoned up enough courage to open the door.

As soon as she stepped inside, she heard her name called, and then Andrew appeared in the hall, lines of worry etched on his tired face. "Where have you been, Dorothy? I've been worried sick! And the children are worried, too! I finally put them to bed." He stepped closer and took one look at her face. "What's wrong?"

he asked. "You're pale as a sheet—and you're trembling. Come . . . come and sit down. What's wrong? Did you have an accident?"

Dorothy said nothing because she could not speak. Finally he led her into the drawing room and helped her into a seat. Her legs collapsed, and as he sat down beside her, she took one look at his ace that was lined with concern. Her heart was ready to break, and she cried out, "Oh, Andrew—" Then she bent over and put her face in her hands and began to weep great tearing sobs that she could not contain.

Andrew was shocked as he watched Dorothy's shoulders heave uncontrollably. "What is it?" he said, putting his arms around her. "Please! Tell me, Dorothy. What is it?"

She could not speak for a long time. The gentle touch of his arms around her and the anxious compassion of his voice caused a bitterness to rise in her. For so many lonely months it was what she had yearned for—but now it was no good. She had wrongfully sought for it elsewhere. Another wave of remorse and shame washed over her, and she began to sob even harder. Finally she cried herself out, and she felt his hands helping her to straighten up. He pulled his handkerchief out and wiped the tears away from her face.

"What is it? Is it your mother? Tell me, Dorothy."

There was no escaping the horrible truth of it all. Dorothy knew that he had to know. Her heart was breaking at the thought of what her betrayal would do to him. If ever there was hope to go on, she knew she had to be the one to confess her terrible sin to him. She pushed herself away from him and whispered, "Andrew, I've got to tell you something—and I can't bear to think of it."

Andrew took her hand and held it. "What is it, Dorothy? Whatever it is, it'll be all right. I'll stand by you. Tell me what is bothering you." There was an urgency in his voice, and he reached out and dried another tear from her face with the handkerchief.

This last gesture almost broke Dorothy. This was the old Andrew she remembered. Full of compassion, full of love, but now it seemed all empty and vain. It was too late.

She straightened herself up, and her voice hardened as she said, "I've . . . I've been having an affair with a man." She saw shock leap into his eyes, and his head flew back as if he had been struck. Disbelief clouded his face, and then she saw anger twist his lips. Knowing she had to face it fully, she went on. "I know this will destroy everything you ever felt for me, and I'm sorry to hurt you. Sorry to hurt the children. I have no excuse for my sin before you or God."

"Who is the man?" Andrew demanded, his eyelids coming down and half shading his eyes. His mouth grew tense, and he removed his hand from her arm and sat there, his back stiffly erect.

"Nolan Cole," Dorothy said flatly.

A wild and tortured look of anger and fear crept across Andrew's face. Dorothy had never seen him look like this. He stared at her coldly as if she were a stranger.

"How long has it been going on?" he asked, his voice stark and bare. He listened as she spoke in a broken fashion, and finally he said, "Why did you do it, Dorothy?"

Dorothy Winslow could not answer. She could not tell him of her loneliness and how rejected she felt by him. It was too late for that now. There was no excuse for the sin she had fallen prey to. She mutely shook her head and was aware that he was standing on his feet over her. She heard his voice then, although she dared not look up.

"All right. Cole will resign. He'll have to go!"

Dorothy could not refrain then from looking up. Her eyes were swollen, and tears blurred the sight of Andrew's face, but she saw how pale he was. "What about us, Andrew?" she whispered.

"We'll have to continue to the world, to the church, as if things were the same—but it's all over between us, Dorothy."

His words rang like a death knell to Dorothy Winslow. As he turned and walked away, never in her life had she felt so alone as she sat on the couch listening to the monotonous ticking of the clock out in the hall.

CHAPTER TWENTY-TWO

ILL TIDINGS

★ ★ ★ ★

Dr. Maurice Gunn was a busy man, as most physicians were. He began his day early and ended it as soon as possible so he could go home and be with his family. But emergency calls often pulled him away from the two-story frame house that he and his wife had designed and built on the beach. Gunn was a mountain man from the Blue Ridge Mountains of Virginia, where he was born and spent his youth. He had done his college work at the University of Virginia and then had moved to Pennsylvania to complete medical school. His move to Los Angeles had been at the urging of his wife, Laura Jones, who had grown up in Fort Lauderdale, Florida. Ever since she was a child, she had been enchanted by the charm of the ocean and never forgot it. When the opportunity had come to move to California, especially to live on the beach in Los Angeles, Laura had persuaded Maurice that the life there would be better for them and for their three young children. Maurice had long since grown weary of the cold winters in Pennsylvania and required little persuasion. The two of them had made the move and never regretted it.

Gunn had looked forward to spending a quiet evening at home, but he was pulled away from his dinner table by an emergency appendectomy. The operation had proved difficult, and he decided to stay to observe his patient for a while. Finally pulling off his operating mask and clothing, he dressed and left the hospital and headed for home. Weariness hit him as he drove along, as it usually did after a long day, and he thought eagerly of the late snack that his wife, Laura, would have prepared for him. With equal longing, he looked forward to lying in bed, where he could listen to the surf for a time, then drift off to sleep.

As he passed the new church, his mind suddenly was pulled away from thoughts of his own comfort to the problems of his pastor and the pastor's wife. He glanced at the new edifice and thought, *It's a beautiful building, but it cost all of us too much—especially Andrew.* Even as the thought flickered through his mind, he glanced up and saw a single light burning on the second floor. Impulsively, Maurice touched the brake of the Reo he was driving and pulled into the parking lot. He shut the engine off and sat there for a moment thinking about the difficult situation.

Three weeks had passed since he and Parsley had encountered Dorothy and Nolan at Cole's house on the beach. It had been a difficult time for all of them. Gunn had practically threatened Harold Parsley physically. Parsley was a man given to gossip, which was exactly what the church did *not* need at this time. Gunn was a deeply spiritual man who would not flinch at the grave responsibility he faced, but he wanted to proceed with discretion and scriptural wisdom in dealing with the offending parties.

He had taken Parsley home that night and sat out in the car with him for over an hour, stressing the fact that the situation, as terrible as it was, would only be made worse if it became public. "We'll have to handle this, just you and me, Harold," Gunn had said. "Since only the two of us know about it, if it gets out, I'll know exactly who it is that spilled the beans. Andrew Winslow is a good man, though mistaken, I think, in some things. And despite what you think, Dorothy Winslow is a good woman who got caught in a trap that many have fallen into. Do not misunderstand me. It is a grievous sin, but let us not forget it's only by God's grace that you and I haven't had the same sort of problems." He had fixed his eyes on Parsley and said, "Harold, you and I will handle this. We'll talk to Andrew, and we'll talk to Nolan Cole. Nolan will have to leave. What Brother Winslow will do, I can't say, but it would ruin his ministry now, and that would be a tragedy for the kingdom of God. We've got to work together and by God's mercy somehow redeem them all."

As Gunn got out of the car slowly, he remembered how Parsley had vowed to keep the matter in confidence. Since then, the two of them had endured two sessions that were bitter to think of. As Gunn looked up at the window of Andrew's office, he shook at the memory of Andrew's face when they had met with him and revealed their knowledge of the guilty affair. The other was with Nolan Cole, and to Gunn this was almost as painful. Nolan, too, was a man who had fallen into the trap that had ensnared men since the beginning of time. They had encountered no problem with Nolan when they confronted him. He had informed them at once that he was resigning and leaving town in two weeks. Gunn had gone back alone and spent several hours with Nolan and encouraged him to take some time off and spend it seeking God's forgiveness and direction. And before Nolan had left, the doctor had gained considerable hope that Nolan would find peace and forgiveness. Though the whole affair would surely take its toll on Nolan, Gunn knew that the young man had great ability and deep down still wanted to serve God.

The brief winter season had brought cooler temperatures to Los Angeles, and the breeze that now blew in off the sea was still brisk but warmer than it had been the last few weeks. Taking in a deep breath as he entered the new church and started up the stairs, Dr. Gunn prayed a brief prayer for wisdom. Reaching the door with the sign "Pastor" on the outside, he knocked, and after a brief pause, he heard Winslow's voice.

"Come in!"

Gunn stepped inside and found Winslow sitting behind his desk. "You're working late, Andrew."

"I'm not working. Just sitting here."

Andrew's face was drawn, and he had lost weight in the past three weeks. His cheeks seemed to be hollow and more drawn in, and dark circles under his eyes told of the agony he was silently suffering. The physician's quick eye took these signs in, but he said cheerfully, "I've been working late, too. Mrs. Olsen's oldest son had a bad case of appendicitis." He sat in the chair across from Andrew and stretched his arms upward and flexed his fingers. "It was a close thing, Andrew. For a time, I thought we were going to lose him."

Andrew sat up straighter, saying, "I'll have to get over there right away. Nobody called me."

"I think it'd be better if you wait until tomorrow. Ted's asleep now, and I've given Mrs. Olsen something to help her sleep, too. You might have Dorothy go by and spend some time with her. Mrs. Olsen is a mighty fine woman. She's had a hard time raising those four children of hers with no husband."

"Yes. She is. I'll speak to Dorothy, Maurice."

Gunn let his eyes run over the backs of the leather books that lined the walls of the large study and said nothing for a while. The awkward silence dragged on, and finally he leaned forward and said, "I got a call from Nolan yesterday. He's down in Alabama. That's where his home is. Just outside of Montgomery. I think he's going to be all right."

"He's a hypocrite and has no business in the ministry!" Andrew said bitterly.

Gunn was not too shocked by the harshness of Andrew Winslow's voice. In the last few weeks, he had already heard similar remarks. And he had spent hours praying and asking God for wisdom to help his pastor through this difficult time. In a voice filled with gentleness and concern, Gunn said, "Andrew, I know this has been the hardest thing you've ever had to face. I'm truly sorry. It's a bitter thing that Nolan failed all of us. He's hurting pretty badly himself, Andrew. I could tell that God has convicted him deeply, and He wants to work in him and restore him."

Andy got up from the leather chair and began to pace the floor, his fists clenched tightly and his brow furrowed. He stopped to look out the window, but the darkness outside only reflected the stygian darkness of his soul. Turning, he came and slumped back down in his chair and shook his head. "What could be in his heart to make him do it?" he murmured, shaking his head.

Gunn hesitated for a moment, then looked directly at Andrew and said, "The same thing that's in my heart—and your heart. You know your Bible as well as any man. You've even preached on why people sin, from a verse in Jeremiah, 'The heart is desperately wicked. Who can know it?' In the time you've been here, you've seen Nolan's dedication to the ministry. I don't believe Nolan set out to do this terrible thing any more than Dorothy did. I don't think any of us ever wake up one morning and say, 'I think I'll rob a bank today. . . .' And yet some Christians have fallen into bad company and done just that. Sin doesn't come to us like this, does it? Why, you preached a sermon on it three months ago. How that sin often comes first as a thought, or maybe one tempting look as it did to David when he looked down and saw Bathsheba bathing on the palace roof. Do you suppose the king of Israel said, 'I'm going to commit adultery with that woman, and if her husband gives me any trouble, I'll have him killed'?"

Shifting in his chair, Andrew stroked his head slowly. "Well, of course not. But still, they could've broken off before they actually fell into an affair."

Gunn leaned forward, his eyes sharp and intent. He said quietly, "You know better than that, Andrew. You've been a preacher long enough to have encountered almost every kind of problem human beings can have. You know that even Christians who love God with all their hearts fall into sin. Maybe not this particular sin, but we are in a battle against the world, the flesh, and the devil. That's what the Bible identifies as our enemies. I'm humbled to have to admit it, but I've had my own trouble with the flesh. No one is beyond temptation." He hesitated for a moment, then added, "Two times in my life, I came that close"—he held up his fingers measuring off a small portion of an inch—"to falling into exactly the same kind of trap. A doctor runs into these things, and I would guess that preachers do, too. I still remember the times I found myself alone with a patient . . . an attractive woman who was lonely and confused. It's easy enough for a man to be brought into the wrong relationship."

Gunn continued to speak for some time, and he got up and said, "Let's pray about it, Andrew." He bowed his head instantly without waiting and prayed for Andrew. Then he prayed for Nolan and for Dorothy, and ended by praying that he might overcome temptation in his own life. He picked up his hat and started for the door, but then a thought came to him and he said, "Good night, Andrew. If you ever want to talk, you've got my number."

Getting up from his desk, Andrew walked over and put out his hand. The visit by the physician had disturbed him somehow, but he said, "Thanks for coming, Maurice. It's been a help."

Once again Maurice Gunn hesitated. He knew it was possible to go too far with counseling, and finally he said briefly, "I'm worried about Dorothy. Laura saw her yesterday, and she noticed she had lost weight. She said Dorothy seemed very nervous. A thing like this can destroy a woman, especially a sensitive woman like your wife. Be very careful, Andrew. She needs you more than she ever has in her life. In a way, I think whether she gets through this and goes on lies in your hands." He started to say something more, but wisdom told him that he could not push it any further. He saw a stubborn light in Andrew's piercing blue eyes. "Well, I'll see you in church."

★ ★ ★ ★

When the door shut, Andrew turned and walked back to his desk. Sitting down, he put his head between his hands and thought about what Gunn had said. The last few weeks had been the most difficult and despairing time of his whole life. Since he had told Dorothy they had to keep up a front, an emptiness filled his heart and a bitterness robbed him of sleep every night. He carried out his duties in a perfunctory manner, preaching mechanically, saying the right things in the right tone of voice. As usual some church members had filed by after each service and congratulated him on his sermon. Each time he shook their hand, he flinched inwardly with a touch of cynicism, knowing that his congregation had not gotten his best. He had comforted himself with the thought: *Well, it's the preaching of the message that's important, not the messenger. God's had some pretty sorry messengers in His day. He's used some pretty crooked sticks, and I guess I'm one of them.*

Finally he bowed his head and prayed for a long time—or tried to. The heavens seemed like brass, and he could not get through to God. Every time he thought he almost made a breakthrough, he would think of Dorothy, and the hardness that had gripped his heart would stop him. After an hour he rose in despair, got his hat, and went home. When he arrived the children were in bed, and Dorothy was in her room. He walked down the hall and glanced toward her door. More than once these last few weeks he had passed by and thought he heard the sound of weeping, but she had kept herself secluded as much as circumstances permitted. He hesitated, and the impulse came to knock on her door, but then he thought, *It's her responsibility to come to me. I'm the one who's been hurt and betrayed. She's the one who had the affair—not me!* Bound by pride and an unforgiving spirit, Andrew turned and went to the guest room, undressed, lay down, and spent the night tossing and turning in a sleepless, bitter state of mind.

★ ★ ★ ★

Priscilla had just sat down to breakfast when a knock sounded on her door. When she rose and went and opened it, she was surprised to see Dorothy Winslow standing there. "Why, Dorothy," she said. "How nice to see you. You're just in time for breakfast."

"No. I couldn't eat anything, Priscilla—but I do need to talk to you."

"Why, of course. Please come in and at least have a cup of coffee." She was somewhat shocked by Dorothy's appearance. She had not seen her friend in two weeks. Priscilla had noticed that Dorothy had not been at church the previous Sunday and had assumed that one of the children was sick. Now she suspected it might have been Dorothy herself. Her color was bad, and there was a dullness to her eyes that bespoke some sort of illness. "Let me just eat this egg and toast. How do you like your coffee?"

"Sugar and cream, please," Dorothy said, sitting down across from Priscilla.

Priscilla served Dorothy her coffee and began to eat. She was somewhat puzzled, for although Dorothy had visited her several times, there was something troubling about her appearance today. Dorothy Winslow had always been a calm person, but now she displayed a nervousness in her manner. She could not keep her hands still, and her shoulders twitched occasionally in a strange fashion. Priscilla watched as Dorothy drank the coffee without even seeming to taste it. When Dorothy was finished, Priscilla said, "Come on over to the divan. We can get more comfortable there." When the two women had seated themselves, Priscilla pulled her legs up under her and put her arm on the back of the couch. "What is it, Dorothy? You seem troubled. Aren't you feeling well?"

Dorothy had slept very little the previous night, and her voice had no life in it as she spoke. "Priscilla, I've got to talk to someone. I've . . . I've . . . done something that is about to drive me crazy. I can't go on like this—!"

"Why, Dorothy!" Priscilla sat up straight and leaned over to take Dorothy's hand with both of hers. It was cold and trembling. "What in the world is it?"

Dorothy Winslow bit her lip. She had steeled herself for this moment. Her guilt had almost destroyed her, and now her lips trembled as she said, "You won't understand this, Priscilla, and I'm . . . I'm ashamed to admit it." She hesitated and then could not go on. Tears filled her eyes, and she suddenly lowered her face and began to weep.

Priscilla moved at once to sit beside her. She still held her hand, but she put her right arm across Dorothy's shoulders. Dorothy turned to face her and suddenly buried her face against Priscilla's shoulder. Priscilla held her tightly and tried to comfort her. She could not imagine what had happened to cause Dorothy such agony. Finally the storm of weeping passed, and Dorothy fished a handkerchief out of her purse and sat there unable to look up. "Whatever it is, Dorothy, it's all right," Priscilla said gently. "It won't change how I feel about you."

Dorothy looked up and whispered, "I've . . . committed adultery, Priscilla!" As soon as the confession was out, Dorothy began to weep again inconsolably. When she had calmed down, she unburdened the whole story—the disappointment in her marriage, the loneliness, Nolan's kindness and attention, and the night at his house on the beach. Her voice broke at various times, and twice she seemed unable to go on. Finally, she shook her head and said, "I know you must think I'm the worst woman who ever lived, and I . . . I guess I am."

Priscilla was shocked by the revelation. Not a word of it had reached her ears. As she sat there holding her friend, vivid memories of the shame she had experienced over Eddie Rich came to mind. She could almost feel the burden of guilt and despair that weighed Dorothy down. At one point, her own despair had driven her to the edge of hopelessness. Then Esther Winslow's gentle and uncondemning face flashed in her mind. Priscilla's heart filled with the same love and compassion that Esther had given to her that day in the hospital when Ruth lay so sick. Looking down at Dorothy, Priscilla knew she could do no less than what God had extended to her that day when Esther prayed with her. She said quickly, her arms still around Dorothy's shoulders, "Dorothy, I know how hard it is not to feel all the shame and guilt. I felt that way myself when my life got off track."

"But you didn't do what I did, Priscilla," Dorothy said, wiping her eyes with the lace handkerchief she had pulled from her pocket.

For the next hour, Priscilla sat there speaking softly. She told Dorothy the whole story of how she had had an affair with Eddie Rich back in New York, and how she had lived with him thinking they were married.

"But . . . but that's different. You thought you were married to Eddie."

"Not at the beginning. I was an adulteress just the same, and there was no excuse for it. I was in rebellion against my family and against God. Let me tell you what God has done in my life since then." Priscilla went on to relate how Esther Winslow had found her almost ready to commit suicide, and how she had brought the good news of the Gospel to her. "That's when I found out, Dorothy, that Jesus was real and His mercy and forgiveness could change even me. Before that time, I only thought of Him as someone in a story in a book. Esther wouldn't give up on me when I already had given up all hope. She kept on telling me about His love. At first I couldn't believe it. But it is true. You know that better than I. You've grown up in a minister's home, and you're married to one. You know the Scripture. I don't know much about the Bible, but I do know it teaches one thing. That Jesus loves us, and not just when we're good, either," she said strongly. "He loves us when we're bad."

Dorothy looked up, her eyes too painful to see. She had been a sensitive woman all her life, and now she shook her head. "I . . . I know that's true, but somehow I can't forgive myself."

"Exactly. I was the same way," Priscilla said. "Do you know that there were times when I was going through all that that I wouldn't pray because I was too ashamed to go to God in prayer?"

"Why, that's exactly what I've been doing."

"Dorothy, you mustn't do that. Running from God now will only make all this worse. What happened with Eddie, and what happened between you and Nolan are grievous sins. And there will be serious consequences, but you can't get through this on your own. Only God can help you. He can forgive and cleanse you."

The two women sat there, and Priscilla's voice was quiet and reassuring as she continued to speak. Dorothy sat listening, and for over an hour Priscilla ministered to Dorothy Winslow's broken heart. Finally Priscilla said, "Have you asked the Lord to forgive you?"

"Oh yes! Over and over again, but—"

"Then let me tell you, Dorothy Winslow." She paused and then said emphatically, "*Your sins are forgiven!* God has said if we confess our sins, He is faithful and just to forgive us our sins. And I always liked the last part of this verse, 'And to cleanse us from all unrighteousness.' Dorothy," Priscilla said earnestly, her eyes glowing, "once we ask to be forgiven, if we are earnest and sincere with our repentance, it's finished as far as God's concerned. You know He promised to cast our sins into the depths of the sea and remove them as far as the east is from the west. You have to believe Him, Dorothy, because that's what God has done with your sin."

"But I feel so . . . so *dirty*! I can't stop thinking about what I did."

"And who do you think keeps bringing that up?" Priscilla demanded. "If I sinned against you, would you keep bringing it up after I asked you for forgiveness?"

"No, of course not."

"Well, do you think you're better than God?"

For the first time Dorothy smiled somewhat wryly. "No, I don't think that, Priscilla."

"Then you know that you have asked a loving God, and a truthful God who never changes, to forgive you. Now, can't you just accept that and believe that you're as clean in His sight as a person can be?"

Dorothy suddenly reached over, took Priscilla's hand, and held to it tightly. "Oh, Priscilla, can it really be true?"

"Yes, it's true. Now, I want you to begin doing something that's very strange. Even though there will be consequences for what you've done, I want you to begin thanking God. I know," she said quickly, seeing the startled look on Dorothy's face, "it sounds strange, and it's probably the last thing in the world you want to do. But when I had such a terrible problem in my own life, Esther taught me that once we've asked for forgiveness, that's what will help us more than anything else."

"Give thanks?" Dorothy said. "Thanks for what?"

"Thank Him for the blood of Jesus for saving you and forgiving you for all of this," Priscilla said firmly. "Thanks for two wonderful children who are healthy and strong. Give thanks to God for your husband, even though right now you're not together as you'd like to be. Give Him thanks for that time when you will be together. Thank Him for your friends, for your health. Oh, Dorothy, I know that life seems dark and bitter now, but God is good, and the Lord Jesus gave His life—not just to save us, but to keep us safe."

★　★　★　★

Twenty minutes later Dorothy left, Priscilla's kiss burning on her cheek. Somehow something had changed in her. The prayer they had prayed together had been cleansing, and for the first time since she had fallen into error, Dorothy Winslow felt a ray of hope break through the clouds of guilt and despair that had settled on her heart. As she rode the carriage toward home, she suddenly changed her mind. "Driver," she said, "go to Faith Temple."

"Yes, ma'am."

Dorothy leaned back in the carriage, somewhat frightened, but yet at the same time strengthened by the words of encouragement that Priscilla Winslow had given her. When she arrived at the front of the church, she paid the cabby and then climbed the stairs to the large church and walked into the spacious foyer. She looked around and hesitated for a moment, almost turning around and leaving. Shaking off the nervousness, she felt a new resolve in her heart. She knew what she had to do. When she reached the second floor, she greeted Mrs. Barnes, Andrew's secretary, with a smile.

"Why, Mrs. Winslow," she said. "I'm surprised to see you so early."

"Is my husband with anyone?"

"No, I think you can go right on in," Mrs. Barnes said.

Dorothy walked to the door of Andrew's large office and knocked firmly three times. When Andrew's voice came bidding her to enter, she opened the oak door and quickly stepped inside. Closing the door behind her, Dorothy walked across the room and stood silently in front of his desk. Andrew was standing beside the window looking out. He turned, and something changed in his face the instant he saw her. He said nothing but faced her squarely, his lips tight.

Gripping her purse between her hands, Dorothy stood there gathering her courage. Finally, her voice quivering with emotion, she looked her husband in the eye and said, "Andrew, I've . . . I've come to confess that I've sinned against you terribly." Before he could say anything, she said quietly, "I want to ask you to forgive me." She stood in silence waiting, hoping, as a tear from each eye trailed down her face.

★   ★   ★   ★

Her words seemed to hang in the air, and shock ran through Andrew. Although he had felt it was her duty to come to him, he could not respond as he looked at her. Deep down he knew that he ought to, and there was part of him, a voice that cried, *Forgive her! Go to her, put your arms around her!* But that impulse and that voice were quickly drowned out by another thought that came to him, and he spoke that one aloud. "It's very easy for you, isn't it, Dorothy. All you have to do is say, 'I'm sorry, forgive me. Let's start all over.' " He shook his head, saying, "You really don't think it's that easy, do you?"

"I know it isn't easy, Andrew," Dorothy said, her voice choking.

When she said no more, Andrew Winslow stood staring at this woman who had been his life since he first met her in Africa. A war of emotions—anger, betrayal, hurt, bitterness—raged inside his heart. He of all people knew how difficult it had been for Dorothy. He had seen her silently suffering. He knew that she was in the depths of misery. He also knew his duty as a Christian, and as a husband, but the last three weeks had affected him drastically, as well. He had stopped praying. Each day he had spent hours mulling over the betrayal and the injustice that had been done to him. He could not escape these thoughts, and after a time he ceased to try. He had thought on them so long that they dominated his heart, and now he could not break loose from the bitterness that welled up in him.

"Don't you realize what you've done, Dorothy? You've broken your marriage vow—you've ruined my ministry. I can hardly preach anymore. I can't do anything!" He continued to speak harshly, standing before her with his hands clasped tightly behind his back. Finally he said, "We'll just have to go on as we are. I don't think we can ever have what we had before you turned away from me to another man."

Dorothy had not spoken during all of this time, and now she simply said, "All right, Andrew." Then she turned and left his office.

The instant the door closed, Andrew had a sudden impulse to go and jerk the door open and call after her to bring her back inside. But pride, not mercy, controlled his heart. It was stiff within him and would not permit him to speak the words of forgiveness. Deep inside a sinister voice seemed to whisper, *She's sinned against you and against God. Let her suffer a little while. That way she'll know how I feel.* Disturbed by the thought, he turned away from the door and walked back to the window. An emptiness such as he had never known made him shiver as he stood at the window and watched Dorothy climb into a cab and drive away. Still, his pride would not let him bend. Turning abruptly, he went back to his desk and began grimly making plans for his next sermon.

★ ★ ★ ★

Priscilla stared down at the telegram she had torn open nervously, and her eyes swept the page. "Your father has been in an accident. Condition serious. Come home at once."

Blankly Priscilla stared at the yellow sheet of paper with her mother's name at the bottom trying to take it in. Then alarm ran along her nerves, and she left her dressing room at once. She knew that Peter was working on a scene that involved a car race, so she hurried to the garage where he and Easy worked on the cars.

Peter looked up and grinned when he saw her. "Hi, sis. Ready for the big race?"

"Peter, I just got this telegram from Mom." She handed it to him and saw the same shock that she had felt wash across his face.

His face turned pale, and he looked up from the telegram and said, "It must be bad."

"I think it is," Priscilla said. "We've got to leave at once. What will be the quickest way to get there?"

"The *Jolie Blonde*," Peter said as he wiped his hands on a rag. "We can drive straight through without stopping. Have you told Cass?"

"No, not yet. You call him, Peter. I think Jason will want to go with us—and I want him to."

"Then we'll have to get another car from the studio. I'll take care of the car. You find Jason, then go get ready. I think we ought to leave this morning as soon as you can get your things together." He reached out and touched her, saying, "Maybe it's not so bad." But the thread of fear was evident in his voice.

Priscilla said, "I'll go get Jason, and I'll be ready to go as soon as I throw a few things in a suitcase."

"What about the picture?" Peter asked as she turned to go.

"They'll have to shoot around me," Priscilla called over her shoulder.

She went first to find Stan Lem and told him the story.

"You go on home and see about your dad, Priscilla," Lem said. "Don't worry about things here. I'll talk to Porter." He put his hand on her shoulder and said, "I hope it goes well for you, and for your dad."

"Thank you, Stan." Priscilla left the lot and walked toward the corral, where she found Jason currying a horse. He was carrying a cane and still limped. His leg had been badly mauled by the lion.

Jason heard someone approaching and turned. When he saw Priscilla, her face tight and pale, he quickly said, "What is it, Priscilla?"

"It's Dad. He's had a serious accident. Mom says we need to come as quick as we can."

"I'm going, too," Jason said instantly and tossed the brush down.

"I . . . I hoped you would, Jason." She stood there unable to move. The initial shock was passing away, and she feared the worst. "I don't know what I'd do if anything happened to Dad."

Jason came over, put his arms around her, and held her tightly for a long moment, then said, "Are we going to drive through?"

"Yes, Peter's picking out a car big enough for all of us. I've got to stop by my place and get some clothes. I think Peter wants to leave as soon as you can get something together."

★　★　★　★

Peter found Porter, and when the producer heard about the telegram, he said, "Take any car we got, Peter. I'm sorry about all this. Make sure you tell Priscilla not to worry about anything here. We can finish the picture anytime."

Peter nodded gratefully. "Thank you, Mr. Porter. I'll take care of the car."

He left Porter's office and decided to take the studio's Maxwell, which was large enough to carry the three of them comfortably. He drove it down to the gas station, filled it up, and then decided to go by and tell Jolie that they had to go to Wyoming. When he pulled up in front of the front porch, he was surprised to find Tom Ziegler there sitting on the porch with Jolie. "What are you doing here, Tom?" he asked. "It's not time for a lesson, is it?"

Jolie was aggravated by his harsh words. "Is it inconceivable to you that a young man might want to come and spend some time with me just because he likes me?"

Hot words rose to Peter's lips, but before he could speak, Ziegler stepped forward, saying nervously, "I've been meaning to talk to you, Peter."

"About what?" Peter demanded.

"About how I feel about Jolie. I might as well tell you that I love her, and I've asked her to marry me."

Amazement flickered in Peter's eyes, and he said angrily, "You're crazy! You hardly even know her. You're just her tutor."

"I'm not talking about right now. I'm talking about in two or three years when I finish college and establish myself in my career."

Peter had been upset about the news of his father's accident when he had pulled up in front of the boardinghouse, and now it all seemed to boil over. "I won't have it!" he said flatly. "Now, you get out, Ziegler, and don't come back anymore!"

"Wait a minute," Jolie said, her face pale. She was shocked at Peter's anger and incensed by the injustice of it all. "You don't understand, Peter. Tom wants—"

"I know what Tom wants!" Peter said. "And I'm telling him to leave right now. And I'm telling you not to see him again! Now, get out, Ziegler!"

Tom Ziegler was a shy young man and not accustomed to a rough scene. He looked at the anger scrawled across Peter Winslow's face and turned to Jolie. "Maybe we can talk later."

Jolie stood speechless by the swing as Tom left the porch and walked rapidly away. Then she turned to Peter and said, "I told you once before, Peter! You're not my father!"

"I'm the closest thing you've got to one!" he said. "You don't have any business talking about marriage!"

"I'm twenty years old! That's answer enough for you!"

Peter knew he was in the wrong, but he seemed unable to control himself. "You don't know what's best for you right now. You're still too young," he said harshly, staring at Jolie. He could see the anger rising in her face before she even began to speak.

"Peter, you can leave now, and never speak to me again!"

"You mean that, Jolie?"

"Yes!" she snapped. She was close to tears, and the quarrel that had sprung out of nowhere had shaken her terribly.

For one moment, Peter stood staring at the young woman, and then he said, "This is good-bye. My father's been in a serious accident. Jason and Cass and Priscilla and I are leaving." Without saying another word, he turned and walked away and leaped into the car.

★　★　★　★

Jolie's emotions were still swirling with the suddenness of all that had just taken place. She had not been able to take in what he had said, then she ran out, crying, "Peter—Peter! I didn't mean it, Peter!" But all she heard was the roar of the car as it sped away. The dust flew in her eyes as she stood in the middle of the street watching the Maxwell disappear in the distance. She turned away, tears forming in her eyes, and walked slowly back to the house.

CHAPTER TWENTY-THREE

A CHANGE OF HEART

★ ★ ★ ★

Andrew Winslow had not thought it possible to be more miserable than he had for the first few weeks after learning of Dorothy's infidelity, but he was mistaken. As the days ran on, he thought almost constantly of Dorothy's visit to his office when she had asked for forgiveness—and he had refused to give it to her. Since then he had been unable to face her. For the past few days he had stayed at the church until the early hours of the morning before going home and slipping quietly into the spare bedroom. When he awoke each morning, he dressed and left the house without a word, going to a nearby restaurant to eat breakfast. He did everything he could to avoid seeing Dorothy or having to talk to her.

Now he sat in the large leather chair behind the walnut desk and looked around his gleaming new office—and it meant nothing. All of his theology books filled the oak shelves that lined one wall, but he had no inclination to pick one up. He had been unable to eat lately, and he had experienced several bouts of nausea more than once. He thought about visiting Dr. Gunn but stubbornly refused to give in and seek help.

A knock suddenly startled Andrew from his thoughts, and his secretary stepped in. "Miss Winslow is here to see you, pastor."

Andrew straightened and forced himself out of the chair. As Priscilla stepped through the door, he came over and said, "Priscilla, how are you?"

"My father's been in a serious accident," Priscilla said evenly. "I'm leaving to go see him at once."

"Sit down, Priscilla, and tell me what happened—"

"I didn't come to talk about my father. I came to talk about you, pastor," Priscilla said in an even voice, her eyes fixed with great determination on the tall man who stood before her.

Instantly, Andrew stiffened. "I don't understand," he said rather harshly, but in his heart he suspected the reason for Priscilla's visit. There was something in her eyes he could not avoid, and he stood there waiting, hoping that he was wrong.

"I should tell you that Dorothy came to me some time ago and confessed her wrongdoing. She was so ashamed and expected me to reject her. Of course I didn't. I told her how I once had made a grave error in my own life, and how your sister, Esther, helped me see how much God loved me and was willing to forgive and help me. I gave Dorothy what comfort I could and prayed with her. I hope I was able to console her a little bit."

"Well, I'm sure you were a help to her," Andrew said, trying to hide the nervousness growing inside.

Priscilla had prayed earnestly about what she would say to Andrew Winslow. She knew the things she was about to say would be very uncomfortable for both of them, but she felt that she must try to help her cousin, even if it caused Andrew some pain.

"It hurts me to have to be the one to tell you this, but you've been no comfort to her, Andrew! You've been a failure as a husband, and as a father—and most of all as a Christian!"

The bluntness of Priscilla's words struck Andrew like a blow. He blinked in surprise and then a surge of anger ran through him. "Get out of here, Priscilla! I don't need to listen to this!"

"Unless you throw me out bodily, you're going to hear what I have to say! And if you do throw me out," Priscilla said, her eyes flashing, "I'll come right in again!"

She means just exactly what she says, Andrew thought with a shock. "All . . . all right. I'll listen. Will you sit down?"

"No, I won't sit down! I can say what I have to say better standing up! First, I want to tell you how you have violated the Scriptures. I've only been a Christian a very short time, and you've been a minister for a long time. Andrew, you know what the Scriptures say about forgiveness: 'If we will not forgive others, then God will not forgive us.' Have you forgotten that? Do you think Jesus turned people away because they had offended Him? Because they had sinned against Him? You know that He didn't. That's the very reason why He came—to offer His forgiveness!"

"I hardly think you're in a position to be accusing me of anything, Priscilla. You're in a business that promotes immoral motion pictures."

"Not anymore, I'm not. God's convicted me of it, and I'll never act again. When I return, I'm finishing the last segment of the film and then I'm turning in my resignation."

Andrew knew how much Priscilla had her heart set on becoming a famous movie star. Her abrupt decision to resign shocked Andrew, and he stood there speechless.

"Andrew, what are you going to do about Dorothy? Did you marry her before a minister?"

"Why . . . why, yes. Her father," Andrew stuttered.

"Did you promise to love her as long as she lived?"

"Yes, I did."

"But you haven't loved her, have you? Ever since you got involved in this new building project, you've changed, Andrew. Dorothy knows how grievously she's sinned against you. But she repented and came to you to make that confession and ask for your forgiveness. And you've shown her nothing but an unkind, ungenerous, unforgiving spirit. And God is going to hold you accountable for it. You'll either break your pride and humble yourself before God—*and* before Dorothy—or else you'll be a miserable excuse for a man, and no minister of Christ at all! That's all I have to say!"

Priscilla's words hung in the silence of the large office. Andrew stood there, his shoulders slumped as he stared at her. He was angry and confused, but inside, all his excuses and arguments began to crumble. Her words of conviction had stung his conscience. The truth of what she had said even now began to pierce the wall of anger he had thrown up as a defense.

Priscilla hesitated one moment, then said more gently, "I've spoken some very hard things today, Andrew, but I have one more thing to say." Sighing, she looked down at the floor for a moment, then lifted her eyes and said, "I love Dorothy—and I love you, Andrew. We're family, and I only want what's best for both of you. I know Dorothy's made a grave and awful mistake. She's hurt and betrayed you deeply—but you've made a mistake, too. You've let your hurt and pride prevent you from giving and accepting the only thing that can help you both—God's forgiveness. I believe your error stems from pride, and if I understand what the Bible teaches, pride is the sin that God hates more than any other. 'Pride goeth before destruction, and a haughty spirit before a fall,'" she quoted. "I have been praying for you, and I will continue to pray that you will seek God, and that you'll find the grace to forgive your wife—who still loves you—as God has forgiven her."

Priscilla turned and left the office, closing the door softly behind her. Andrew stood looking at it as if blinded, then with a jerk of his shoulders, he walked over to stand before the window. As he watched Priscilla drive off, her words seemed to hang in the air. He could not avoid them, and he knew that wherever he went they would follow him.

Grabbing his coat, Andrew quickly told his secretary that he would be gone for a while and headed for his car. His mind was a whirl of mixed emotions as he drove toward the beach. Whenever he wanted to escape and be alone, he had gone there to think and pray. Parking his car, he walked along the beach toward a promontory of rocks that jutted out into the deep blue-green water. It was a secluded spot with a niche where he could sit and watch the waves curl in. They were larger today than he had remembered, and the pounding of the surf matched the pounding of the turmoil that churned inside him. With each wave that crashed against the rocks, something began to give inside Andrew Winslow's grieved heart. The anger and bitterness began to lose their hold as he realized the truth of the Scriptures Priscilla had dared to confront him with. He remembered his first sermon that day long ago when he had been invited to preach at Faith Temple. *Christmas is when we exalt the Lord Jesus Christ not only in our hearts but in our acts and in our words every day of the year. He is love—He is mercy and goodness and splendor.*

"Lord, I have not done that. . . ." His voice choked, and the pain and sorrow he had carried alone for all these weeks tore deep within his soul. *How can I ask your forgiveness when I refused to give it to Dorothy.* Waves of grief welled up inside, and he began to sob uncontrollably as he had never done before. "Oh, God, be merciful to me. My pride and unforgiveness blinded my heart, and I have sinned grievously against you and against my wife."

★　★　★　★

A March wind tossed fluffy clouds across the azure sky as Dorothy pushed Phillip on a swing. It was such a beautiful day that she had decided to take the children out to a park, where they had stayed all morning. Now she knew they were tired from running and playing. She was exhausted herself. By the time she got them home, gave them lunch, and settled them down for a nap, she was ready to lie down herself and rest. She was washing her face in the bathroom when she heard someone calling her. She straightened up rapidly, and her face turned pale as she realized it was Andrew's voice. Quickly she dried her face, ran a comb through her hair, then turned and left the bedroom. When she stepped into the hallway, she stopped abruptly. Andrew had come to stand right before her bedroom door. She had never seen his face so pale and drawn, and yet—there was a look in his eyes she had not seen in a long time. His piercing blue eyes were fixed on her in a strange fashion. He cleared his throat and said, "Dorothy, may I talk to you?"

"Why . . . yes," Dorothy stammered. "Shall we go into the living room?"

"No, this is good enough right here. It doesn't matter where we are. I've got something to say . . . and it wouldn't be any easier there than in the hallway here." He suddenly dropped his head and his voice broke. Dorothy stood watching him with shock. She realized that he was struggling with some powerful emotion. When he lifted his head, she saw tears in his eyes!

"What is it, Andrew?" she whispered and came forward and touched his arm gently.

Andrew reached out slowly and put his hands on her arms. He waited for her to withdraw, but she did not. She stood looking up at him, her lips trembling, and he said hoarsely, "I've just had a meeting." He tried to smile, but it was a miserable failure. "You've heard that before, haven't you? Me and my 'meetings'!"

"A meeting with who, Andrew?"

"A meeting . . . with God." Andrew could no longer control himself. He tried to stop the sob that rose in this throat, but he could not. Another followed, and then his shoulders began to heave and shake. His face became contorted and he cried, "Oh, Dorothy! I've been so wrong!" He could not control the tears as they streamed down his face. Suddenly Dorothy put her arms around him and pulled his head down to her shoulder. She was weeping, too, but it was tears of joy. She held him as he sobbed great, long, hoarse sobs. His arms were around her, and he clung to her as a man would cling to a life preserver in a rising sea.

Dorothy said nothing but kept her arms around his neck, pulling his head ever closer. His tears stained her cheek, and finally when the sobbing stopped, she said, "We'd better go in the living room, Andrew." She led him there, and his shoulders were slumped as they sat down on the divan. There were hollows in his eyes, and she said, "What's happened?"

"Priscilla came to me this morning and told me exactly what kind of a man I've been. She said some pretty hard things, but I realize now she was right. Believe me, she's the best evangelist we've got in this country!" He tried again to smile, and this time partly succeeded. He shook his head, saying, "Then as soon as she left, and I got over being mad at her, God began to deal with me. I drove down to my favorite spot on the beach and spent the rest of the morning praying." He paused again, his voice choked with emotion, then he went on. "God showed me what a rotten man I am."

"No, you mustn't say that!" Dorothy said quickly. She reached over and took his hand and held it tightly. He squeezed hers, enfolding them with his other hand. They sat there, and Dorothy listened as Andrew described brokenly how he had confessed his pride and lack of forgiveness to God.

"And now I've got to confess it to you, Dorothy," he said, his voice cracking. "I've failed to love you at times, and . . . and at times when you've needed my understanding I've been too busy and insensitive to your needs. I've not lived up to all of my marriage vows." For some time he spoke, almost bitterly, and finally Dorothy put her hand over his lips.

"That's enough, sweetheart," she whispered.

"Will you forgive me?" he said, tears streaming down his face.

"Andrew, of course!" she said as she began to weep. "And will you forgive me, Andrew?"

"Yes, with all my heart."

"Then neither of us must ever mention this again—never! We've confessed it to God and each other, and now we must go on and find ourselves again."

For the first time Andrew smiled. He reached out, pulled her close, and kissed her lips gently.

Dorothy felt the strength in his arms, and suddenly she felt like a bride again. She could tell that his longing for her was real, and she knew that the loneliness she had faced for so long was being replaced by Andrew's promise of renewed love.

Suddenly he pulled back and gave her an odd look. "While I was praying this morning, I felt God speaking to me. I'm going to resign from the church."

"Oh, Andrew. . . !" Dorothy gasped.

"Yes. The church building is built. It's time for another man to come in now."

"But where will we go?" A slight fear came to her and she said, "I know. You're going back to be Superintendent of Missions again."

"No. That kept me from my family with all the traveling." He reached out and stroked her smooth cheek and said, "I'm going to take you back to where I courted you and won you for my wife."

Dorothy stared at him blankly, and then joy rushed over her. "Back to Africa?"

"Yes, I got a letter from the Mission Board. They want us to go and take over your father's mission station."

"Oh, Andrew! My old home, and my mother. . . !"

"Yes, and your mother will be there, too. She needs you now, and we need her."

Dorothy's face was radiant. "And just think, Andrew—it would be *home*! And we'd be with Barney, and Katie, and their children."

"Yes. I feel it as clear as I ever felt anything from God. I know He would have us return to Africa." Smiling, he felt a peace fill his heart. He pulled her to her feet, then wrapped his arms around her. He kissed her, then put his lips against her ear. "We'll go start all over again, sweetheart—and I'll court you a lot better than I did the first time. . . ."

★   ★   ★   ★

Hope Winslow sat quietly beside the bed, her chair drawn up close enough so that she could reach over and hold her husband's hand. Since the accident, she had been sitting almost constantly beside Dan's bed and praying steadily. Dr. Rayburn had been faithful to stop by regularly, but each time he was less optimistic. His last words had been on the morning of March the twentieth, three days after the accident. "Hope, he's getting weaker every time I see him. There's only one end to that, I'm afraid. You must be ready."

Hope had responded, "God can do anything, Dr. Rayburn. If He chooses to heal my husband, He will do so."

The long hours had passed, and though she saw no change in her husband's condition, Hope never faltered. She spent every waking moment sending up a constant stream of prayers for her injured husband's recovery. At times when her faith would seem to falter, she would pick up the Bible and read the promises of God out loud, claiming His faithfulness.

When the hall clock finally struck six, Hope was startled out of a fitful sleep she'd fallen into. Quickly she peered at Dan's face, then sat quietly stroking his hand gently. After a time Dan's eyes fluttered, and instantly she leaned over and said, "Dan, can you hear me?"

Dan Winslow's eyes opened suddenly, and Hope saw with a sudden joy that they were clear. "Sure I can hear you," he said as he stirred. His voice grew stronger, and he said, "I'm sore as a boil, Hope!"

"Dan, you're better!" Hope stood up and bit her lower lip. "How do you feel?"

"Why, like I've been stomped by a whole herd of Brahma bulls—but I'm okay." He saw her face tense with strain and squeezed her hand. "I guess I was pretty low on the limb, wasn't I?"

"Dr. Rayburn thought . . . he thought you wouldn't live. I sent for the children."

Surprise filled Dan's eyes, then he said, "God knows more than the doctors. Now, don't be crying, Hope—you know I can't stand that. . . !" Hope sat down abruptly and bent over and put her face against his chest. The sobs came hard, and he stroked her hair until they passed.

Hope dashed the tears away and sat there quietly for a time. He looked up at her and spoke about how happy she had made his life, and how he had loved her more than he could ever say. "I never had just the right words," he said, "but I did the best I could. I love you as much as a man could love a woman on this earth."

She held his hand tightly and leaned over and kissed him. Then she told him what was in her heart of hearts. A few minutes later he fell asleep again. She bowed her head and prayed silently.

From time to time she looked up to see if he was awake.

★　★　★　★

The Maxwell pulled up with the Reo right behind it. Peter jumped down and gave Priscilla a hand. Her legs were stiff from the long, tiring ride, and she stomped the ground for a moment while Jason got out. Looking back, she saw Cass and Serena climbing stiffly out of the Reo with their children. "It was a hard trip, Peter, but you did so well."

"Cass didn't do bad, either," Peter said soberly. "He kept right up with us the whole way."

They all moved toward the porch, and as soon as Priscilla's feet touched the first step, her mother came out the door. Priscilla ran up and threw her arms around her, and Hope whispered, "I'm glad you're here, dear."

"How is he?"

"Much better, thank God!" Hope's face was wan with strain, and she said, "Cody just left, and your uncle Tom went home to get some rest. Both of them have hardly left the house since the accident."

"What does the doctor say?" Peter demanded.

"He almost gave up hope—but last night your dad took a turn for the better. It was from God—no other way to explain it." She shook her head, wonder in her eyes. "He's been waiting for you. He's been asleep, but he'll wake up soon."

They all filed in, and Serena whispered, "You go ahead, Cass. I'll keep the children."

"I'll wait outside, too," Jason said. "This is just for family."

"He's been asking for you, too, Jason," Hope said. She smiled sadly and said, "He's missed you something terrible. You mean a great deal to him. More than you know, I think." She saw Jason's face change, then he turned and looked blankly at the bunkhouse across the way where he had spent so many years as foreman of the ranch.

Hope led the three into the room. Moving over to the bedside, she whispered, "Dan, the children are here. Are you awake?"

Dan's eyes fluttered and then opened. His gaze swept the four gathered beside his bed, Priscilla standing beside her mother, and his two sons on the other side. His face was pale, but he smiled and his eyes were clear. "Never should have sent for you," he protested. "You've got more to do than fiddle around with me."

Priscilla leaned over and kissed him and brushed back her tears. For a moment she was unable to speak. "Oh, Dad, I've been so afraid!"

Looking up, Dan saw her tears, like diamonds in her eyes, and whispered, "I guess it's all right to cry a little bit." He turned and looked at the two stalwart sons of his and said, "It's all right for men to cry, too. I do it myself sometimes, you know."

Cass leaned over and squeezed his father's shoulder. "Dad," he whispered brokenly and then stopped. He could say no more.

Peter took the hand that was lying on top of the comforter and whispered, "We got here as soon as we could, Dad."

All three of them were so relieved at their father's improved condition. Throughout the whole trip, they had all faced the same fear. *Can we get there before he dies?* Now that they saw the big man clear-eyed and out of danger, their emotions choked them all up. They wanted to express their relief, but it took some time. They stood beside the bed for a short time, then Hope shooed them out, saying, "Plenty of time to talk—he needs to rest now."

But Dan was not finished. "I'll bet you broke every law in the book with that fast car of yours," he said to Peter.

"Sure did," Peter tried to smile.

"Didn't Jason come with you?"

"Yes," Cass answered.

"He's outside, Dad," Priscilla said quickly.

"Go get him—and Serena, too."

"She's keeping the children," Cass hesitated.

"Bring them in, too." He waved Hope's protest away, saying with a sly grin, "I'm a sick man—and deserve to have my own way."

"All right, but just for a minute," Hope said as she left the bedroom and went to get the rest of the family.

Dan greeted Jason warmly, then Serena and his grandchildren. He looked around the room and said drowsily, "Shame a fellow has to get piled up to get his kids to come and pay him a visit. . . ."

"I'm right glad to see you doing so well, boss," Jason said, clearing his throat, then he wheeled away and left the room with his head down.

Dan dropped off to sleep, and then the rest of them left the room for the time. When they were outside Peter said, "What happened, Mom?"

"There was a drunken driver. Your father was driving the buggy, coming in after dark from town. I don't think the driver ever saw him. It killed the horse, and your father took a bad blow." Peter's face hardened, and his mother saw it. "I know you love cars, son," she said, "and it wasn't the car. It was the whiskey that did it. I wouldn't have you feel bad about this because you like automobiles."

Dan slept well that night, and the next afternoon he insisted on getting out of bed and putting on his pants—but Hope put a stop to that. The doctor had ordered him to stay in bed a few more days, and she was going to make sure he did. He growled but at least won the right to have visitors.

Priscilla sat beside him for some time. She was glad to see the pleased look on his face when she told him about her decision to leave the acting world. "Dad, something's happened to me. I've been worrying for a long time about what the theater means, and it's all right for some," she hesitated, then leaned over and whispered, "but it's not for me."

Dan's eyes opened wide and he smiled broadly. It made him look younger then, and almost healthy. "I'm so proud of you, Priscilla. Don't worry about anything now. When you put God first and follow His will for your life, He will take care of the rest."

Priscilla shared a warm smile with her father, and a deep peace that things would turn out right filled her heart.

"You know that Jason saved my life?"

"Peter told me all about it." He looked at her fondly and said, "He's a good man, Priscilla."

Priscilla had not formulated her thoughts, nor her emotions, but ever since Jason had thrown himself on top of that wild animal, throwing his life away to save hers, she had thought steadily about it. She could not help making comparisons between him and the other men who had pursued her. She knew that neither Eddie Rich nor Todd Blakely would even think of risking their lives to save hers. She squeezed her father's hand and said, "I . . . I guess I was all mixed up, Dad—with all the world of the theater, and the glamor of it. I guess I got my fill of it."

Dan smiled again. He was very tired but he said, "You've made me very happy, daughter. That makes me feel like the family is all right. Peter still needs the Lord. I'm trusting God to save him, and I'm praying that you'll help him, you and Cass."

"I'm coming back to the ranch," Priscilla said. "I'll never go on the stage again!"

Tears filled Dan's eyes and he said, "That's . . . good to hear, Priscilla. It's what your mother and I have been praying for!"

★ ★ ★ ★

Later in the day, Dan insisted he had to see Jason. Hope found him outside leaning against one of the pillars that held the slanting roof up. "Jason, Dan wants you."

Slowly Jason looked up with an odd expression in his eyes. He hesitated so long that Hope had to insist. "Come along now, don't be so slow."

When Jason Ballard entered the sick man's room, he found Dan Winslow sitting up in bed drinking a tall glass of lemonade. "Haven't been babied like this for a long time, Jase," Dan smiled. Motioning to the rocker beside the bed, Dan said, "Got two things to say to you." Setting the empty glass down on the oak table beside the bed, he carefully took a deep breath, then released it. "I'm getting old, Jase."

"Don't say that," Jason quickly replied. "You can still outwork most of these young fellows who think they're tough as leather."

"Maybe so, but Hope and I have been talking—and what it amounts to is that I'm stepping down from most of the work. Can't say as I mind it. I'd like to take a long vacation to Los Angeles and visit with Cass and our grandchildren. . . ."

Jason Ballard listened as Winslow spoke of his plans, then a shock ran through him as the owner said, "I couldn't do this— step down, I mean—unless I had a good man to take over. And you're the man to do it, Jase."

"Me! Why, Mr. Winslow—!"

Waving his hand to cut off the tall puncher's protest, Dan said, "Hope and I have been planning it for quite a while. We were just waiting for you to get back from California before we said anything. Will you take it on, Jase?"

"I'd be proud to work for you, Mr. Winslow. I always have been, but—"

"What's wrong?" Winslow's quick glance told him that Ballard was uncertain. He waited and asked, "Can you tell me what's bothering you, Jase? Maybe I can help."

Ballard lifted his eyes to Dan Winslow and said abruptly, "I'm pretty low on the limb, I guess, sir. Never been so miserable in my whole life!" Rising from his chair, he paced the floor like a caged beast and his words tumbled out. "Something's been eating at me for a long time. I can't get rid of it—and I know it's God." Abruptly he wheeled and came to sit down. His hands were trembling, and he held them up, laughing shakily. "Look at that! I'm not fit to run a ranch—or anything else!"

For a long moment Dan let the silence run on, then he reached over and picked up the thick black Bible on his table—the same one that Hope had read for days while he was unconscious. "I've been waiting for a long time to see you come to this place, Jase," he said, his eyes filled with pleasure. "I remember when you first came here. You were as wild a boy as I ever laid eyes on! But there was something in you that I saw and liked from the start. But sometimes a man has to come to the end of his tether before he'll let Jesus Christ into his life. I was the same as you, but the day I called on the Lord—that was the day everything changed for me." He opened the Bible and read, " 'All have sinned and come short of the glory of God. . . .' "

★   ★   ★   ★

Hope grew worried about Jason's long visit. "He's been in there with Dan long enough," she muttered. She opened the door and stepped inside—then stopped dead still. Her eyes took in Jason, whose eyes were red with weeping, but who had a broad smile across his face. She turned to Dan, questioning him with her eyes.

"It's all right, Hope," Dan said quickly. He turned to the tall man who sat beside him, adding, "Jason's just joined the family of God!"

CHAPTER TWENTY-FOUR

A NEW TIME

★　★　★　★

As her father recovered with a swiftness that amazed Dr. Rayburn, Priscilla found herself strangely free from all the burdens and cares she had faced at Imperial Pictures. She knew Porter would be furious with her for not coming back to complete the serial, but she hoped that deep down he would understand. There were plenty of other young women in Los Angeles anxious for an opportunity to take her place. Edwin would find someone else, someone he could mold into the kind of actress who was willing to do whatever he wanted on the big screen. She was certain she had made the right decision to stay. Something about the spacious horizon of the plains seemed to release her spirit, and each morning she found herself riding the trails that led to the low hills bordering the ranch. The long silences out in the open land were soothing to her after the hubbub of the world in New York City and Los Angeles. The warm rays of the sun and the smell of earth and the vigor of life soaked into her and revived her. She also rejoiced in the conversion of Jason Ballard—though he seemed to keep to himself a great deal. Her father said, "He's sorting out some things, Pris. He'll come around."

Finally she became aware of one element that was missing from her return to the ranch. At first she could not put her finger on what it was—but a week after Peter, Cass, and Serena had returned to Los Angeles, she spoke to her mother about her future. The two of them were sitting on the front porch watching the clouds skim over the hills. After a long pause, Hope said, "You seem restless, Priscilla. Is anything wrong?"

"Oh no, Mom," Priscilla said, staring off in the distance.

Hope turned her gaze on her daughter, and after studying the girl's expression, she asked, "Do you miss all the excitement of Los Angeles? I know the ranch isn't very thrilling after being a star."

Quickly Priscilla shook her head, answering, "It's not a good life—not at all. Why, I can't think of more than two or three actors or actresses who are really content. They're all worried about being done out of a juicy role—or about getting old. I'm glad to be out of it," she said firmly.

"I'm glad, too, and your father is happier than I've ever seen him. He has all sorts of plans to set afoot when he gets all healed up." She rocked back and forth slowly, but something seemed to be troubling her. She started to speak, then changed her mind and shook her head doubtfully.

Sensing her mother's concern about something, Priscilla asked, "What is it?"

"Nothing."

"Yes, there is. What did you start to say?"

"Oh, I was just wondering what you'd do with yourself now. Do you have any idea what kind of work you'd like to do?"

Priscilla turned restive, and rising to her feet, she said briefly, "I haven't thought much about it. Something will turn up. I'm just going to wait on God's direction this time."

Priscilla patted her mother's hand and assured her that something would work out. Then she left the porch and strolled over to the corral. Her mare trotted up to her, and she saddled her, then stepped into the saddle and rode out, raising a cloud of dust. The muscles of the mare bunched under her, and Priscilla leaned forward, urging more speed. Her hair flew out behind her, and she felt a rush of exhilaration as she sped over the dry earth. Reaching the line of trees that marked the downward slope of the ranch, she slowed the horse, then sat balanced in the saddle as the mare picked her way down to the creek that bubbled over small stones, making a pleasant sound.

Dismounting, she tied her animal to a slender cottonwood sapling, then sat down beside the brook. Darkness was coming on and she listened to the sound of a cow bawling far off in the distance. After that the silence seemed to cover the earth, and as the sun dropped lower, falling behind the distant range of mountains, she clasped her knees and hugged them. This was the thing she'd missed most in Los Angeles—the privacy that was never there.

For a long time she sat still—so still that once a dog fox came trotting briskly down the bank of the stream sniffing around. He shied at her horse and took a detour. He never saw Priscilla and passed within ten feet of her. She could see the bright glitter of his eyes and the gleam of his white teeth as he came by.

Overhead the sky turned a dark azure tinged with pink at the horizon, and a few pinpoints of light began to glimmer. Finally it grew so dark that she knew she must ride home. With a sigh she rose and started for her horse—but at that moment a shadow appeared. At first it was just a blur, but it was moving toward her. Fear leaped into her heart, but then she heard her name called and a wave of relief washed over her.

"Priscilla?"

"I'm here, Jason." Priscilla stood still as Jason approached her in the long shadows that had fallen. "What are you doing out here?"

"Looking for you. Your mother is worried." He bent over to peer at her face, then added, "She was afraid you might have gotten thrown."

"Not very flattering, is she?"

"Never was a horse couldn't be rode—"

"Never was a rider couldn't be throwed," Priscilla finished the old saying. "You told me that enough back when I was giving you a hard time."

"Sure did. You still remember that?"

Smiling, Priscilla said, "Of course! I remember all the times I drove you crazy. I don't see how you put up with me. You should have roughed me up."

"Did that once, too," he said, then laughed.

"Yes, you did, didn't you?" She felt strange and did not know why. All of the restlessness that had bothered her lately seemed to stir now, and she asked in a low voice, "Jason, what are you going to do?"

"What I've always done."

"You're going to stay here on the ranch?" Suddenly a gladness welled up within her. "Are you going to work for my father?"

Ballard nodded, then said, "I've been talking to your father a lot lately. He and your uncle Tom have been talking about combining their ranches into one big one—and a good one, too. The two of them came to me with an offer yesterday I couldn't refuse. They want me to manage the spread when it's combined. I told them they should give it to Cody and Laurie, but they already have one as large as this one will be, and they said they didn't want to take on any more."

"Oh, Jase, that's wonderful!" Reaching out her hand, Priscilla caught Ballard's arm. Looking up at him, she exclaimed, "You'll do so well at it. You always were the best foreman in all of Wyoming!"

"Don't know about that," Jason answered, acutely aware of her touch on his arm. "Might be a better one in China or someplace like that."

As he spoke a coyote yelped, then began to make a mournful howl that carried across the plain. The two paid no heed, and for a time they stood there, each waiting for the other to speak. Finally Jason asked casually, "What about you, Priscilla? What will you do?"

"I won't go back to making movies—that much I know!"

"Sure about that?"

"Yes!"

A sigh of relief escaped from Jason's lips. "Your dad told me so—but I thought he might have misunderstood you. Be hard to give up all that, won't it?"

"Not really. I thought it was what I wanted—but lately I've been looking at what that life is all about, and I don't want it."

"I'm mighty glad to hear it, Pris."

She warmed at the old name he'd called her long ago. "Would you like to know when I decided to leave the movie business?"

"When was it?"

"When I was locked in the cage with that lion. I thought that beast was going to kill me—and that I would die before I'd find out what kind of life I wanted. And then you jumped down from that cliff and saved my life. I was so afraid for you, but ever since that moment, I've known that I had to find some other way besides the movies to make a living."

Her words held Jason Ballard still—so still that Priscilla finally said, "Jason—"

And then Jason said roughly, "I guess I wanted to hear that more than anything in my life, Pris!"

"Why, Jason—!"

"As long as you were a big star and I was just a bronco-riding cowpoke, I didn't dare to hope—but now I can say what I've felt for a long time." Jason reached out for her and said, "I love you—"

Priscilla knew suddenly that the restlessness that had plagued her for years was a need to be loved—to be loved by a man of strength and honor. Jason had waited and proven himself, when others had led her astray. He had always been there for her, thinking of her, never demanding. She came to him, surrendering her lips, and as she felt the strength of his arms, it was like coming out of a dry desert into the cool shelter of the oasis. His kiss was gentle but firm, and she knew the stirring in her heart was deep and real. The wound in her heart had finally been healed, and she knew he was a man she could love and trust and who would always protect her.

Finally he lifted his head, saying, "Do you feel what I feel, Pris?"

"Yes, Jason!" She buried her face against his chest, happiness flooding her. They stood there quietly, and finally she whispered, "Can you believe that it's always going to be like this?"

He tightened his arms and laughed deep in his chest. Lifting her face he kissed her, gently and then again with a possessiveness that she loved.

"Yes, Pris, it's always going to be like this for us!"

Overhead the stars glittered, and the mare lifted her head and nickered. The wind blew suddenly across the creek, touching her cheek—and then Priscilla said, "Take me home, Jason!"

★　★　★　★

Jolie opened the door and blinked with surprise to see Peter standing there, his head bent and his shoulders slumped. His clothes were wrinkled, and he had not bothered to shave, nor did he offer to come in. "I . . . I just came by," he said quietly, "to tell you I was wrong the way I spoke to Tom before I left for Wyoming to see my dad."

"Why, Peter. . . !" Jolie managed to whisper—and then she could not respond for a moment. She had wept over the argument for hours that day after he had sped off in the Maxwell. She knew he had been upset about the news of his father, but the words between them had been harsh and still hurt. She now said, "Come in, Peter."

"No, I won't do that. I just wanted to tell you how foolish I acted."

Jolie quickly said, "I was wrong to scream at you like that. I wanted to apologize right away, but you drove off before I could even think."

Peter stood there with a strange sense of loss. He finally said, "Priscilla's getting out of the movie business. She and Jason are staying back home. My dad's decided to join the farm with uncle Tom's, and they've asked Jason to manage it. Jason and Priscilla are finally going to get married."

"Oh, I'm so glad! I thought it was the most marvelous thing I ever saw when he threw himself on that lion to save her."

"That was pretty good," Peter nodded. "It was like something out of a storybook, wasn't it?"

"Better than a storybook, I think. He's such a good man—and your sister, there's nobody like her."

"I'm glad you think so." Peter hesitated, then shuffled his feet and twisted his hat, which he had removed and was holding in his hands. "I came to say good-bye, Jolie."

"Good-bye?" Jolie's voice was desolate. She stared at him, her eyes enormous. "What do you mean, Peter? You're not leaving, are you?"

"Yes, I am. Easy and I are going back to Detroit. He's already left, driving the car through. I've got to stay around here and take care of a few things for Jason, but I'll be leaving tomorrow on the train."

He tried to smile and said, "It's been a long time since we came in on a train. This time I won't have to ride the rails as a bummer. I can take a Pullman."

Jolie could not speak. His words seemed to have stricken her dumb, and to her horror she found herself having to swallow to keep from showing the growing emotion she felt inside. She blinked the tears away and could only say, "I'll . . . I'll be sorry to see you go, Peter."

"Me too." Peter hesitated awkwardly, then stuck out his hand. "Well, good-bye, kid—no, not kid," he said, holding her hand tightly. "A fine young woman! I'm mighty proud of you, Jolie!"

Quickly he released her hand and turned, saying, "Think of me once in a while." He jammed his hat on his head, walked off rapidly, then got into the car and drove away.

Jolie stood watching him and sighed, "Oh, Peter. . . !"

* * * *

The train jerked abruptly with a clanking of cars as the engine huffed and puffed. Peter settled back in the comfortable seat as the large coal-burning engine slowly pulled its burden out of the Los Angeles station and headed east. He sat there unaware of the talk of the passengers that buzzed around him. For the next two hours, from time to time, he looked out the window, but felt nothing. He should have been feeling excitement about returning to Detroit to try his luck with the stars of the automobile racing world, but something was missing. He didn't want to think about the words his father had shared with him the day before he left. He knew his father was right, and that he needed God, but he still had so many things *he* wanted to do with his life. He shut his mind to his father's final words and closed his eyes for a time as the train made its rhythmic clicking over the rails.

Finally the mountains reared up before him, and he abruptly recalled coming out of them with Easy and Jolie. The memory saddened him, too, and he shook his head and closed his eyes and tried to catch some sleep.

He had almost dropped off when suddenly a voice right beside him said, "Pardon me, is this seat taken?"

Peter knew that voice! He yanked his hat off, then whirled to see Jolie Devorak standing beside him. She was wearing a close-fitting dress in a light blue flannel with a high lace collar and falling lace cravat blouse. Her lips were turned up in a smile, and her deep blue eyes were sparkling. She laughed as she saw his astonishment and said, "Do you mind if I sit beside you, Mr. Winslow?"

Peter blinked and could not answer, and Jolie took that for an affirmative. She plumped herself down beside him, saying, "A little bit different from the last time we rode a train together, isn't it, Peter?"

"What are you doing here?" Peter finally managed to say.

"Why, I'm going on a trip, just like you are."

Peter was confused. For some reason she looked more grown up. If it had not been for the scar on her face, she would have been the most beautiful young woman he had ever seen, perhaps, except for Priscilla. But she did not seem to be thinking about her scar right now. She was looking out the window.

"You remember when we came out of those mountains? I'd

just shot a man, and you threw him off the car. That was an exciting time, wasn't it?"

Peter shook his head. "Jolie! What are you doing on this train?"

"Why, I'm going to Detroit."

Peter stared at her for a moment, then a smile began to turn his lips. "So am I," he said.

"That's right," Jolie said. "Do you want to know what I'm going for?"

"Yes. Why are you going?"

A roguish smile came to Jolie's lips, and she said, "Somebody has to look after you."

The train suddenly gave a jerk, and Peter threw his arm across Jolie to keep her from hitting the seat in front of them. Then easing her back into the seat, he sat there staring at her, a smile playing around his lips. "I guess I need a keeper," he said finally. "You're sure this is what you want to do, Jolie?"

"I'm sure." She looked anxiously at him then, showing doubt for the first time. "Is it all right, Peter? Do you want me to come?"

Peter reached out and squeezed her shoulder. "We're going to have a great time, Jolie Devorak!"

"Yes, we are, Peter Winslow."

The train rumbled on, passing over plains and mountains, but the two inside were more interested in the exciting days that lay ahead of them than the picturesque scenery flashing by outside. Finally the train gave a lonesome whistle, but neither of them heard it, for they were busy listening to each other talk about all the car races Peter was going to win.